Also by Bruce Macbain

Roman Games: A Plinius Secundus Mystery (Book 1)
The Bull Slayer: A Plinius Secundus Mystery (Book 2)

odin's child

a novel

BRUCE MACBAIN

Blank Slate Press | Saint Louis, MO

Putterham

Blank Slate Press
Saint Louis, MO 63110

For information, contact
Blank Slate Press at 3963 Flora Place, Saint Louis, MO 63110.
www.blankslatepress.com
www.brucemacbain.com

Blank Slate Press is an imprint of Amphorae Publishing Group, LLC

Manufactured in the United States of America
Cover and Interior Illustration: Anthony Macbain
Cover Design by Kristina Blank Makansi
Set in Adobe Caslon Pro and Viking

Library of Congress Control Number: 2015938961

ISBN: 9780991305865

To Carol with love and gratitude

odin's
child

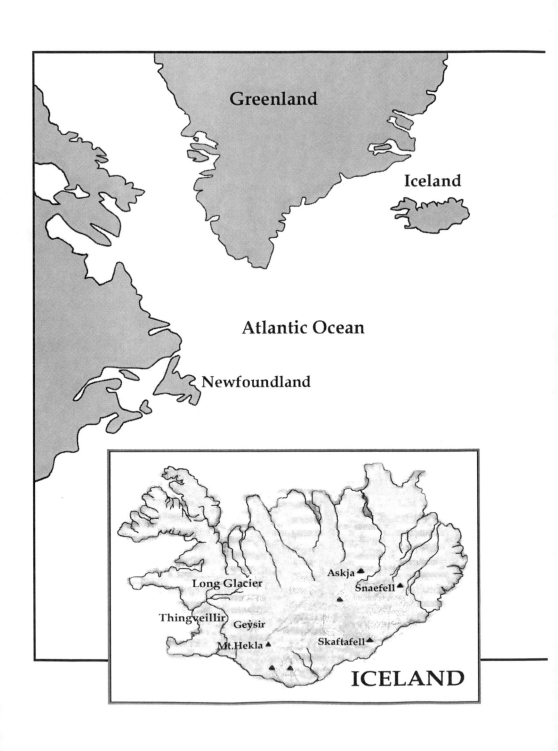

Greenland

Iceland

Atlantic Ocean

Newfoundland

Askja

Snaefell

Long Glacier

Thingveillir Geysir

Mt.Hekla Skaftafell

ICELAND

The Viking World

ICELAND
AD 1029

1

The Stallion Fight at Thingholt

On that morning in May, as we rode to the stallion fight at Thingholt, my fate was revealed to me. A raven flew low across the sky into the rising sun, and the moment I saw it I knew Odin had spoken to me and that he would give me the courage to do what I had already secretly made up my mind to do. Only now, half a century later, do I see what a long text was folded into that swift vision.

The spring of my sixteenth year had come early to the South Quarter of Iceland, with days hot and cold, and thunderclouds sweeping up over the mountains. The stallions, smelling the air, trembled and kicked against their stalls. If you staked out a mare where the stallions could smell her, they would fight like berserkers to get at her. The great ones would die before they broke and ran.

Black Grani was such a one. This was his fourth spring and the time had come to take him to the South Quarter Thing and fight him. Thorvald, my father, grumbled and held back, but I gave him no peace, until, at last, he flung up an arm, which meant *yes*.

My brother Gunnar and I set out early from the farm that day, and it was nigh dusk before we came in sight of Thingholt plain and heard the distant shouts of men and the whinnying of horses. We left Grani and our mounts at the horse lines and walked across the sparse heath into the holiday crowd. And as we pushed our way through, there were some who knew us. A few old men came up and in low voices asked to be remembered to our father. But one red-faced woman, seeing us, cried, "Jesu!" and dragged her little daughter from our path.

Gunnar—six years older than me and as reckless as he was handsome—stopped short, favored her with his wickedest grin and purred, "I've eaten my breakfast today, housewife, or wouldn't I just love a bite of your fat girl! Now, my black-headed brother here, who is greedier than I...."

The woman elbowed herself out of our way. Some, standing near, laughed, though others eyed us coldly and shook their heads.

"I've too sharp a tongue in my head," Gunnar allowed to no one in particular. "It's my single fault."

Ahead of us a crowd gathered for the horse fights. We worked our way to the front until the clearing lay before us, a haze of dust hanging over trampled grass. At the edge, the mares were tethered, while in the center two farmers, stripped to the waist and backed by a knot of shouting friends, shoved and goaded their snorting stallions into battle. It was a good match and we watched, shouting with the rest, until the loser, foam-flecked and streaked with blood, charged into the crowd, scattering spectators to right and left. Winning horse and master both threw back their heads and cried victory.

In the days before the White Christ, the winning horse would have been sacrificed to Frey, whose horse's prick fertilizes the fields, and the meat cut up and sold to the folk to eat. Christian priests put a stop to that, but they were too shrewd to make us give up our sport entirely.

While pieces of silver changed hands and horns of ale went round, Gunnar fingered his yellow beard and looked over the crowd for a likely competitor.

"I will goad Grani." I had waited for this moment to speak.

"Maybe next year, Tangle-Hair," he answered, not looking at me. "When you've got more size on you. You'll get yourself trampled."

Our younger sister had given me the nickname 'Tangle-Hair', as well as 'Black-Brows' and 'Half-Troll' and several others. Our father resembled a black bull—short, thick, and dark. Not handsome according to the taste of our people. And I was the image of him, black and shaggy-haired from birth. How much did I resemble him beneath the skin? That question gnawed like a worm in my belly.

"Gunnar," I said, "I goad him or no one does."

My skin was cold. What Gunnar could do smiling, I did with teeth clenched. That was the difference between us.

"That's not how you put it to Father."

Not even to my brother could I confess the real reason. I could scarce admit it to myself. We fixed our eyes on each other. I would know today, I swore to myself, whether my father's blood—the blood that gave me his looks and his temper—had also infected me with his sickness. I would master my fear today or die. I didn't mind which.

"If it goes badly, you'll face him by yourself."

"I know."

"I oughtn't to let you." But then he smiled. "I hope Grani knows what to do because it's certain as rain and fire you don't. Just promise me you won't lose your temper, it'll only worry the horse."

While he went back to fetch Grani, I drew a long breath and stepped into the circle to yell my challenge. This was the first time I had put myself forward in a group of strange men. I had a lump like a fist in my throat and hardly recognized my own strangulated voice. In answer there was only a little laughter and scattered shouts of "Brave boy!" Then anger welled up in me and I cried out, "Odd Thorvaldsson does not leave this circle with his horse un-fought!"

For a long moment, nothing. Then a stir in the crowd. "Hold on! Hold on!" Some jumped aside and others turned to look as a man thrust his way through from the rear. He launched himself toward me across the open space.

"Don't burst your lungs, boy, Hrut Ivarsson still has one good ear left to hear you with!"

There was laughter from the crowd at this joke, which he acknowledged with a wave of his arm.

I knew who he was. Even to our remote farmstead, the story had made its way of how this man Hrut had got his ear torn off in a brawl last Yule Feast. Strife-Hrut, as his neighbors called him, was a bully who couldn't enter a strange hall without starting a fight and who never paid blood money for his killings, though he was plenty rich enough. He farmed down on the Whitewater, near the coast, and spent a part of each summer over the sea, trading in his own ship.

He thrust his face at me—red and meaty, with small eyes, and a scrappy beard. He grinned, showing broken front teeth, and said, "I've a roan stallion, ugly as me and less good-natured, that I'll match with yours for the stakes of a silver ounce." He pulled a bit of hack-silver from his purse and waved it under my nose. "And seeing as you're only a young'un, my boy Mord, that isn't much bigger 'n what you are ,will goad him."

He had two sons, Mord and Brand, who had followed him into the circle and stood behind him now, one to either side. Both of them were closer to Gunnar's age than to mine and no prettier to look at than their father.

"Mind you," Hrut tapped my chest with a thick forefinger, "I take up your challenge out of kind regards for Thorvald, for I know whose son you are. He had a shrewd head and a heavy hand once upon a time, and I call it a shame he keeps himself so close nowadays." It was meant as a sneer and was said loud enough for many to hear.

"He has his reasons," I said.

"I expect he does."

With a nod to his sons, Strife-Hrut went off to round up his horse. A moment later, Gunnar appeared at my side, grim-faced.

"Tangle-Hair, these are men who don't like to lose. They'd sooner kill a horse—or his driver."

"What would you have me do?"

"In Christ's name, Odd, let me handle the horse." Whenever Gunnar swore by Christ it was as if to say, *Our mother would ask this.*

"Give me the goad," I said.

They were coming back now, leading their scarred animal, the survivor of many a fight, and the crowd gave them room, for the horse was side-stepping and his ears were flat against his head. I laid aside my sword belt and tunic and picked up the iron-pronged club, while Gunnar, with his hands tight on Grani's halter, brought him to the edge of the clearing. The moment Grani saw the roan, his lips drew back over his teeth and he rolled his eyes like a battle-mad berserker.

"He won't need the goad," Gunnar shouted over the noise of the crowd. "Keep close and let him hear your voice. That's all he wants."

Round and round the stallions circled each other in the dusty ring, lashing out with their hoofs, thrusting with their necks, snorting with the same sound that the earth makes when it steams and heaves beneath our feet. And I, with the choking dust and the hot reek of horseflesh in my nostrils, danced alongside Grani, shouting his name and rushing in to throw myself against his flank as he charged.

We fought like brothers, he and I, side by side, the same blood, foam, and sweat soaking us both. The battle-joy rose in my throat and swept me up so that I had scarcely a mind left with which to tell myself, *You have conquered fear—the sickness hasn't touched you.*

Hrut's horse was a fierce biter and soon Grani was bleeding from his face and neck. But his strength began to tell against the roan. He drove his foe back on his haunches and, rearing up, lashed him with his fore-hoofs. Mord used his goad frantically, raking his animal's back until long ribbons of blood ran down its flanks. His brother Brand rushed in, too, to throw his weight against the beast and the two of them shoved and flailed and swore, but the roan had no heart left in him. Wide-eyed with fear, he shied away, tumbling Brand over in the dust.

"One more time, Grani!" I shouted.

Then Mord raised his arm. I saw what he was going to do and I tried to throw myself in his way—too late! The goad went up and came slashing down at Grani's head. My beautiful stallion rose on his hind legs and wheeled round, showing only a red well where his eye had been. In the same motion he struck me on the brow with his fore-hoof, knocking me down, and with a scream of terror and pain plunged through the crowd.

The next thing I remember, Gunnar was holding me up under the arms, wiping the blood from my eyes with a strip of his tunic. Together we stumbled after Grani. A dozen men held him down by his head and legs as he writhed in the dirt. What happened after that comes to my mind now only in sharp splinters of memory: my brother forcing my fingers around the haft of a spear, his mouth working, saying that the horse must not live mutilated, the spear shuddering in my fist, sinking deep, until half its length was buried in Grani's chest, and his hot blood spurting over my hands.

"A good sacrifice," said someone in the crowd who was of the old religion. "Frey is glad of him."

I pressed my face against Grani's neck, letting my blood and his run together, until Gunnar pulled me away. "There is a reckoning," he said.

Followed by the crowd, we walked back to the clearing. There Hrut and his sons with four of their hirelings stood close together, looking truculent and just a little frightened. There was a numbing pain in my forehead over the right eye. My legs barely held me up.

"Stay behind me," ordered my brother.

He was holding the goad—I suppose he had pried it from my hand—and, without a word, he went straight for Mord. Quick as a cat he swung it, aiming for the eye, and Mord let out a howl and fell to the ground. Instantly, the rest of them had their swords out. We would have died there and then if bystanders hadn't rushed between us, throwing their cloaks over the blades and pushing us in opposite directions.

Next moment, there came a shout to make way. Hjalti the Strong, big and barrel-chested, shouldered his way into our midst and roared for quiet. He was the godi of Tjorsariverdale, a respected and powerful man.

He stamped his foot and glared around him. Devil skin him, he would stand for no brawling at his Thing. If folk couldn't enjoy a simple horse-fight without falling to blows, then damn him if he wouldn't see it all put a stop to!

But Hrut appealed to the crowd to pity his boy that was all bloodied and who knew but what he was blinded for life.

"Hold!" cried Hjalti. "Enough! The harm's equal for both. Mord's wound for the horse's. No blood money owed on either side, nor any more blows to be struck, or you'll have me to deal with. Agreed?" It wasn't a question.

He looked to us. Gunnar, after a long moment, let the goad drop from his hand. "Agreed," he said between his teeth.

Hjalti looked to Strife-Hrut. Hrut said nothing, but he and his men turned their backs and stalked off, dragging Mord behind them.

"Well if he murders you," confided Hjalti, watching them go, "it'll be flat against the law."

Hjalti-godi was renowned for his keen legal mind.

The crowd began to drift away, except for a few who approached us and asked quietly if they might buy a haunch or a side of Grani to take home for their table, the horse having so much strength in him, and bugger the priest that didn't like it.

I walked apart and let them bargain with Gunnar. I hadn't the heart for it.

When he came back he threw an arm around my shoulder. "You want to stay a bit?" he asked. "Watch the wrestling, stone-lifting? Listen to the lawsuits?"

I shook my head, no.

"Not anxious to go home and deal with *him*, are you?"

"He must be told, Gunnar. And maybe he'll see what fate lies ahead of us—the feud, if there is one. He has the gift, you know he does."

Gunnar spat and ground the spittle into the dirt with his boot. "Much good it does him."

2

BLACK THORVALD

We spoke little going home. Sullen clouds heavy with rain hid the sun, and a cold mist gathered in the hollows and low places along our way, creeping into our bones, although we huddled deep in our cloaks. The lump from Grani's hoof oozed blood and throbbed. But the real pain was in my heart. *They haven't paid enough*, I thought, not enough for Grani's life, whatever Hjalti-godi says.

We reached the top of the ridge overlooking our home-field. The sun was sinking below the horizon draining the light from the sky. We gazed down at the silver ribbon of the Ranga, swift-flowing with the water of glaciers. Beyond the river rose Hekla's snowy peak, a plume of smoke drifting up from its cone. Between the river and the volcano's barren flank lay our farmstead – good land, although far from the coast and out of the way of travelers.

As we splashed across the ford, our grass-green house came into view. Long and low and walled with turf, it looked not so much built upon the ground as sprouted from it. A cow shed and stable joined the hall at one end, sheep pens ran along one side, and nearby were the smithy, the hay barn, and the thralls' cabins —the sum total of our estate.

Because no freeborn tenant or hired man would stay on the place, we were forced to rely on the grudging labor of thralls. Two of them, idling outside the door, looked up when they heard us coming. If they noticed the absence of Grani, they gave no sign. We gave them our horses to stable and, stooping through the doorway, passed into the dim space within. The fuggy chill seemed to follow us inside and, as always when the air was damp, a haze of peat smoke filled the room, unable to find its way out through the smoke hole.

Before we took another step, Gunnar's new-wed wife, Vigdis, ran to us, kissed him, and thrust his little son into his arms. While he gave him a squeeze and a toss, she eyed us anxiously.

"Jorunn Ship-Breast," she called over her shoulder, "there's been trouble. Odd is hurt."

My mother's head appeared through the doorway of the weaving room. She covered the length of the hall with swift strides.

"Odd, what have you done to yourself?"

She started to put her hand to my head but Gunnar got between us and told her I had been bloodied like a man and needed no women to fuss over me. She took a step back. Gunnar was her darling, he had that sort of influence with her.

"What has happened, Odd?"

"Mother, you'll hear it all when he does. He must be told first."

Gunnar and I strode down the hall and stopped before the smoke-blackened pillars of his high-seat. Thorvald's rings and chains glowed dully in the pale light of the hearth-fire and his shadow trembled large on the wall behind him. Always he sat so in the evenings: silent, frowning at his knees while the life of the house flowed quietly past him as water in a stream laps the stone.

Only his hands had life. In one he held a knife, in the other a stick of kindling, planed smooth on its sides. For hours at a time he would bend over such a stick, working slowly along its length, carving the runes, which are Odin's gift to men. First, he would cut the long uprights, then add the hooks and cross-strokes until all sixteen letters of the futhark were complete. And always, while he carved, he mumbled in a low singsong their names: *Fe ... Ur ... Thurs ... Ass ... Reid ... Kaun ... Hagall ... Nauth ... Iss ... Ar ... Sol ... Tyr ... Bjarkan ... Mathr ... Logr ... Yr.* When he was done, he would fill up the empty spaces that remained with interlocking spirals and twining serpents until every bit of the stick was minutely covered.

If this was magic, it got him nothing. He neither prayed nor cursed as he carved; only the act itself absorbed him. When he was done, he would throw the thing into the fire, choose another stick, and begin again.

Gunnar and I stood waiting to be noticed until, finally, I spoke his name. Only then did he raise his eyes—dark, deep-set eyes under sweeping black brows like the wings of a raven.

"You've an unlucky look about you, boy." Ignoring Gunnar, he looked straight at me.

I said, "Grani is dead and we're at feud with Strife-Hrut Ivarsson." I added the circumstances short and plain. While he listened, the corners of his mouth drew downward and the furrow between his eyes deepened. A vein, like a twisting worm, pulsed at his temple.

I waited, tense with expectation, hoping to hear the words that would send us into battle. His knife-blade bit deep into the stick; a sliver of wood flew at me.

"You!" he snarled. "You would plague me about the horse. O, you brave Stallion-Fighter, don't you know men like Hrut Ivarsson grow fat from feuding with their neighbors? You gave him his opening—I blame you for whatever happens now."

Gunnar started to defend me.

"Shut up!" Thorvald shouted him down. "You think I haven't seen it? Three nights ago in my sleep—twelve riders approached a desolate house and entered it. Inside were women standing before a loom—the Norns. Men's heads were their loom-weights, guts were their weft and warp, a sword their beater, their shuttle an arrow. While they worked they sang a bloody song."

He sank back in his seat and passed his hand over his eyes. He had visions often—though never one I could recall as gruesome as this.

"Husband, dreams are sent by the Devil to delude us." My mother had come up behind us while he spoke.

"D'you think so? Did the foreign priests teach you that? Well ..." he began in a truculent tone but seemed to shrink under her steady gaze and an uncertain look crept into his eyes. "... well, anyway, here it ends. We'll not feud with Strife-Hrut. No, not for all the stallions in Iceland. Now leave me in peace."

My chest ached so I could scarcely breathe. "At least we weren't cowards!"

The word burst from me—I had never dared say it aloud before. There was a long moment's silence. Then the hand that held the rune-stick lashed out and struck me across the forehead where my wound was. My knees gave way and only Gunnar's grip on my arm kept me from falling.

"Coward? *To me?* Say that again, boy, and I'll have the lungs out of you! If it shames you to live in my hall, then go to sea and earn your bread with your spear as I once did. You'll soon have your belly full of fighting. But while you eat my bread, you'll take my orders. There will be no feud. Just as I have done these thirty years, I'll have naught to do with Strife-Hrut or any of the rest of 'em." And almost to himself he added, "You know why."

All the world knew why.

Twenty-nine years before, when Iceland became a Christian country, Black Thorvald, alone of the forty-eight godis, had refused to accept the new faith.

It happened this way. Missionaries came from Norway; in particular a man named Thangbrand of Saxony. At first, the people laughed at him, but Thangbrand frightened them with stories that the world was soon to end in fire and the dead rise from their tombs, for it was nearing the thousandth year, he said, since the birth of the White Christ. This Thangbrand was a fighter, too. He attacked some who disputed him and killed three or four—one, a famous berserker, whom he beat to death with a crucifix.

Then there began to be conversions and the country was deeply rent. At the Althing that summer, open fighting nearly broke out between the new believers and the old until, at the last moment, a compromise—or so they called it—was proposed. In order that the country not be split into warring camps, both sides would let one man decide for all of them and take their oath to uphold his decision.

The story goes that he lay for a night and a day in his tent, his face covered with a cloak, while outside the people waited. When, at last, he came out, he gave his verdict. Let there be one law and one belief for all, he pronounced—and let it be the religion of the White Christ!

My father and a few like-minded friends were stunned, furious. But they had sworn. More than that, they were outnumbered. The godis knew that if they did not lead the way to conversion, others would, and they would soon see their old-time influence usurped. Thus they rushed to lick the Christmen's boots. That, at any rate, was what my father shouted in the face of their leader, the rich and powerful Snorri of Helgafel.

The following day, when people left the Althing, they dipped themselves in hot springs and let the foreign priests say words over them. All, that is, but Thorvald the Black. He stood apart and railed at them, scorning their new religion and calling it a feeble thing, unbecoming to war-like men. But, though many in their hearts agreed with him, none stood with him, and he left Thingvellir Plain alone.

Within a few years, the exposure of infants was banned as well as the public eating of horseflesh. Soon after that, even private sacrifice to the old gods was forbidden on pain of outlawry. Then old folk, especially old women, who clung to their fathers' faith, were called witches and some were drowned in the deep pool at Law-Rock.

In the end, my father made two concessions. First, he gave up sacrificing to Thor, whose temple had stood on our land for five generations. Not because the law forbade it, but because he was enraged at Old Redbeard for letting this new god make a fool of him. And secondly, he allowed our mother, whom he had lately married, to have herself baptized together with the others of her family. This may seem strange, but he loved her very much. He even allowed her to go to church twice a year and to wear a cross provided she did not expose it near the fresh milk or the beer when it was brewing.

His stubbornness cost him dear. In the year one thousand, Black Thorvald was a vigorous man of two-and-thirty, full of fire and ambition. His voice was heard with respect at the Althing, and men had begun to seek his support in their lawsuits and to promise their allegiance in return. He had made a name for himself as a viking too, spending a part of each year at sea and enjoying the guest-friendship of the great Orkney jarls.

All this he let slip from his hands. He had never made a secret of the fact that he knew rune-lore and that he had the second sight. Now folk began to whisper against him, and the more they whispered, the more he despised them. As the years passed, his thingmen, whose fathers and grandfathers had been dependents of our family, deserted him for happier halls and fewer and fewer sought his help. He, being too proud to seek theirs, turned from them and ceased to attend any of their gatherings. Finally, he let his chieftaincy be purchased for a song, as though it were a thing of no worth.

While godis like Snorri and his friends grew great by feuding and suing, trading and marrying, and lavishing their money on the new churches that began to dot the land, Thorvald the Black, ignored and nearly forgotten, only grew angrier.

And little by little his mind gave way to melancholy, indecision, and sudden frights, until there was no spirit left in him. That was the worst of it. He was only a rag of the man he had been. Oh, he could rant and threaten us, but he walked on his knees.

My father's voice broke in upon my thoughts. "What are you gaping at, moon-calf? I said leave me. I'll not change my mind. I've chosen my way and that's an end of it."

"Oh, yes!" I shot back, for I truly hated him at that moment. "Yes, and your way has led us to this, that we crawl before bullies like Hrut!"

"Odd!" My mother saw his face darken and the worm writhe on his temple. "Drop this quarrel at once. Beg your father's pardon and vex him no more."

She looked from me to him, her eyes full, near to brimming over. She could still summon her tears for him.

My anger died even as she spoke. I too had tears though I kept them inside. I made my apology to his stony face and let her draw me away.

She sat Gunnar and me down on the wall bench and served us bowls of skyr and boiled mutton, and, for Gunnar, a big marrowbone she had saved especially for him. Our sister Gudrun Night Sun sat beside me and touched my forehead with her fingertip. She, too, was close to tears. She was a pretty girl of thirteen, all leg and no bosom, and hair so long she could tuck it in her belt. "Tangle-Hair, I'm sorry about Grani. He was beautiful, and I loved him as much as you. We'll fight those men, won't we?"

I shrugged. "You heard Father."

At that Gunnar laughed harshly and said in a low voice, "What did you expect?"

For him it was simple. He despised our father in a quite uncomplicated way. For our mother's sake, he did not fight with him. He shouldered the work of the farm and managed it well, for underneath all his dash he was a serious farmer; but in his heart he was only living for the day when he would be master of this hall.

He cracked his marrowbone and scooped it clean with a finger. "Why don't you clear off and go to sea for a bit, Odd?" he said. "The farm could spare you and any trading ship would take you on. I know all the captains." Gunnar managed our yearly bartering expeditions to the coast. "You moon about strange places all the time."

That was true. But something held me back. I was Black Thorvald's child, a part of him in some way that Gunnar—blond and bold and good-natured—would never understand. My father and I had unfinished business, though when or how it would ever be finished I did not know. But it was pointless to say this aloud.

"What, and leave you here to wolf down all the best bits?" I grabbed his marrowbone. He pushed me back and we wrestled, laughing, ending up in a pile on the floor.

3

A walk in the night

Late that night I lay awake in my place on the wall-bench, listening to the breathing of the others. My head ached and my brain teemed with restless thoughts.

A creaking noise—the door to my parents' bed-closet swung open. Ulf, my father's old hound, heard it too, heaved himself up from his warm place by the hearth, and trotted over to the shadowy figure that filled the doorway. The two shadows glided to the outer door, the bar was slid back, and they went out into the gray half-light of a northern spring night.

Going to piss, I thought idly. But another thought stirred in me. Visions come clearer out of doors, he always said. Our mother had scoffed at his dream vision, but he believed. *I believed.* Was he going out to seek a waking one? I lay still for a while, waiting to see if he would return. When he didn't, I pulled my cloak around my shoulders and followed.

A milk-white mist covered the ground. I stood shivering by the door, searching for a sight of him. Out on the heath, a nightjar cried. Behind me the river whispered between its stony banks. Black against gray, the slumbering bulk of Hekla floated in the distance. I had lived all my life under the shadow of the volcano. From that direction I caught a movement. Ulf raced back and barked around my legs.

I could just make him out. "Father, wait!"

"Go back!"

He started away and I followed, walking quickly because I knew what great strides he took. I remembered too well how my little-boy legs had to work to keep up with him when he would take me on those midnight marches that filled my childhood with such terror and wonder. I didn't need to catch up. I knew where he was going.

Ulf raced back and forth between us, but soon tired and fell back, leaving us alone—two shadows in the void. I thought, as I did when I was a boy, that Chaos must have looked like this on the day before creation.

For it was of such things that my father would rant, as we tramped the countryside on those restless nights long ago. Dragging me behind him with his hard hand gripping my small one, the words would pour out of him, for whole hours at a time, in a howling mad torrent. He taught me how Odin All-Father hung for nine days and nine nights on the windswept tree, on Yggdrasil the Sacred Ash, pierced by a spear, himself a sacrifice to himself. How he peered into the depths, grasped the runes and, screaming in his frenzy, flung them up. And he told me what natures the other gods had—guileful Loki and handsome Balder, and Frey, who makes the grain grow, and Red-Bearded Thor, bluff and jolly, except when he stands on the thunderclouds and hurls his hammer. But always and always he came back to Odin—Sorcerer, Rune-Master, Lord of the battle-mad berserkers. The more that darkness closed in around his mind, the more my father turned his hopes on One-Eyed Odin.

But where was there room for hope? He had had a vision, he said, of the end of things.

First would come a long, killing winter, and after that an Age of Axes, an Age of Swords, and an Age of Wolves. Kin would slaughter kin. The sky would split, the sun turn dark, and in Hel's Hall a cock would crow, and the fettered monsters would wake and break their bonds—Garm the Hel-Hound and the Wolf Fenris, whose gaping jaws stretch from earth to sky.

Then would gather all the enemies of gods and men—the giant, Hyrm, driving from the east in a boat made of dead men's nails, and the Midgaard Serpent, hissing and dropping poison, and all the dead, marching back along the road from Hel. They would ring Asgard round, they would storm across the Rainbow Bridge, and the armies of gods and giants would clash on a dark plain in the Last Battle. The wolf would swallow Odin and in the end, all would be dead—gods, giants, ogres—all. He called it Ragnarok, the doom of the gods.

*A hundred paces ahead of me I could see his back
bent over double as he toiled upward.*

After such a night's excursion I would creep under my covers and shake. My mother would hold me then and, in comforting me, try to make me tell what I had heard. I told her nothing.

In the mornings I would reason with myself, for I am a reasoner by nature. If the gods were dead, or doomed, then why not let them go? Why not accept the Christian god as nearly everyone did and let life be simple? My mother believed in the White Christ and she was a good woman.

No. Almost ... but, no. My father's hold on me was too great for that.

He raved because he knew things so deep that they drove him mad. He shook and bullied me because these were things so hard to tell that the words stuck in his throat. And he taught me—this above all—because I was his spirit-child. I was everything to him.

For his sake, then, I thought, let these doomed gods have my prayers, for what little good it may do them. The White Christ has all the rest.

That was what I said to myself in the morning. But oh, how he frightened me at night.

After some years the night marches stopped. His bouts of melancholy, which earlier had come only at intervals, mostly in the dark of winter, grew longer and more frequent. He would sink into brooding silences that lasted for days. It was then that I began to think he was bewitched.

I did everything to keep him from slipping away from me. Because I was gifted with word-wit beyond my years, I could recall every word he had ever spoken to me. Tales by the dozen, not all of them gloomy, and fierce poems on the deaths of heroes, composed in that knotty, riddling skaldic style of verse of which he, like many an old warrior, was a master. He used to declaim them to the mountains sometimes in a ringing drumbeat voice. Now, in an effort to please him, I shaped poems of my own, devising the most complex meters, the most elaborate kennings. Always only to please him.

As he had taught me the shapes and names of the runes, I begged him to reveal to me their secret uses, too. And he did teach me a little, but soon lost interest. He would grunt and put me off when I pestered him to teach me more, until at last, I ceased to ask. Perhaps he'd begun to doubt the magic himself and was afraid to put it to the test. But I feared it was some secret flaw in *me* that unfitted me to learn it.

Finally, I could find no way to break through the wall he had built around himself. As I grew older, I turned more and more to Gunnar, whom I adored. I saw how my father hated that, and so I did it all the more. Let him choke on it!

✝

We had tramped for miles now and the ground began to rise and leave the mist behind. A hundred paces ahead, I saw his back bent low as he toiled upward. I scrambled after him, my feet slipping on the loose pumice stones and the fractured lava rocks with edges like knives. I called his name, but he went on as though he didn't hear.

I remembered the boy I was, no more than ten, who came flying down this mountainside one night, half running and half falling, cut to ribbons by the stones and blinded by tears. In all the years since then I had not dared to go back.

But now—since the stallion fight, I told myself—I was no longer afraid. I had mastered fear itself. And so I climbed.

Hours passed. Now I had come as far as the snow-filled crevices that reached like skeleton fingers down the blue-black mountainside. The going was very steep as I neared the top. My palms and knees were bloody. An icy wind tore at my clothes and wailed in my ears like the shrieking of ghosts.

Here began the bottomless fissure that split the mountain lengthwise. A sulphurous steam rose from it. I climbed for another hour, working my way along the edge. I knew where my father would stop.

"Get away from me! Why d'you follow me?" He stood tottering on the rim of the crater. I sank down in the snow at his feet.

"To see what you see. Our fate."

"I've seen that already. I told you."

"Then, to see the Old Ones in the mountain." I scarcely knew what I was saying, I only wanted to be near him.

"You had that chance, boy. It wasn't to your liking."

"I was only a child...."

He had dragged me here one night, snorting like a bull in his fury, and pushed me to the edge to show me my tomb. For into Hekla, he said, die all the men of our family. In terror, thinking that he meant to kill me, I broke away from him and flung myself headlong down the slope. By the time I reached the bottom I was half dead and lay in a brain fever for three days. When I recovered, I tried to excuse myself to him, but he only turned from me with a scowl and never mentioned that night again. Though later my mother told me he had not eaten or slept during those three days that I hung between life and death.

"Well, if it pleases you now," he said, "look your fill."

I crept to the edge and peered over. Far below, the fiery red muck rolled and spat like blood soup in a cauldron. I felt its scorching breath on my skin and sweat broke out on me. The stench of sulfur made my stomach heave.

"Well, boy, d'you see them? The Old'uns? Sitting at their stone table, feasting, banging their mugs, roaring for ale? D'you see how they grin and howl at us? They wait for us, boy, they wait for us!"

I stared until I could stand it no more. Weeping and retching from the fumes, I drew back from the edge. I had seen nothing. I shook my head, afraid to look at him.

For a time he was silent, and then he said in a gentler voice, "You haven't the sight, boy, and you're better off without it. It's a curse. If I could, I would never see again, for it can steal the heart from a man." He sounded suddenly weary.

"No, Father, don't say so. Your heart is still in its place, ready to beat again. Believe me."

"Believe *you*? Why, what have you seen of the world?"

"None of it, Father, I'm sorry."

He gazed at me in silence for a time. "Well, not your fault. Not your fault. Go away now, Odd. We'll talk another time. Go home and sleep."

"What about you?"

"I sleep best here."

I stood, uncertain what to do. He turned me around by the shoulders and I began to pick my way down the mountain track.

"Odd," he called after me, "the horse fought well?"

"Like a hero, Father. I never had to touch him with the goad."

"You say so? Never touched him? Well, bravely done, boy. You are a stallion fighter. I was one once, too."

"Yes, Father."

I left him to the volcano, which he loved, and to the dead, with whom he spoke more easily than with the living. But I thought that, maybe, I had made a small beginning on our unfinished business.

✝

The sun was high in the sky by the time I reached home. Mother and Vigdis were working in the garden, Gudrun was chasing piglets, Gunnar and the thralls were at work shoring up the hay barn's sagging roof. My brother stared at me in frank curiosity as I passed. So did the others. Our mother, kneeling to pull out weeds, avoided my eyes. They all guessed where I had been.

I went inside and threw myself down to sleep.

4

A WHISPER FROM ANOTHER WORLD

Heyannir is the month of haymaking. In the home fields of Thorvaldsstead, the sweet-smelling hay grew as high as our heads. Brown-shouldered under the sun, we worked late into the white nights, Gunnar and I with the thralls, swinging our scythes in long straight lines across the field. Scraps of straw clung to our bodies, stuck in our hair, filled our nostrils and throats, and often we stopped to sluice ourselves with buckets of cold river water and shake our heads like wet dogs to fling away the droplets.

Behind us followed the women and children, gossiping and playing as they gathered the hay with long-handled rakes, spread it on the racks to dry, and heaped it on the wooden sledges to be dragged by oxen to the barn.

It's hard work and happy work, haying.

And dangerous. An open field is a bad place to be found by your enemies. Always, while we worked, we kept our weapons close at hand and posted a man on the ridge to watch for riders. But none came to molest us and the summer passed without incident. It was a better summer than many we had seen. We made three crops of hay and one each of barley and rye. Now winter could do its worst, but the animals would not starve and we would have enough to eat and drink.

Meantime, the sheep grazed placidly in their upland pasture. We men took it in turns to spend a day and a night there, camping out in the little stone shieling that perched on the rim of the high valley. And Gudrun often sneaked away to join us. There was a certain hillock up there where elves lived and she was determined to surprise them into showing themselves. If an elf man wanted her for his bride, she told us, she would happily go with him into the hillside.

I looked forward to these hours up in the pastures, too, but my love was no elf girl. Morag was an Irish woman, neither young nor old, with a strong thick body, an open face, and a giving nature. Thorvald had bought her as a child from a band of vikings who'd lifted her in a raid and brought her home to sell. We owned about a dozen thralls and treated them decently, feeding them good porridge every day and beating them rarely. When Morag was fifteen or so, Thorvald made her his concubine. However, when the melancholy grew so great in him that his spear would no longer rise to the challenge, he sent her back to the thralls' quarters to be a bedfellow to Aelfric, his freedman. Morag resented this bitterly. Her revenge was to cuckold Aelfric, and not just with anyone, but with the master's sons. She found us willing accomplices. First had been Gunnar, and now me.

I liked Morag because she said my looks reminded her of her own people and she didn't mind them a bit. On such flattery, I throve.

As often as we could manage to find ourselves alone in meadow or pasture, I would assail her with my ardent young kisses and we would couple in a hot and hasty rush, she with her skirt under her chin, crooning as I rolled between her muscular thighs. Such moments came seldom enough and were too short. And sometimes they were not as private as we thought.

One hot afternoon as we lay stretched on the earthen floor of the shieling, there came a muffled giggle from the doorway.

With my trousers down, I lurched toward Gudrun Night-Sun. She danced out of reach before I could get my fingers around her neck.

"Shame on you, Tangle-Hair,"—wagging her finger at me—"for tumbling dear old Morag, who's practically one of the family, and do pull down your shirt, you look ridiculous. Now, what will you give me not to tell Father?"

"It's what I'll give you if you do, you little sneak!"

She would settle for nothing less than my best belt with the buckle of silvered brass, which happened, at that moment, to be around my ankles.

Clasping that treasure around her, she raced away shrieking with merriment down the hillside.

I was cross, but Morag chuckled and pulled me down to her again. "Never mind, darling," she whispered into the hollow of my neck, "we'll catch little sister here one day and pay her back."

It is frightening how words come true in ways we never meant.

✝

As autumn drew to a close, we girded ourselves against the coming of the long nights. Now our mother took charge—marshaling her army of women and girls, and scolding the men out of her way.

Jorunn Ship-Breast was as strong as a man, with a broad face, big hands, and shrewd blue eyes. It was said she'd been a beauty once, and you could still see a little of it when she smiled. For one smile of hers, she told us, young men had whiled away hours in her father's hall. But it was the fierce, black-haired viking she'd chosen, and her father, of course, had been delighted to marry his only daughter into the family of a godi, one of the forty-eight chieftains of Iceland.

But now she was nearing fifty, and her beauty was mostly gone. She had born ten babies and buried seven, had labored like an ox in the fields, had seen her bold young husband change into a hateful stranger—yet she had steadfastly refused to divorce him for his heathenism, even though her family begged her to. She was a brave-hearted woman such as only Iceland breeds, and it was her strength that held us together. I admired her more than loved her. What was in her secret thoughts, I never knew.

Under her watchful eye, the thrall women poked the cakes of soot down from the rafters, scrubbed the tables with sand, and lay new straw on the floor. They made ale, seething the malted barley in foaming caldrons over hot stones; they churned the milk into tubs of butter and great yellow wheels of cheese; they packed our soiled clothes, stained with the summer's sweat, onto the backs of the horses and carried them to the hot pools. Like an officer at the head of her column, rode Jorunn Ship-Breast, and it was four days' scrubbing and boiling before they marched triumphantly back.

It came time now for Gunnar to go down to the coast and trade. Gunnar loved trading. Though he cared little for anyone's religion, he'd gone to the trouble to have himself prime-signed by a priest, so that the Christian merchants would feel easier doing business with him. In his dealings he always made a shrewd bargain and never lost a friend.

Often I had gone with him. But this year, though the name of Strife-Hrut was not mentioned aloud, it was understood that one of us should stay at the farm. Early one morning then, with all the packhorses loaded and four armed thralls to accompany him, he set out.

As soon as they were out of sight we felt naked. Vigdis was tense, and her baby turned colicky, crying night and day. Thorvald kept himself in his smithy, hammering furiously all the day long at horseshoes and bucket hoops. I spent my days in the bog with a crew of thralls cutting peat for our winter's fuel. And I never went out without my sword.

A week passed, then two. Gunnar had never been gone as long as this. Fear gathered round us like a fog. I was just debating with myself whether to go after him when, about midday, we heard his *halloo* from the shoulder of the ridge where it slopes to meet the river. We looked up to see him on his sorrel mare, plunging down in a spray of stones with the pack animals skittering after.

Springing from his horse, he swept Vigdis up in one arm, threw the other around our mother's neck, and kissed them both. "It was a capital trip if I say it myself!" he laughed. "Wheat flour, dried fish, seaweed for our salt, all the usual, and more!"

"Gunnar," Vigdis squealed. "What have you done to your face?"

"What—oh, this? Saw a Norwegian fellow with his beard combed to a point. Fancied it myself. And then I thought an earring would go nicely with it. What do you think?" He kissed her again and we all stood laughing at him. "But look here," he said, "I've brought presents for you all. We need a bit of cheering up, don't we?"

With a flourish, he reached inside the folds of his cloak, playfully mumbled magic words, and materialized his treasures, one by one. "New combs of walrus-ivory for mother and Vigdis and—where's the Night-Sun? Gone to find her elf-lover in the pasture? Well, she never combs her hair anyway. And for mother a breast-brooch, and for Vigdis three ells of fine linen to make me a shirt...."

"Gunnar, the way you spend!" Vigdis scolded, but she was smiling in spite of herself.

"And for Odd ... now let me see ... what have I done with it? Ah!" Turning away, he fumbled in his purse, then stretched out his closed fist to me.

"Well, let loose of it," I said, prying at his fingers until he opened them. In the hollow of his palm lay a silver coin, scarcely bigger than my thumbnail. I held it up to the sun, turning it this way and that, while the others crowded round.

"Some great king for sure," said Jorunn. "See his crown."

"And see how the eyes hold you," said Vigdis.

"Who is he, Gunnar?" we asked.

Gunnar shrugged. "Won it at dice from a Saxon captain who had it from a Dane who had sailed far to the east. The Dane said it was Greek, but that was all he knew."

We studied it some more. One side of it bore the head and shoulders of a bearded man—gaunt, thin-lipped and solemn, who stared at us out of round eyes. The other side of the coin was covered with writing—half a dozen words in letters none of us had seen before.

"They aren't runes," I said.

"Nor priests' writing," said our mother.

While they talked, I rubbed the little precious thing between my thumb and forefinger, trying to imagine what other fingers had touched it; fingers of gaunt, round-eyed men and women who glided in jeweled robes through unimaginable landscapes somewhere at the ends of the earth. My mother, laying her hand on my arm, begged me to treasure the coin for it was sure to bring me luck.

Whatever luck it brought me was mixed of good and evil. I finally lost it during my years of slavery, long before I reached Golden Miklagard. Still, I happened to think of it one evening when I was strolling with the Empress Zoe in the gardens of the Great Palace. A tear trickled down her cheek to think that her grandfather's face had reached the shores of Ultima Thule and stirred my young heart.

We hadn't noticed Thorvald trudging from the smithy until he was suddenly upon us. Gunnar turned quickly to rummage in a packsaddle and brought out a parcel wrapped in chamois. "The chisels, Father. The ones you wanted."

Thorvald let him put the chisels in his hand. They avoided each other's eyes.

"What's that thing?" He took the coin from me and squinted at it. "Keep your Christian king out of my sight or I'll take a hammer to him." He flung it on the ground and stalked away.

Gunnar clenched his fist and looked as if he would go after him, but Jorunn held him back, her eyes pleading. In embarrassed silence we all turned to unloading the horses.

That evening, after an early supper, we sat with our ale horns, talking quietly across the long hearth, except for father who kept his usual silence while he whittled.

"Did you hear anything of Hrut?" I asked Gunnar.

"Only that he's back from his summer trading voyage. They say Mord's still got both his eyes, worse luck, though he isn't so pretty to look at anymore."

There was a scratching on the outside of the door, close to the ground.

"But what do you think?" Jorunn pressed him.

"Well, it's been four months, hasn't it, and they haven't stirred a finger against us. I expect we gave Strife-Hrut more of a fight than he'd bargained for."

"No," I said, "I don't believe it."

"Or, don't want to believe it, Odd?" asked my mother. "Must we feud to make you happy?"

The scratching came again.

"Let's talk about something else," said Vigdis, taking the baby from her breast and handing him to her husband to bounce. "Did you stop off to see my brothers?"

Again, the scratching.

Jorunn in exasperation said to Vigdis, who was nearest the door, "Daughter-in-law, shoo the pig away or let it in, I don't care which."

Vigdis opened the door and screamed.

5

BLOOD FOR BLOOD

Gudrun Night-Sun lay on the threshold, her face pressed against the stone, her hands clawing the ground. A trail of blood led out through the garden gate. Her face was dead white, the eyes glassy. She looked as though she had no blood left in her body—her dress was sodden with it. It oozed from a wound in her chest.

Jorunn gathered her up and lay her on the wall bench. Thorvald stared at her, his eyes almost out of his head, then staggered away. I heard him groan.

"Christ Jesus!" cried my mother. "How? Where was she?"

She knelt beside Gudrun and lifted the blood-soaked dress from her legs. "Ahh!" she moaned when she saw the blood between her thighs where she had been ripped. "Baby, who did this to you?"

Gudrun's lips moved, but no sound came out. Only saliva bubbled at the corners of her mouth.

Vigdis dashed to the river and came back with her hands full of moss to press against the wound. But we all knew it was too late for that.

"Where was your sister?" Jorunn demanded of Gunnar and me.

"Up at the shieling," I said. "Looking for her elf lover."

"And dragged herself all this way?" Vigdis murmured. It seemed almost impossible.

"Elves didn't do this," said Jorunn between her teeth, her breath coming short.

"Trolls, then?" I said.

"Or men no better than trolls," Gunnar said.

We looked at each other and knew.

"I'm going to the shieling," I said, reaching for my sword. "Father—?"

But he had retreated to his high seat and wouldn't look at us.

"Leave him," Gunnar snarled. He grabbed up a spear and ran out the door.

I raced after him.

In the high pasture we found a bloody shambles. Slaughtered sheep lay everywhere, and the bodies of the three young thralls who had been with her, too—all dead. Inside the hut, I noticed something glittering in a corner—my belt with the silvered buckle. They must have pulled it off her when they raped her. We ran farther up the slope to the rim of the valley and looked out. Nearly lost in the glare of the sun were some black specks moving rapidly away from us—toward the coast where Hrut's farm lay.

Back at the house we told what we had seen.

"Send us after them, Father!" I cried.

But he pressed his hands to his temples and squeezed his eyes shut.

"Send us, you useless, pitiful old man," shouted Gunnar, nearly in tears, "or we'll go anyway."

"No!" Thorvald backed away from us toward the door. "How do you know it was Hrut—doesn't the whole world hate us? It might have been anyone. Time enough to act when the girl recovers."

"Recovers!" Jorunn hissed, kneeling by the body. "Husband, in Christ's name...."

With a sudden swift motion, he snatched his sword from the wall and planted himself in the doorway. He was breathing hard and sweating.

"Listen to me, all of you! I know what you think of me, but I'm telling you the truth. Listen to me. We are defenseless. We have no allies, no friends. But this man, Hrut, isn't he a Christman like the others? They'll back him up. Oh, don't I know how it's done? They'll combine against us. They'll wipe us out. Can't you see that? Except that we'll not give them their chance—oh no, not for a few sheep, and thralls, and a ... and a girl. We won't let them destroy us just for that!"

He swayed in the doorway, making menacing thrusts at us with his sword. His eyes were mad. We would have to kill him to get past him. Gunnar would have done it gladly but for our mother.

Instead, we turned to doing what we could for Gudrun.

Whoever stabbed her had a faltering hand and missed her heart. He would have been kinder to have done the job cleanly. It took her long to die.

Meanwhile, Jorunn bided her time. For so long she had submitted herself to her husband—out of love, or duty, who could say? But the savaging of her child changed that.

All evening Thorvald kept his post by the door, haranguing us in wild, incoherent sentences. Terrified himself, he was terrifying to us. We kept our eyes averted—I especially, for I felt that his were constantly on me. Instead we busied ourselves with changing the compresses of moss every little while, and bathing Gudrun's cold face and hands.

Mercifully, she never woke up.

I must have sunk at last into an exhausted sleep, for I was struggling in a violent dream when I opened my eyes suddenly and sat bolt upright. Hours had passed. The room was silent and dark as pitch except for the flicker of a lamp flame above my head. Behind the flame hovered my mother's face, pale as a ghastly moon in the black sky, her unbound hair streaming loose over her shoulders.

Not saying a word, she took my sword down from its peg on the wall and put it in my hands, leaning so close that her damp hair brushed my face. Still half in my dream, I rose and followed her outside. There I found Gunnar standing with two of the thralls, armed with spears, and four horses. A night wind had risen. It whipped his hair against his face.

"I told her to wake you, brother. Even now she wasn't going to make you disobey him. Did I do right?"

"Where is he?"

"Out there," he pointed with his chin, contemptuously, toward the mountain, "wandering and talking to himself. Mother leads us now."

I felt sick to my stomach. "May the gods help him, Gunnar."

"May the gods fling him down the bloody crater and have done! Are you coming or not?"

I eased my sword a little from its scabbard and tested its edge with my thumb. Its name was 'Neck-Biter'. It was an old weapon, heavy and plain-hilted, that had belonged to several men before it came to me. Others, no doubt, had killed with it. I, at the old age of sixteen, had never drawn it in anger. Time to change that.

I swung into the saddle and kicked my horse hard. Gunnar led us at a dead gallop into the dusk. The rest of that night and all the next day we followed the river, stopping only once along the way to beg some curds and milk from a farmwife for our breakfast. Late in the afternoon, we reached the coast, and turning northwards, rode up along the black sand beach toward the mouth of the Whitewater.

Before we'd gone half the distance we found them. A big finback whale had beached itself and Hrut's two sons were there with a couple of their hired men and some packhorses to cut it up for meat.

Brand, the eldest, who was standing spraddle-legged on the whale's back, saw us first and shouted a warning to the other three. They spun around to face us. Plainly they hadn't expected us to come after them or they wouldn't have been so few and so far from home. How they must despise us, I thought.

We dismounted and started towards them, Gunnar striding ahead, loose-limbed and balancing his crescent-bladed axe in his hand—easy as could be, although I knew he had never fought a man to the death before.

When we were close enough to see the ragged scar on Mord's cheek, Gunnar asked mockingly if he might have another chance at that eye. "'Second time perfect' as they say."

"What for?" said Mord, edging sideways. "We're quits, Hjalti-godi said so."

"Quits, you dog-shit, *You* say that?"

"Get back to your mountain, you sons-of-trolls, you haven't any business with proper men."

"Fight me!"

But fighting wasn't to Mord's taste. "Bork!" he shouted. At his command, the broad-shouldered fellow standing beside him ran forward and swung at Gunnar with his billhook. Gunnar crouched, leaning to the side, then sprang forward and brought his axe down so hard on the man's head that it split him to the jaw and his teeth spilled out on the ground.

This was too much for Mord. Before Gunnar could regain his balance, he dashed past him, leapt on his horse, and galloped off. An instant later, Gunnar was on his own mount, and, followed by both our thralls, was pounding after him down the beach and out of sight.

Their other man, deciding that this fight was no business of his, threw down his gaff and ran away.

Which left me and Brand face to face.

He was taller than me by a head, and he held a long-handled axe that he had been using to carve the whale.

"Are you coming down, Brand Hrutsson," I shouted, "or must I come up?" It sounded like a fine, brave thing to say.

"Either way, Blackie, it's more meat for my axe!"

I threw a stone, which struck him on the shoulder. He gave a shout, jumped down from the whale's back, and ran at me.

His axe head whistled past my face, missing me by an inch. I sprang back in pure terror. Then, with one swooping cut after another, he drove me backwards into the water until both of us were thigh deep in the surf and there was nowhere left to run. He coiled himself for another swing.

The thought flashed through my mind that I was about to die and that my life, so far, had been nothing to boast of. As the axe came down, I shut my eyes and dashed in low, grappling him around the chest. The force of his swing threw us both off our feet and down we went, rolling over together in the churning water.

Then it was hands, knees, and teeth. I bit his hand, making him let go the axe, but he kicked free of me and we came up spluttering and pawing our hair from our eyes. He pulled his sword and waded in close, cut at me once, and again. I still had my sword in hand and, half-blinded by the streaming water, struck out wildly with it.

Neck-Biter bit deep. Brand's head lolled sideways, and, turning around, he took five steps toward the shore before he pitched over on his face.

I sank down beside him in the reddening sea-foam.

A little time passed while I sat in the water, my chest heaving and my limbs shaking. Then, hearing the thud of hoofs on the sand, I looked up to see Gunnar and the thralls coming back.

"Tangle-Hair!" cried my brother, throwing himself down at the water's edge.

"It's all right, I'm not hurt."

"Look at you."

I hadn't noticed. Brand's point had gone deep into my left biceps when he lunged at me, and the blood was dripping from my fingertips. As I looked, pain lanced me like a hot needle.

"Mord?" I asked, when I got my breath.

"Too fast for me. And I didn't care to chase him all the way to Hrutsstead, they keep a small army there. We can't stay here in the open." Looking from me to Brand and back again, he gave a low whistle. "I wish I'd seen it."

"I fought like a plowboy. I was scared out of my wits."

"Brother," he laughed, "any fool can be fearless, just look at me." He touched Brand's body with his foot. "There's a funeral gift for our sister, paid for with your fear. There's nothing dearer bought than that. Cut his head the rest of the way off. Go on, do it! Skidi Dung-Beetle,"—he motioned to one of our thralls— "give us your cloak to wrap it in."

Gunnar sawed off the cloven head of the man called Bork, and together we hurriedly covered the two corpses with stones, as the law requires. That done, we mounted and rode away, stopping only at the farmstead we had passed earlier that morning to give notice of our killings, which the law also demands.

The sun was low when we slid wearily from our saddles in the yard of Thorvaldsstead. Jorunn Ship-Breast watched us from the doorway.

"What have my sons done?"

We tossed the heads in their bloody wrapping at her feet. At the sight of it her eyes caught fire.

"Your sister will have joy of it," she said. "She died in the night. Her grave is dug. We've waited for you."

The words she spoke were plain, but black hate and battle joy rang in her voice.

I felt it, too. Round and round in my head ran the words, *You are a warrior. Never mind the fear and the pain, nothing that a man does is better than this.*

That night we busied ourselves with preparations for the coming of Hrut. By dawn the weapons had been sharpened, the thralls armed, lookouts posted.

But when Strife-Hrut Ivarsson came, it was with no army of killers at his back. He came instead with nine farmers as witnesses, as the law prescribes, and from his saddle screamed at us the formula of summons to the next summer's Althing on a charge of murder.

In amazement we watched them wheel their mounts and gallop off.

"Murder!" I exploded. "It's not murder, it's manslaughter, rightful killing in feud. We declared it so at his neighbor's farm."

Gunnar shot me a worried look. "Odd, did you not recognize that selfsame neighbor just now among the nine witnesses? Either bribed or frightened, it makes no difference, he'll swear to Hrut's version of the facts, not ours."

"Oh wife, oh sons of mine," said Thorvald in a voice like doom. "D'you begin to see now what you have done?"

He had come back from his wandering just after Gunnar and I reached home. I had expected him to be furious at us, but as so often happened with him, his frenzy had given way to dumb resignation. After his daughter's burial, he had taken to his high-seat again, and from there, all night, he watched us—not helping, but at least, not hindering our preparations for battle.

"You may cry to the mountains that Hrut murdered your sister, but you have no proof. Instead it is *you* now who face trial for murder."

"But the law—" protested Gunnar.

"Bugger the law, you fool. You've tossed a sword at Hrut's feet—for law is the sharpest sword of all. And he is not the man to let it lie. He will go away from the Althing with our lives, our land, with everything that is ours, and the law will smile on him."

There was a deep silence in the room. For this sounded to us not like a madman's ravings, but the hard-earned wisdom of a man who had once sat among the forty-eight godis of Iceland. Vigdis moved closer to Gunnar and put her hand in his. The thralls traded tense, stealthy glances.

"No, Husband," cried Jorunn, "you are wrong. Whether you like to admit it or not, there *is* one who can save us, for nothing is beyond his wit."

"Shut your mouth, woman, a troll has twisted your tongue! Even if he could do what you say, I would not beg my life of that man."

"No, but *I* will, and he'll do it for me and his nephews—and because it's his Christian duty. Thank God for my brother, Hoskuld Long-Jaws!"

✝

Soon after this, black night came down on us like a cover on a kettle. It was a brief and pale light that drifted down the smoke hole when the feeble sun got his head up over the horizon, only to sink back at once, exhausted, into the sea. Snow piled high against the door, sealing us in our smoky tomb. We huddled with the animals for warmth, drank much, but without cheer, and thought our own gloomy thoughts. Yuletide came, but we, holding neither to the old religion nor the new, scarcely knew how to keep it.

Winter wore on. And then one day, the Ranga loosened in its icy sleeve, the sun grew stronger, and the rains came. Thorvald would not sow the barley seed that spring, for he said he did not expect to reap the crop. But, under our mother's eye, Gunnar and I took his place.

Our neighbors took their fighting-stallions to the South Quarter Thing, and no doubt, recalled to each other, shaking their heads, that bad business of a year ago. People with little to remember forget none of it.

We kept to ourselves and waited.

And at last the day came when it was time to ride to the Althing.

6

FRIENÐ KALF

Jorunn bustled about the yard, ordering, haranguing, directing. "Daughter-in-law, set down the bedding and help me with the cooking things. Skidi Dung-Beetle, is this how you tighten a girth? Skin the man, must I do all?"

The fat-bellied horses shifted patiently under towers of sheepskins and tenting, cauldrons and tripods, clean clothes and weapons, while we scurried back and forth between house and yard.

Our caravan complete at last with everything needful for a week's camping on Thingvellir Plain, Jorunn called out with forced cheerfulness, "Husband, take your place in the lead." She did not want to shame him in front of the thralls, who were gathered to see us off. He obeyed her like a sullen child, but it was Jorunn who gave the signal to advance. Looking, with all our baggage, like a family of tinkers, we lurched up the stony track that led from our home-field, out into the wild country beyond.

Our first destination was Hoskuldsstead.

Hoskuld Long-Jaws was my mother's brother, a widower who farmed at Hawkdale-by-Geysir, in the house where he and Jorunn had grown up. Not being designed by nature for an active life, he had devoted himself to the pursuits of farming and law. He had succeeded so far in both that his fifty milk cows and two hundred milking ewes were the fattest in southern Iceland, and his law-wit was sought after by many. Even powerful godis were not ashamed to take his advice in their lawsuits.

My mother wanted more than advice. She would ask him to be our advocate and plead our case at the Althing. Being fifteen years younger than he, she saw in him more a father than a brother, and her faith in him was boundless. She had already sent him word of our troubles, and it was arranged that we should break our journey at his house before going on together to the Althing.

And what had Black Thorvald to say about this? Not a whisper of a word. During the winter he had grown ever more listless and despondent, his energies so low he could seldom even rouse himself to a rage. He gave up washing and combing his hair, and very nearly gave up eating. By winter's end he had aged ten years.

For myself, I was determined to be hopeful, and so clung to my mother and Gunnar, whose optimism never flagged.

✝

Our way lay northwest across an open heath ribbed with steep, stony ridges cut by swift rivers. We rode for hours, it seemed, before the great glittering rampart of Long Glacier began to grow large on the horizon. And meanwhile a ribbon of smoke curling up from Hekla's peak still smudged the sky behind us, as though the volcano were unwilling to let us go. The heath gave way to a stretch of watery meadow in which treacherous bogs lay hidden. Beyond the meadow, we came to a range of gray, stony hills that rose like whales' backs from the mossy earth. The track we followed wound between them and brought us suddenly to Gulfoss, a thundering cascade of water that spilled into the river below us. We broke our journey here, and while the women saw to supper, we men found a hot pool and soaked ourselves in the steaming, milk-white water.

Next morning, we traversed several miles of smiling farm land, passing any number of farmhouses along the way, until abruptly, as by a line drawn across a map, the tilled land ended and the great lava field began. Here stood pillars of black and twisted rock that were said to be the bodies of night-trolls caught and frozen by the sun.

Scrabbling up a hill of cinders, we saw spread out before us the red, cracked plain of Hawkdale, overhung with the pall of countless smokes. We kept tight rein on our mounts now, for they hated the sulfur stench and shied at the spitting pools of hot mud and the roaring jet of Geysir.

More hours of riding brought us, at last, out of the reek of Hawkdale and to the edge of Hoskuld's fields. With the sun already slanting toward the hills, we straggled into his yard and slid from our horses.

My uncle was an elongated man: long of neck, long of nose, long of tooth, and his body, too, was put together of long, brittle limbs. He stood in the doorway, peering owlishly at us until he could discern our shapes and a little of our features, for he was nearly blind. He put out his arms as we approached and embraced us gravely, one by one.

"Sister," he pronounced in his mournful bass—a single word as good as a speech—stern, tender, and reproachful all at once. Jorunn leaned against his chest and dabbed at her eyes. "Gunnar the Handsome," he spoke over her head, "you look fit as ever. And Vigdis Sveinsdottir. He bent down for her to kiss his cheek. "Odd Tangle-Hair, what a black, hairy face you've gotten." He held my chin in his big-knuckled hand, turning me critically this way and that." And of course, Thorvald ... welcome to my hall."

The two men barely touched hands. There was no love lost here—not for these thirty years past, ever since Hoskuld took up the new religion and did everything in his power to get Jorunn to divorce her heathen husband. This was the one instance, as I have already said, in which she had disobeyed her brother.

As hirelings and thralls took our horses, we trooped through the door into the glow of Hoskuld's spacious hall, far larger than our own.

In honor of our visit, the wooden walls were hung with tapestries— fine stuffs crowded with scenes of warriors and sailing ships, which I never tired of looking at. On the wall-benches, thick fleeces were spread where we would sit to dinner and later sleep. Along one wall stood tubs of butter and barrels of milk and beer, and over the long hearth hung simmering cauldrons of meat that filled the air with its savory aroma. My uncle lived well.

"Towels to wipe away the dust of travel," he ordered. They were brought promptly by the servants. "Ah, but don't sit down yet, kinsmen," he said, "for we've still time before dinner to walk the farm."

We always walked the farm. This was our ritual every spring upon arriving: to admire his new lambs, foals, and calves. Husbandry offered the only safe subject of talk between Hoskuld and my father.

Kalf Slender-Leg came in the nick of time to rescue me. Kalf was

Hoskuld's grandson and my closest friend—to tell the truth, my only friend, besides Gunnar.

"Odd, how goes it with you?"

"Pretty well, friend Kalf."

We always began shyly like that. Months at a stretch passed between our meetings and we surprised each other every time by being taller, gruffer, hairier, different in a dozen small ways. He was half a year younger than me, gangling and lean, with curly red hair and eyes quick to smile. His whole nature was brisk and lively.

He had a sheaf of arrows in his belt and two bows. He handed me one.

"Heh, what's this?" said my uncle, frowning down on us from his great height. Even though he had a stoop, he was quite tall. He made some rumbling and expostulating noises but ended with the observation that, "Young dogs must go off on their own," though, he warned, we should get no supper if we were late returning.

We were always 'young dogs' to Hoskuld, which we took to be an affectionate name, for he was a kindly man at bottom, though inclined to be pompous.

Promising to be prompt for dinner, we raced out the gate, followed by Kalf's black-and-tan bitch and by an envious look from Gunnar.

"Hel's Hall!" I swore, punching him on the back, "it's good to see you!"

"And you, by Odin's crow!"

Kalf liked to imitate my speech, swearing roundly by Hel, Thor, and Odin, though he was a baptized Christman, as well as following my lead in every other way. I loved him for it, I admit it. I craved admiration, and Kalf Slender-Leg was one who gave it gladly and unstintingly, even when I had done nothing to deserve it.

Though this time, of course, I had. I had killed a man.

"With this?" he asked, touching my sword in its scuffed old scabbard.

"Aye."

"Tell me everything."

I had no intention of telling him how, when the fight was over, I had sunk down on my knees in the water, sick and shaking. But in the end I told him that, too.

"Yes," he murmured, "it would be like that the first time."

"The first time, but not the next," I said in a hard voice. "The father and the brother still live."

"You mean to kill them too?"

"If it comes to that."

"Which it might, you know. You've never been to the Althing, have you?"

I shrugged, not liking to be reminded of the solitary life I was forced to lead.

"I've been lots of times with Grandfather. Thor's beard! The year before last, two families wrangled over a boundary stone, armed to the teeth and with all their supporters around them. When it was over eleven men were dead. It happens all the time."

"So much the better."

"Though I suppose Grandfather will get you through it all right, he's never lost a suit."

"He's never had the sons of Black Thorvald for clients."

Kalf knew me well enough to be cautious on the subject of my father. "Come on, Tangle-Hair, let's hunt!" He gave me a friendly push and raced away up a hillside, a fleet and tireless runner.

In a high boulder-strewn meadow we startled a brace of moorhens. They flew up with a beating of speckled wings, but one tumbled back instantly with Kalf's arrow through it. Then, seeing my shot go wide by a mile, he drew and loosed again. The second bird fell.

"Fair bit of shooting, Kalf."

"Well," he flashed me a grin, "it's a poor fellow who isn't good at something."

After that, we joked, wrestled, ran with the dog, and came to rest at last, out of breath, on a grassy hillside. We threw ourselves down and stared into the blue sky.

"Odd."

"Hmm."

"You remember the cliff?"

We always talked about that.

Two summers ago we had hiked from Hoskuldsstead all the way to the coast at Reykjanes and gone climbing on the cliffs with ropes and long-handled nets to gather puffins' eggs. The coast-dwellers pursue this dangerous activity from childhood. We, being inlanders, had never tried it before.

On the portion of cliff we selected, there happened to be a girl—a plump little thing about our age, who sat in the sling of her rope, with her skirt around her thighs, and swung from cranny to crag, with a great deal more confidence than we felt. Once we had secured our ropes with pegs and lowered ourselves down the sheer cliff side, she began to tease us and then to fling eggs at us, which seemed to amuse her greatly.

I could think of nothing better than to curse her, but resourceful Kalf climbed back up to the top of the cliff, saw where she'd pegged her rope, and cut it half way through. He lay on his belly with his head and shoulders over the edge so she could see that only his thin arms—which were stronger, fortunately, than they looked—were keeping her from falling to the rocks below. She screamed her head off, but there was no one about to hear. After a good long time, he and I together hauled her up.

She called us filthy names for a while and then we became friends. Her name was Thorgrima, she said, the daughter of a local fisherman. We spent a happy afternoon together exploring the caves in the neighborhood. Along the way, we explored Thorgrima, too. It was Kalf's first time with a girl.

"I went back there last month," he said.

"Not looking for our little friend, were you? Nobody could be that lucky twice."

"No, no. Just to watch for ships and talk to the crewmen. I can't stick it here much longer with only Grandfather and my sister Katla for company."

"Old Long-Jaws isn't a bad sort."

"I suppose not, though I never seem to profit from any of his advice."

"I can't say as much for your sister...."

"God, how I want to leave this island! In my own ship or another's, it wouldn't matter, only to be gone."

He spoke with such sudden passion that it made me sit up and look at him. But I understood. It was something we shared. Just as I had, so had Kalf a viking father, the only difference being that, while mine lived on as a squeaking ghost, his was gloriously dead.

Flosi Hoskuldsson had been a fierce pirate, the owner of two sleek dragons, and had gone on many a foray in Irish waters. In 1014 he joined the army of King Sigtrygg Silk-Beard of Dublin in his war against the Irish rebel, Brian Boru. Things turned out not as they wished. At a place called Clontarf, the Norse were routed and Flosi, who stood his ground to the last, was taken prisoner.

It was told later, by men who got away, how the Irish slit his belly and marched him round and round a tree until his guts were all unwound. Still he had smiled, they said, up to the very end.

Flosi had been Hoskuld's last child and his favorite. Four other children and his wife had all been carried off by fever years before. When word was brought to him of his son's death, the old man shut himself up in his bed-closet without food or drink for five days and never afterwards would speak Flosi's name or allow it to be spoken in his presence. Flosi's wife, who was pregnant at the time, came to live with him, and there she was delivered of Kalf and his twin sister Katla—dying in the process.

"Grandfather will never let me go," Kalf said bitterly. "Whenever I bring it up, he turns his face to the wall and reminds me that I'm his eyes. But it's not so. Katla can lead him as well as I. The truth is, he's afraid that someday they'll come and tell him *I'm* dead. But, One-Eyed Odin, what sort of a life do I have here? One day I will sail away and not come back, I swear it."

"Kalf Slender-Leg, one day I'll go with you."

Just for a moment, we looked in each other's eyes and understood why we were friends.

The sun touched the distant hills, where it would hang throughout the endless day-night, and our stomachs told us it was dinnertime. Tying the moorhens to our belts and whistling up the dog, we turned our steps toward Hoskuldsstead.

✝

By the time we got there, the hall was packed with Hoskuld's people— his tenants, his hirelings, his thralls, and an assortment of poor relations, whom he fed from his table. Long boards were set up on trestles and heaped with all the good things his farm provided. There were pickled eggs and bowls of skyr, steaming pans of flatbread, fermented shark, boiled mutton, beef, swan, and, an especial delicacy, the head of the sheep, carefully singed. Hoskuld himself was directing his servants to pour out the mead, made from English honey. At home we drank mead seldom, and this was a treat for us.

"I am not a rich man." Hoskuld addressed the room in his deep voice. (He was, in fact, a very rich man by our standards.) "Nor a traveled one—being not robust enough for the seafaring life. All the same I know how men live in the wide world. They drink this precious stuff, and so shall you, down to the humblest of you, for neither am I a niggardly man." From his high-seat he beamed complacently at all the gathered company.

Kalf and I slid onto the wall-bench next to Gunnar and Vigdis.

"Ah." Hoskuld squinted at us down the table. "Are the young dogs back? And have you had good hunting?" Katla, my dear, pour your kinsman's mead, there's a good girl."

How utterly different from Kalf was his twin. A hatchet-faced girl, plain as a turnip, and with a sour disposition to boot. Well-dowered though she was, she had no suitors. Tonight she was especially brusque in pouring my drink and raised an arrogant eyebrow at me. What's this about? I wondered, and then it struck me that it was Gudrun's death. As if Katla were saying, *I'm not pretty, but I'm alive.* The wretched girl!

"Thank you, Katla Thin-Hair," I said coolly, coining her nickname on the spot and seeing her stiffen with anger. Kalf snorted in his cup.

For a while then, there were only the sounds of hungry folk eating—or, in the case of my father, drinking, for I noticed he barely touched the dishes, though he honored the mead cask again and again. At last, when our bellies were full, we washed our soiled hands and Hoskuld signaled for the boards to be cleared and hoisted to the rafters. We settled down now to the evening's real business.

This was the moment I'd been waiting for. With a tremor of nervousness and a prayer to Odin, god of poets, I begged my uncle's permission to recite a poem.

I had labored over this creation of mine during many a long winter's night, saying nothing about it to anyone, intending it for this very gathering. Its title was *The Slaying of Brand Hrutsson.* It's a poor warrior, I told myself, who can't sing his own praises in passable verse, and I've been better taught than most my age.

It was an ambitious affair, done in the high skaldic style that my father was a master of, full of complicated word-play and ornamented with every obscure kenning I could remember or devise. The fight was a *helm-storm.* I, the victor, was *wolf-crammer* and *crow-fattener.* My battered sword was a *wound-snake,* and even the whale around which we fought made an appearance as *mountain of the sea-god's meadow.*

What a magical thing is poetry that can take a brawl between two clumsy farm boys and clothe it with ancient splendor.

My poem rose to a climax, and died away in a keening lament for Gudrun Night-Sun. I stood still, with my eyes lowered, not daring to breathe.

There was a moment's silence, followed by an explosion of stamping and pounding all across the room, from the hirelings in the back to Kalf and Gunnar at my elbow, who jumped up and let out piercing yells. My mother, too, was deeply moved, sitting silent and erect with a tear stealing from the corner of her eye.

Yet the eyes I wanted most to read were veiled. Had something flashed there for an instant, or was it only a trick of the firelight? My father sat impassive, his hands fooling with his knife and stick. He might have been alone in the room.

My uncle, on the other hand, seemed positively pained.

"I am not a poetical sort of man, nephew, and have nothing to say about wound-snakes and such, all very fine, I'm sure. But I am a legal man, and I tell you plain that the occasion for this poem of yours is very, very much to be regretted."

"Which brings us," said Gunnar, "to the subject."

"So it does."

Hoskuld Long-Jaws, sallow-skinned and saturnine, leaned back in his seat with his eyes half closed and the tips of his long fingers pressed together under his beaky nose, every inch the lawyer. To me he looked like nothing so much as a large, ancient, and dusty bird.

He continued in this way for a full minute, regarding us solemnly, and ruminating before he spoke again. "The trouble, you see, is that you've killed the wrong man."

My mother looked at him horror-stricken. Gunnar and I jumped up from our seats. Unperturbed, Hoskuld continued in his precise lawyer's way.

"It isn't simply the lack of witnesses to Gudrun's death—that's to be expected. But has Strife-Hrut, to our knowledge, ever bothered to deny a killing before, even a cowardly one like this? Did he not brag all over the district when he burnt up Illugi the Silent in his house, though women and children died in that fire? And then there's the matter of Brand and

Mord the next day—as young Odd has just been good enough to remind us—miles from home with only a couple of hirelings for protection? Men who are conscious of provoking a feud are surely more careful than that."

Gunnar shot me a worried look.

"No, my friends," Hoskuld summed up, "it just won't wash."

"Who, then, Uncle?" asked Gunnar angrily.

"Upon my soul, nephew, the countryside is full of wandering ruffians. Things like this happen every day. You would have considered it yourselves if you hadn't let this fellow Hrut prey on your minds so."

"But slaughtering the sheep?" I said. "That was no part of a casual rape and killing."

Yes, Hoskuld conceded, there was that. We might never know for sure. But it didn't signify against all the rest, and no jury, he pronounced with finality, would believe our charge.

We sank down, crushed, stunned. My beautiful verses lay in ruins.

"Come, come," he said with a touch of impatience, "it's a lawyer's job to bring out the facts of your case, even those you'd rather not hear."

My father, who had not said a word up until now, looked up suddenly from his whittling and said, "Brother-in-law, you have spoken my very own thoughts. No doubt they will get a better hearing from your lips than from mine." There was malice in his eyes.

"Thorvald," cried Hoskuld with feigned delight, "you've decided to add your voice to our deliberations. I am relieved. I address myself to you, then, as head of the family." How slyly he said it; it hadn't taken him long to see how matters really stood between my parents.

"Let us come down to cases. Anyone who goes up against Strife-Hrut Ivarsson isn't likely to wear out many new shirts, as the saying goes, unless he's willing to make some slight compromises with his honor. Well now, what is our situation? For the murder of his son and the other fellow, Hrut can demand six marks of silver in blood money. A large sum, no doubt, but it would be the easiest way out for you, Thorvald. I, of course, am ready to put at your disposal...."

"He doesn't want my silver, you fool. He wants my sons!"

This outburst brought no change in Hoskuld's expression, except a slight paling around the nostrils. "Yes, quite. Outlawry. Well, he has the right."

"Outlawry," echoed Jorunn, seizing her brother's arm in both her hands. "But only for three years, is it not, brother?"

"That is the lesser outlawry, my dear, awarded for justifiable homicide. But if the jurors believe Odd's assault on Brand was unprovoked, the plaintiff can demand outlawry for life against both brothers—permanent exile, never to see Iceland again under pain of death."

"And," added Thorvald grimly, "if they haven't left the country within two weeks after the verdict, the law allows Hrut to kill us all and seize our land for damages. And that, my dear wife,"—he mimicked her brother's patronizing tone of voice—"that is why he drags us to the Althing. Strife-Hrut will be well repaid for the death of his worthless son by the time he's done with us."

My mother's shoulders sagged. She looked helplessly from one man to the other.

"But," said Hoskuld, "all is not lost. What are lawyers for? Evidence and argument aren't everything. Dear me, no. Iceland's laws are complicated and deep—like your poetry, young Odd. There's always an advantage for the man who knows where to look. Why, I've seen suits overthrown by the tiniest flaws—a witness improperly summonsed, a declaration in the wrong form of words. Oh, there are endless possibilities."

"You waste your breath, lawyer," sneered my father. "You forget I was a godi once. I *know* how it's done. Money, force, and friends, Hoskuld. Money, force, and friends—without those your piddling lawyer's tricks aren't worth a bite from a mare's backside. Now, Hrut has money, hasn't he? And force is his nature, is it not? And we know, brother-in-law, who his friends are, don't we?"

"Do we?" Hoskuld's eyes narrowed. "Who?"

"Your accursed Christmen, that's who! Those wolves who have circled me these thirty years, contriving against me, waiting for their chance to strike home. Isn't he one of you? Isn't Hrut a Christman? You know he is, brother-in-law. And they'll all come together against me now!"

He hacked so hard at his stick I feared he would take his thumb off.

Now it was out in the open and Hoskuld was so angry he could hardly speak. "And I?" he sputtered, "and your own wife, you sorry man, are we plotting against you? You've driven yourself mad with religion, Thorvald. I swear you spend more hours in the day brooding about Jesus Christ than any of us Christmen do. Yes, Hrut has friends among the godis. He's a merchant, he lends them money when they're short. Only that. But I, too, have friends, and, if it comes to that, money—which, God help me, I wouldn't spend for your stinking heathen hide but only to save my sister's children. Now say no more to me about religion."

"But that's the heart of it! Why else does the high-and-mighty Snorri of Helgafel hate me?"

"Hates you, does he? Well, we mustn't be too hard on poor Snorri for that!"

They were both half out of their seats, glaring at each other across the table. Hoskuld, I imagine, couldn't see clearly the expression on my father's face, but I could. And I saw his knuckles whiten on the hilt of his knife.

"Gunnar, sing!" I cried. The gods alone know what put it into my mind.

My brother stared at me perplexed for an instant and then understood. He only knew one song, *Finnbogi's Daughter*, which he always sang with spirit—though without a noticeable melody. He roared out the first line, and I came in on the second, both of us pounding the floor with our feet. Then Kalf added his voice, and so did the others in the back of the hall, stamping and shouting lustily.

Hoskuld and my father looked about, equally astonished.

Jorunn did not lose a second. Snatching up a horn of mead, she abandoned her brother and ran to her husband's side. His shoulders were bunched, and he was snorting like a bull.

"Drink, Husband," she urged, sitting down by him and putting the flagon to his lips. "Enough gloomy talk for one night. The young'uns are right to be impatient."

She covered his hand with hers and brought it slowly down to rest on her thigh and as she did so, looked past him and caught my eye.

Every shade and hue of pain was in that look. She understood that this meeting, on which she had fastened all her hopes, was a disaster—that her husband was just possibly not as mad as she had thought, and her brother, perhaps, not as wise. Between these two angry men she did not know where to turn. The only thing certain was that we dared not let them come to blows.

We sang ourselves hoarse. Finnbogi's Daughter has a great many verses, each dirtier than the last, and after a little, you could see the tension begin to go out of Thorvald's shoulders and the fingers uncurl around the hilt of his knife. Even his foot began to move absently in time to the music. Who would have believed it? Jorunn drew a deep breath and slowly let it out. It would be all right now.

Hoskuld, on his side, had regained a little of his composure. Katla hovered about him in her fawning way, patting his forehead, arranging his ruffled hair until, exasperated, he pushed her away.

When Gunnar's song was done, Kalf brought out his bone whistle, which he always carried on a cord around his neck, and began to pipe. He piped *The Dun Mare*, which, after a few times through, turned into *Old Haakon at the Well*, and so on, without stop through half a dozen more.

Gunnar led Vigdis to the middle of the floor and they danced together, face to face, hands on one another's shoulders, as they used to do in their courting days. And soon others in the hall joined in, mostly men partnered with other men, as sailors do, for there weren't enough women to go round. After a while, my mother prodded me to dance with Katla Thin-Hair, which I did, though she held me at arm's length with the tips of her fingers and gazed steadily over my shoulder with a look of distaste. Kalf doubled over with laughter watching us.

There was one fellow in particular, one of Hoskuld's hired men, who caught my eye with his antics. His face was battered, pockmarked, and villainous, and his close-cropped hair was as spiky as a patch of thorns. I believed he was the ugliest man I'd ever seen. I had noticed him earlier in the evening, sitting well back from the fire, speaking to none nor spoken to by any, with a sort of dreamy look in his eyes. And yet I felt he paid very close attention to everything said and unsaid.

Now he leapt into our midst, with a savage grin splitting his face, and all alone began to execute the wildest and funniest capers with great skill, not clumsily or drunkenly. He kept this up for a good long time, until just as suddenly as he had begun, he stopped and withdrew again to his place in the back.

What a strange man, I thought, but soon dismissed him from my mind.

As the evening passed, my eye strayed now and then to my parents. Gunnar's little babe had gone to sleep in Jorunn's lap. Thorvald's hand rested on the child's head, and he ran a calloused thumb gently back and forth over its pink scalp. The two of them did not look at each other or speak, and yet something was there between them. I caught myself wondering, not for the first time, what secrets these two shared that we children would never know.

Uncle Hoskuld was no more a dancing sort of man than a poetical one, but he put on a show of good spirits, grateful, I think, for the respite. In truth, we were all glad to send our troubles away for a little while. They were greater troubles than we had thought, and we made ourselves the merrier to forget them.

7

ALL ICELAND ASSEMBLES

Our great-great-grandfathers, newly come from Norway, fashioned a government for our kingless land: a *thing*, an assembly, to be held during two weeks in June on a wide, well-watered plain in the southwest quarter. Here, free men come together to hear the laws recited and sit in judgment on their peers. Nowhere else in the world does such a gathering exist.

Approaching, as we did, from the east, you ride down into a grassy plain that stretches for miles, bounded on the south by the vast sheet of Thingvalla Lake and cut by the meandering streams of the Axe river. The plain is a sea of color: the tents and booths, roofed with homespun cloth, where the folk from Skagafjord and Snaefellsnes and Ljosawater, from the Eastfjords, from Breidavik and Eyr, and every inaccessible corner of our island are encamped. In a land without towns, without villages even, we create, briefly, a city of the whole nation.

At the far edge of this plain you can see a thin ribbon of black. As you draw closer, that ribbon grows thicker and darker, and becomes, at last, the immense black and jagged rampart of Almanna Gorge. The walls and floor of this gorge, dense with shouting and jostling farmers, is the arena, the cockpit where we must stand and face our enemies.

My uncle's booth was a snug little cabin of turf with a roof of striped awning that he brought with him each year for the purpose. Besides the godis, not many kept such permanent quarters on the plain. Our family had had one once, too, but it had long since passed from our hands along with Thorvald's chieftaincy. Here we stopped while Kalf and I got Hoskuld's awning up and all the baggage unloaded with the help of his two servants. One of these was that ugly man who had performed the wild dance. I heard my uncle call him Stig. He seemed to me, as before, an uncomfortably silent and watchful fellow and disinclined to talk when I tried to sound him. I wondered why Hoskuld kept him.

We pitched our own two little tents some ways away, and soon had a fire going. We all supped together on the leavings of yesterday's dinner and tried our best to be cheerful.

Kalf, washing down a last hunk of bread and mutton fat, licked his fingers, and said, "Tangle-Hair, let's explore. Who'll come along?"

To our great relief the old folks begged off and only Gunnar, before Vigdis could get a good grip on him, jumped up, shouting, "Off to the fair!" and with an arm around each of us, plunged into the roiling crowd.

Everyone was out and about, as hungry for the sight of new faces after winter's long solitude, as they were starved for the sun's light. A human river wound slowly up from the lake to the great gorge and back again, turning aside in chattering eddies around every oddity that fairs attract—dealers in charms, sellers of falcons, sword-grinders, wrestlers, stone-lifters, and storytellers.

I was listening to one of these, when I noticed that Gunnar and Kalf were no longer beside me. A twinge of alarm pricked me, but I ignored it and drifted again with the crowd, expecting at every moment to see their faces. When after some time I still hadn't found them, the twinge became something stronger. With gathering panic, I realized I was lost.

You will laugh if you are accustomed to the ways of cities, but remember that I grew up in an empty country, whose few solitary landmarks were known to me from infancy. I had never been lost in my life, had never even imagined the condition.

I pushed my way through the resisting mob, going faster and faster in my agitation. The sun, by this time, was below the mountains, leaving the plain, not in darkness, but in soft deceptive shadow where every striped canvas looked like ours, and every bulky shape that sat or sprawled around a campfire seemed, for a moment, familiar.

I thought that if I steered toward the distant mountains, I must eventually come out at about the right place, and before long, I glimpsed with relief the blue and black striped awning—I was positive—of my uncle's booth.

Coming upon it from behind, I failed at first to notice the strange shields propped against its turf walls, or the unfamiliar faces of the men who sprawled in the grass nearby. In my eagerness, I very nearly yelled out Hoskuld's name before I heard a sound that froze me in mid-step. A voice I knew well—and it wasn't my uncle's.

Taking advantage of a passing horseback rider to shield me from view, I worked around to the front of the booth and made myself as inconspicuous as possible in the milling crowd. The man whose voice I'd heard sat on a three-legged stool in front of the booth's little doorway, with a drinking horn in his hand. There was no mistaking that brutal face with its missing ear.

But it was his companion who riveted my attention. Strife-Hrut was a good-sized man, but he looked like a puny child beside this other one who overtopped him by half a head and whose blond beard was streaked with gray. Though I'd never laid eyes on him before, there wasn't a shadow of a doubt who he was; I'd heard him described often enough at home. My father's nemesis, the man whom he had denounced here thirty years ago for delivering Iceland up to the Christmen—the great and powerful Snorri-godi of Helgafel.

While I stood hesitating, one face in the gang of men near the booth happened to glance my way, and the eyes—I could almost swear it—fixed on me with a look of surprise.

Snorri's thingmen were handsome and well dressed, but among them was a smaller number of scruffy looking characters, who, I guessed, were Hrut's bullyboys. It was one of these who seemed to watch me now, a snaggle-toothed fellow with a frayed white cap pulled down to his ears and a hank of hair falling over his dirty face. Feeling his eyes still on me, I slipped away into the crowd.

Again, I ran, pushed, searched—driven now by urgency more than panic.

"Odd?"

Gods! I'd just about stepped on her, sitting by the last embers of our campfire. I dropped onto a campstool and heaved a deep sigh. "Mother, where is everyone?"

"Why, your father's just over there, resting in the grass, and your uncle's napping in his booth. Vigdis is with her family, and as for Gunnar and Kalf, why, I thought they were with you."

"We must get Uncle and Father up at once."

"Heh? What's that—Odd? What is it, boy?" His tongue was thick with drink and he could scarcely sit up. 'Resting' wasn't the word for it. He was drunk. The wine skin, which had been full when I left, lay beside him nearly flat.

"Father, you were right...."

"You're a good boy, Odd ... good boy ... and you don't hate your father, do you?"

"What?"

"Good boy. I don't say it often, do I? Well, if I don't say it again, you'll remember, won't you? You'll remember I said it."

"Thorvald," Jorunn commanded, "hold your nonsense. Can't you see the boy's trying to tell us something?"

Before I could speak, there came the sound of a scuffle behind the tents and Gunnar and Kalf stepped into the firelight, holding a figure between them who kicked and struggled to get free.

"Here you are!" cried Kalf, seeing me.

"We looked everywhere," said Gunnar, "and finally came back here, just in time to catch this fellow skulking about, looking for something to steal, no doubt."

"I never!" bleated the figure, twisting helplessly in Gunnar's grip.

I peered into his face. It was the same dirty one that I'd just now seen at Snorri's booth. He returned my gaze with the beginnings of a smile.

"You know me, don't yer? I know you, and your brother here. It didn't take me a minute to say to myself, when I saw you back there, 'Sigmund'—for Sigmund Tit-Bit is my name—'Sigmund,' says I, 'here's your chance, don't yer lose it.' And so I slips away and comes after you. Christ and Thor, didn't you lead me a chase—dashin' about from tent to tent like you done, and me runnin' after, bendin' low to keep out of sight of them as might recognize me. Now just you tell these two fellows to unhand me, sir, if you please, and after I've moistened my throat—for I am pitiful thirsty—let us have ourselves a nice talk."

Kalf and Gunnar, looking doubtful, released him. He swept off his cap and made a clumsy bow toward Jorunn and Thorvald: "Housewife and Master, a good evening to yer from Sigmund Tit-Bit."

"That's no name I know," answered my father, somewhat soberer than a moment before. "What's your business?"

Sigmund grinned, plainly enjoying his little mystery. "I am so pitiful thirsty—just a little sip from that skin of yours would make me a new man."

Kalf went and shook out the last few drops into a cup and gave it to him.

"Ahh." He drew a dirty, out-at-elbow sleeve across his lips. "Mead? I don't believe I've ever had the pleasure, being that no one gives such stuff to a poor hireling in our hall. Very nice it is, too."

"Well?" said Gunnar, laying a heavy hand on the man's neck and squeezing till he winced.

"On the beach, masters," cried Sigmund wriggling free. "By the whale—don't yer remember? When one of you killed my mate, Bork, and took off after Master Mord Hrutsson, and the other one killed Brand, though I didn't stay to watch it, but run away as fast as I could."

Gunnar's hand went to his sword.

"Oh no, sir, no, it's nothing like that. I haven't come to finish that fight."

"Then what?"

He narrowed his eyes and looked at us slyly. "When I tell you that, I expect yer *will* want to take sword to me. You must swear to me first that yer won't."

"We don't swear oaths to thralls' sons like you."

"Be still, Gunnar." It was our mother, her voice icy calm. "Say your piece, man, no one will harm you."

He doffed his cap to her again. "Thank 'ee, Housewife."

He told his story, halting at every few words to fidget or shrug or glance up hopefully. And Jorunn, listening, never took her eyes from his face. Her stare must have felt like two points of fire on his flesh.

When he had done, we looked at each other in silence.

"Wake the lawyer," said Thorvald.

Hoskuld was fetched, and it all had to be gone through again. Only this time my mother turned aside and covered her eyes with her hand when Sigmund came to the part where two of the men held Gudrun down on the floor of the shieling while she screamed, and Hrut, Brand, and Mord and the others took turns getting on her until she didn't make a sound any more, and then someone stuck a knife in her chest.

No, he didn't see who because, Christ and Thor be his witness, he wouldn't take part in such low stuff, but just went outside and killed sheep like he was told. But all the way home master Hrut and his sons laughed and joked about it with the boys and said how everyone knew that Black Thorvald and his sons were such cowards as wouldn't stir a finger over it. Afterwards Master Hrut had flogged him half to death for leaving Brand to die alone and had treated him like a dog ever since, making him sleep out in the barn in all weathers. And so that was why he was here now to tell his story and would tell it in open court, too. By Christ and Thor he would, if only we would protect him from Hrut's vengeance and afterwards send him out of the country with enough silver to live comfortable until things cooled down.

To this I added my information about Hrut visiting Snorri's booth just now. And as I spoke, I realized that we had the answer to my uncle's objection to our case. Hrut, left to himself, was a braggart—no crime so cowardly that he wouldn't make a boast of it. But if Snorri, for his own good reasons, had gotten hold of him right afterwards and ordered him to keep his mouth shut...?

Hoskuld stroked his long jaws with the tips of his fingers and frowned.

"Well?" Jorunn burst out when she could stand it no longer. "Bless you, brother, you were wrong! Admit it. God has heard us!" She stood between me and Gunnar and hugged us both to her. "No outlawry for these sons of mine!"

But Hoskuld shook his head. "The word of a landless man like him won't carry much weight. Not unless we find someone of standing to take an oath on his truthfulness." He was silent for a bit and then straightened his shoulders. "Kinsmen, I change my mind. I am cheered by this, indeed I am. And as for having been wrong, why I make nothing of that at all, not being a proud sort of man. Now then, my task lies clear before me, to enlist a powerful ally or two. We must seek friends."

"How is it, brother-in-law," said my father, his voice dripping irony, "that you always come round at last, and with such certainty, to my own view?"

8

ACCUSED

At the pealing of the morning bell, the whole plain stirred and moved toward the gorge. Carried along by the crowd, we entered at its shallow end and filed down between its black walls toward Law Rock. There was a crush of people there already, giving their attention to the Law Speaker. The ancient Skapti Thoroddsson, who had held this post for a generation, stood upon the jutting boulder above the crowd and recited from memory one-third of the laws of Iceland. I stole a look at my father and wondered what thoughts were going through his mind, seeing all this again after the passage of so many years. But his face told me nothing.

The recitation completed, the day's business could commence. Now it was time for the proclamation of lawsuits

Wrapped in a skin cloak, his pig's eyes screwed up tight, Strife-Hrut charged out of the crowd like a boar from a thicket and, scrambling onto the Rock, bawled his accusation, the words nearly drowned out by the loud cheering of his men.

"...notice of an action against Odd and Gunnar Thorvaldsson ... did afflict my son with gut wound, brain wound, and bone wound, the which did cause his death ... full outlawry." *Full outlawry*—the rock walls flung the words up and down the chasm. "To have no harbor, help, nor hand, no friend, and no food in this island forever!"

He flung out an arm in our direction and every head turned toward us. On that cue, his men commenced to bang on their shields and chant his name. Snorri's men, who were there in force too, joined in. Here and there in the crowd others picked it up, people, who a moment before had had no notion of who we were or what we had done.

"Hrut—Hrut—Hrut—!" Strife-Hrut, gesturing and grimacing, danced like a troll on his mountaintop, whipping them on.

Being at the bottom of a chasm in the middle of a thousand angry Icelanders is not for the faint-hearted. If a hand had so much as brushed the hilt of a sword, we might have been cut to pieces on the spot.

We didn't let out our breath until we were up on the plain again and walking rapidly—I won't say running—to our tents.

"Hah!" cried Hoskuld, putting on a brave face. "We'll see who packs up and says farewell to Iceland come tomorrow morning. It shall be Strife-Hrut, much to his surprise, who finds himself facing a charge of unprovoked murder."

My mother responded by giving him a smacking kiss on his forehead and then got busy at once clanging pots and pans together and chivvying Vigdis and Katla and the servants to get our midday meal. It was her way, I suppose, of keeping down fear.

Roused by all this bustle, the source of our new found optimism poked its head out through the tent flap. "Let a man sleep, at least. Christ and Thor, there's naught else to do in all this wearisome time that I must stay holed up here."

"No call for such a sour tone," said my uncle sternly. "You'll come out of this affair better off than anyone—as well you knew when you came to us. 'Twill all be over shortly."

"Well then, I am hungry," said Sigmund yawning, "*and* thirsty. I will have some more of that mead, if you please."

Gunnar frowned at the man's impudence and doubled up his fist, but Hoskuld stopped him with a look. "Just get our friend some mead, would you, Katla?" he said quietly. "There's a good girl."

When the porridge was ready we took our bowls and drifted into separate groups—Kalf and I sitting in one spot, Jorunn, her brother and Katla in another, Gunnar in front of his tent with his wife and baby, and Thorvald, alone in front of our tent—simply staring out over the peaceful lake, while his porridge got cold.

In fact, only Sigmund ate heartily, sitting in the dirt with his leg tucked under him, shoveling the mush into his mouth with the serving spoon and washing it down with our mead. At the rate that he and Thorvald were going at it, my uncle's store of that tasty liquid would soon be exhausted.

Our meal was barely over when the gorge emptied its human burden up onto the plain. The day's session was over and Iceland streamed back to its tents to eat and drink and stroll and argue and gawk and bargain and wonder and drink again for another afternoon, evening, and night on which the sun would never set.

Now, it was that each of the forty-eight godis would sit in state in his turf-walled booth, flanked by his thingmen, his sword laid across his knees, to receive petitions.

"And so," said Hoskuld, getting creakily to his feet and arranging his cloak on his shoulder, "to business. Brother-in-law," he spoke to my father's back, "asking favors is not—ah—your particular talent, is it? And anyway, these affairs are best conducted with the smallest possible audience. I will take only Kalf to guide my steps." He waited as long as politeness required, not expecting an answer, and got none.

But when he had gone, my father spoke—in so quiet a voice that we scarcely heard him at first.

His sword was in his tent, lying where he or someone had tossed it when we unpacked. Obeying his order, I went and fetched it for him, while the others stood by, as silent as if they all had water in their mouths. He took it from me and with great deliberation in his movements, laid it on his knees. Like a godi.

✝

We got through the time until uncle Hoskuld returned as best we could. The sun, by then, was once more brushing the mountaintops.

Even with Kalf to lean on, my uncle's steps were slow and faltering. We lowered him gently onto a stool and waited for him to get his breath. Katla, meanwhile, flapped around him like a lunatic bird until he shooed her off.

"It is a bitter day," he began with a sigh and a shake of his head, "when one finds that a friend is false. Today I have found more than one false friend."

We did not dare speak.

After a pause, he went on in a trembling voice that scarcely resembled his usual rich bass. He had gone first, he said, to the booth of Hjalti Skeggjason, a godi of Thjorsariverdale—the same who had intervened in the scuffle at the stallion fight a year ago. This Hjalti was deeply in Hoskuld's debt owing to a scrape that his son had gotten into some years back. The high-spirited youth, it seems, had assaulted a bride on her wedding day. Thanks to Hoskuld, the damages sought by the lady's husband were quite a bit less than they might have been. Notwithstanding, Hjalti had begged off with feeble excuses about his own suits going badly and having no room in his house just now for another man's bad luck.

After that, he had gone in turn to four other godis and all had been delighted to see their old friend, but all had pleaded one excuse or another to put him off—even when a bribe was discretely offered. Hoskuld's chin was on his chest as he concluded this catalogue of rebuffs.

"Here!" struck in an all-too-familiar voice behind us—Sigmund Tit-Bit, looking full of consternation. "What's all this about, then? Friendless, d'yer say? Christ and Thor, if I'd but known that yesterday, I never...."

"Quiet, you," snarled Gunnar, raising the back of his hand. But Hoskuld's weak eyes sparked to life.

"Did I say friendless? Not quite. Disappointed, yes. But friendless? No indeed!" And suddenly, it was a different Hoskuld—shoulders squared, chin up. "Forgive an old man his love for the dramatic—I've saved the good news for last.

"I paid my final visit to young Hall Thorarinsson who, you may know, has recently become a godi in my own district of Hawkdale. I was his father's thingman for many a year, though the son I scarcely know. To my delight, I found him a most agreeable young man, polite, generous, frank—every inch the image of his father.

"To be brief, I explained our case, and laid our evidence before him. He did not even wait to hear it all, so eager he was to oblige me with both money and men."

Hoskuld leaned forward to speak in a confidential whisper. "He will attend us tomorrow with a force of a hundred thingmen *and* will swear in court to the truth of our case." My uncle spread his hands on his knees and looked triumphant.

Expressions of thanks and praise burst from our throats. Jorunn threw her powerful arms around her brother and near squeezed the life out of him.

Throughout Hoskuld's long recitation, my father had sat impassively, hardly seeming to listen. Now he said in a weary voice, "Hoskuld Long-Jaws, what does this godi want in return for supporting us?"

"Why, he does it to oblige me, his father's friend."

My father shifted his weight sideways on his stool and farted. "I would feel happier if he had named a price, for I never knew the godi who didn't have one."

"Rubbish!" snapped Hoskuld. "The young man's word is as good as gold. He is a faithful Chri...." He thought better and swallowed that word.

We got no more speech from Thorvald that night. While Hoskuld preened and basked in the admiration of us all, my father fell to work on another wineskin until he toppled off his stool, whereupon Gunnar and I dragged him by his heels into the tent and threw a cover over him.

That night, as I lay close alongside my parents in the little tent, I was awakened by my father's thrashing and muttering in his sleep.

What night-hag rode his back? What gruesome visions did he see? I was getting up the courage to touch him, when my mother put out her arms and pulled his head onto her lap. Without waking, he sighed and became still.

I crawled outside to leave them alone.

9

ChE BULL'S
LAST BELLOW

The air had grown hot and thick overnight, smelling of rain, and ragged dark clouds hid the mountains.

The morning bell dinned in our ears, and again all Iceland tumbled out of its tent, plunged its face in cold river water, brushed its teeth with a birch twig, and put on its finery—all in a great state of excitement, because today was the day set aside for trials. Before this day was out, there would likely be corpses on the grass.

What else but this, after all, drew the gawking crowds and made the Althing worthwhile?

Sigmund Tit-Bit began complaining as soon as his eyes were open. Gunnar flung a hooded cloak at him, telling him to put it on and stop his squawking until time came for him to testify. "And then just you do your part, my friend."

"Do my part? Christ and Thor, don't you worry about me doin' my part. Just you see to it that Strife-Hrut doesn't have off my head first ... friend."

"Odd," said Jorunn, crawling out of the tent, "your father wants you." The look in her eyes told me something was wrong.

I found him crouching at the back of the tent with his arms around his belly.

"I won't go, I'm sick."

"Well, then, you won't. Why tell me?" Seeing him yesterday with his sword on his knees, a spark of hope had caught fire in me. How foolish. Of course he would fail us when the moment came. I just wanted not to look at him.

"Don't leave me yet—"

"Take your hand off me!"

"Just for a minute. I ... I have something for you." He put his hands behind his neck, under his hair, and pulled a cord over his head. From the end of it hung his Thor's hammer, the iron polished smooth with years of rubbing against his skin. Even when he had stopped sacrificing to Redbeard, he kept that hammer for the magic in it.

You don't see them much nowadays. It was an amulet in the rough form of a hammer but shaped enough like the Christmen's cross so that a man who wore it could pass it off as one thing or the other depending on the company he was in.

"I don't want this."

"Take it. It'll protect you when the waves come over your gunwales, for even the Christmen call on Thor in a storm!"

"What storm? What are you talking about?"

"Out there, boy. When you measure yourself against Hrut and Snorri."

"I? And where will you be, Father? Hide now and you'll go on hiding forever."

"I'm sick, I told you. Take the hammer!" He thrust it at my chest and pushed me away from him.

Outside, I told the others.

"I'll change his mind," said Jorunn grimly.

"Leave him, Mother, what's the use?"

But I hung the hammer around my neck. Maybe there was a little luck in it yet, though I doubted it.

Gunnar looked at me quizzically as he handed me a shield and a spear from the arsenal we had brought with us. He was armed in the same way.

Forcing a cheerful voice, I said, "Kalf, where's your bow and quiver? We have bigger game than meadow hens to shoot this morning."

He flashed me a brave smile, but Hoskuld, staring with sudden fright out of his clouded eyes, cried, "No! No, I forbid it! Kalf, come here. Give me your hand. Come, you'll do no fighting here."

Kalf stopped. He stood torn between us, his fists clenched, his face hot with shame and anger.

"Best do as he says, Kalf ... " I urged in a low voice, pressing his arm, "this time."

"Odd Tangle-Hair, you'll see one day how I can fight." He was close to tears. He took hold—not gently—of his grandfather's hand. A look of peace spread over the old man's face.

"Well, Uncle," said Gunnar, "where is this godi of yours? Wasn't he going to march up with us?"

"Don't you worry about that, Handsome Gunnar," Hoskuld replied. "His quarters are at the far end of the gorge. No doubt he'll meet us along the way."

With Gunnar and me in the lead, our party started across the plain to the spot appointed for the meeting of the South Quarter Court. There we found, seated on a curving row of wooden benches, the thirty-six jurors who would hear our case. Around them, a crowd of the curious had already collected. There were just ten of us, including the womenfolk and Hoskuld's two servants, who wore swords and, perhaps, could use them. Sigmund, his face well hidden by the hood, stayed in the back as we'd told him to.

At the opposite end of the row of benches were Hrut and his son, backed by a mob of armed men. Also in plain sight was Snorri, whose head overtopped them all. Altogether, I figured there were three or four hundred fighting men there, and every one of them hoping to warm his sword in our guts before the day was done.

"Jesu," said Jorunn in a hushed voice to her brother, "they have come for war, not justice. Where is this Hall Thorarinsson of yours?"

"Quiet!" he snapped. "He'll be here. And if it's bloodshed they want, it's bloodshed they shall have."

To my surprise, Snorri detached himself from the throng around Hrut and made his way toward us. He reminded me of some great dragon ship: his belly like a prow, making the waters part, and his cloak of red wool the size of a small sail, billowing around him. He was armored in a coat of mail that two ordinary men could have stood up in. At his heels a white bull mastiff trotted.

He came to rest puffing and blowing in front of us. When he spoke, the voice, coming from that cavernous chest, was surprisingly light. "Good morning to you, friends. What a pity that it takes a sad business like this to bring us together at last, eh? But where is he? Where is my old comrade? I'm told he was at Law Rock yesterday, though I didn't see him myself."

"Thorvald is ill," replied my uncle. "I speak for him and his sons."

"Hoskuld Long-Jaws, of course! Upon my life, man, I am deeply hurt you did not call upon me yesterday. What now—am I to be treated as an enemy? Blind me! I'm no such a thing."

"You mean you deny being Strife-Hrut's ally?"

"Why, absolutely. I've only joined the fellow's suit to soften his harsh nature. Why, I should like nothing better than to see us all friends again."

"Yes, well, that is kind of you, Snorri-godi," my uncle, won over in an instant, began to stammer. "I mean damned kind, taking this line. Of course, we—"

"And these are the sons!" cried the battleship, abandoning Hoskuld with his mouth open and turning his smile on us. "Gunnar, is it? Blind me, what a fine looking young man. Father's pride, I'll wager."

He swung his gaze then to me. "And you're Odd!" He squeezed me by the upper arm just hard enough to cause pain. Noticing the Thor's Hammer hanging on my breast, he said, "What is that, boy—you don't mind saying, do you? Is that a cross or a hammer, boy? Would it be rude of me to ask what you believe in?" He held it between thumb and forefinger and pulled on the cord until it began to cut my neck. I locked my knees against the force.

"I believe in my own strength, Snorri Thorgrimsson."

"Heh? Hah, hah! Listen to him. Spoken like a viking! Yes, that's how the old pirates used to talk before they got religion. You're Black Thorvald's son, boy, blind me if you aren't!" He laughed and let go of the hammer, smiling all the time, but there was no mirth in those ice blue eyes.

I said, "What do you want with us, Godi?"

He put on a look of mild surprise. "Why, nothing much, Odd Thorvaldsson. I'm sorry your father isn't here. Perhaps, if he could be asked to attend us, sick as he is? It's a little thing but a nagging thing. You see, he had hard words for me once, thoughtless words, said in the hearing of many. No doubt, you've heard somewhat about it? And it has occurred to me that thirty years may teach a man wisdom. Humility even. Now, if he should regret those hasty words of his and beg my pardon in front of these jurors and this crowd of onlookers, and if he should oblige me further by becoming my thingman, deeding his land to me, and living as a tenant on my home farm. If he should do all that, why I venture to think that Strife-Hrut will settle for a modest return on his son's life."

So that was it. Only that to save us.

Not that I picture Snorri brooding over Thorvald's harsh words all these years; he would have had to be as mad as my father to do that. But when the chance to pay off an old score dropped into his lap, neither was he the man to let it slip away. And it was Snorri, of course, who had recruited the other godis. My father, it turned out, had been right exactly where he seemed most foolish: his old enemies were uniting around Hrut to bring him down.

There was a long moment's silence. "Brother," I said, "what are we to tell this great godi?"

Gunnar, smiling, answered, "Bag of guts, start your trial!"

Snorri's mastiff, sensing anger, bared its teeth and growled in its throat. In a swirl of red sail, the battleship put about and sailed back to his own side.

Then the trial began.

At a sign from the jurors, Strife-Hrut stalked into the clearing before the benches to swear his oath and name his witnesses.

"Kalf," Hoskuld said quietly, "just run over to the booth of Hall Thorarinsson and ask what is detaining him."

The crowd of onlookers, which was sizable now, stood on tiptoe to hear Hrut tell how we two lawless ruffians had set upon his defenseless boys for the purpose of stealing his whale meat, how we had murdered his son and hired man, and, to excuse our crime, concocted some revolting charge of rape and murder of a little girl, which on his word before Almighty God he flatly denied.

After that, Mord took a turn at describing how we had ambushed and overpowered them, despite the fact that he, Mord, fought like a lion until all hope was gone.

All this took time. The sun inched up the dome of the sky. Hoskuld paced and gnawed his lips.

Then, "Look over there!" cried my mother. We looked to our left and saw a tall young warrior splendidly equipped and behind him, rank upon rank of armed men advancing at a trot.

We clapped our arms around each other, we whooped. But ahead of them sped Kalf. He was white-lipped and could scarcely speak. And

Hall Thorarinsson marched past us to take his place with Snorri and the others. He did have the decency, I will say, to avert his eyes as he passed Hoskuld.

Maybe he'd even meant his promise when he gave it. Maybe Snorri had not gotten to him yet.

Then, all the godis on Hrut's side stepped forward one by one to take their oath on the truth of Hrut's story, and to urge these honest jurors to pass the sentence of outlawry upon us.

Hoskuld's face was the color of tallow. He sagged against his sister's strong shoulder.

"Uncle," I said, "I will speak for us. I have the words."

He nodded. He could make no sound.

"You think words can save us now?" asked Gunnar bitterly.

"Sigmund's testimony is all we have. At least the truth will be told before we go down fighting."

The words came out somehow—"lawful feud ... a life for a life"—they aren't important. But I remember what a sudden hush there was as I faced Hrut and told him there was a witness to his crime. "Hrut Ivarsson," I cried, "do you recognize your own man?"

That was Gunnar's cue to seize Sigmund, push him into the circle, and tear off his hood.

Hrut took a menacing step towards us, looked hard at the cloaked figure, and began to laugh. Then Snorri, too, and the thingmen, and the jurors, and the crowd—all held their sides and laughed.

For it wasn't Sigmund Tit-Bit at all. It was a bald, toothless old man, frightened out of his wits, who piped, "That fella give me this copper penny just for to wear his cloak and stand back there..."

"How long ago?" I screamed, shaking the old man till his few teeth rattled.

"Not long, sir, on my life! About when the young godi marched by. You won't kill me, sir?"

"Gunnar, find him!"

"Where, for God's sake?"

"Don't bother," came a voice from behind us. "Here's your lost dog."

"Father!" Dragging Sigmund by the scruff of his neck, Thorvald marched into the clearing. "He came sneaking up to Hoskuld's booth to help himself to the last wineskin and a fast horse. He found me instead.

And so...." my father looked around him, blinking, as though seeming to notice for the first time where he was. "And so, I've brought him. Heard the end of your speech, boy—fine speech. Now you make him talk, and I'll ... and I'll wait at camp."

He had fought down thirty years of dread to get this far. Our desperate need had given him the strength to come face to face with his enemies—but only just. His nerve was failing him again, he couldn't stick it. Releasing Sigmund, he took a faltering step backward.

"Father, look out!" I yelled.

Hrut, with his sword in his fist, covered the space between us in a few bounding steps and flung himself with a curse upon Sigmund. The blade took off the top of the man's skull in a shower of blood and brain. Whirling, he came at my father, who stood flat-footed and helpless, with a dazed look in his eyes. Hrut aimed a blow, and then things happened fast. Black Thorvald bent low and drove his shoulder into Hrut's stomach as he rushed in, and Hrut made a circle in the air and landed hard on his back.

Bystanders scattered in all directions. Two of Hrut's men were right behind him, and they went for my father, who—I saw with horror—had not bothered to strap on his sword. Gunnar was quicker than I. With a warning shout, he threw his spear butt first at father. Thorvald plucked it from the air, and in two swift movements drove it into one and then the other of his attackers.

But this was a hopeless fight. In a moment they were all over us. Gunnar, father, and I crouched inside a steel hedge of sword blades, awaiting our death.

But death didn't come. Instead, the hedge parted and Snorri stood before us. His thingmen, too, rushed in between Hrut's fighters and us, shouldering them out of the way. At a word from Snorri, some held up their shields to protect us, while others wrenched away our weapons and twisted our arms behind us.

What were they saving us for?

"Black Thorvald," Snorri smiled. Malice glittered in his eyes. "What a long time you've made me wait. I won't lose you now. If I let our friend kill you, why, these good jurors might call the honors even and dismiss his suit. And that would be a pity. Gunnar, tell your father what I require of him."

My brother bit his lips and said nothing.

"Perhaps the young troll will oblige me," said Snorri indicating me.

I turned my head away.

"The wife, then?" Snorri barked, letting his exasperation show.

The shield wall parted to let in Jorunn, with Hoskuld behind her. Tears streaked her cheeks. "Husband, he wants you to ask his pardon, and if you do, he'll make Hrut give up the suit. I've been a true wife, Thorvald. These thirty years I have shared your misery. I ask you this one thing now—save my sons for me."

I hated her at that moment.

"Brother-in-Law," Hoskuld urged, "do one sane thing to redeem your wretched life. There's no shame in begging pardon of a Christman. It allows him to forgive you, and so God loves you both."

Thorvald turned his face to them, his bull's chest heaved.

"Father, don't!" I cried.

Cowardice had become a habit with him, and Snorri's scorn was nothing compared to the scorn he felt for himself. What spirit had he left to fight them with? But he had fought! Just for a few moments, thirty years had dropped away and he had wielded his spear like a young viking on the deck of his ship—*the viking he had been.*

"Husband, I beg you," Jorunn pleaded.

"Odin!" He screamed his god's name. With a twitch of his big shoulders he shrugged off the two men who held his arms. Snorri threw up his hands to defend himself, but Thorvald had him down, tumbling over with him on the ground, searching for the man's jugular with his teeth.

It took the bullmastiff and five men to get him off, while others forced Gunnar and me to the ground. All the while, Snorri, in a hoarse voice, was shouting, "Don't kill them! Don't kill them!"

It would have been too easy a death, you see. He wanted to give us time to see it coming, to taste the fear.

✝

The trial was soon over.

Poor foolish Hoskuld, gabbling his legal gibberish, was shoved aside. The jurors looked grim. They knew what was expected of them. Gunnar and I were dragged forward to hear sentence passed against us: "For the unprovoked slaying of Brand Hrutsson and the hireling Bork, exile for life, to be accomplished within two weeks from this day, the penalty for refusal, forfeiture of your land and your lives to any man who cares to take them."

While these words were being spoken, Hrut crowed and capered about, showing us his backside and screaming filth. Snorri watched him for a moment with an expression very like disgust, then turned and strode away, his spearmen falling in behind him.

✝

The next hours I pass over quickly—they aren't very clear in my mind. Perhaps I said with bitterness to Hoskuld, *We never had a chance, did we, lawyer?* Perhaps I only meant to say it. Kalf touched my arm, but I spun away from him—I cannot bear the sight of friends when I most need them. In that way, as in so many, I am like my father. Thorvald, Jorunn, Gunnar, and Vigdis—I suppose we said words to each other. Somehow the tents came down and the horses were loaded up.

Then we were crossing Thingvellir Plain and parting where the way divides—one track to Hawkdale, the other to Hekla. I don't think anyone called, "Farewell."

That ride home still finds its way into my dreams. A storm had been brewing all day and it erupted with booming thunder and sheets of rain that beat the meadow grass flat: such a wild, unseasonable storm as Black Thorvald might have conjured up out of his own black heart had he really been the sorcerer he was said to be.

"Please, husband," cried my mother, her voice almost lost in the roar of the wind, "Vigdis and the baby, pity them at least." All she could do was beg. For better or for worse my father had made himself master of our house again. He ignored her pleas and rode like a man with a demon at his back. And we followed over forty miles of rain-lashed heath and five swollen rivers, stopping only once to cram handfuls of sodden bread down our throats.

As I shrank in my saddle from the driving rain, long-buried memories of those wild childhood rambles with my father crowded in upon me—his fearsome description of the Doom of the Gods, which would be heralded by great whirlwinds and the falling of the sky. In the state of mind I was in, I half feared and half hoped that I was seeing it now in real truth.

It might have been midnight or noon when we reached the farm. I had lost all sensation of time in the indistinguishable grayness. My horse was stumbling from exhaustion, and all I knew was the clawing wind, the ache that throbbed from my buttocks to my shoulders, and the numbness of my fingers frozen to the dripping reins.

Then Ulf, our yellow-toothed hound, came howling up the ridge to meet us. His barking roused the thralls, who gathered round us, watching silently. They weren't fools, they wouldn't stay to be slaughtered. Soon they'd begin to slip away, hoping to join some bandit gang. Even Morag. I saw it on her face.

Inside, we hung our dripping clothes by the fire and wrung out our hair, then threw ourselves down to sleep. Tomorrow would be soon enough to take stock.

But Thorvald did not sleep. He fumbled in the kindling pile for a stick, took it, and sat down heavily in his high seat. He drew his knife and began to carve: "*Fe ... Ur ... Thurs ... Oss....*" The slivers flew.

I lay on the wall bench opposite, wet and shivering under my fleece. "Father," I whispered, "it was good to fight again, wasn't it?"

He didn't answer, and before my lips could shape another word I was asleep.

That night I dreamt of Grani, my brave stallion. In my dream I stood beside him in the ring, saw the goad descend in aching slowness through its arc, and heard myself scream ... *Too late!* The iron hook clawed out the red gobbet of his eye. But instead of the shriek of pain and hoofs beating the air, he turned his blood-streaked face to me in silence. And as I took his head between my hands, it seemed to dissolve, becoming instead the head of a bull—a black bull, from whose eyes streamed not blood but tears, rivers of tears. When I thought on it later, it seemed obvious that the bull was my father's *fylgia*, his spirit animal. Then I felt a crushing weight: a nightmare sat on my chest, pressing down, suffocating me. I thrashed and struggled to wake up and finally, with a wrenching effort, broke free. I lay still for a few moments.

When I opened my eyes, I saw that the rain had stopped and bright sunlight sifted down through the smoke hole. No one else was awake. It was very still.

The next thing I noticed was my father's knife lying on the floor by the side of his chair. Raising myself on an elbow, I was surprised to find him still sitting just as he had been when I fell asleep, only that his right hand hung down, and his head, turned a little to one side, rested against the carved chair back.

And his furious dead eyes looked into mine.

10

JORUNN SHIP-BREAST REMEMBERS

For the length of a heartbeat I simply stared. Then I dropped to the floor and rolled out of the path of his gaze. With my heart knocking against my ribs, I circled the wall until I was beside him. Then snatching his cloak from its peg, I threw it over his face. Feeling a little easier once his eyes were covered, I woke the others.

That morning while Thorvald sat—indifferent as always and only a little less animated—in his high-seat, we tried to make our brains, numbed already by so many shocks, take in this one too.

Jorunn, pale and lifeless as a corpse herself, sat on the bench close by her husband's side, unable to speak a word. It fell to the cool-headed Vigdis to set us moving.

"Find a big plank, husband," she said to Gunnar. "Odd, fetch water and cloths."

We began the ritual of preparation: laying him on the plank as best we could, for he was already stiffening; sealing his eyes and nostrils, and wrapping up his head. With an effort, Gunnar and I got him stripped, washed, and clothed again in clean breeches and a fine embroidered shirt that we discovered lying in the bottom of his chest. I didn't remember ever seeing him in that particular shirt, but my mother's cheeks colored for a moment when I brought it out.

Then Vigdis said to us in a low voice, "You know you must put him out through the wall, for he was a difficult man when he lived and I don't imagine death will improve him."

When Gudrun Night-Sun died, we had carried her out by the door, but of course, no one feared her little ghost if it should find its way home again. Thorvald was a different case. A *draug* is a terrifying thing—especially so when the living man died in anger, still more so if, like our father, he was uncanny.

Gunnar replied sarcastically that he would enjoy nothing better that morning than to tunnel through five feet of sod wall, but that we mustn't hope to get rid of father as easily as that. "He'll be back to stamp on our roof and kill our cattle however we carry him out, that grim man."

"Hush, Gunnar," said Vigdis, with a nervous glance at Jorunn. But our mother, sitting with her hands limp in her lap, gave no sign of hearing anything we said.

So Gunnar and I, with Skidi Dung-Beetle to help, set to work to break a hole in the rear wall, the farthest from the door, just large enough to admit the plank and body. While they dug from the outside, I applied the bow-drill and sawed through a section of the wooden planking that lined the inside of the room.

The day was a hot one. By the time we had dragged out the last basketful of dirt, the sun beat down straight above our heads, so that we got no shade even in the angle where the stable adjoins the house wall. Luckily, the river ran close by this end of the hall. We drank the icy water and rested a little.

"Now then, Tangle-Hair," said Gunnar, "you at his head and I at his feet."

We shoved our burden through and trudged with it over the stony path that followed the river.

"Brother," said Gunnar over his shoulder, "doesn't he seem a little heavier than you would have guessed?"

A draug's weight, it's well known, grows in proportion to its mischievousness. I thought this a poor joke and didn't answer.

'The Barrows' was not a place we visited often. Here the heath was humped up all around in grassy mounds which gave the appearance of a range of foothills as it might look to a strolling giant. Within each barrow, like a worm in a cocoon, an ancestor kept his vigil and thought his patient dead man's thoughts—or so, at least, they did when not feasting inside the fiery mountain. One little mound was new, the grass not yet thick upon it. There Gudrun Night-Sun lived.

Altogether, six generations of our kin rested under our feet.

Thorolf Braggart had been a priest in the temple of Thor back in Norway. It was a large temple that boasted a man-sized statue of the god, covered from top to toe in gold leaf, and seated in a chariot drawn by wooden goats.

In those days, because of the tyrannical rule of King Harald Fair-Hair, thousands of Norwegians loaded their families, their cattle, their tools and weapons into any leaky tub that would stay afloat and braved six hundred miles of open sea to make their home on this island, only recently discovered. They found a country by no means rich, the interior nothing but ice and lava, the seacoast and river-valleys able to bear only hay and a little barley in the south. In place of the magnificent pine and oak forests that they'd left behind them, they found nothing here but stunted birches. Despite these drawbacks, immigrants continued to arrive until, within sixty years of its discovery, all the useable land was taken.

Thorolf, too, decided to join this migration—in his case, impelled by neighbors who had chanced to find their missing cattle in his barn. Arriving at the mouth of the river Ranga, he soon discovered that all the decent land along that coast had already been claimed by others, and he was compelled to follow the river and seek land up country. He could find no place that suited him, though, until he came in sight of Hekla. Here, at any rate, his horse lay down and refused to go another step, and he took this as an omen.

So there, beside the riverbank, Thorolf Braggart set down his high-seat pillars and built his hall around them. The pillars in our hall are those very pillars, and the hall has changed little in two hundred years.

Not far from his new hall, Thorolf built a temple, just large enough for himself and his neighbors to sit comfortably in when they drank ale and ate the consecrated horseflesh on feast days. And in it he placed images of Thor, Odin, and Frey, all carved with his own hands, as well as a table to hold the bowl and twig by which the sacrificial blood is sprinkled on the worshippers, and the silver arm ring, which a man touches whenever he swears an oath.

Now, Thorolf was gifted with the second sight, as many of our family have been, and was able to see how the land-spirits from round about came up out of the ground to see this new temple of his and appeared to be favorably impressed with it. When he died, his barrow was built within sight of it, and all his descendants thereafter were buried in this same place.

From that time on, every father in his turn served as Thor's priest, beginning with Thorolf's son, Amundi Twist-Foot, who was the father of Olvir the Childish, who was the father of An Bow-Bender (the first of our line to be a godi), who was the father of Stein the Fast-Sailing, who was the father of Odd Snout, who was the father of my father.

But Black Thorvald, as I have already described, being angry with the god for letting the White Christ make a fool of him, neglected the temple and it soon fell to ruin. The idols within it, punished by the weather and gnawed by mice, shrank away until they were nothing but misshapen stumps.

Ironically, there seemed to be no other space large enough to contain our father's mound than this very spot. With the help of the thralls, who trooped along with us, carrying their spades and mattocks, we broke up Thor's earth.

Jorunn came up behind us as we worked, so quietly that no one noticed her until she spoke. By that time the grave was nearly dug and a mountain of dirt and stones lay heaped up beside it.

"Odd, will you do a thing for me even though it doesn't please you?" She knelt at the edge of the hole and held down to me a wooden crucifix. "He wouldn't have one in the house, but I have kept this all these years hidden in my chest."

"He won't like it any better now, Mother."

"I want you to carve runes on it the way he taught you. I want you to carve *Thorvald, do not walk.* We will lay it on his breast when we bury him."

This was the woman who only the day before had begged him to grovel before Snorri. Who could blame him now if his draug should haunt her?

"Ask a priest to write it in priest-letters, why don't you? It's no job for me."

But she persisted. "Your father can't read the priest-letters, what good would it do? Carve the runes for me, Odd." She thrust the thing in my hands, turned, and took a few steps. Then she came back. She said, "Odd, carve on it too *God help his soul.* Then she went quickly back along the path to the house.

75

Sitting down on a nearby rock in the shade of a barrow, I began to carve, and, as I carved, sadness and pity filled me. For the runes represented to me all that unfinished business between my father and me: questions never asked, understanding never gained, comfort never given. It would never be finished now.

Gunnar, laying his spade by, came over to watch. "He tried that with me once, you know, before you were born—the runes—but I didn't take to 'em. When he set me to carving, I threw the stick away, and he flew into a rage and beat me so hard I couldn't move for a week. After that we went our own ways." The bitterness in his voice surprised even me.

"Gunnar, I never knew that."

"Lots you never knew, brother."

"Do you have no tears for him even now?"

"For a coward?"

"But he fought, Gunnar! At the end, he *fought*. You saw him."

"Oh, he fought—like a weak man goaded to it, not joyfully as a warrior fights."

"I call that hard words for a dead man."

"Odd ... Brother!" Gunnar put out his hands to fend me off, for I had jumped to my feet and swung at him with the crucifix, like a club. An instant before, nothing could have been farther from my mind.

"Odd, don't!" he said. "I wouldn't have us fight for anything—not now of all times. I take back what I said."

Putting his hand on my shoulder, he sat me down again. I poured my anger into my carving and made the slivers fly, just as if Father himself wielded the knife. Was his spirit raising its awful head among us so soon?

But anger with me has a way of rushing in and out like a madman on an errand. Before long it went its muttering way, and I mumbled words of apology to Gunnar.

I finished the inscription and drew the knife blade across my thumb. My blood flowed into the deep lines and notches of the runes. Rune spells are weak, so my father had taught me long ago, without the added strength of blood.

"Gunnar, if you haven't tears...."

"Aye."

He took the knife from me and sliced between his thumb and finger, cutting deeper than he needed to, and let his blood run together with mine over the crucifix. "May he have good of it."

I knew Gunnar did it only for me. I loved him very much at that moment.

✝

That morning the sun had been bright and hot in an empty sky, but by afternoon, rain clouds stood again over the mountains.

We laid Thorvald in his tomb, placing next to him a joint of mutton on a platter, his silver-rimmed drinking horn, his blacksmith's tools, a pair of spears, and his sword—first bending the blade to consecrate it. I whistled for Ulf and, when the old hound loped up, I scratched him behind the ears and cut his throat, laying his body at Thorvald's feet. Then Jorunn placed the crucifix on his chest and folded his hands over it. I thought I heard Hekla grumble in its sleep as she did this, though it might have been only the echo of distant thunder. After that we shared ale and mutton at the graveside and, lastly, covered the crypt with planks, shaped the mound over it, and bade Black Thorvald farewell.

Our mother did not weep. It isn't our custom for women to wail and claw their cheeks at funerals in the appalling fashion of Greeks or Arabs. Nevertheless, she bore it hard.

Little Gudrun's death had stirred rage in her. Thorvald's, once the first shock was past, affected her in a different way. All that evening she stood at her loom, her hands never still, weaving and talking, talking to herself more than to any of us, recalling the man that she alone remembered.

"Lord," she said, "the day I came here to live. His old mother was still alive then, the daughter of a king in Ireland, as she claimed, and maybe she was. Anyway, she thought I wasn't good enough to wed her son, though I came of a proud hall. 'We'll see about that,' thought I to myself, and I stood at this loom, just as I'm standing here now, to weave him as fine a shirt as ever man wore. But, as often as I would set the heddles for my pattern, that old mother of his would curse me for a stupid girl and pull them out again, until I grew so vexed that I cried and begged to go back to my own hall where they treated me kindly.

"Your father just put back his head and laughed—you know his eyes would dance when he laughed—and said that a man in a house with two women was a thing to be pitied. 'Mother go back in your corner,' says he, 'for I'll wear no shirt at all but what fair-haired Jorunn weaves me, and as winter's coming on, I'll be glad if she hurries at it.'

"He took off the shirt he was wearing then and laid it on the very bottom of his chest. After that, he went bare-backed for a week in the cold until I'd finished him his shirt."

"And where is that shirt now?" we asked.

"Ah well, nothing lasts forever, does it?"

"And the one he took off?"

"Why, I guess he's wearing it now," she smiled sadly. "But it was such a long time ago."

And she remembered other things. How she would stand down by the riverbank each day as summer drew to an end, listening for the sound of his war horn and watching for his ship to come in view, its oars flashing up and down. And how our hall would ring at night with the shouts and laughter of the warriors boasting of their high deeds and hailing Black Thorvald of Hekla as their godi and their Ring-Giver.

I heard all this with astonishment. I could just recall as a tiny child playing among the bleached ribs of that ship, its timbers soft with rot, as though they were the outward image of his own decaying soul. Finally, one winter we burned what was left of it for fuel. All the brave crewmen had long since gone off to luckier halls.

With these bittersweet memories the day stole to its end.

✝

The next night at dinner Gunnar did a surprising thing. He sat down in the high seat. Vigdis shot him an anxious look and said it was too soon, for decency's sake, but Jorunn said, "No, he has the right, and the sooner done the better."

"I do have the right," said Gunnar, his expression uncommonly serious, "but it isn't long I plan to sit here. It's up to me now to say what we will do and so I mean to. We are leaving Iceland—all of us, now."

"Ahh!" Jorunn's face looked as if he had struck her.

Seeing how she took it, he pressed his reasons. If he and I went into exile, he said, what would become of her, a woman alone? If we defied the ban and stayed—well, that was just what Hrut and Snorri were hoping for. They would have our lives and our land in short order.

"Now then, hear me well," he continued, addressing all of us. "I know a certain ship captain, a Greenlander. I've traded with him many a time. He's an honest man and sails a fair little tub of a ship. I calculate he'll leave within the week from Reykjanes, and he could take us with him. There's land for the grabbing in Greenland, or, still better, in Vinland. Why, it's so mild there, they say, that grapes grow on the bushes. We could drink wine every day in the year. I can taste it already! You're with me, Odd, aren't you? Odd's with me."

I hadn't said anything. What a change had come over my brother. The recklessness, the mockery were gone, and in their place an earnest, cautious head. How long he had waited to sit in Thorvald's seat!

But Jorunn, in a choked voice said, "Leave here? Leave Thorvald alone in his tomb, and the Night-Sun, and all my little ones?"

Suddenly and without warning the river that ran deep inside her, that none of us had ever seen, broke to the surface and burst from her eyes. Leave her babies! She was strong enough for anything but this. Great sobs shook her, throwing her forward and back.

Gunnar waited. When the sobbing lessened a little, he put up his last argument against her. We could deed the land to Hoskuld, he said, and he would pass it on some day to Kalf or Katla when they married, and this way it would stay with kindred, and the dead would be content. But if we waited for it to be taken from us—here he made her look him in the eyes and spoke in his gravest tone—Hrut would come here to live, mow our hay, reap our barley, and no doubt piss on the graves of our ancestors.

While he spoke, Vigdis put her arms around Jorunn and added words of her own.

Our mother sat for a long time then, looking into the fire, but at last stood up, pushed back her hair, and smoothed her dress with her big hands. "Handsome Gunnar," she said, "the man who sits in the high seat sleeps in the bed-closet."

"There's no need...." he started to protest, but she hurried on.

"You and Vigdis have made love on the bare straw long enough. It's a good bed. Enjoy it while you may, it won't be going to Vinland with us."

Gunnar jumped up from the high seat and kissed her. He was her darling, no one but he could have won her over.

That night as I lay waiting for sleep to come, I thought again of my father's gods. As I have said, he turned his back on the bluff and genial red-bearded Thor. As the darkness swallowed his heart, he turned instead, to one-eyed Odin, god of poetry, of war, and of madness. I decided that I, too, would put myself under his protection, for he is, besides all else, the patron of outlaws and outcasts—exactly what the Christmen had made of me. It pleased me to think that, as I was Black Thorvald's child, I was in a way, Odin's child too, for the two of them seemed to mingle in my mind.

11

COWARD

The following morning Gunnar was up early, rummaging around for food to put in his knapsack. Being a light sleeper, I awoke.

"Well, brother, how was it in the bed?"

"I shall ignore that, young Tangle-Hair." With a flourish he twirled the tip of his pointed beard and grinned wickedly.

"Where are you going?"

"To Hoskuld's, about the land—we've got no time to waste. Then on to Reykjanes to arrange our passage. Expect me back in three days, four at the most. Meantime, get everyone stirring here—Mother especially. Keep her busy. I want us packed and ready to go by the time I get back, you understand?" He bit off a hunk of bread.

"Gunnar—?"

"What is it?"

"Nothing. If you say Vinland, Vinland it is. Only I was wondering last night ... if shirking a fight was cowardice when our father did it, how has it now become prudence?"

He stopped in mid-chew. Strange as it seems, he really had not thought of this. It showed on his face. "Well, damn it, Odd, I mean, if it was just you and me we'd go down fighting, wouldn't we? But there's the womenfolk to think of, and young'uns, and the land, and...."

"And all those things that weighed on his mind, too."

"Well, that is, but I mean to say...."

But he couldn't quite think what he meant to say and so chewed his bread ferociously instead.

For the second time in as many days the chattering madman, Anger, rushed upon me—that my brother should be so blind to this one thing, my father's memory, that mattered so much to me. But I held my tongue and begged the madman to leave. How could I fight with Gunnar, who meant more to me than anyone? "We'll be ready when you get back, brother, I promise. Ride fast."

✝

The next days passed quickly, for me at least. I drove unhappy thoughts away and concentrated my whole mind on this new adventure—and what an adventure it would be! To sail over the sea to a new land, with new faces, with riches for the taking, with dangers for a certainty. Red-skinned Skraeling warriors, painted and feathered, as we'd heard them described, lurked in my imagination, behind every rock. Sloe-eyed Skraeling girls peeped from every bush. What a swath I would cut through them both!

From time to time, I thought of Kalf and felt sad. I would miss no one in Iceland but him. Couldn't I rescue him somehow from his bondage to Hoskuld? By the Raven, I'd find a way.

On the third day Gunnar returned. I was the first to see him, as I happened to be at the river end of the house at work with Skidi Dung-Beetle fitting new blocks of turf to the hole we had dug for father.

Gunnar was in high spirits, for everything had gone according to plan. Our uncle had pressed on him far more money than the farm was worth. Gunnar emptied his knapsack onto the table and out spilled a heap coin and hack silver that you could scarcely pile on a plate without it spilling off. The ship's master had promised to squeeze us in among the bolts of homespun and sacks of eiderdown, and guaranteed we would sail to Greenland as snug as a family of mice.

"And so, my friends," concluded Gunnar triumphantly, "we leave in the morning."

"Then," said Jorunn, "each of you is to name his favorite dish, for I will never cook a meal in this house again."

The thralls were staying behind, the Greenlander not having space enough for them, and would pass with the land to Hoskuld. It seemed only right they should share this last meal with us, as for so many years we had shared the same labors under the same sky.

Fewer of them had slipped away over the past few days than I would have predicted when you considered our contagious bad luck. I did note the absence of Padraig, a quarrelsome man whom I'd never cared for, and a couple of others, but there still remained six able-bodied men and four women and a gang of young'uns.

That night Jorunn and Vigdis spread wild flowers on the tabletops and we slaughtered liberally—it was Hoskuld's stock now—so that joints of mutton simmered over the longhearth. We were generous, too, with Hoskuld's ale.

I began to get drunk.

And the drunker I got, the more I discovered that I was not happy. *How Hrut and Snorri will laugh to see the sons of Thorvald run away!* I thought bitterly. *Just like their father, cowards to the bone.*

The prospect of a new life over the sea was no cure for this.

I kept these thoughts to myself, for they did not seem to trouble Gunnar at all. There was no cowardice in Gunnar, and he knew it. And because he knew it, he could retreat when it suited him without a pang of self-hate. But he was only the son of Black Thorvald's body, while I was the son of his spirit. I hadn't the freedom to run away laughing.

"May you have better luck hereafter, masters," called out Skidi Dung-Beetle, offering a toast. "And us'll think fond of you, for you have been good to us, as Northmen goes." Skidi had been with us from childhood, and Gunnar this day had granted him his freedom. Looking round the table with his blunt, honest face, he got everyone's assent, and the thralls lifted their stone mugs all together and brought them back down with a clatter on the table.

But there was not much warmth in the eyes of Aelfric. He was a burly Saxon who had been scooped up six or seven years ago by a Danish raiding party that struck his village in some English fen on his very wedding day, or so he said. It was with him that Morag slept nowadays, although he suspected that he didn't have her all to himself.

I watched her sitting beside him. She was four months gone with child (his or mine she couldn't, or wouldn't, say) and her breasts were beginning to swell and her face to grow rounded and soft. Did I say there was no one in this land that I would miss but Kalf?

There was her.

In the days since our return from the Althing, I'd been too distracted to seek her out. But on this last evening, a great longing for her took hold of me.

She saw me staring at her and hesitantly smiled back. Stiff with desire, I went over to her and gathering a bunch of her dark hair in my hand, pushed myself between her and Aelfric on the bench. Why should I wait and watch like a thief to steal a minute alone with her? Tomorrow I would own nothing on earth—not land, or country, or honor. Tonight, at least, I would take what I wanted.

"I will miss you, darling Morag," I said, "link arms and drink with me for old times' sake."

She tried to laugh and turned her head away, saying I had drunk enough already. Did she fear Aelfric? Well, rot the bastard, I didn't! "Give us a kiss, sweet Morag." I pressed my mouth hard against hers and felt her yield—*what else could she do?* Along the bench the happy sounds of feasting died away, and the thralls glanced nervously at us. Even Skidi frowned at his plate.

"What?" I cried. "I beg your pardon friends, I didn't know. Must I have permission to fondle a slave's bed-mate?"

When a man talks like a fool, we say that a troll has twisted his tongue. Mine was twisted clear around my neck. But it wasn't Morag, really, that I cared about. It was only that I must have a little power over *someone*.

Aelfric sat still as a stone, his fingers digging into his knees.

"Come now, sweetheart," I wheedled, "sit on my knee. We'll never have the pleasure again."

"Odd, don't force me."

"Force you? By the Raven, when has anyone needed to force *you*?"

"Odd!" Gunnar's voice reached me across the room like a whiplash.

"Later, brother," I answered, not looking at him.

"Come here to me." It seemed, now, the voice of my new master, not a brother.

With desperate bravado I got to my feet. "Well, darling Morag, it seems that anyone can have you but me."

"Friends," called Gunnar, "go on with your drinking. Someone fill Aelfric's mug for him. Christ, where would we be without his broad back! Excuse my brother and me if we talk a little in private." Their eyes followed me to the foot of the high-seat, where I stood shaking with anger.

"You shame me, Gunnar."

"Sit," he hissed, keeping his voice low. "Sit down and cool your head. I only ask that we not have the hall a bloody shambles and you laid up with a cracked skull or worse the day before we sail. They are six fighting men to our two, and despite Skidi's pretty speech, there is precious little right now keeping them in their place. Now, don't sulk. Just clear the fumes from your head, and turn your thoughts to something more useful than Morag's pretty ass, because we *do* have things to talk about."

Sounds of merriment swelled again from the thralls' benches as the ale flowed. Gunnar made me sit beside him and began another enthusiastic speech on how we would make a new home in Vinland.

In my miserable state of mind, I was only half listening to him.

The *thuck* that rattled the door might have been just the rap of a heavy fist, but it roused me from my stupor. While the others looked up curiously, I went and put my hand on the latch and stood there a moment, not breathing.

I'd never thought I had the second sight, or ever wished to, but at that moment I knew, as certainly as I have ever known anything, what I would see when I opened that door. Knew it and welcomed it. A chance to die, sword in hand!

I flung the door open. A spear quivered in it. I looked up at the face of Strife-Hrut.

"Young Odd Thorvaldsson," he said with mock politeness, "how pleased I am to find you at home. And your brother, too? Where is he? Not gone, I hope? Ah, then I'm not too late."

Gunnar stood beside me in the doorway. Jorunn and Vigdis peered between our heads.

Hrut sat his horse a dozen paces away, flanked by a line of mounted men. All of them wore visored helmets. But nothing could conceal the bushy whiskers or the enormous girth of the man on Hrut's left.

In a steady voice my brother said, "Hrut Ivarsson, the two weeks allowed us by the law are not yet up. This is treachery."

"Treachery?" Hrut cried. "No, young peacock, it would be 'treachery' if you was to get away with your lives after killing my boy. Is it true your father's died, damn his eyes? Your runaway thrall's been telling it all over the countryside." He turned toward the big man on his left. "The old bear's cheated you, Godi but by Christ, the cubs won't do the same to me!"

Snorri, of course! Not in command of this outrage—oh, far too upright for that—but willing to be a spectator of it. So much for the laws of Iceland.

"Their exile doesn't satisfy you, you pig-faced man?" shouted Jorunn behind us.

"That it don't, Housewife. What will satisfy me is to cut these two boys of yours meat from bone and nail their heads up to my hall door, as I should have done before now. Now then, sons of Thorvald, look to yourselves!"

Gunnar leapt back, pulling us with him, and barred the door. With a smile on his handsome lips, he put his back against it. "Well, brother Odd, our corpses will feed the Iceland crows and not the Vinland ones after all. I think that suits you better?"

"If only they feast on Hrut's eyes too!"

He threw an arm round my neck and laughed. "So they may, brother! We've men enough here to give 'em a fight. We may live to see another day yet. Would you sail away happy then?"

"Never happier than I am at this minute, Gunnar!"

He was my brother again.

Outside, fifty throats raised the battle cry. The door shook under the blows of axes. Gunnar and I shouted orders: "Vigdis, get the baby ... Get the women in the back ... Mother, bolt the stable door ... Skidi, Aelfric, you others, arm yourselves, hurry!"

I snatched our shields down from the wall, tossing one to Gunnar with his sword. The door planks shivered, and two men burst through, their shields over their heads.

Gunnar and I faced them side by side. I caught mine with a backhand cut under the shield that sliced through his right leg at the knee. He hadn't hit the floor before another man leapt over him and thrust at me with a spear held low, aiming for my balls. I leaned to the right, and as we collided, drove my shield into his face, sending him reeling backward.

On my left, Gunnar slashed about him like a whirlwind. Two men went down, howling. A third turned to get away, and my brother, seeing him, cried, "Here I am, murderer, strike!" The fellow turned back, and it was Mord Hrutsson. Gunnar let out a yell and leapt for him, but caught his foot on the body of a dead man. As he lurched forward, Mord held out his barbed spear, bracing the butt of it on the floor. Its long blade went into Gunnar's belly right up to the crosspiece. I aimed a blow at Mord's arm and severed it at the elbow. Kicking him out of the way, I threw my shield over Gunnar while Jorunn dragged him away by the heels.

Such a battle-rage fell upon me then as I had never felt before. My war cry echoed in my ears, and Neck-Biter's steel tongue wove back and forth before my eyes. It cut bone with every stroke and men went down before it, screaming.

My mother, leaving Gunnar in his wife's arms, now stood beside me. Gripping an axe in her big fists, she brought it whistling down on shields and heads and wherever she struck, the blood flew up like sea-spray.

Behind me I heard Gunnar order Vigdis to draw the spear out and I heard him groan. The barbed blade took big pieces of his flesh with it. Holding his guts in one hand and his sword in the other, he stumbled back into the fight.

In the narrow space before the door, our attackers could not come at us all at once. Still, the fighting was hot. Hacking, stabbing, shoving, we drove them back a step at a time. The floor was slippery with blood. Men lay groaning everywhere. I had wounds on my right arm, my head, and my legs—though none were mortal. Incredibly, Gunnar was still on his feet, still hacking and thrusting, while the blood leaked out of him like water from an old bucket.

Our only advantage was that these men were not fighting to defend their homes. Their attack faltered. One man lost his nerve and tried to push his way back through the door. That was all the others needed to make them turn tail.

As the last of them cleared the doorway, we upended a table to barricade it. Behind it, Gunnar sank to his knees. He was finished.

Meanwhile, our thralls had pulled down the remaining arms that lined the walls and handed them round, but although they shouted and waved their swords about, not one had stepped into the blood-storm alongside us.

Then one of them cried, "The roof!"

Over our heads Hrut's men were hacking at the sod, prying clumps of it loose from the rafters. There a man crouched above it, one foot planted on each side, throwing the sod away behind him. I snatched a spear from the floor and sent it straight up, catching him between the legs. He screamed and fell backwards. But in other places, too, they were breaking through.

From outside came Hrut's voice crying, "The heathens will burn in the next world, roast 'em in this one, too!"

Torches were tossed up to the men above, who began to put them to the bare rafters.

"Not fire!" Gunnar whispered. Pulling himself up to where there was a little space between the table top and the doorway, he put his mouth to it and called, "In Christ's name let us send out the women and children!"

"Don't name Christ to us, Troll-brat!" came Hrut's voice back. But another voice—surely Snorri's—commanded, "Send 'em out then, damn you, we'll burn no babies here."

"Vigdis," called Gunnar faintly. She ran to him, clutching their baby. "You have a son to raise .... Tell him who I was."

"Husband, no!"

"Obey me. Get out!"

When she didn't move, he appealed to me with his eyes. Shouldering the table aside, I pushed her out, though she screamed and tried to claw my face. Two of Hrut's men went for her, both at once.

"Odd, behind you!" Morag's voice. Then a fist like a beam end struck me between the shoulders. Aelfric's face, twisted with hate, looked into mine and snarled, "Burn, Master!" He shoved past me, out the door, dragging Morag behind him. Behind them tumbled all the rest, even Skidi, flinging their arms away in a mad rush to get out the door.

You may say they would have bolted anyway. You may say that if they had stayed to fight, we were still too few to save ourselves. You may say what you like. I lay against the doorway and groaned, "I have done this."

Now the rafters were a mass of flame. Falling sparks ignited the straw that covered the floor. Smoke poured into the room through the cracks in the wall panels. Seconds later, the sweating wood exploded in sheets of fire. Fear, deep and unreasoning, gripped me.

Here stood Jorunn Ship-Breast in the middle of the room, swaying on her feet, still clutching the axe, her bare arms bloody to the elbows, and her dress clinging damply to her side where a blade had pierced her.

"Run!" I screamed, but she was past hearing. With the flames leaping up around her and her hair flying loose in the cluttered wind, she seemed to me like Brynhilde in the ancient lays, lusting for death. Her lips formed words, but the roar of the flame carried them away.

As I went toward her, a flaming timber cracked overhead and struck her to the ground. I wrestled with it while the flames licked my hands, and nearly had her free when her hair began to burn, and I shrank back.

Nearby lay Gunnar doubled over, his handsome face all staring eyes and twisted mouth. But still the lips managed a smile. "Fate's a trickster, eh, Tangle-Hair? Now, get away if you can—out through the stable...."

"I can't leave you."

"Brother, one of us must live for vengeance. Promise me—"

"Yes, all right, Gunnar, yes. "

But the door to the stable was aflame. I could hear the horses on the other side pounding the walls with their hoofs. There was no escape that way. And I didn't seek one. I didn't want to survive this slaughter that I'd brought upon us. This son of Thorvald would not run away.

Gunnar's fingers clutched at my shirt. "Look for me one day, Tangle-Hair, in Valhalla or in Hel."

"Sooner than you think, brother," I answered. "Don't be angry with me."

The fingers tightened in a spasm, then uncurled, leaving bloody prints.

Handsome Gunnar with your brave pointed beard. I rolled him on his back, pulling his blood-soaked tunic over his thighs and putting his legs together so that his body would not be found indecent. Then I stretched myself out beside him.

Against the command of every pleading nerve, I willed myself not to move. Over my head the ridge beam groaned and sagged.

"Now, Brother!" I cried aloud, waiting for it to fall and crush out my life. Instead, only a rain of embers showered down on me.

But this was the end of my little courage.

In terror, I leapt up to beat the glowing scraps from my face and hair. Oh, just let me get away! Let Gunnar bleed out his life a hundred times over, let my mother's long hair smoke and flame, let dishonor follow me to the ends of the earth. Only let me get out of here!

With my cloak over my head, I plunged through the smoky inferno of our house to the rear wall where the hole in the wall still gaped open. But there was no escape this way, either. Only this morning Skidi and I had filled in the outside with fresh cut sods to an arm's length before Gunnar's arrival distracted me from it. I told Skidi to finish the job, but how much more had he done?

I crouched before the opening, paralyzed with fear. I knew I would suffocate long before I broke through to the outside, or else the wall would collapse and bury me alive. But the heat in the room was searing and I could smell my crisping hair. I had no choice. Throwing my sword ahead of me, I plunged after it into the mouth of the tunnel.

We had made the space wide enough for Thorvald's shoulders, but mine were nearly as broad. I could get no purchase with my elbows or knees. Digging my fingers into the dirt and wriggling like a snake on my belly, I inched forward.

I got to the barrier where a shower of loose soil filled my mouth and nostrils. I lay on my side, working my sword into the dirt, jerking the blade this way and that, but a mountain sat on my chest and the blood pounded in my ears. I could move neither forward nor back. My feet! The flames licked at my toes. I squeezed forward with all my might but couldn't draw them away from the fire. In a frenzy, I began again to stab at the dirt with my sword point, heedless of how the blade cut my fingers. Hopeless. Hopeless...

A hot wind brushed my fingertips. I braced myself and pushed with the last of my strength. My head burst through a shower of dirt into the acrid air. I was out!

I huddled, retching and trembling, at the foot of the wall.

Hrut's men clustered around the front of the house, expecting us to make a sally there. No one saw me crouching in the back. I rolled through the pall of smoke and cinders down the embankment to the river, and from scorching heat passed to shocking cold. Forcing my head under, I wriggled along the shallow bottom to the little islet that lay mid-stream. Coming up for one gulp of air, I dived again and worked around to the far side. I dragged my body, numb as a stone, onto the bank behind a clump of sedge and lay there gasping.

With the last of my strength, I crawled to where I could look back through the parted grass and see our house, just as the roof collapsed in a cloud of sparks that whirled up like a thousand fireflies into the blue midnight sky. Far away, I heard Hrut's men shout their victory cry.

After that, I heard no more.

12

STIG NO-ONE'S-SON

Somewhere beyond thought, a monotonous halting rhythm throbbed in my bones. My eyes fluttered open, showing me two black and bloody hands dancing at the ends of ragged sleeves, while, miles below them, the pebbled ground lurched past. The odor of sheepskin and horse's sweat was in my nostrils, ropes ran across my back, cutting into my flesh. In an instant I was awake and screaming, my head bursting with the weight of my blood, my skin on fire.

"Sst!" A hand seized me roughly by the hair, pulling my head back, and another hand covered my mouth.

I struggled until the darkness rolled over me again, leaving once more only the distant awareness of that jolting rhythm.

✝

My delirium continued, so they told me, for a day and a night. At times, I was faintly aware of faces swimming above me—my uncle's mournful eyes, Katla Thin-Hair's sharp nose, and the ugly face of a man who watched me without emotion—though I had the feeling that his hands touched me skillfully and eased my pain. But more constantly than all of them, I saw the anxious face of Kalf Slender-Leg.

Sometime on the second day I sat up suddenly.

"Grandfather!"

"Heh? Kalf? Oh, God in Heaven! Be still, dear boy. Just lie still. Katla, the posset, hurry!" Hoskuld rushed over to me. His shaking hand held the warm milk and wine to my lips, pouring most of it down my cheek.

"Uncle Hoskuld?" My voice rasped in my throat.

"Yes, I'm here. Don't try to talk, dear boy. Drink it all down. There."

"How did I get here?"

"We found you in the long grass on the island—or rather, Kalf did with his eagle eye.

"How...?"

"Lie still, now. You really must. Kalf, tell him he must."

I let him push me back on the mound of fleeces they had heaped around me.

"Oh, to see you alive, dear boy! You've got young Kalf here to thank for it. It was the morning, you see, that Gunnar visited us with his sad news of Thorvald dying and all of you leaving. After he left, I took to my bed. I confess, I lay in my bed moaning and weeping for half the day, a thing I have not done since—well ..." Since the death of Flosi, his son, he had started to say. "For I'm not an unfeeling sort of man, not a stone, by God, not a tree stump!

"But Kalf made me ashamed of myself, saying it wasn't right to let kinsmen go away without a proper farewell. It was God, of course, who made you say that, Kalf, seeing as how things turned out. So the two of us set out on horseback after Gunnar."

"I saw the smoke a long way off," Kalf broke in. "'By Odin's crow,' said I, 'they're being murdered!' and I galloped to the brow of the ridge from where I could see your house. I wasn't there a minute when I saw you crawl up onto the island. By the time Grandfather and I got to you, you were stiff and stony cold. I thought sure you were dead."

Hoskuld resumed, "I put my ear to your lips and could feel a little breath stirring. 'Not dead yet,' said I, 'but as good as, if Hrut searches for his body and doesn't find it.' Right away I saw what was to be done. I'm a cunning man when need be. We watched and waited on that island for hours until the fire was nearly burned out, chaffing your poor arms and legs all the while to warm 'em up. You don't remember it at all? Well, by time, the lot of them were drunk, helping themselves to what was left in your brew-house. Then I took that heathen medal from off your neck, that cursed Thor's hammer, for I recollected how Snorri had fingered it...."

"Snorri was there! I burst out. "I saw him!"

"Let me tell it now," said Kalf. "I took the Thor's hammer with me and waded across the river. I crept up along the bank until I was just by the house. I got in the way you must have gotten out, through that gaping hole in the wall. How it came to be there, I can't imagine."

I explained in a few words.

Kalf gave a shudder at the thought of Black Thorvald's draug. "No evil but has some good in it, though," he said. "Without that hole I don't know what I would have done. I wriggled in and had a look round until I found a body about your size—one of Hrut's men. He was so charred I didn't like to touch him, but I had no choice. I stripped off his sword and jewelry that his friends might recognize him by, blackened his hair with soot, and hung your hammer around his neck."

"But he didn't have my face."

"He hardly had a face at all. Then it was just a matter of getting you home. You did give us a scare once, when you woke up screaming before we were out of earshot."

"Kalf Slender-Leg," I said, "you're the bravest fellow in all the world. Ask me for my life whenever you need it."

He blushed to the roots of his hair.

"And it worked!" crowed my uncle. For just yesterday who comes knocking at my door but Snorri himself, looking mighty uncomfortable—admitting nothing, mind you—but saying how he had heard about what happened, and wasn't it a pity, and he had seen to it that Gunnar's wife and baby were delivered alive to her father's house, and that all the victims got a Christian burial, the mother and *both* sons—his exact words—both sons. And you lying under a fleece not six paces away. You're safe, Odd, for a while, as long as you stay hidden here. God has not forsaken us altogether." He put out a blue-veined hand and stroked my forehead.

✝

In the long days that followed, the outside of me healed. They made poultices of moss and marsh marigold and put them on the palms of my hands, which were sliced and torn, and on my scorched toes, and every other part of me that was bruised, burned or cut.

I'd been lucky. My face was untouched except for where my hair and beard were singed on one side, and elsewhere on my body the wounds did not mortify. Within a month the worst of it was past.

The outside of me, as I say, healed well. But I saw in all their eyes the dawning knowledge that there were things amiss with me that no poultices could cure. You are never the same man afterwards when you should have died but didn't.

I began by taking mead or ale to deaden the pain of my wounds. As the pain grew less, I found that I still could not sleep without drink, and, despite great quantities of it, I slept badly, waking in the middle of the night, my shirt soaked with sweat. I would grind my fists into my eyes to squeeze the pictures out of them. But nothing could take the stench of burning hair and flesh out of my nostrils. Hoskuld placed under my pillow shavings of goat's horn, in which he put great store as a cure for sleeplessness, but neither that nor any other remedy gave me ease.

In the daytime, when the rest of the household was occupied with the work of the farm, I tottered from one end of the hall to the other: from the bed-closet to the stable, and from the stable to the pantry, from the pantry to the bed-closet again; past the hangings, past the ornate high-seat posts, past the old weapons that lined the walls in an unceasing, aimless, and distracted round of movement.

And in the evenings by the fire I talked endlessly, telling the gruesome tale over and over again, jumping up to circle the room, then returning to my place at the bench only to abandon it a moment later, but always talking.

"Gunnar ordered me to run away, Uncle, or else I would not have lived...."

"Yes, dear boy, and thank God for it."

"Kalf, he made me promise him. 'Avenge us,' he said—his last words."

"Yes, Odd, you've told us, and someday you surely will."

"Gunnar held me by my shirt—like this—and ordered me..."

"Yes, yes, I know."

They listened to me at first with sorrow, then with perplexity, finally with fear.

"Odd," said Kalf, when a little drink spilled from the ale horn I was holding and wet my tunic, "your hands—"

After that I was careful to hold them close to my body, to put one on top of the other, to sit on them.

Waking and sleeping I dreamed of revenge, rehearsing to Kalf, or anyone who would listen, the most fantastic schemes, only to reject each one in turn. Any act of mine would draw attention to Hoskuld and make his life forfeit for harboring a fugitive.

Not that he seemed to care much for life now. The past weeks had aged him like so many years. In his heart, I think, he blamed himself for bungling our case, and even for what happened afterward. I, the 'young dog' of happier days, had never been his 'dear boy' until now. This unaccustomed tenderness was the measure of his guilt.

For myself, I could have forgiven him, but even his own god, it seemed, would not do so much, despite all the mumbling hours that he spent upon his knees. And meanwhile, his cloudy eyes grew cloudier, the skin around them dark and drawn, and his clothes hung looser from his shoulders. Kalf watched helplessly as the two of us, man and boy, wandered our separate ways into the dark places of the soul.

But there was another who watched, too, one whom I have already had occasion to mention—the man called Stig.

Not Stig the Silent, nor Stig the Ugly, though either of those nicknames would have suited him. Not Stig Sveinsson or Einarsson, or any such patronymic, since he claimed to have no father. He was, therefore, for lack of anything better, called Stig No-One's-Son, though usually simple Stig sufficed.

I had seen him for the first time, you'll recall, on that night in Hoskuld's hall when he danced like a wild man, and then again on our journey to the Althing—a tight-lipped man who seemed to care little for being a servant. Finally, it was his villainous face—pockmarked, broken-nosed, and shock-headed—that watched over me in my delirium. And they were his skillful hands that tended me.

He was, according to his own terse account of himself, a bit of a farmer, a bit of a surgeon, a bit of a sailor.

"A bit of a brigand," Hoskuld added ruefully, "though the rascal has his uses."

He was not a thrall, as I had thought at first, but a landless freeman who had arrived at my uncle's doorstep seeking work some summers previous, and had stayed on to tend the forge, to doctor the household and the stock, and even to barter the produce and handle money.

These talents outweighed his defects, which were, in my uncle's eyes, considerable. He had no religion; he suffered bursts of manic energy, which appeared without warning, although (fortunately for the crockery and the furniture) not often; and lastly, he had a habit of going off unexpectedly on long expeditions of indefinite duration, whose purpose he never cared to disclose.

He was a man who kept to himself and had little to say most of the time, but I began to notice, as much as I noticed anything in those brain-sick days, how he would often follow me with a cool and appraising eye.

It was on a warm evening in high summer, about the fourth week of my captivity—as I now thought of it—and we were ranged around the hall in our usual attitudes: Katla at the loom, Kalf by the fire, fletching arrows, Hoskuld fretting, and I drinking—as I had been doing steadily since morning, though I felt no better for it. Stig sat in a corner, stitching a patch of leather on his shoe.

"Nick his ship," he said to the wall.

No one quite heard, and after a few moments he took the wall into his confidence again, repeating in a louder voice, "Nick his ship."

"What's that, you scoundrel?" said Hoskuld, giving a start as if he had been shaken out of a slumber.

Stig glanced around and lifted an eyebrow. "Hrut's ship," he said. "Nick it."

We all stared at him.

"What—take it?" said Hoskuld. "But he's gone off a-trading already, man. The sailing season's half over."

"Hasn't."

"What d'you know of it?" I demanded, thick-tongued and surly with drink.

It was Stig's habit never to look quite at you when he spoke, but rather to squint past your shoulder as though his keen mariner's eye descried some distant coastline on the horizon. So it appeared that he spoke to walls.

"Talked to a man who happened to mention that your friend Hrut's ship sprung a leak and they had to re-tar her. Then he got sick in his stomach for a while. No sooner recovered than his white gyrfalcons that he'd meant to sell abroad went and died on him, and they had to find more. Troubles that man has had could make you weep." He allowed himself a quick smile.

"And she's still in the river?" I asked, hardly able to believe him.

Stig scratched his spiky head. "Was yesterday." He had come back only yesterday from one of his mysterious rambles. Finally, he looked straight at me with the same cool, searching look such as I had caught him at before. It seemed to say, *What are you made of, boy? What are you game for?*

"Still moored in the river," he said, "but not for long. Fellow tells me she'll sail in three, four days' time, now that the new falcons are old enough to live through the voyage."

"Three or four days!" I cried. "And just waiting to be plundered and burnt. A blow against him where he'll feel it the most!"

"You wicked, thankless boy, "Katla Thin-Hair screeched, wringing her thin hands. "It's no different from all your other plans. If you're caught at it, you'll be your uncle's murderer. It won't take them long to guess who has sheltered you all these weeks. They'll come and burn *us* up in our beds!"

"Sweet darling Katla," I laughed, "I won't be caught. I've just this second thought of a better plan. Now listen everyone. We don't plunder her, we sail off in her. We'll get away clean with no witnesses left alive. By the Raven, I'll wear a sack over my head, if it'll make you feel better. I promise you Hrut won't know who's to blame for the theft of his ship until the day I come back and throw it in his face."

I looked at my uncle. "Hoskuld Long-Jaws? I owe you everything. There'll never come another chance like this. Give me your leave."

For a long moment he sat silently. Then raising his hands toward the rafters, cried out in his deep, strong voice of old, "Praise God, who rejoices in the broken bones of his enemies! Praise Him for He has heard our prayers!" He folded me in his arms and his tears wet my cheek.

"Of course," resumed Stig, "I mean, before we all fall to kissing each other—there is one little thing. It needs half a dozen lads to sail a ship like her. Seafarers, I mean, not plowboys."

"But you could get them, Stig!"

"In three days?" he shrugged. "Not likely."

"Rubbish," said Hoskuld. "Why the countryside's teeming with rough-edged rascals like yourself who'd as soon cut a throat and steal a ship as spend the summer stacking another man's hay."

"Why, Hoskuld Long-Jaws," Stig leered evilly, "I'm overcome to hear myself so well spoken of."

"But he's right, isn't he? You could find us a crew?"

With some hesitation he allowed that he knew someone here and perhaps another one there, who might be game for a summer's cruise."

"Now Stig," I said, "make this plain to them—that my name, for the time being, is none of their business, but it's my vengeance we're about. I, and no other, will command this ship."

"Don't worry, young Captain, I'll tell 'em so. No need to look so fierce about it." Again, that momentary smile. "And ... you've sailed a ship before, have you?"

"You'll teach me all I need to know."

"I? I teach you? Did I ever say I meant to risk my skin? Why it's been longer than long since I held a tiller stick under my arm, and I've a warm berth right here. I fancy myself a farmer nowadays."

"D'you fancy yourself swinging from a tree, damn your eyes!" sputtered Hoskuld. "You'll either steer that ship for him and teach him seafaring, or I'll hang you here and now for the thief that you are! But I'll make you a bargain, Stig," he added, lowering his voice. "If you serve my nephew faithfully for one year and still fancy the life of a farmer after that, come back and find a purse of silver waiting for you, and you can buy yourself as tidy a farm as you'll ever see. Would that suit you?"

Leaning his back against the wall, the brigand gave his spiky head a good scratch and seemed to gaze at some imaginary horizon. "Part with old Stig as easy as that, is it, sir? And just when I thought we was getting on famous. But it's a tempting offer to be sure—lick this young 'un into shape for a purse of silver. You did say she'd weigh five pound, eh, sir?"

"Praise God!" cried Hoskuld again, and this time sent Katla running to the bed-closet to take down the crucifix from over his bed and bring it here to hang above his high-seat. "And we had better all fall on our knees—yes, especially you, Odd Thorvaldsson, and thank Him properly, for vengeance is His specialty!"

Hoskuld had us on our knees a good long while. I looked sidelong once or twice at Stig, kneeling dutifully with his hands folded under his bristly chin and his eyes turned reverently upwards. He might have been a bishop in that pose. Add acting to this man's many talents, I thought. How far can a rogue like that be trusted?

I stole a glance, too, at Kalf, who knelt beside me, and nudged his elbow. Long-limbed Kalf, who could spit a moorhen on the wing with one arrow, and who loved to swear oaths by Odin and Thor to please me. I hoped for a wink. But Kalf's mouth was hard set, and he turned his face away.

I knew why. That night, after Hoskuld had gone to bed, Kalf and I talked quietly for a long time.

†

Stig was away for the next two days while I suffered such a state of excitation—torn between visions of revenge and a sickening fear that the ship would sail before we were ready—that I nearly gave up sleeping altogether, and my nerves were as raw and ragged as, a month before, my skin had been.

In the intervals between these bouts of despair, however, I pondered my future, taking Kalf and Hoskuld into my confidence. "I won't come home just to be an outlaw in my own land. And I won't go to Vinland either, there are no riches to be had there. I must gain wealth and fame enough, somehow, to pay back the butchers of my family and force the Althing to restore my rights. Does anyone doubt that a man with a hundred warriors and a full purse can do as he pleases in this country of ours?"

No one doubted it.

"Will you turn viking like our fathers?" asked Kalf. I saw Hoskuld wince, pained by even this allusion to his son, so long ago tortured to death by the Irish.

"Maybe," I answered. "In any case, I'll begin by sailing to Norway—to Trondelag, where our ancestors came from. It's where exiles from Iceland go, I'm told. There rules a king there who keeps a great court and is a friend to our countrymen. Once there, I'll look for my opportunities."

My uncle nodded sagely and approved of my plan. Being not a traveled man himself, but not ignorant either, he felt himself well informed about life in the wide world.

So Norway it was—or rather, would be—if only Stig returned in time. I plunged my horn into the ale barrel again and resumed my fretful pacing.

Just when I thought I could stand it no longer—it was about midnight of the second night—I heard a commotion in the yard and threw open the door to find Stig and five others straggling in through the gate.

"Captain, your crew," he called, with a wave of his arm. "You might find prettier than these but none more willing when it comes to robbery and murder."

They trooped inside and sat down in a row on the wall-bench.

"Now these two galumphing lads," Stig said, "are Stuf and Otkel. Cousins. Never go anywhere one without the other. Not brainy, but good-natured and energetic as you could want. I've known 'em for a while."

They were somewhere between my age and Gunnar's. Stuf had hair like a haystack and a pendulous lower lip and was very strong. Otkel was slighter of build and seemed afflicted with shyness, for he seldom lifted his eyes from the floor.

"And this rat-faced man is Starkad."

Starkad had sad eyes and a sharp nose with a brush of brown moustache under it, which gave him the appearance of an unhappy rodent. But there was intelligence in his face.

"Don't be fooled by his puny size. We've taken many hard knocks together, Starkad and me. Now these last two I haven't had the pleasure of knowing so very long, but they claim to know their way around a ship and don't object to a little rough and tumble."

I didn't doubt it. The one called Bald Brodd was an oldish fellow, gone to fat, but with muscle under it. His manner was gruff and deliberate and with his shiny head and small eyes, made me think of an ancient sea turtle.

The other called himself Hogni Hard-Mouth, a man of about five-and-thirty whose heavy grinding jaws were constantly at work, and whose wide mouth was set in a scowl, as though he were condemned for life to chew some morsel that did not agree with him. He was the only one who didn't touch his forehead or his cap when Stig introduced him. I paid it no attention at the time.

Altogether, not an imposing lot, I thought. Not quite the sea rovers of ancient song. Landless men, all of them, or even the sons of thralls, who lived hand to mouth as laborers at harvest and haying time or as seamen when they could get a berth, armed with nothing more than knives and sickles—though with those they looked well-practiced. I was in no position to be finicky.

"They're right good-looking men, Steersman," I said, addressing Stig by the title I meant to give him. "I'll gladly 'plow the sea's furrow' with these."

My poetic kenning must have appealed to Hogni Hard-Mouth for he laughed out loud.

"We had a look at your ship," said Stig. "Moored at the mouth of the Whitewater and heavy laden with cargo. If the weather holds fair, I guess she'll go out on the morning's tide."

"Then there's no time to lose! Uncle, I need arms for these men and me, and your fastest horses with a trusted thrall to lead them back again. With hard riding we'll be aboard Strife-Hrut's ship before he's drunk his morning ale."

Hoskuld strode about bellowing orders at his people. Swords, axes, shields, and steel caps, all grimy and rusting from years of disuse, were pulled down from the walls and handed out amongst us.

"Dear boy," he said, "you haven't a sword yourself." I had lost Neck-Biter in my escape. "This one wants sharpening, but it fits the hand well." It was his own sword, which hung beside his high-seat; a heavy weapon with spots of rust on the blade.

"What's its name, Uncle?"

"You give it one, it'll answer."

"Then I name it 'Hrutsbane' and 'Snorrisbane'—to remind me whose lives I am sworn to take."

In the cool night air the horses stood sleepy-eyed, tossing their shaggy heads and snorting while we flung saddles on them and fumbled in the near-darkness with knots and buckles.

Kalf was beside me. Now there remained only one last thing to do. Though it was a sad train of events that had brought it to pass, still, this was the day that he and I had dreamt of for so long. Leaving the others in the yard, we went together to the doorway where Hoskuld stood.

"Grandfather, I'm going too," said Kalf. "You know I must."

"How's that, you young dog, what d'you say?"

"I said I am leaving—not for good, but for a while, to seek my fortune with Odd. May I have your blessing?"

"Blessing? That you may not!"

"Then I go without it, I'm sorry, Grandfather."

"Must I lose son and grandson both?" He put his hands to his ears and reeled back into the room. His loud lamentation brought Katla flying from her perch by the loom to throw herself between us.

"Wicked Kalf!" she screamed. "What are you thinking of to leave us like this and go off with these outlaws—and with *this* one especially," directing her pointy chin at me. "I don't say anything about myself without a brother to protect me from ... from assailants and such, but the poor old thing here, lone and lorn, and...."

She would have gone on longer, no doubt, for she was just warming to her subject, but Hoskuld, recovering himself, silenced her with a look. I had often suspected that he disliked Katla, for all her fawning on him, and couldn't bear to hear himself defended by her as if he were a pitiful, doddering invalid. Her outburst against us did more to change his mind than anything Kalf or I could have said. Still, it was no easy change of heart that he underwent. If you could have looked through the filmy windows of his eyes, what a battle you would have seen raging inside him.

"Be still, girl," he snapped. "Your brother is right after all. I have seen it coming this long time. The son of Flosi the viking has better things to do than lead an old man about."

Flosi—that name that was never to be spoken.

Kalf went to embrace him, but Hoskuld held him at arm's length and bent his brows sternly. "Now Kalf, you must promise me. Stay with Odd. Never leave his side. And mind this, too, damn it all. I am not a lecturing sort of man, but there are wise words in shriveled skins, and young dogs ought to heed 'em. You listen, too, Odd. Keep silent in a strange hall. Answer lying with lies. And don't think that everyone who laughs when you do is your friend. When the ale goes round, drink your share, but don't hold on to the cup. Above all, never trust what a woman tells you or believe 'em constant, for their heads are turned on a potter's wheel and their counsels are cold. It takes sharp wits to wander in the world, you young dogs, and a fool is soon found out."

"Yes, Grandfather, yes," Slender-Leg answered impatiently to all this preachy stuff.

"And Kalf, even though you swear like a heathen to vex me, try to remember that you are a Christian boy, and say your prayers sometimes. And you, Odd Tangle-Hair, God help you. Not even guarded by the armor of baptism. What can I say?"

"Hurry up in there," came Stig's rough voice from the yard. "We're mounted and ready."

"Hoskuld Long-Jaws," I laughed, taking his dry hand in mine, "live easy. And charming Katla, too. We'll be back to drink your mead again one day soon."

But it wouldn't be soon.

They were all long in their graves before I saw these shores again.

Kalf scooped his bow and quiver from their peg on the wall, flashed a last smile at the weepy old man, and dashed out the door with me.

"Young dogs," murmured Hoskuld to our retreating backs.

13

GRIM VISITORS

The rising sun threw our shadows ahead of us as we trudged along the sandy spit that divides the mouth of the Whitewater from the sea. We had left the horses out of sight and walked the remaining distance with our packs and shields slung on our backs. Just within the bar, Hrut's ship rode at anchor, and nearby three of his men hunched over a small fire, warming themselves against the morning chill. They jumped to their feet as we came in sight, though we were careful to walk slowly, keeping our hands well away from our swords.

"Halloo," I called when we were within hailing distance. "We are men from over Skalholt way, looking for a berth. Can you use a few good seamen?"

Coming closer.

"You've wasted your time," one answered, surly-voiced. "Strife-Hrut Ivarsson's her master—you passed his hall four mile upstream. And he sails today with a full crew."

"We'll ask him just the same, friend, if you don't mind—always room for good hands at sea. Meantime, won't you let us have a look at her? We won't sail in just any old tub."

Almost close enough.

We were too many for his liking. He hesitated, with his hand on his signal horn. His two companions stood close at his side, fingering their weapons.

"No farther," he warned, "not without the master's say-so. Wait there, if you want to talk to him."

"I'd like to, friend, but not just now." I ran the last few steps, drew, and thrust all in one motion, bearing him to the ground with my sword in his side. Stig and the rest leapt in after me and in a moment the other two bled out their lives in the black sand.

"Captain," said Stig, "best we get aboard and cast off. The tide's already running and Hrut'll be on his way."

But I scarcely heard him. Blood frenzy blew through me like a gale.

"Here, now what are you doing, Captain? We haven't got time for that."

What was I doing? On my knees beside the sentry's body, cursing Hoskuld's dull old blade, I struck and sawed at the bleeding neck, picturing to myself that it was Hrut's neck—Snorri's neck. Not enough for me to steal a ship and sneak away like a common thief. No, let them find this, and ponder it!

"Will no one lend me an axe?" I cried between sobs of breath.

They looked at me sidelong, unsure what to do.

"Be here all day at this rate," muttered Stig, taking an axe from Brodd and tossing it on the sand by me.

With a crunch of bone the head came away and I swung it up by its hair, the blood running down my arm to the elbow, and shouted, "This for Gunnar!"

Stuf and Otkel grinned, Bald Brodd likewise, and Starkad, and even Hogni Hard-Mouth, as much as his grinding jaws would allow. But Kalf looked wide eyed at me. Poor Kalf. Never seen a severed head before?

I flung myself on the second body, raining blows on its head, its back.

"Captain, that's enough of that," Stig said sharply. "Look over there!" He pointed up the riverbank where a pair of oxen appeared about a quarter mile away, pulling a lumbering cart. Two figures walked alongside it. Their shouts reached us faintly. Then others came into view behind them, and all began to run.

For one wild moment the thought flashed through my mind: "Never run away. Fight them here and either live or die—what does it matter which?" With my sword in one hand and Brodd's bloody axe in the other, I took a step forward. But Kalf held me back. "Odd! If any of them recognize you and live to tell it?"

"Let me go!"

"You gave Grandfather your word."

The wind of frenzy blew out. I shook my head to clear it. *Where had I been?*

"Yes—yes, you're right. Aboard her then, boys, be quick!"

We swarmed up the side, hacked through the mooring line, and ran out the oars—as many as we could man.

The shouting of Hrut's men grew louder. A short-handled throwing axe whirled through the air and arced downward, burying its blade with a smack, a hand's breadth into the deck.

"Heads down now, lads," I shouted, "and break your backs!"

While Stig crouched by the tiller, we pulled till our muscles cracked and the veins stood out on our necks. For an awful moment we didn't move at all, and Hrut was not a hundred feet away. He would see my face, and then there would be no reason to run. I tightened my grip on Hrutsbane.

"Pull!" roared Stig. "You girls! You babies!"

The ship creaked, rocked, and shook herself. The sandy bank moved—oh so slowly, but it moved. With scarcely enough speed to make steerageway, Stig swung the tiller hard over and pointed her nose into the middle of the channel, just as a shower of spears struck us and hung quivering in the bulwark. Then the current caught us, sweeping us through the channel, past the bar, and into the open sea.

On shore little clownish figures danced with fury and soon were lost to sight against the gray horizon.

We looked round at each other and laughed—we had done it!

At Stig's signal we shipped oars and stepped the mast. The breeze found us at once, bellying our red and black striped sail, and the ship leaned over and shot ahead, leaving me breathless with the speed of it.

Hrut's ship was no sleek viking cruiser, but only a fat-bellied knorr—high-stemmed, broad-beamed, and hard to steer. Still, in a good wind she was a fast sailer and as the water hissed and the spray flew up around me, I thought she must be the swiftest, sweetest ship in all the world.

"Well, you're a pirate now, Odd Tangle-Hair," called Stig from the poop. "How does it feel?"

Kalf and I looked at each other and, together, we let out a whoop that startled the gulls overhead.

"Let's have a look at her," I cried. "Kalf—Stuf—Otkel, lend a hand with the tarpaulin. I want to see my prize." But the two cousins made no move until Stig said, very quiet, "You heard the Captain, lads."

I was too excited then to pay it any heed.

Leaning over the hatchway, we looked down on a mountain of riches—bundles of fleeces, bales of raw wool, rolls of homespun, great round cheeses piled next to sacks of eiderdown and casks of sulfur, and a teetering pyramid of wicker cages from which glared the yellow eyes of falcons. Stig gave a low whistle. Strife-Hrut of Whitewater had just become a poor man.

Of provisions for the crew, we found in the stern two barrels of fresh water and one of beer, a tub of salt fish, some turnips, a cauldron with cooking things, and a pile of skin sleeping bags, each made to hold two men.

The sun climbed up the brilliant blue sky and the breeze freshened. Stig, with his arm draped over the tiller, worked us through the choppy in-shore currents while Stuf, who knew this bit of coast, called our course from the prow.

What a fine day! What an excellent day! Over our heads gulls swooped and hung in the dazzling morning air. As we bore along past the rocky needles of the Westmann Isles, fishermen putting out in their boats waved us a good morning. And on the white cliffs that rose above the bright, blue water, boys and girls hung from ropes—looking, at that distance, like flies on a wall—to gather puffin eggs with their long-handled nets.

Kalf winked at me. "Remember Thorgrima?"

The sun was at his zenith by the time we rounded the south coast and stood out to sea. Our last sight of home, from many miles away, was the glittering dome of Vatna Glacier, whose glassy fingers seemed to run down the mountainside right into the sea itself.

Alone on the white-haired ocean, as the deck rolled under me and the spanking, salt-sharp breeze stung my cheeks, I felt as free and powerful as a god must feel. Oh, my limbs ached with tiredness from too many nights without sleep, yet never had I felt more awake or alive than at that moment, with the past behind me and the future all ahead—glittering, like the glacier, with a thousand lights of possibility. I was Odd Thorvaldsson—warrior, sea rover, poet. Verses hummed in my head faster than I could con them. I loved Kalf, I loved Stig, and I loved those others whose names I barely knew.

I almost forgot that my hands still shook.

"Captain," said Stig, "are you ready to become a sailor?"

"Steersman, I know as little of boats as a cat does of fiddling, but you'll see how quickly I can learn."

So began my instruction. All that day and the next I learned to work the rigging and the corner poles so as to angle the sail just so to catch the wind, and how to handle the little tiller-stick that by some simple miracle moves the great stern steering oar. A captain ought to know how to pilot his own ship, said Stig, even if he leaves most of the steering to his steersman. I learned to drop a wood chip from the bow and count my heartbeats until it passed the stern in order to gauge our speed. I even learned to mix my porridge with a bit of sea water to improve the taste of it.

And I learned a little, too, of that greatest mystery of all. On our second day out, when the breeze had dropped to a gentle push and the sea was running in long even swells, Stig gave the tiller to Starkad and pointed me toward the sun. The others also came round to listen, for by no means is every seaman a navigator.

"We set our course by him," Stig began, "and you must know where to look for him at dawn and dusk in every month of the year, for he's a wanderer and doesn't stay put. Knowing that, you can set a course, provided you've got one of these."

He rummaged in his kit bag and produced a wooden object consisting of a handle to which was attached a wooden disk, its edge marked with notches. In the center of the disk stood a bronze needle, the shadow pin, with a similar needle, perpendicular to it, projecting over the face of the disk so that the notches could be rotated under its point. This contraption he called a bearing plate.

"By sighting the sun at his rising and setting," he explained, "we can read our heading from where the shadow falls. Right now we're making south-east to the latitude of the Faroes."

"And how long, then, 'til we reach the Norwegian coast?"

"Maybe a week, maybe two, depending on the winds."

"Or maybe never if we lose the sun for long," struck in Bald Brodd. He was a blustering, argumentative man, as I was beginning to learn.

"Ah," said Stig, "but now I'll show you a real wonder." Once more into the kit bag, and this time he drew out a flat wafer of some kind of stone, set in a frame of wood, the whole thing no bigger than my palm.

"Hold it to your eye, now, Captain, and move it across the sky, turning it this way and that, until you find the sun."

I did as he instructed and cried out in astonishment when its milky light suddenly went black. I let Kalf look through it and then the others, for they were all eager to see this marvel.

"And it'll do that through a fair bit of cloud," said Stig, "when the sun don't appear to be anyplace at all to the naked eye."

"It's magic?"

He shrugged. "Not the black sort, anyway."

"But not even your sun-stone can pierce the fog," Brodd kept up in his wrangling way, "not real fog. There's nothing can pierce that."

"No, and that's the truth." Stig scratched his spiky head. "Best not to talk about that."

Perhaps it was the wind turning colder just then that made me shiver.

"Captain?"

"It's nothing, Steersman, go on."

"Are you feeling all right?"

I clapped my arm round his shoulder. "Never better, only a little tired."

"Lay up a bit, then. You look to me like a man that's been ridden all night by a hag."

"Blast you! What d'you mean saying that?"

"Eh? No call for hard words."

"I told you I'm all right. Starkad, give me the tiller again."

Puzzled, they moved away—except for Kalf, who faced me with a worried look.

"Odd, you woke me up last night, fighting in your sleep and groaning."

"Share someone else's sleeping bag, then."

"What is it, Odd?"

"I'm sorry. I have ... dreams. But it's nothing. I'll be well enough soon. Why, by the Raven, I'm much better already—best thing in the world for a man, the sea!"

I said it with all the conviction that was in me, praying it was true. Praying that my unwelcome night visitors would come no more.

✝

Day after perfect day we ran before the wind, making our course southeast toward the Faroes. Stripped to the waist under the sun's unblinking eye, we lay out on the warm planks, letting the breezes play over us, or else hung over the gunnel to watch the humpback whales breech and the yellow-nosed porpoises dance alongside us. We fished, we mended tackle, we sharpened our weapons till they shone, we gambled, and we yarned.

"Old Bjorn Butterbox, so they say, went and died while on a visit to a kinsman of his who lived away in the Westfjords—it's where I come from," said rat-faced Starkad, a quiet man who, after a few horns of beer, became genial and funny. "And so, the story goes, they lay the poor fellow out on the bed and sent for his son to come and fetch him. Now, when the son arrives, what does he see but Bjorn's corpse sitting up in the bed with his arms around the farmer's daughter and trying to steal a kiss. 'Old man, what are you thinking of?' cries the son. 'You're to be buried today.' Well, the old man grumbled and said it was hard treatment he was getting, but he lay down again and shut his eyes. When they asked the lassie about it though, she had no complaints. 'God knows,' says she, 'we get little enough company in the Westfjords!'"

✝

Long, perfect days, but for me, never far from the dread of night. I took to sleeping by myself, after seeing how Kalf watched me. What business did he have to spy on me? And what was he telling the others? Oh, I saw him sometimes talking to Stig, keeping his voice low so I shouldn't hear. Stig liked him; they all did. From now on I would have to watch him closely.

Drink helped. One evening, when the lights on the northern horizon spread a weird, pale sheen on the water, we sat on deck by the ale cask and talked about the days to come. Stig, who had been there before, told us about Nidaros Town, Trondelag's bustling port and King Olaf's capital, where we would sell our cargo and live fat all winter on the profits, each of us with a plump girl in our beds to warm us.

"And come the next spring," cried I, lifting my ale horn, "we'll sail out and see the world and make our fortunes one and all. What say you to that, boys? For, by the Raven, I've grown fond of you all!"

There was a hesitant 'Aye' from Kalf. How slyly he looked at me then. The others were quiet and glanced toward Stig.

"Well, then, lads,"—I forced a smile—"run along home if you like, and with my thanks. There's nothing to stop you, your condition is not like mine."

"And just what might your condition be?" said Hogni between his grinding jaws.

"Why Hogni, I'm an exile, did you not know? Odd Thorvaldsson the Outlaw, I am. Every godi in Iceland wants to drink my blood—all of 'em, truly. If you like, I'll recite you a poem about it, for I have no little skill in that."

Hogni, for answer, hawked loudly and spat over the gunnel. He misjudged the wind, however, and had to wipe the spittle from his eyes, which made me burst out in a loud laugh.

"Hogni, by the hammer of Thor, let me be your friend. For a man who spits into the wind is his own worst enemy. Ha, ha!"

There was good-natured chuckling at this, but I ... I laughed until I was helpless, I pounded the deck and howled and nudged the others to keep the laughter up. "His own worst enemy, I say—Ho! Gods!" Gradually I realized it was only my own voice that I heard, cracked and piping in the immense silence of the night. And I felt suddenly like a small animal in the dark wood—with wolves in the shadows between the trees.

"Only a little joke—eh, Hogni? There's a good fellow."

None would look me in the eyes.

"Enough," said Stig, getting to his feet. "Time to sleep. I'll take first watch."

With muttered good nights, they crept off to their favorite corners and angles of the ship, leaving me alone—alone in the dark with my Unwelcome Ones, who came to me nightly on the wind's invisible sigh, who whispered horrid things to me while I slept, who were driving me mad.

✝

Four days out and the wind veered round and began to blow steadily from the southwest. The sky grew overcast, and the sea turned the color of lead.

"Dirty weather," said Stig.

The squalls hit us with sudden fury, driving the rain in our faces and lashing the sea into heavy swells. We tried at first to hold our course, beating as near to the wind as we dared, and taking turns at the tiller, which fought us till our arms ached. But the wind blew stronger until we had no choice but to shorten sail and let her ride where she wanted.

Drenched and frozen, we crawled about the streaming deck from handhold to handhold, securing what we could, while great green, foam-streaked seas broke over us, and the ship staggered and heeled over on her beam ends as she wallowed into the troughs. Though we bailed frantically with buckets and helmets, we were near foundering.

"Throw out the cargo or we'll sink!" screamed Stig to me over the howl of the wind. "Give the order!"

"No!"

"You want to kill us?"

"It's my prize. I won't throw over a penny's-worth of it."

"Odd, do what he says," begged Kalf.

"Cowards!" I shrieked into the wind.

For five days and nights we labored in the gale, while we called on Thor and Jesus and bailed for our lives. I tied my sword to my wrist, lowered myself into the hold, and swore to kill anyone who came near the cargo. They believed me and bailed harder.

On the sixth day the gale blew itself out. We lay on the deck like spent dogs, weak and wretched; our clothes, our hair, our beards caked with salt, our lips cracked, our skin whipped raw.

"Stig," I whispered, "we're still rich."

He turned his face away.

"Kalf," I called. He was lying limp and dead-white up against the mast where he had tied himself. "Kalf we've been through the worst thing in the world and lived. Heh? Give us a smile."

But I was wrong. The worst thing in the world was still to come.

As the wind died to a whisper and less than a whisper, rags of fog drifted toward us over the flat surface of the sea. Wreathes of fog gathered about the rigging, thick fingers of fog felt along the deck, curling under benches, reaching into corners, twining and winding around our feet, our chests, our faces. Soft mountains of fog rose over us and silent avalanches of fog fell on us. Sea and sky ran together until the whole world shrank to the little circle of our deck. We were swallowed alive by that gray animal in whose belly there is no distinction of night or day, no past and no future, but only the unchanging, unending, unbearable present.

We could have rowed, but in what direction? Stig's sunstone was useless now, and Brodd took a grim pleasure in that. We sat shivering, with our arms around our knees, moving little, talking little. Waiting. Every man wrestled with the fear inside him, for all sailors dread the fog.

But my terror was greater than theirs.

Willful and alive, the fog explored me, though I shrank against the bulwark and struck at it with my arms. It touched me everywhere, creeping inside my clothes, putting its wet mouth against my skin and sucking out my juices. My teeth chattered, I moaned and shut my eyes for fear of what I might see. They were there—the grisly visitors of my dreams. They plucked at my sleeve with their smoky fingers.

The first voice to speak was Gunnar's. *You killed me, Brother, meddling with the girl, turning the thralls against us. Look at me, Brother, look at me.*

"I won't!"

But I could not help myself. His eyes were dark pools of smoke. His blue lips dripped and ran into his beard.

Why do you live, Brother, while I am dead?

"To avenge you," I croaked. "You told me...."

Liar! You ran away because you feared the flames. You are not the man to avenge me.

"But I've stolen this ship of Hrut's."

The farther to fly. No, brother, better die now ... die now....

"Go away ... please."

You ran away, said Gudrun Night-Sun, her white face wrapped in her streaming hair.

You ran while I burned, said Jorunn, putting up her hands to hide her melting cheeks.

You've always run, boy, and always will, moaned Black Thorvald, his face twisting in grief. *Cowardly son of a cowardly father—better die ... better die....*

"Don't say that to me!"

Behind them, crowded others—all my ancestors, runny-faced and indistinct, ancient men and women with wispy hair floating round their heads, and little round-eyed mites, mewling and piping like the ghosts of birds. And all of them crooning, *Come down with us. Oh, come down with us. Better die, Odd Tangle-Hair. Better die....*

"O, Mistress Hel," I cried, "for pity's sake take them away!"

I heard other voices, too, rough, earthy ones.

"Devil take him!"

"What'll we do?"

"Pitch him overboard, say I."

"Aye, if his dead friends want him, for the love of Christ let 'em have him, or else we'll never see the sun again."

So, the living and the dead agreed what I must do, and what could I say against them?

At last my weary will gave way and I began to weep—whether aloud or to myself, I do not know.

"Yes, all right. Yes ... better to die, to just slip over the side ... to sink into the fog and the deep sea." I struggled up against the bulwark. "Gunnar ... Father," I swung my legs over. "Take me now." The fog licked my feet, and the black water, invisible beneath it, sucked at the ship. I let go....

A rope snapped taut around my chest, jerking me backwards. Kalf pinned my arms to my sides, threw me back against the mast, and looped the rope around it.

"Let me go!" I wailed, but I was too weak to fight. There was surprising strength in those thin arms of his. I sagged against the ropes while helpless tears ran down my cheeks.

"Stand away from him, boy." It was Hogni's snarl. As I faced the prow, they were all behind me, but I knew them by their voices. "Stand away, and we won't hurt you."

But Kalf ducked down, reached into the fo'c'sle, where we stowed the arms, and pulled out his bow and quiver. "I'll put an arrow through any man who takes a step forward!"

✝

All six were huddled aft, around the water barrel, from which they never moved, being unwilling to trust each other alone with its dwindling contents. Their shields and spears were all in the fo'c'sle.

"I've seen him shoot, mates. He can do it." Stig's low voice. "Now, young Slender-Leg, you're a good lad, and be damned if I don't feel responsible for you to your Grandpa, though that was no part of our bargain."

"Was *this* part of your bargain?"

"He's bad luck, boy. You can see that. Now stand away from him."

Someone must have moved, for the arrow flew. I heard it strike wood. "I mean what I say," said Kalf. "The next one will stick in your throat."

"Why, boy?" Stig again.

Kalf stared doggedly ahead of him. "I promised Grandfather never to leave his side."

After that they kept to their end of the ship. None wanted to be the first to taste Kalf's arrow.

Time—if there was such a thing in that gray void—passed. Water slapped against the hull and the mist stirred a little as a breath of wind took us. For a while the men continued to call out to Kalf—bullying, wheedling, tempting him with water. After a time they stopped.

From the sounding fog my Dead Ones spoke to me still, but I had sunk into a lethargy and answered only with tears and groans. Kalf looked sidelong at me, and quickly looked away. He never spoke to me during all that time, nor I to him.

More hours, I suppose, crept by. The ship rocked gently, drifting from nowhere to nowhere.

Kalf's head began to droop. He shook himself once, and again, then his eyes closed and his fingers on the bow uncurled.

The scrape of shoes behind me ... a rustle of cloth ... a breath upon my neck....

Die, moaned pale Gunnar in my ear.

"Yes, Brother...."

NORWAY
AD 1030

14

A DOCTOR OF SOULS

But no one dies before his time.

In that frozen moment when Hogni Hard-mouth—as I later learned—stood behind me with his axe upraised, we heard the cry of a gull, then the crash of surf, then timber grated against stone and everyone but me was flung on his face as the ship scraped bottom, wallowing slantwise onto the strand of an invisible shore.

In the confusion that followed, Kalf and I were forgotten. The men scrambled past us on the tilting deck and craned over the side to peer into the mist, where the outline of a hill could just be made out. They leapt the gunnel and splashed up the pebbly beach and blundered about like blind men, calling out to each other in excited voices. Kalf untied me and took me by the hand. Obediently, I stumbled after him.

It is hard to tell the story of the next few hours. The truth is I barely knew where I was or what I did. Much of what follows comes from what Kalf and the others later told me—and I can't say they troubled to spare my pride.

The men huddled at the water's edge and turned to Stig, who picked up a handful of pebbles and studied them in his palm, as if they could speak.

"I'm glad to be anywhere," said Starkad, "but I'd be even gladder to know where 'anywhere' is."

"It was a southerly wind that hit us," the steersman replied, "and there's a strong current, too, that sets to the north all up along the Norway coast as far as—well, as far as anyone's ever gone."

"As far as the Edge is what you meant t'say," growled Brodd. He poked the fog with a blunt finger. "And d'you know what lies out there, you young'uns, or did your elders neglect to teach it to you? It's the Midgard Worm, in the deeps of ocean, coiled all 'round the world. The same, they say, as even Thor and Hymir the Giant couldn't catch when they went fishing for it. And come to speak of giants, they're as thick as fleas here, as any fool knows."

"That may be," Stig broke in sharply, for he could see that Brodd would frighten the others worse than they were already. "What I know for a fact is that we've no place else to go until this fog lifts."

The fog. That reminded them of me.

"Aye," said Hogni Hard-Mouth, hefting his axe, "and that'll be as soon as we rid ourselves of our bad luck. Out of my way, young Kalf, you'll not stop me this time with your little bow and arrow."

Kalf put himself between us and appealed to the others.

"But the smell of death's on him, lad," said Starkad, speaking all their minds. "We'll never prosper as long as he's among us."

"Be fair," Kalf pleaded. "Has anyone seen these ghosts but him? I don't know what ails him. Oh, Odd Tangle-Hair, stand up!" I had sunk to my knees and was crying again. "Just wait a little while. The fog may lift yet. Please, he's my friend."

"You deserve a better one," muttered Stuf.

"He isn't like you and me—he feels things more. Stig, give him a chance."

Stig gazed away and thought, while Hogni, eager to finish me off, scowled. "All right," he said finally, "we'll give the weather another day—I owe that much to old Long-Jaws. But if we're still fogbound after one more tide rolls in, it'll be the end for Tangle-Hair. Hogni, put away your axe."

"I'll put it away in his goddamned head!"

It was only for Kalf's sake, because they liked him, that the others surrounded Hogni and kept him off me.

"Now then, back aboard ship," ordered Stig. "We'll be safer there."

But no, damn them, they weren't budging. Not after so many days confined in that oaken prison. They'd take their chances on these solid stones, come giants or no.

So it was agreed. They returned to the ship only to unload their gear and the last of the rations. Then they spread their cloaks out on the shingle and sat down to wait.

"I do believe she's thinning," said Otkel to Stuf.

"Piss on what *you* believe," replied his bosom friend.

Kalf, for fear I would wander off or try again to kill myself, took away my sword and knife and tied my right wrist to his left one with our two belts looped together. From my own recollection, I can remember thinking that I should warn him lest the ghosts, when they came for me, should take us both, not bothering to untie us. But a great weight seemed to press upon my chest, stifling the words in my throat.

"Captain," asked Stuf—meaning, of course, not me but Stig, "You'll set watches while we sleep?"

"I will. I'll have no crowd of giants creeping up on us. They're sly and quiet fellows, as I've heard." One corner of his mouth turned up in a smile. The cousins laughed a little at this and felt better. Bald Brodd harrumphed and frowned at his feet.

In spite of Stig's promise, they were all of them so worn out that soon after finishing a cold and cheerless meal on the stones, they crawled into their skin bags, as near to one another as could be—though keeping a distance from me and Kalf—and were soon asleep.

I was wearier than any of them, but sleep I could not and would not. While Kalf tossed uneasily at the other end of our tether, I sat still as a stump, my eyes and ears open to the speaking fog—waiting for my death.

So it was, as the hours crept by, that I alone saw what happened.

Around me the salt-bleached stones took on lights and shadows. Soon out of the mist crept the rounded hills nearby, and then, very far away and very high up, a gigantic range of mountain peaks appeared, floating in space like a rack of white cloud on a dark horizon. Gradually, as I watched, the whole massive barricade of mountains took shape in the thinning mist, while above them, glowing in the haze like an old coal, hung the sun. In my distempered brain something stirred.

"Gunnar?" I whispered. "Gunnar? Father?"

All this time, the faces of my Dead Ones had not left me alone—but when I looked for them now, in the transparent air, they were gone! I cannot describe the feeling of utter desertion that overcame me. I clutched myself and rocked back and forth, repeating through numbed lips, "Come back. Don't leave me. Where is my death?"

Bruce Macbain

I had no right, you see, to remain in the world of the living. I was already more than half dead—my ghost tied to my heavy limbs only by a thread. "Oh, Lady Hel," I moaned, "don't play such tricks with me." Twisting my hands in an agony of doubt, I rocked back and forth, back and forth.

It was in this state that I happened to see the band of little people who stole silently toward us from around the curve of the nearest hill.

Signaling to one another with gestures, they divided and circled to the right and left so as to approach us from both sides at once. When they saw me looking at them, they froze, but when I made no sound, they crept closer.

Were they the dwarves of old men's talk, I wondered, for the tallest of them would barely reach my shoulder. But dwarves are rough and bearded folk, while these men were as hairless as babes.

The band numbered about fifteen and they stood quite close now, studying us out of black slits of eyes and pointing their weapons—bone-tipped harpoons and long, wicked-looking arrows—at our sleeping forms. It appeared to me that they meant to kill us. I put my hands to rest in my lap and smiled at them. My death had come at last.

One aimed his arrow at my heart and drew it back to his ear. I watched him unblinkingly. But an instant before he would have shot, their pack of mangy dogs made a sudden dash for the remains of our dinner and fell to snarling over it. Our lads awoke in a fright—cursing, rubbing their eyes, and groping for their weapons all at once. Kalf, forgetting that we were attached, leapt to his feet, nearly yanking my arm out of its socket. Starkad, followed by Hogni, ran at them with swords drawn, but Stig roared, "Hold! Strike no blow!"

For a tense moment we stood this way, face to face. They had the advantage of us in numbers, but it was obvious that they feared our size and our steel blades.

At last, cautiously, the one who had aimed at me eased off his bowstring, took a step forward, and addressed us in a strangely accented version of our own language.

"Brave Norsemen," he began in a reedy voice, "you waste your time here. It is a bad year for the Lapps—bad for the reindeer, bad for the walrus. We have nothing for you. You go away now and tell your king— maybe next year." He did his best to look apologetic.

His face was round, brown and smooth as a hickory nut, and his age as likely fifty as thirty. His costume, made all of greasy buckskins, consisted of boots with turned up toes, tight trousers around his little bowed legs, a loose short-skirted coat, and on his head a leather cap with three peaks to it, each pointing in a different direction.

He was altogether a comic little manikin. They all were—except that all the while he spoke, they held their weapons pointed unswervingly at our breasts.

Stig answered the little man by sheathing his sword and holding out his open palms. "Friend," said he, "we are not the king of Norway's tax gatherers and I don't envy the man that is. But I've been in Norway and heard the Lapps mentioned with respect. We're merchants from Iceland who've lost our way, and we would take it kindly if you'd allow us to camp here awhile in peace, for we've been a weary time at sea."

This was the longest formal speech ever known to have been uttered by the laconic Stig.

'Iceland?' The name clearly meant nothing to the Lapp, but "merchants" he understood, and his eyes brightened. "Colored cloth?" he asked. His leather coat, I should say, was embroidered all over the shoulders and front with bright strips of red and blue wool, and balls of the same stuff hung from the three peaks of his hat.

"A boat-load of it," said Stig with his crooked smile.

The manikin turned and spoke some words to his people in a tongue that sounded like rippling water. While he did so, Stig spoke quickly to us.

We were hundreds of miles north of our destination, as he had guessed, in a vast country of mountain and forest from which the Norwegians levied tribute, though they hardly could claim to rule over it. "These Lapps are hard folk to deal with. Don't be fooled by their size. They spend most of the year wandering with their reindeer—it's a sort of tree on legs, Otkel—and they can fairly outrun man or beast up the sides of those mountains yonder."

"My God!" exclaimed Starkad as if he had only now noticed them, "the mountains!"

And Kalf cried, "You see, Stig? Hogni, you see? The fog lifted—by itself!"

"No need to shout," replied Stig, "I'm neither blind nor deaf—we'll worry about your friend later. Hear me out now. In the summer, these folk come down to the coast to fish and hunt the seal and sometimes they'll wander down into Norway for a while—that's where our friend here must have learned his Norse. Now this is the main thing about 'em—whether they be dwarves, or elves, or imps, or God knows what—they have powers. Leastways, I've heard it said their sorcerers can call up thunder and lightning and wind and I don't know what all. They're nobody to fool with."

The manikin turned back to us with a hesitant smile. "I am Nunna," he offered, touching his breast. "I speak—oh, so badly—for these fellows. It is possible these poor Lapps might find a little antler, a few sealskins to trade for colored cloth. How we Lapps do love that stuff! We would cover our whole bodies in it if we could, and look like Norsemen." He repeated this to his friends and they chuckled at the absurdity of the idea.

The weapons came down on both sides. Stig took Nunna's small hand in his paw and gave it a squeeze.

"And who is that one?" inquired the little man then, pointing at me with his chin. "He saw us a whole horizon away and did not warn you. He is your prisoner?" Of course, I was still tied to Kalf, and unarmed.

"He's our Captain," answered Kalf.

"*Was* our Captain," said Hogni, at the same time giving Stig a clumsy nudge and a wink. "Pay him no mind. He's cursed, or mad, or—"

"In that case," Nunna interrupted matter-of-factly, "it is your good fortune to have come here."

Without another word, the Lapp hunting band turned and trotted off down the beach, moving swiftly on their short, muscular legs. We hurried to keep up.

A brisk trot of two miles or so along the rocky shore brought us, foot-sore and breathless, to their campsite, which was no more than a few untidy huts clustered round a small inlet. The huts themselves were cone-shaped and made from strips of birch bark tacked onto a framework of poles tied together at the top. The whole thing gave the appearance of a badly made haystack. From the top of each hut curled a wisp of wood smoke, nearly invisible against the white sky.

The camp dogs, leaping and growling, announced our approach. After them streamed the rest of the population—an antic crowd of little women, children, and old folks who formed a chattering circle around us that moved as we walked, all jabbering and pointing. The bravest ones even ventured to touch us. Starkad bent down, scooped up one little mite of a girl, and popped her on his shoulder. There was a gasp from the elders, but shrieks of excitement from all the children who flung themselves upon him, clamoring to be picked up.

But no one touched me. I shambled along on my leash behind Kalf, whey-faced, hollow-eyed, and palsied. The little people drew back from me and looked away.

Nunna halted before the entrance to one of the huts, which was larger than the others, though not any better made, and told us to wait. Inside a muffled conversation went on for some time before his round face reappeared in the entrance.

"Go, please, to any of our houses," Nunna said, addressing himself to Stig and the others. "Eat and rest. The man with no soul"—he looked at me—"is to come inside."

He drew the reindeer-skin curtain aside for me. "The noaidi has agreed to see you, Man-With-No-Soul. Your keeper may come, too."

"*Who* will see him?" asked Kalf warily.

"You have no word for it, I think. Just come."

The ripe smell inside the hut—smoke mingled with sweat, rancid grease, and old meat—nearly made me retch.

Taking a cautious step into the darkness, I found my feet entangled in a prickly mattress of twigs. I tumbled to my knees alongside Kalf. From somewhere close at hand came muffled laughter.

"Begging your pardon," said Nunna, "we crawl. This way."

Like clumsy infants, we followed him on hands and knees over the twiggy floor. In the center of the room a fire flickered within a ring of stones, and over it, an iron kettle hung on a chain whose other end was lost in the haze of the smoke-hole. The fire gave off just enough light to reveal the outlines of a dozen or so figures who lay stretched head to toe along the circumference of the wall, their glistening faces propped on elbows, their eyes watching us.

Reaching a spot on the side of the hut exactly opposite the entrance, Nunna stopped. In front of us, there lay what appeared to be a sleeping child. He spoke softly to it. It stirred, lifted its head, and answered in a voice that was as dry as the rustling of dead leaves.

I peered at the tiny face. Its skin was the color of beeswax and infinitely wrinkled. The nose and chin caved in around a toothless hole of a mouth. It was a face shriveled and soft as a windfall apple and old beyond sex.

Nunna listened a moment to the rustling leaves and then turned to me. "The noaidi wishes to know why you do not go to the sorcerers of the Christmen for help? He wonders if they are not as powerful as they claim."

I think that I just shook my head in dumb wonderment. Kalf let it pass with a shrug.

Again the leaves rustled.

"The noaidi," said Nunna, "wishes you to know that what he will do is very hard for him. He asks what you will pay him?"

"Ten ells of blue cloth," said Kalf quickly, indicating the length of his forearm from elbow to fingertips and holding up all his fingers.

"The noaidi is disappointed."

"Twenty, then."

Nunna translated and listened to the dry rustle of the response. "The noaidi is content and wishes you and your friend to know that he is not greedy, but it is his belief that what is not paid for is not valued. See the wisdom of our noaidi!"

The wizened face acknowledged our presence now for the first time with a toothless smile in which there was just a touch of cunning.

While our bargain was being struck, other Lappish men and women crept through the low doorway, jostling and squeezing in wherever there was a bit of room, until soon the hut was entirely filled, save for a little open space around the noaidi and ourselves. The heat and the smell were getting worse by the minute.

Now a man crawled to the hearth and dipped a wooden cup into the steaming cauldron, drawing off some evil-smelling liquid, which the noaidi downed at a single gulp. The cup was refilled and emptied several times.

"So he hardens himself," whispered Nunna. "Neither iron, nor steel, nor water, nor fire can hurt him now."

The Ancient raised his body to a sitting position. Putting out a scrawny hand, he fumbled behind him under the heap of skins that served as a pillow, and brought out two objects—one a drum, flat like a plate with the skin on one side only, the other a small hammer of carved antler. There was an intake of breath all around us in the dark.

"Here is his power," said Nunna in a low voice to Kalf. "See the pictures on his drum."

Three dark stripes were painted across the drumhead, dividing it into zones that were filled with a jumble of shapes and figures.

"Here is the whole world—look closely." Nunna pointed to one figure after another with his finger, being careful not to touch them. "The rivers, the lakes, and the mountains, fish, reindeer, wolves, and bear. All here. The gods, too. And the sun and moon, and the Mountain Men, the spirits whom the noaidi commands. You understand? Ours is a very great noaidi, few are greater. He commands fourteen spirits. With these he will cure your friend."

Again the dead leaves rustled, and Nunna translated, speaking this time to me. "Now you must tell the noaidi—omitting nothing—how your sickness began."

I could more easily have climbed a glass mountain with greased shoes than I could voice one single syllable of my numbing despair. I shook my head while the tears ran down my cheeks.

"You must talk," he said gently. "Try."

"I ... am waiting ... to die."

"Yes, yes, the noaidi understands this, but he must know the reason for it. Try harder please."

Kalf, seeing my helplessness, spoke up and said that he knew my story from my own lips as well as from what he himself had seen, and would they let him tell it in my place? Nunna interpreted and the Ancient nodded.

So he began, telling a long story about someone with my name, whom I scarcely seemed to know. "The best friend in the world, but strange in his ways, given to moods and tempers, and his father stranger still—a sorcerer, so they said...."

The noaidi's eyes flickered with interest.

Then Kalf told about the house-burning.

"Kalf, you filthy liar," I pleaded in silent anguish, "how can you say such things about me? Running, hiding like a rat in a clump of weeds! Must you tell everything just to shame me?"

The noaidi stopped Kalf and made him go back, asking questions about this detail and that. And all the time his black eyes in their deep folds never left mine. Gradually, Kalf's voice began to sound to me as if it came from the end of a long tunnel, and soon I stopped listening altogether. There were only those eyes.

"Now," said Nunna, shaking me by the shoulder. "You must do as I tell you." He untied the belt that still attached me to Kalf. "Your keeper must step outside, but I will stay. Lie down. It begins."

With a muscular arm around my shoulders, Nunna pushed me over on my side and pulled my legs straight out in front of me—the way we straighten the legs of a corpse for burial. My father—*Gunnar!* This image flashed like an arrow through my mind and I began to shake, but Nunna knelt by my head and held me down.

The noaidi brought his face close to mine and began to tap his drum, and at the same time he chanted in a high sing-song that rose and fell, rose and fell.

Nunna whispered in my ear. "He calls the Mountain Men. He will catch them in his drum and make them obey him. Can you hear me?"

I nodded.

"Your Dead Ones miss you. They have captured your soul. It is a common thing. Now the noaidi must send his own spirit down to Jabmiidaibmu, where Jabmiidahka rules, and make them give it back. You understand?"

"Yes."

The drumming grew faster and the old man's eyes stared, looking past me, past the faces that ringed me, past the ragged wall of his mean hut. Looking to the mountains. No part of his body moved except the hand that held the little hammer—almost a blur as it struck and rebounded from the drum.

Hours passed this way, or minutes—who can say? I knew nothing, *was* nothing, but the sound of that drumming and humming.

Then abruptly it stopped.

The Ancient's head snapped back as if jerked by an invisible cord, his eyes rolled up showing the whites, and the pink tip of his tongue protruded from his mouth. His little body arched up and back until his head nearly touched his heels, and he gave out a sharp cry like a woman in childbirth. The drum and hammer dropped from his hands, and he pitched over on his side, crumpled in his loose clothes like an empty wineskin. His chant was taken up now by the others in the hut—a droning hum that sounded like a swarm of bees.

Now I saw things that I would be happier not to tell about. I was waking and dreaming and seemed to be in many places all at once. The stinking haze that filled the hut was Hekla's sulfurous breath, and I was a child of ten again, stumbling down the mountainside, flying in terror from my terrible, mad father. But also, it was the smoke that reeked of bodies turning black in the flaming shambles of my home when I leapt up from my brother's side, shrieking and beating the sparks out of my hair, with no thought for anything but to save my life. I was in both dreams at once, and both of them more real than reality itself. Everything happened not once, but again and again until it was all one heat, one stench, one fear, one pounding of the heart and pumping of the legs. I was running ... running ... running away....

I thrashed on the floor, tossing my head from side to side, while four men sat on my arms and legs and Nunna's sweating face hung over me.

Sometimes I knew the face was his and sometimes not. For sometimes I believed I was looking into my father's face, and sometimes Gunnar's, and sometimes Mother's or Gudrun's, and all of them giving me such piteous looks that, if I could have moved, I would have torn myself apart in despair.

Through it all, the bees hummed, drawing out their long, vibrant syllable—thirty voices, or a hundred, or it might have been a thousand. I heard it even through my chattering fear, a sound like summer in the fields—the droning of bees in the hot sun and the humming of the women while they bundled sheaves. Nunna's cradling arms were my mother's, then Morag's. In my nostrils was the smell of new hay and women's hair. A low voice sang in my ear, "It's all right ... it's all right. Rest now."

For the first time in five weeks I sank into a deep and dreamless sleep.

15

MUTINY

I was alone when I awoke, except for a young boy who squatted on his heels beside me. Seeing me stir, he gave a shout. Instantly Kalf and Nunna came in, and behind them, creeping like a little ancient baby, the noaidi. Kalf helped me to sit up and told me that I had been asleep for more than a night and a day.

I had an evil taste in my mouth and felt light-headed with hunger. I looked from Kalf to our companion. "Nunna," I said, "bring me food."

"Hah! You know me, do you?" His good-natured face beamed.

It did seem strange, but I knew his name, and I knew where I was and why. Or, thought I did, anyway. Later, when I tested my memory against Kalf's, I realized how much out of those days I really had lost.

"All right, you wait." Nunna went out and presently returned carrying a wooden trencher piled high with a steaming mess that turned out to be boiled salmon and cloudberries pounded into a paste. Nothing ever tasted so good. I asked for ale to wash it down.

"This the poor Lapps do not have," he made a sorrowful face. "Probably for the best. Drink this instead." He pushed a bowl of some dark, thick gruel at me. "Hot water and reindeer blood. Very good."

Meantime the noaidi had sunk into his usual place against the wall and regarded me through half-closed lids.

"He is tired," Nunna said, seeing me glance at him. "His spirit was gone many hours."

"Nunna, he really spoke to my Dead Ones?"

"Gently, you'll spill your bowl."

"Please, I have to know."

"Tell me, friend Captain, are you cured?"

"Maybe ... yes."

"So then, why do you ask? It's as I told you. The dead, you must know, are always jealous of the living. They can't help it, poor things. It's their nature. And so they will catch a man's soul, knowing that his body must soon follow. But the noaidi spoke very sternly to your dead. They were hard to deal with, like all you Norse. Oh, how they grumbled and complained. But in the end they had to confess the truth, that they are no braver than you, only unluckier."

"They *said* that?"

"Oh, yes. And they are quite ashamed of the tricks they played on you. They have given you back your soul and will bother you no more—except that, from time to time, your father may make himself known to you, if you want his help. He hopes you will not hate him."

I sat for a while, turning this over in my mind. "All the same," I said at last, "they have a claim on me. They have a right to vengeance. Nunna, will I avenge them someday? Can the noaidi tell me this?"

He shrugged and scuttled over to the old man's side and they had a long whisper together. Coming back, he hunched down on his heels in front of me and said, "The noaidi sent his spirit into the gray wolf, and into the albatross, and into the seal. Everywhere he searched for the end of your fate, but it lies a great way from here, and even he cannot see all the threads of it. He says that you will travel far and, for a time, will forget your home. But one day, he says, the time of your returning will come, and when it does, you will know it without a doubt."

"There will be a sign? A dream?"

"You will know it, just as the reindeer know when it is time for the winter trek, who can say how? Then you will go back to your country and do what is necessary—though it may not make you happier."

"Why not, Nunna, can't your noaidi speak more clearly?"

The little man smiled. "Our noaidi is very old. He loves riddles as a child does. But his riddles come true." From the shadows the dry leaves rustled. "The noaidi says that he has done enough for you now. He will answer no more questions."

I struggled to my feet, dizzy with the sudden motion. "I have no more questions, Nunna. Tell the noaidi I thank him from my heart."

Outside, I stood by the door, blinking in the bright sunlight. Across the wasteland of stone and scrub, the great, gray mountains—the Sacred Mountains—half filled the sky. Even to an Icelander it was a bleak and forbidding landscape. But the air was clear and fresh and tingled deep down when I drew in a lungful of it. I shivered and sneezed three times—big sneezes that rang in my ears like three magic handclaps, waking me from a poisoned sleep.

"Goodbye, Dead Ones," I said aloud. "I don't forget you, but I put you away for a while. One day we will see each other again—but not today, not today."

I held my hand out in front of me—it no longer shook.

Kalf came out and stood beside me. "How are you feeling?"

"Weak as a baby and glad to be alive. For the second time, Kalf, I owe you my life. How will I ever repay you?"

"There's no reckoning between friends."

"Fate stole my brother from me, Kalf. There's a saying, 'One's back is bare without a brother.' Take his place, my friend. Be my sworn-brother."

He hesitated. "Brothers fall out sometimes, Odd."

"But we won't. I'm not what you'd call a steady sort of fellow, Kalf Slender-Leg. I need your sound head and good heart. Will you do it?"

For answer, he drew his dagger and cut his thumb and mine. We mingled the blood together with earth, and then knelt and swore that each of us would avenge the other like a brother.

"Brother, I must tell you," he said, "that you'll soon need more friends than one. Come and look."

I followed him 'round the side of the hut to where there was a view across the inlet. There lay our ship with a good portion of her cargo strewn on the beach, and beside it, my crew with a crowd of Lapps amidst heaps of furs, whalebone, and antler. With much wagging of heads and waving of arms on both sides, a lively barter was going on.

"Who ordered this?"

"Stig's taken over as captain."

"And the others?"

"Hogni's his strongest supporter. He hates you—the rest only fear you. Who knows why? He came within a whisker of splitting your skull when you were, ah, distracted."

"What d'you think they'll do when they see me alive?"

"Kill you. They'll have to. Mutiny's a hard thing to take back, even if some are willing. Odd, I was talking to Nunna before—it's possible to go to Norway overland with the Lapps, on their winter trek. Let the ship go, Odd. The two of us can—"

"Can run? Let them bury me here first! Where are my weapons?"

"Inside. Don't, Odd, you haven't got the strength of six."

"Brother, I haven't got the strength of one—but they don't know that. Nunna," I yelled through the bark wall, "bring me my sword!"

The manikin appeared in the doorway accompanied by a boy, his youngest son, who struggled with both hands to carry my sword, trailing the belt on the ground behind him. Giving me a cautious eye, he stretched up to his father's ear and whispered something.

"Please," said Nunna, "he asks if the battle will be very ferocious, for he has never seen the giants fight before."

Kalf and I looked at each other and burst out in laughter. It hadn't occurred to us that *we* were the terrible giants of the North!

"Say to him, friend Nunna," I replied, "that he will tell his grandchildren of it."

The cacophony of bartering faded away when we were spied coming along the beach. The Lapps shooed their women and children to safety while my men gathered around their two ringleaders and grimly stood their ground. Ignoring Hogni's glowering looks, I walked straight up to Stig. He stood at ease, facing me squarely with his arms hanging loose at his sides.

"Steersman, I don't remember telling you to do anything with this ship's cargo."

Before Stig could answer, Hogni struck in: "I guess you don't remember much of anything, seeing as how you was out of your wits!" He held up his hands and shook them, imitating my palsy. "And you've been up to some black sorcery, too, haven't you? We heard the wailing and the drumming. Now, I say the thing to do with madmen and heathens is drown 'em. Stig for captain, and the deep water for this one, eh lads?"

There was a chorus of 'ayes,' though not as loud as might have been expected. They liked Stig all right but not Hogni, who was a bully—and not much of a seaman either. During Hogni's speech, Stig had said nothing at all but only watched me with that same cool, inquisitive look that he had turned upon me in earlier days—the one that asked, *What are you made of? What are you game for?*

I decided to stake all on that look.

"Hogni Hard-Mouth," I said mildly, "what is it that puts you in such a temper? Is it being deprived of a diet of mare's ass to which you're addicted or is it heart-sickness for that troll who uses you as a woman every ninth night?"

A snort of laughter came from Stuf and Otkel; thin smiles from Starkad, Brodd, and Stig. Hogni's jaws began to work like two millstones.

"Hot to kill me, are you, Hogni? Good. No need for anyone else to bleed. Hogni and I will settle this." The truth was, I doubted I could beat Stig on my best day—which this was far from being.

Suddenly Hogni changed his tune. "What if they've made his hide so as it can't be cut, or what if they've charmed his sword? They can do that, these sorcerers...."

He looked from face to face, and the faces looked stonily back. They might share his fears, but all the same they didn't respect a coward. Hogni sensed it. "Make him use a different weapon, that's all. I'll fight him, him and his ghosts. Jesu, he looks like a bleeding ghost himself! Ha, ha!" He cleared his throat to spit as he always did when he wanted to seem cocksure.

"Mind the wind, now, Hogni."

The men brought shields and helmets from the ship. Hogni chose to fight with his axe. I chose an ash wood spear because I knew I was too weak to manage anything heavier.

"Finish him fast," said Kalf—advice I didn't need. Nunna, coming close to my elbow, whispered encouragingly, "The noaidi has not seen your death in this place, my friend, and our noaidi is never mistaken."

"Well, let us by all means not embarrass the noaidi!" I said under my breath.

The fight started badly and got worse. Hogni was a clumsy fighter but a strong and determined one, and he knocked me about pretty hard, aiming smashing blows against my shield until it was battered to pieces and my arm was numb.

I feinted and retreated. In seconds I was gasping for breath. My legs wobbled. The faces of the spectators swam in front of me. In Hogni's eye was the gleam of victory. Desperately, I flung my spear and pierced his shield. With a snort of contempt he tossed shield and spear away. He raised his axe in both hands and drove in for the kill.

But hadn't my father stood weaponless when Strife-Hrut went for him at the trial? Hadn't my father crouched and thrown his shoulder against the charging man and flung him into the air?

I don't say that those thoughts passed knowingly through my brain, but somewhere near me—and not for the last time in my life—I caught a strong scent of Black Thorvald in the air and knew the noaidi spoke truth.

Hogni was coming too fast to stop himself. He went up and came down on his back. The axe flew out of his hands. I picked it up and split his head.

Taking my sword back from Kalf—and praying that my legs would hold me up just a little longer—I walked to where Stig stood and leveled the point at his breast.

"Is this hand steady enough for you, Steersman?"

With an eye on his distant horizon, he allowed that it seemed pretty steady.

"You're a good man, Stig. I want you with me. But by the Raven, you'll take orders from me or you'll take a long walk with the Lapps come winter."

Of course, it was all bluff. The ship and crew were his, if he wanted them. He knew that. But somehow I didn't think he would do it.

He looked me up and down, then held my sword point lightly between his thumb and forefinger and drew it away from his heart. "Odd Tangle-Hair, I don't know what all that was about back in the fog—and I don't want to. But anyone that can be house-burnt, haunted, brain-sick, and beaten as you have been and still talk so bold is a tough man or a lucky one. Maybe a little of that luck will rub off on me, for I've never had much of my own. I'll take your orders, Captain."

"Starkad, Brodd, Stuf, and Otkel?" I looked at each in turn.

"Let old quarrels lie and we're your men," they answered all together.

Such are my countrymen. You can be a raving lunatic, but be a fighter and they will follow you cheerfully to the gates of Hel.

✝

We stayed on a few more days with the Lapps. They were shrewd traders and wheedled most of our cloth away from us. It was a poor Lapp who couldn't wear a blue coat and leggings now. But we did well out of it, too, and gathered a haul of bear and marten skins that would bring a handsome price on the quays of Nidaros.

Meanwhile, I found time to study our hosts. It astonished me to learn that there were people in the world with ways so different from our own. In fact, this was the beginning for me, I think, of that lust to see and to know that has dragged me over half the earth.

We were invited to sleep with them in their huts, which, even with the stench, seemed preferable to camping out on the stony beach. I elected to stay in Nunna's hut, which he occupied with his two aged parents, his little black-haired wife, his three sons and two daughters, and his kennel of half-starved curs. Added to this mob was an unending stream of visitors who marched in uninvited at all hours of the day just to sit and stare at me.

My host grumbled that he must soon build a bigger hut but in fact, he loved the celebrity, although he was kept in a fever preparing food for us all. I say *he* because among the Lapps it is the man who cooks—this task being thought too important to entrust to women—and they keep their provisions, along with their fetishes, in the sacred part of the hut where no woman ever goes.

While Nunna cooked and fussed, his wife and daughters made it their task to fashion a pair of leather boots for me. They make their boots large and loose and stuff them for warmth with handfuls of springy moss. Once a year a Lapp takes off his boots and replaces the moss.

Nunna's eldest daughter, a girl of fifteen or so named Risten, was tracing around my feet, which are pretty large, with a stick of charcoal. She said something in their twittering tongue that sent everyone in the room into peals of laughter. Her father explained: "She only wishes to know if what she can't see is as large of its kind as what she can—excuse her rudeness." Then he looked thoughtful for a moment. "You may, if it pleases you," he said, "allow her to find out."

Handsomely offered, I thought. And at the first opportunity, I did. She had a pretty face, round and shiny as a penny, a trim little body, and no modesty. We spent that night together under the furs while everyone around us kept up a steady, loud, and unconvincing rumble of snores.

And the next morning when we gathered for breakfast, the girl was fairly bursting with jolly conversation, which the others greeted with gasps and clucks and smiles. Her papa, especially, kept giving me large and encouraging winks and speculating on the likelihood that I had gotten his daughter with child, until it began to dawn upon me that his whole design—good stock-breeder that he was—was to become the grandfather of a giant. Well, I wasn't one to complain.

"Not that you are so very tall," he mused, "not like some of the others."

"Ah, but my mother's people, friend Nunna, are extraordinarily bulky—like pine trees, like mountains. Of course, you understand that nothing so large as that can be conceived in a single night."

He understood perfectly. Could I exert myself again? He would vouch for his daughter. I thought perhaps I could.

Visitors had arrived already to share our breakfast and to gawk—and the girl was happily launched on her second recitation of the morning—when Nunna and his sons got up to go about their chores.

We walked together up into the foothills beyond the camp where, as far as the eye could see in every direction, reindeer grazed.

Reindeer are a Lapp's pride and his wealth. A rich man like Nunna might own hundreds of animals. I watched as his dogs dashed into the herd to cut out particular animals and drive them towards us. His purpose today was to castrate some of his bucks.

"It is coming time for the trek," he remarked, coiling his lasso and measuring the distance with his eye.

"How far will you go?"

"Oh, many horizons up into the mountains. You are lucky, you know, that you found us this summer. I fear the old noaidi will not live through one more trek. Even for the young it is very hard."

He flicked his wrist. The lasso snaked out and dropped over the rack of a young buck. The animal jumped, snapping the sealskin rope taut, and Nunna dug in his heels. Quickly, his two biggest boys wrestled it to the ground and held it down with its hind legs spread apart.

"For the old folks," he continued, coiling up his rope again, "a time comes when they cannot keep up with the herd anymore."

"I suppose you must leave them to their fate, then?"

He had just buried his face between the buck's legs, put its testicles in his mouth, and bit. With a squeal the animal regained its feet and shot back to the herd. Nunna raised his head and regarded me with a look of pure horror.

"Leave them? *Leave them!* Do you take us for savages?"

I searched for words to apologize.

"Of course we do not leave them. No, no, no. It is like this: the children and grandchildren bundle the old one into a sledge at the top of a precipice. Everyone says goodbye—and they push. In a moment, spirit and body are parted. It is a fine thing to see. And in the case of a great noaidi like ours, the spirit will dwell in the Sacred Mountains with those of other sorcerers who have gone before. One day, when we beat the drum to call the Mountain Men, his spirit will be among them and, being dead, he will be even wiser than he is now."

While we talked, the boys had caught another buck.

"*Leave* them," Nunna muttered, still shaking his head, and knelt once again to his work.

✝

My crewmen's adventures, each entertained by a different family, had been quite as interesting as my own. Stig had impregnated four daughters in a single night—or so he boasted, and Kalf was obliged to visit several huts on successive days where they hoped to breed his long, runner's legs to their stock. Still, after a week had gone by, we were growing restless.

"Let us leave this place," grumbled Brodd, "where the mosquitoes are as big as hummingbirds, no beer is brewed, and you can't tell the women from the reindeer by smell alone."

That evening I told Nunna we were going.

"Yes, my friend, quite right. We will soon break camp ourselves. Time to be off, time to be off."

From this I gathered that our appetites were beginning to make a dent in the Lapps' provisions, and they were now confident that the spring would bring them a crop of grandsons as tall as trees.

The weather had been holding fair, with only a little early morning mist each day. Still, Nunna pressed me to make a sacrifice, in the Lapp fashion, for a good wind.

The next morning, he chose two white male reindeer out of his herd and we led them into the center of the camp where stood a low platform of rough planks. There sat Nunna's gods: two squat stumps of birch with sticks for arms and nothing much for faces.

"Wind Man and Thunder Man," he explained. "Thunder Man holds his hammer, you see,"—he pointed to a cudgel tied to one of the stick arms—"just like your Thor, yes? And Wind Man has his shovel for serving out the winds, and his club for beating them back again. Oh, they are rough fellows, these gods," Nunna laughed. "They roar and bluster. But feed them well and they will be your friends."

My crew, seeing what we were up to, gathered round—some with uneasy looks.

"You'll do as you like, Odd Thorvaldsson," young Otkel said, screwing up his courage, "but I'm not going to stay where devils are. I wasn't brought up to it, like you." And he retreated a few steps to what seemed like a safe distance.

"Boys," I said, "you may call on the White Christ as much as you like and Nunna here won't mind a bit, will you, Nunna?" He shook his head vigorously. "But let's not be quick to slight these wooden friends of his. Take help where it's offered, say I. And for that matter, I recall a few voices calling on Thor when the storm was like to have sunk us."

There were guilty smiles all around at this.

"Otkel was one," brayed Stuf treacherously. "I heard him. Don't you deny it now, it's true."

"T'ain't," muttered his cousin, kicking at a stone. But having gone too far to back down, he turned and marched down to the seashore.

The others stayed. Stuf and Starkad, who were Christmen, crossed themselves hurriedly. Bald Brodd, who was heathen and didn't care who knew it, glared at them. Stig, to whom all religions were equally uninteresting, gazed at us with faint amusement.

"Brother of mine," I called to Kalf. He stood not far away, his eyes fixed on the ground. "You'll lend a hand, won't you? Brother? Ho, Kalf, d'you hear me?"

"Aye, brother" he answered in a loud voice that sounded unnatural in him. "Give me the knife quickly. Where do I cut?"

Kalf, my loyal friend, my sworn brother. Kalf, who always swore by the old gods just to please me—why were his movements awkward and his features strained? I felt the beginning of anger stir, but the next moment he seemed himself again, and I dismissed it from my mind.

Following Nunna's instructions, we stabbed the two beasts to the heart, making sure that plenty of blood splashed over the idols. Then we worked over them for half an hour. From each one we took the muzzle, an eye, an ear, the brains, a lung, the prick, and a bit of meat from every part of its body. These were for the gods. The rest of the meat would be cooked and eaten. When we had finished, Nunna placed the bones in a bark coffin, poured blood over them and buried them. He gave me a satisfied smile.

And I? What did I feel? The truth is, I felt self-conscious, like an actor in one of those plays the Greeks love so much—wearing another's face, speaking another's words. My father had sacrificed to Thor long ago. He would have pierced some animal's heart, felt its blood run over his hands, uttered a prayer. For him it was simple. He knew, he *knew* Thor heard him and was glad of it. But I, for all that I called myself a 'heathen', had never sacrificed. How could I, when every temple, every image of the gods had been erased from our land before I was born? I *wanted* to believe. Nunna's Thunder Man was surely Thor by a different name. But where was he? Could I feel his presence truly? Or Odin's, or any of them? Or was it only a hope, a wish?

✝

That day we sat all together on the beach and feasted on venison and blood gruel. Kalf struck up a tune on his whistle, and then the Lapps, seated in a circle, chanted their songs, just as they had done in the noaidi's hut.

From time to time I looked around for the Ancient. I had not seen him since that first day.

"He sleeps," said Nunna. "He sends his spirit here and there, he dreams for us. Let him be."

"I won't forget him."

"No indeed, my friend, you will not."

Nunna's daughter stepped forward and shyly handed me my new-finished boots. She patted her belly and smiled.

"The old women say it will be a boy," said her father. "What shall we call him?"

I thought a bit. "Call him Suttung, for he was a famous giant."

"Ah."

"Feed him on meat and milk, beat him if he's lazy, make him tough and shrewd as you are. Here. Here is the axe I killed Hogni with. Give it to him when he's big enough to swing it, and tell him he's an Icelander's son."

Well, I was young and this was my first bastard. With the next one ... and the next, you stop giving away weapons. I only hope little Suttung didn't turn out the runt of the litter.

When the tide ebbed, we said goodbye and sailed away.

Wind Man and Thunder Man, as Nunna promised, played us fair. I never thought to ask him who their war god was. I would soon wish that I had sacrificed to him, too.

16

STIG RENEWS AN OLD ACQUAINTANCE

"Strange," said Stig, scratching his bristly chin. "Damned peculiar." He had just come aft to where I stood at the tiller.

"Eh, Steersman?" I barely heard him, I was so excited.

We had been fifteen days at sea since leaving the country of the Lapps, following the coast southwards to Trondheimfjord. I had taken the helm all the way, even to working us through the tricky entrance to the fjord, with Stig calling directions from the bow. I was beginning to be the master of that little tiller-stick. Stig said he'd soon have nothing more to teach me.

The sun was high in a cloudless sky as we glided, silent and solitary, up the great fjord which reaches like a crooked finger deep into the Norwegian land. The wooded hills that rose sheer on either side of us tinted the glassy surface of the water with their reflected color.

It was from these same shaggy hills, two centuries ago, that my ancestor, Thorolf Braggart, had sailed for barren Iceland. How he must have missed these great trees. For his descendent returning, the sight of them was astonishing.

Thus, I beheld my first forest, and prickling with anticipation, was about to set foot in my first town. Dead ahead, across the green-glass water, where the little River Nid spills into the fjord, lay Nidaros, the largest port in the district of Trondelag, and lately royal capital of Norway.

The site had been virgin forest in Thorolf Braggart's day and for long thereafter. It was just thirty years ago that Olaf Tryggvason—not the present King Olaf but his predecessor—had built his hall, his church, and his shipyard. His reign had been bloody and brief, but what he built had prospered, and by now, according to Stig, the site enclosed some hundreds of merchants, shopkeepers, shipwrights, sailors, and willing girls within its wooden palisade. The babble of all their voices carried to us across the water.

"Brodd, Starkad, drop the yard and secure," I called, "the rest run out oars!" I held the tiller over, aiming for a clear bit of stony beach to run us up on. "What's that you say, Stig?"

"I said 'peculiar' is all. In all the months I spent here I don't recollect a single day when there wasn't smoke rising from the roof of the king's hall yonder above the town. Winter or summer there was always meat roasting by this time of the day."

"Well, I suppose he's off hunting or warring if he's any sort of king at all. Why should we care, anyway?"

Still with his face screwed into a frown, Stig moved away.

The harbor was a confusion of birds. Some filled the sky with their complaints while others sat motionless on the ridgepoles of the houses. Some flapped away, protesting, as I nosed us on to the beach.

In short order, we stood together on dry land, sucking in great breaths of pitch and pine, wet hemp, herring, and dried cod, while we gaped about in wonderment at civilization.

There was, first, the harbor itself.

Along a front of three hundred paces, fishwives shrieked and loafing sailors browsed the merchant's stalls or tumbled noisily through the doors of a dozen tiny alehouses. Here and there bales and sacks and casks in endless procession were trundled in and out under the watchful eyes of hawk-faced captains.

The town proper crawled up the hillside that rose from the wharf: acres it seemed, of thatched roofs, golden under the autumn sun, that gave the appearance from a distance of a mountain meadow all neatly mown and stacked. Narrow lanes ran down between the houses to the wharf, and here housewives and children, artisans, and farmers-come-to-town mingled with the harbor crowd.

"Just look at 'em all," whispered Stuf, awestruck, "just look."

"Well, Stig," I said, glancing about, "what now?"

"Now is when the king's harbormaster must come and inspect us and tell us where to unlade." He peered into the crowd.

"That's him now." I pointed out a beet-faced man who was struggling through the crowd in our direction.

"Not unless the king's taken to hiring drunkards."

The perspiring red face with its plum-colored nose, framed with tufts of white hair above each ear, came to a wheezing halt in front of us and produced a series of gasps and gurgles like a man drowning.

I was ashamed to have mistaken this old ruin for the harbormaster, and so, in my sternest captain's voice, demanded of him, "Who is in charge here, fellow?"

With more desperate gasps he built up enough wind for a wheezy laugh: "In charge? Why, nobody's in charge, friend. They all do as they please nowadays. Name is Ketil, *Old* Ketil as I'm generally known, and I haven't got all day to stand here talkin' t' you, for I am a workin' man."

"And what trade do you work at, Grandpa," asked Starkad with a chuckle, "that can be carried on in a tavern?"

"*This* is what I'm working at, damn your eyes. You'll be wanting a snug hole to lay up in, won't you? Maybe you plan to winter over? There's not many sail home this late in the year. Well sir, a warm fire, plenty to eat, best ale in the town—"

"Come to the point, old man," growled Brodd.

"The point is that the woman I work for keeps an inn for sailors and I'm supposed to bring 'em there—which is what I am trying to do, if you'd shut up long enough to let me say my piece!" With that long speech he ran out of air and was reduced again to wheezes.

Stig turned me aside and spoke softly. "I say maybe we sail on to Skiringssal or Birka. Something here I don't like the smell of."

"You worry too much," I replied. "You don't mind the smell of silver, do you? There's plenty of it here, from what I can see. Anyway, we need to get drunk. We'll stay a day or two and look the place over."

I turned back to our friend, but he had already started off, head down and listing dangerously to port, without a backward look, as if the matter of our staying was settled. With a word to Brodd to do his drinking near the ship—his rough manners would keep the wharf rats at bay—the rest of us set off in pursuit of Old Ketil.

The narrow street wound up through the town. The place still had a raw, new look, it being only a generation old. But a generation's filth had accumulated in ripe, rotting piles in every alleyway. It came to me with the shock of a brand new thought, that people close together will make a mess.

"It's like living at the Althing the whole year round," said Starkad. "You wonder how they stand it."

"But wouldn't it be fine," said Kalf, "if there was a place like this at home!"

"That there never will be," answered Stig. "Two things make a town—kings and timber. Iceland doesn't want the first and hasn't enough of the second."

He was right about the timber, anyway. The main thoroughfare from the harbor was paved with logs laid crosswise; the houses, too, were mostly log-built, and in the kitchen gardens behind each one, mountainous stacks of cordwood stood heaped up against the coming of winter.

Our way took us through the center of the town where, in a square formed by the crossing of its two principal streets, stood the cathedral.

Who would have thought wood could play such tricks? I had once seen a church in Iceland that Snorri-godi had built, but that was nothing to compare with this. It was six stories high from its square foundation to its slender steeple. The walls were of split logs, cunningly carved, and the sloping eaves were shingled so as to resemble the scales on a dragon's back.

Old Ketil was glad of a minute to stop and catch his breath. "Saint Clement's," he gasped. "King Olaf Tryggvason built her when there was nothing here but a clearing in the woods. When the workmen come to the top, it baffled 'em how to put up the steeple."

"How did they?" asked Stuf.

"Hah! Troll come along, took that steeple in both his arms, like this,"—he made a circle of his arms—"and set it on for 'em, easy as you please."

"But trolls hate churches. Leastways, they do at home."

"Well, this were a *Christian* troll, dammit!"

Otkel had his mouth open to reply, but his words were drowned by the sudden pealing of the bell. Swinging high up in the steeple, it sent its iron voice out over the town—over the hills and over the dark green water. Its name was 'Glad,' said Ketil, and it was the gift of Olaf Haraldsson, the present king. To my ear, its voice was harsh and heavy—a voice meant to afright the ancient spirits of the land.

As the bell tolled, a procession marching two-by-two filed into the square.

"Curse me for a sinner!" Ketil suddenly cried. "Assumption Day morning and me laid up in the alehouse drunk! Here she comes. Here comes Our Lady, bless her!"

Borne above the crowd, a palanquin swayed. On it, under an arch of flowers and fruits, stood a painted and gilded wooden statue.

Stuf's mouth gaped open, and he seized hold of his cousin. "That's God's mother, Otkel, as they're always talking of. I'm sure of it. Look, ain't she a beauty, heh? What a beauty!"

"Takin' her round the fields to bless the crops before harvest. And me laid up drunk again," Ketil lamented more. He bent his knee and made fervent crosses as the palanquin swayed past us.

The procession concluded with a gaggle of shaven-headed priests and a troop of boys, singing in clear high voices, and after them the townspeople, jostling and milling, until the square was entirely filled with them.

In this great throng, I couldn't see their leader, at first. I saw him now, though: a man of middle age with a smooth-shaven face and deep-set eyes, robed in red and white. As he passed, knees bent and hands reached out eagerly to touch his robe.

"Bishop Grimkel," wheezed Ketil reverently, nudging us and pointing, "Holy Bishop Grimkel!"

He passed close by us, his right hand upraised to make the cross over us, his left—a strong, big knuckled hand—holding a tall gilded staff, crooked at the top.

There's his magic rod, for sure, I thought, backing away from it in spite of myself. I could have had no inkling then what a long shadow that rod would cast over my life.

He went in through the cathedral's open doors, and the shuffling line of worshippers filed slowly after him.

"Old Ketil," I said firmly, "enough standing about. Lead on to this inn of yours, for we are thirsty men."

We skirted the crowd of spectators who loitered in the square. Some of these were singing and some were on their knees. But there were others, I saw, and not just a few, who looked on with cold eyes.

146

"Odd," said Kalf, "I'll stay for just a bit."

"What? Don't be silly, you'll never find us again. Come on."

As we walked, Stig plied Ketil with questions about King Olaf, whose absence from church on such a holy day struck him as especially strange, but the old fellow, having hardly enough wind in his sails to navigate, could say nothing intelligible.

Our way brought us at last to the edge of the town. There, shouldering itself in between the rampart and a straggle of mean huts, was the inn.

It was a sprawling, ramshackle affair of sun-bleached timbers and old thatch. A small brew house, a bath house, and a dairy stood near it, all joined together with wattle fences to enclose a dirt yard where chickens pecked and an ugly dog barked at the end of its tether.

Ketil ushered us into the hall's cavernous interior—dark but for the glow of a few candles flickering in the corners and a dusty sunbeam that fell through the smoke hole high above. It was a moment before my eyes could pick out details: an enormous copper cauldron hanging above the hearth, a row of nail-studded sea chests along one wall, and four men leaning over their ale horns at one of the scarred tables, laughing with a couple of girls.

But what caught my eye, almost at once, was the carved and painted dragon's head, all white teeth and round, red eyes, that overhung the doorway where we entered.

"Ketil? Have they thrown you out of the tavern, then, you useless old fool? Don't think to creep back here and drink up the wages you haven't earned." It was a voice that might crack a stone, and it came from a woman who advanced on us from one of the side doorways. "I haven't had a lick of honest work from you in an age, and I ... Suffering Christ, it's Stig! What ill wind blows *you* here?"

Stig grinned all over his ugly face and rolled his eyes. "You've gotten a might older, Bergthora Grimsdottir."

"Well, the devil skin you, you've grown no prettier yourself!"

She swooped at Stig, nearly knocking Old Ketil off his wobbly legs, threw her arms around his neck, and planted a kiss full on his mouth. He pried himself loose and they stood back to look at one another.

She was a raw-boned, long-legged, angular woman, with a good deal of beak and a good deal of neck—altogether something like a stork. In age, not young, as Stig had been so unkind as to notice, probably about forty, give or take.

She was dressed like a proper housewife, in a long tunic of dark blue wool whose sleeves were rolled up to the elbow and an apron, none too clean, that was pinned on at the shoulders with plain brooches. A housewife's scarf covered her hair except for one straw-colored lock that clung damply to her forehead.

Yet she would have stuck out strangely in any Iceland farmer's kitchen. There was an air of the town about her. She had a man's eyes, and when she spoke, she ran her words together like a sailor.

"Bergthora and I are old friends," Stig explained over our laughter. It's been ... how long? Three years?"

"Five, you whore's son," she shot back.

"Has it really? Well, let's not speak of that, my love. It pleases me to see you've come up so far in the world. You were ever a friend to Icelanders, and I hope you're one still."

She noticed the rest of us now. "Stig, are you the captain of this bunch?"

"I am not. Here is our captain. Don't be fooled by his young looks. Odd Tangle-Hair's his name."

"Why should I be? I've known boys half his age to go a-viking. How d'ye do, Tangle-Hair."

I introduced the others.

"Seen worse."

I liked her at once.

"And as for how we come to be here," Stig resumed, "well, I'll tell you the truth, my girl. We borrowed a ship in Iceland, you see, which just happened to be loaded to the gunwales with cargo. Believe me now, the first person I thought to share my bit of good luck with was you. And me being the navigator, why—here we are."

She replied to this speech with a word that I'd never heard a woman use before.

Sitting us down, she called to one of the girls to fetch a bucket of ale. "Wash the salt out of your whiskers with that," she said, filling our horns for us. "'Friend to all Icelanders' indeed. I was a friend to only one, and how does he serve me, but runs off one day with not as much as a by-your-leave."

Stig, in his customary manner, squinted into the distance. "Love, I'm not a man for goodbyes. Had a bit of trouble—nothing to speak of now—

saw a ship in the harbor bound for home and thought it might be time for a move. Don't take it to heart so. Though we did get on well, didn't we?"

And how had he fared since? she asked.

"Ah, not near so well as you, love." Turning to us, he explained, "She was only in a small way in those days—little place on the wharf with just three girls in it. I tumbled 'em all, but in the end, it was the lady herself I liked best—and it wasn't so much her beauty as her wits, I may say. And look at you now, darling." He took in the place with a sweep of his arm. "You didn't come by all this from picking sailors' pockets."

Straightening herself and putting on a somber expression, she gave us to understand that 'Poor Karl' was her benefactor.

"Poor Karl?"

"Him." She raised her eyes to the carved dragon's head above the door. "Or, what's left of him. He was a shrewd trader but a careless sailor. His ship went down one day in a squall in the fjord. They only found bits and pieces of the wreckage, but he'd left a bag of silver in my safekeeping. We were that close. Well, there was no use in letting it go to waste, was there? I put it down on this wreck of a place, and Karl, such as he is, has the overseeing of it. I do miss him, poor thing. But," she added quickly, "it was always you, Stig, that I favored most. You know that. Lord, the place does want a man."

"Captain," Starkad spoke up, "will we stay a bit or no?"

How much would she want, I asked, to bed us all down.

"Well, now that'd depend on how long you mean to stay. If it was for the whole winter, the rate goes down, and you'd have the place almost to yourselves."

I tried to catch Stig's eye, but he gazed steadily away. "Let's say a week then, Bergthora Grimsdottir, and after that we'll decide again."

Businesslike, she named her figure and explained that for our money we would get a place to stow our sea chests, room to sleep on the wall-benches or up in the loft, whichever, and a seat at the table for dinner."

"And women?" I asked, trying to sound like an old hand.

"Oh them, too. Lord, yes."

✝

The rest of the day passed quickly. I marched the lads back to the harbor, arranged with a warehouse, and set about unlading our cargo—a task that, with frequent stops to quench our thirst, occupied most of the afternoon. From time to time I saw Stig glance upward and followed the direction of his eye to the king's hall, high up behind its spiked palisade. There was still no smoke.

As we made our way back again through the town, the sun was going down, and the 'Troll's Steeple' atop the cathedral cast its shadow across the square. I turned around to say something to Kalf. We had just been talking, and I thought he was behind me, but he wasn't. Stig nodded toward the church.

"Right," I said, making my voice sound easy, "he knows his way back." But it annoyed me more than I would admit.

✝

At Bergthora's inn, which we had decided amongst us to call *Karl's Doom*, a side of venison now turned on the spit, filling the hall with its crackle and smell. In a steady stream, men and women trooped in, shouting hellos and pulling benches noisily up to the tables. Some were seamen who lodged there, others were townsfolk drawn by the inn's reputation for thick ale and good company.

Of the latter there was plenty to go round. Country girls, too poor to be dowered or just bored with the hard life of the farm, drifted into Nidaros, bedded down in one little shack or another on the waterfront, and lived by their wits. Six of them lived here, working for wages as well as what they could make off customers. Together with Old Ketil and his grandson, a scruffy boy named Toke, they got busy serving. Bergthora brought us ale and meat and sat for a bit, with her hand on Stig's knee, while we tucked into it.

But a good innkeeper can never sit still for long. She would tolerate a good bit of roughhousing from the guests, but when things got ugly, which happened often enough, she was instantly in the middle of it with a smile and a line of banter and if this was insufficient, sterner measures. One noisy fellow, swearing he'd been cheated by a girl and brandishing his knife, went down hard with Bergthora's knee in his balls. It didn't seem to me that she was any the worse off for the absence of Poor Karl.

This was the first time I had gotten drunk with my men—which is the best thing you can do, next to leading them into battle, to make them yours. We roared with laughter and poured ale on each other, drank to our good luck, and named all the things we would buy as soon as we were rich.

We told each other all over again how we had lifted Hrut's ship right from under his nose, and ridden out the fiercest gale that ever blew, and gotten children on the daughters of the dwarves—and said nothing at all about those other, grimmer, things—ghosts, madness, and mutiny. By silent agreement, we were creating a past for ourselves that would bind us together.

Then Stuf and Otkel danced a jig. Stig, not to be outdone, leapt up on the table, balancing right on its edge, and with wild shouts executed those mad capers I remembered from that night at Hoskuld's. All the room clapped and stamped, Bergthora more than any.

How many places like this one, I wondered, had my father seen the inside of in his viking days? How often had he laughed and danced like this, and felt as free and happy as I felt now?

By and by, Kalf came back, slipping quietly in through the door and sitting down quickly at the foot of the table. What in Hel's High Hall had he been doing with the Christmen all this time? Well, he could do as he liked. Anyway, I was too full of good cheer to ride him for it. I threw my arm around his neck and made him drink out of my horn, pouring the liquid half down his front, and he laughed and cuffed me. In a moment he seemed himself again and none the worse for wherever he'd been.

Some girls gathered around us, none of them beauties, but sturdy and willing. Soon they were sitting on our knees and brooches were unpinned and aprons lifted.

"Give me a girl with flesh on her!" cried Brodd as he buried his face between a pair of tits that were as fleshy as any man could want.

So the evening passed. I made good progress with a plump lass who squealed every time she was squeezed. We linked arms and drank from one horn, rolled in the straw, and afterwards drank more. Aud was her name, one of Bergthora's girls.

Sometime during the night, our hostess took Stig by the hand and led him to her bed-closet.

"Go to, Steersman!" I called after him. "For I suppose you know her channel as well as you know the fjord's."

With a leer and a wave, he disappeared inside.

I began to grow muddled and drowsy. I remember only one other thing clearly. Kalf was sitting down the table from me. The plump lass slid over to him, shedding the last of her clothes. She pressed against him, her belly, which made three folds, thrusting into the curve of his lap while she swung a thigh over his legs.

"Hi, Kalf," I called, "remember the fair Thorgrima? Bears a strong resemblance, no? Give her your best, old friend!"

But Kalf sat frozen-faced, his head pulled down between his shoulders like a petrified animal. He shot me one ghastly look before his hands, as if by a will of their own, began to move on the girl's body.

About then, I think, I fell asleep.

17

BROTHERS FALL OUT

Through the fog of sleep came Stig's voice booming in my ear, sounding too cheery by half. "Sun's up, hey, and we've work to do. Captain, get 'em on their feet, or must I do it myself?"

All around me, bodies lay sprawled amidst the wreckage of last night's celebration.

"You do it," I groaned. The base of my skull felt as though someone had taken an axe handle to it.

He proceeded around the room, dragging our lads from the arms of their girls, rolling them out of puddles of beer, and cursing them generally for drunkards and weaklings.

Except Kalf.

Kalf sat bolt upright before Stig touched him, his eyes red-rimmed as though he hadn't slept at all. The plump lass nowhere near him.

"Fortify yourselves, my boys," said Stig. "It'll be a busy day for us."

We foraged amongst the remnants of the feast, finding hunks of bread, slivers of cold meat, and a few swallows of flat ale from the bottom of the cask. I wasn't the only one of us who held his aching head in his hands.

One of Bergthora's girls, whose name was Thyri and who could almost be described as pretty, fetched a basin of cold water from the well and we plunged our heads in it. She wrung out our hair and clucked sympathetically at our groans.

Last of all, Bergthora emerged from her bed-closet, dressed in yesterday's clothes, but minus her housewifely headscarf, as though a single night with Stig had made her a girl again. She motioned her ugly lover to her and after a short consultation, trumpeted in her brass-throated voice, "Master Ogmund! Hey there, Ogmund Pot-Belly, where are you hiding?"

The man so called poked his head out from under a bench, yawned heavily, and rubbed his eyes. "Really, Bergthora Grimsdottir, I protest—"

"Oh, don't do that, Master Ogmund." Taking him by the shoulder, she lifted him to his feet and proceeded to give him a vigorous dusting off. "Master Ogmund, I've a favor to ask you, and I know you won't refuse, being as you're one of my oldest and dearest customers."

"Yes, and one that likes to be let sleep after a night's exertions, as you well know."

He scowled peevishly at her while arranging his clothes and running a hand through his sparse hair. He was a man of middling age, round-shouldered and paunchy. I had noticed him last night drinking his beer in neat, small sips while one of the prettier girls nuzzled him like a puppy.

"Now then, Ogmund," said Bergthora, " I want you to meet this young ship's captain here and see if you can't help him out a bit. It would mean so much to me." With a hand on his shoulder, she propelled him in my direction.

"Master Ogmund is a wool merchant from Skiringssal in Oslofjord," she explained, "and spends a part of every summer here trading. He's lodged with me since, oh, since donkey's years. Likes the beer and the fun, don't you Master Ogmund? Doesn't bother the girls much, but they do love him for his little gifts."

We acknowledged each other without much enthusiasm, while the rest of my crew drifted over to listen.

"Now, coming to the point," Bergthora went on, "Ogmund Pot-Belly knows every merchant and shop owner in the town by name, as well as every little trick of the trade. If you've never done business in Nidaros, he'll be a great help to you. You've only to ask him, the dear man won't say no to any friends of mine."

Bergthora gave the round shoulder an affectionate squeeze.

"Delighted," he said sourly, taking my hand as if it were a day-old fish. "Icelanders, is it? New at trade?"

"Yes, well, we bought this cargo—"

"Please!" he said quickly, holding up a hand. "I never ask a man how he came by his cargo, that's his business. You'll find it a useful rule." Bergthora beamed at this instant demonstration of her friend's deep knowledge of affairs. "I'll fetch my scales."

Going to his sea chest, he brought out a cunningly made little pair of scales with iron arms folded up double and the brass pans tucked neatly under them. With a flourish he hooked the instrument by a brass chain to his belt, where other men wear their swords.

"Not going to weigh our sealskins in those little things, are you?" brayed Stuf. Stig told him to shut up.

Squaring his round shoulders, Master Ogmund Pot-Belly marched to the door. With winks and smiles we fell in behind him.

✝

I needn't say much about the week that followed. One glorious day ran into the next, while up and down the bustling waterfront we hawked our cheeses and our eiderdown, walrus ivory, antler, seal skins, fleeces, and furs—everything, in short, that we had left Iceland with or acquired from the Lapps, excepting the falcons who had all, sadly, died during the storm.

We soon learned the value of Ogmund's little pair of scales. Any sort of outlandish coin was good currency here: Arab dirhems, English sceattas, and a few which resembled that mysterious Greek coin that Gunnar had given me long ago and that I still wore on a chain around my neck.

Ogmund taught us to nick the edges of the coins to test if they were silver clear through, and to weigh them up and calculate their value. And not coins alone, but anything made of silver—rings, buckles, chains, and so forth—usually hacked into tiny pieces so as to make the amount come out exact.

For four days, under Ogmund's canny eye, we boasted, bargained, and roistered our way from one end of the harbor to the other, and in and out of taverns, where the best trading was done over horns of ale, until we had sold the lot.

Before that week was out, we were, without stretching the point, rich.

Bergthora fairly glowed when we displayed our wealth, and from then on, our position was secure as the lords of Karl's Doom. The choicest morsels of food were saved for us, and the girls, who hungered for presents, were our willing slaves.

Like all rich men, we buried most of our treasure in the woods, each man going alone with his share and finding his own spot. But saving wasn't in my nature. I'd never had silver to spend before. Indeed, until I saw the wares of Nidaros Town, I hardly knew what there was to spend it on. I became wonderfully greedy, and haunted the shops of the weavers, the jewelers, and the armorers from morning 'til night.

Behold me swaggering along the waterfront on a sparkling autumn morning. A blue head-band bordered with silver thread, confines my hair, gold rings are in both my ears, my long-sleeved tunic is scarlet with wide embroidered bands of blue and black rosettes around the hem and collar. The links of my belt are silver snakes, my cloak is of dark blue tufted wool caught at the shoulder by a silver brooch and thrown back over my right arm so that one corner of it trails the ground as I walk. My trousers are fine white linen, snug-fitting and cross-gartered below the knee, and my shoes are fastened with silver latchets. These are the first clothes I have ever owned that my mother did not weave and stitch for me.

I bought myself arms, too: a helmet whose visor was made fierce with scowling bronze eye-brows, a shield of lime wood, covered with three layers of bull's hide and painted in quadrants of red and black to match the colors of our sail, a ring-shirt of the finest make—supple and light, a bearded axe and a spear, both decorated with silver wire pounded into the steel. And a sword. Not that I despise Hoskuld's gift of Hrutsbane, it will have its use one day, but a man can own two swords, can't he? And what a sword this is! Of Frankish make, the armorer told me, the edge so hard it will split a helm in two and still draw blood from the wind. The mysterious name +*ULFBERH*+T is inscribed on the blade. There are only a few hundred like it in the whole world. I have scratched victory runes on it and call it 'Wound-Snake'. I carry it in a scabbard of red leather, lined with oil-soaked wool.

What a figure I cut, swaggering down the wharf at Nidaros. *If only handsome Gunnar could see me now!* I thought.

✝

Behold me swaggering along the waterfront...

Those carefree days came to an end one afternoon in our second week as Kalf and I browsed among the shops.

"What do you make of Stig these days, Brother?" I had gotten in the habit of calling him 'brother,' as I truly felt he was. "Have we lost our steersman to his old love?"

"What? Sorry—did you ask me something?"

"Doesn't matter."

A jeweler, smiling eagerly, spread out his stock of brooches before us—beautiful filigreed pieces set with glowing amber beads—and then moved away to tend to another customer. I wanted something to give Thyri, to whom I'd taken a fancy.

"Kalf, which one is your favorite?" I said carelessly.

"They're all well made."

"I don't mean the brooches—which *girl* is your favorite? The Squealer or which?"

"No, not her. I don't know—none really." He bent over the shopman's table, pretending to examine some ornament.

I was beginning to be sorry I'd begun this, but I was determined to see it through. I had planned this day for the two of us to be on our own and talk, which somehow we had not done in a long time.

"Kalf, look at me." I held him by the shoulders. "Still in the same clothes you left home in. You wear a gloomy face all day long and go off by yourself for hours at a time. What ails you?"

"Odd, if only I could tell you." There was a tightness in his voice. "I can't find the words. You do nothing nowadays but throw your money away, drink, and whore—not that I judge you. How could I? I'm no better. When the girls walk past me swinging their hips, when they touch me, I'm on fire—I can't help it. In the end, I roll with them like a dog in the straw, but I can't stand myself! Every morning I confess my sins, and every night I sin again, until even God's patience must surely be at an end. I'm damned, Odd. I'm bound for Hel!"

He broke off and started down the street away from me, walking fast, almost running, but I kept pace with him and wouldn't let him go.

"It's that priest, isn't it, Grimkel. He's bewitched you. By One-Eyed Odin, I'll have his heart out of him for this!"

"No, not bewitched. I was asleep, and he woke me. I never intended it, Odd—it's God's will." He kept his eyes straight ahead of him as he walked, while the words tumbled out in a torrent such as I never thought to hear from his lips.

"I went to the church that first day just to light a candle to the Virgin, only because—I don't know—it was her day, and I'd promised Grandfather to pray sometimes. The bishop was there. He took me aside and asked me who I was, where I was from, and where was I living."

"You should've told him to mind his own business."

"I told him everything. And he looked sorrowful and said the inn was a wicked place where the Devil rejoiced to see men and women acting no better than beasts, and that I oughtn't to stay there if I valued my soul. He begged me with *tears* in his eyes—with tears, Odd—to heed his words. "No priest—no man at all—ever spoke to me before like that. When I left the church I walked for hours, feeling heartsick, until, at last, I fell on my knees and promised God I would change my ways."

"All right, then, Kalf, leave the girls alone. What difference does it make?"

"But that very night, God help me, I sinned again, and for days after that I couldn't find the courage to make my confession. When I did go again to the church, it was the hour of Mass and the bishop was preaching a sermon. Oh, Odd, if you could have heard him! 'Put away drunkenness and gluttony and whoring,' he said. 'War against the body, for it is there that sin enters.' He bade us live like the blessed monks and hermits, all alone in caves, on mountaintops or islands. Satan sends his army of demons to tempt them with visions of ale and meat and naked women, but they only pray harder, and the demons run away howling, burnt by their prayers."

"Pah! You mean like those scrawny wretches who lived in Iceland when our forefathers arrived? We sent *them* away howling!"

"No, Odd, they have power. They heal, even raise men from the dead—not with witchcraft, but by the grace of God. Odd, I want to be one of them, and I *will* be! But oh, there is so much wickedness in me."

He put his hands to his head as if he would pull out his hair. I thought I knew something about madness, but I had never seen the like of this. I didn't know him.

"Kalf Slender-Leg, it's all nonsense. Healing and raising the dead— how can you believe such stuff? Only the Valkyries of Odin can raise the dead, and maybe not even them anymore."

"You see!" He turned on me with a look of triumph. "You doubt the power of the old gods yourself. Wake up, Odd, before it's too late. There is but one God. Believe in Him!"

Sudden fury took hold of me. "Why, Kalf? Why only one? This is what I cannot understand about you Christmen. Why must everyone be wrong but you? Maybe your bishop can cure souls, but surely the noaidi cured mine. There's room for all—your wooden Virgin, the wooden Thor that once stood on our land at home, and even Nunna's rough wooden fellows. With what right do your priests order us to turn our old friends out?"

"Nunna! When I think of that deviltry we did with him, the sacrifice. Oh, Christ, I want to cut off my right hand. God breathed on my neck when I picked up the knife. I felt Him, but I did it anyway because it was you who asked me, and because I hadn't even Otkel's courage to walk away from it. Oh, I'm far worse than you, Odd. You're unbaptized and in darkness, but I denied Him knowingly. And God help me, I still do. The pure will have eternal life, Odd. But for me, there is the Fire."

"Damn you, don't speak to *me* of fire! I've *been* in a fire, and I know the good Christmen who set it, too."

"Odd, it was a sign, that fire, a warning of what you must suffer hereafter. Heed it."

"Why must I fear anything hereafter? Why must anyone burn for the love of women and ale and every other good thing? These starving fools of yours on their islands and mountain tops will pine someday for what they've missed when it's too late to enjoy it."

I struggled to hide my anger, but could not. How could my truest friend—who followed me in everything, who had twice saved my life, and to whom I had sworn brotherhood—how could *he*, knowing what the Christmen had done to me, turn on me like this?

"Slender-Leg," I forced myself to smile, "you're too sensible a fellow for this rubbish. That priest has done you some mischief, but you'll soon be yourself again. Come now, and let's not quarrel. Aren't we brothers? Come back to the inn with me, and we'll pour down a horn of ale together."

He stopped suddenly and faced me. We had been walking all this while, talking too loudly and drawing stares from passers-by. He took my hands in his, and tears shone in his eyes. "No, Odd, you come to the church with me, and we will kneel together and beg God's forgiveness for our sins. I ask it on my knees, Odd. Unless we become brothers in Christ, we can never be brothers at all."

I hit him so hard that he staggered back against the wall of a shop, upsetting a pyramid of wooden bowls. We stared at each other in dumb pain.

Just then, from somewhere in the next street there came the whinny of a horse and a man's voice shouting. Next instant, horse and rider burst around the corner, the horse's hoofs scrabbling on the slick paving planks. They pounded up the street toward us—the animal was lathered and snorting, the man mud-spattered from helmet to boot. A pig leapt squealing over a wattle fence, and a flock of terrified geese flew straight up in the air, making the horse rear and nearly flinging the rider off. He kicked it savagely, yanked its head around, and came on again.

With the other human traffic, I pressed up against a house wall to give him room as he thundered past. Everywhere, people poured out of shops and houses to run after him up the street toward the cathedral square. Glad to turn my back on Kalf, I ran with them.

In his right fist, the rider brandished the war-arrow, and in his mouth was the name of Olaf, the king.

18

ΤΗΕ RETURN
OF ΤΗΕ KING

Of course, we knew by now why smoke rose no more from Olaf's royal hall. His history, as I gathered it from Bergthora and others, was, this:

Norway had had kings since time past remembering but had never submitted to them easily. Jarls and yeomen alike preferred the pleasures of lawlessness.

After Olaf Tryggvason died, unlamented, in the year 1000, the throne remained vacant for the next fifteen years. In the meantime, southernmost Norway fell subject to the Danes while the rest of the country reverted to a patchwork of petty 'kingdoms', none larger than a single fjord or valley.

One of these was ruled by a certain Harald, who could claim a distant connection to the ancient royal line of the Ynglings. His son was Olaf.

At the age of twelve, Olaf went off a-viking, plundering the coasts of Frankland and England. And sometime during these years he turned Christman—not one of your starving and meditating sort of Christmen, but rather of the fierce variety, in keeping with his character. At the same time, he decided to make himself ruler of Norway.

In the year 1015, he sailed for home with a force of one hundred and twenty men in two leaky tubs. He was met, at first, with little enthusiasm, except in the more populous and Christianized south, where his own people came from. But before the year was out, he had defeated the most powerful of the northern jarls and was able to sail along the whole coast of Norway, hailed everywhere as king. He was just twenty-two years old.

Like his predecessor, Olaf Tryggvason, this Olaf made the northern town of Nidaros his capital, despite—or maybe because of—the fact that his popularity was thinnest there. And also like that earlier Olaf, he set about to convert the region to his new religion, even if he had to shed an ocean of blood to do it.

In that same year, oddly enough, another twenty-two year old viking gained a throne. This one was fated to be Olaf's doom. His name was Canute and he became, upon his father's death, king of Denmark and soon thereafter, of England, too.

Even an ignorant Icelander like me had heard the name of Canute the Rich, who bestrode our northern world as no king before him ever had, and whose ambition was as boundless as his luck. It was inevitable that Canute and Olaf would collide.

Olaf began it by attacking Denmark in 1028. But Canute's double kingdom was immensely richer, and his power far better founded than his rival's. His spies reported the restlessness of the Norse jarls, especially those of Trondelag, and a judicious use of silver did the rest.

When Canute's splendid long-ships—each one mounting on its prow a great gilded bull's head whose horns flashed in the sun—approached the Norwegian coast, Olaf found himself suddenly deserted. Without striking a blow, this stern, intolerant king was forced to flee over the mountains to Sweden—and, in time, much farther than that, as I will tell in its place, though nothing was known about these other adventures then.

Like plucking an apple from a bough, Canute added Norway to his empire. He was hailed as king everywhere he went—and nowhere more enthusiastically than in the eight shires of Trondelag. After appointing Jarl Haakon of Lade to oversee the country for him, he went home to London. The Tronder jarls were well pleased with their obliging absentee ruler.

But Jarl Haakon, the overseer, drowned in a shipwreck the very next year, and word of this somehow reached Olaf in his distant exile. In the autumn of 1030, he re-crossed the mountains with a hired army to take back his throne.

The jarls were alerted. A fast ship, no doubt, was already speeding the news to London, just as gallopers, brandishing the war arrow, were carrying it to every Norwegian village and farm. Olaf was encamped at a place called Stiklestad, at the head of Trondheimfjord. The jarls called upon every able-bodied man to oppose him and his army of Swedish freebooters.

✝

Now, in the crowded streets of Nidaros people milled about the square, talking in worried voices and cursing the Fat Man (for so the king was called by those who didn't love him). If Olaf the Stout had any friends in that crowd, they kept their voices low.

After loitering for a while, overhearing conversations, I decided to go back to Karl's Doom and console myself with a jug and a girl. I already felt wretched about my quarrel with Kalf.

Entering the inn yard, I heard the excited voice of Ogmund Pot-Belly, whom I had seen in the square just a while ago. He was digging furiously in his sea chest, throwing things out to left and right, while he ranted at Stig, Starkad, and Bergthora. They watched him with amusement.

With a grunt, he hauled from the bottom of the chest a large and heavy sword in an old scabbard, and fumbled with the belt, which barely closed around his middle. It had been a long time, I imagined, since a sword had swung from his hip in place of his precious scales.

"Odd Tangle-Hair!" he called out. "Thank Heaven! You heard, didn't you? I appeal to you—will you not join me and command your men to do the same? Our King Olaf needs every Christman's sword."

"Fight *for* him?" I thought I must have heard wrong.

"Of course, for him. Dear God, man, don't listen to what these northern savages are saying. Oh, they'll burn for it one day!"

"Now then, Master Ogmund," warned Bergthora, standing in front of him and giving his sword belt a wrenching tug. "Fight for the Fat Man if you like, but your opinion isn't the popular one, and I don't care to have it shouted from my rooftop. It's bad for business, if you know what I mean."

Ogmund slapped a fist into a soft palm. "Some things matter a deal more than your business or mine, Bergthora. It was our King Olaf who brought this country out of darkness, throwing down the filthy heathen idols with his own hands wherever he went. And when mice and snakes would scuttle out from underneath them, he'd tell the people, '*That's* what you've been feeding with your milk and bits of meat.' He brought 'em to Christ by the hundreds. There are plenty in the south who bless his name for it. But these ignorant Tronders of yours—half of 'em out-and-out heathens and the rest not much better."

"Now really, Ogmund," Bergthora stopped him firmly, "'T'isn't near as simple as you make it out—heathen against Christman. Why, I'm a Christian woman myself, more or less, but Olaf was too harsh, and there's the truth of it. Too many heads and hands lopped off, too many hangings and eye gougings when people came slow to be baptized—and him a foreigner from the south to boot. And it isn't only heathens who oppose him. King Canute's a good Christian as I've heard, and so are our Tronder jarls, Christian to a man."

Ogmund spat. "Your jarls are fools. They're playing Canute's game, and the day will come when they'll regret it."

"Why, he's left us alone so far."

"Look you," cried Ogmund exasperated, "if a man stands with one foot in Denmark and the other in England and pisses, who gets wet, eh?"

"Well, you've a quaint way of putting it, Master Ogmund, and maybe you're right. All I know is, when war starts, silver goes into the ground, and that's bad for my trade. As for the Danes, they drink beer like other men—and piss like other men, too, I daresay."

Stig and I laughed while Ogmund rolled his eyes. "God save us. Only a fool disputes with a stone! Odd Tangle-Hair, I appeal to you again, will you and your men offer your swords to the king?"

I took a thoughtful pull from the ale horn. "D'you know the old saying, Ogmund, 'When wolves fight, the sheep rejoice'? No? Well, I just made it up. It means I don't care for your Christian king or your Christian jarls.

"I see," he said stiffly. "You speak for all your men, do you?"

"I won't see them cut to pieces for no good reason."

"Would there be profit in it?" wondered Starkad.

"Not likely," answered Stig. "Farmers on the one side and vagabonds on the other—wouldn't have enough loot between 'em to make the trip worthwhile."

"In that case," said Starkad with a wide yawn, "I'm content to stay here."

At that moment, in walked Kalf. Without a word to any of us, he went straight to his sea chest. A worried look came over Bergthora's kindly face. She went and laid an arm on his shoulder. "You look bothered, young Slender-Leg, what have you been up to?"

"Looking for Bishop Grimkel."

"Whatever for, at a time like this? 'T'isn't the Sun's Day, is it?"

"To ask his blessing. I'm going away." Stig and Starkad looked up in surprise, first at him, then at me, but they said nothing. "But the church is empty," he went on, "not even a deacon about, and I could find no one to tell me where the bishop has gone."

"No mystery there," replied Bergthora. "He's gone up-fjord to join up with the king. He's not lost a minute. I shouldn't be surprised if he secretly had some word from Olaf before now. He's the king's man."

"He is indeed," seconded Ogmund. "If you want his blessing, lad, then come with me to Stiklestad."

"They say there's to be a fight there."

"So there will. Are you afraid?"

"I would fear nothing, standing by that holy man."

"I'm glad to hear you say it. Any man who fights in Olaf's cause will surely have God's blessing."

"And remission of sins?"

"I shouldn't doubt it. What d'you say, lad?"

"I'll go!"

Thor's Billy goat! I thought. Kalf's no fighter. He'll lose his life for sure, and it'll be my fault if he does. What an ungrateful dog I am. When I lost my wits, did he hit me? Did he curse me? Did he abandon me? Now, I have a chance to repay him. Until he returns to his senses, I'll keep him safe, even if it means tying him to a tree, just as he tied me to the mast.

"Ogmund Pot-Belly," I said, "I've changed my mind. I'm coming with you."

"Don't," said Kalf sharply, not looking at me. "What's this to do with you?"

"Well, I'm a poet, aren't I. And poets sing of battles, don't they? Now, isn't it disgraceful that I've never even seen a battle—not a real one, I mean." I could see he didn't believe a word of this.

"Suit yourself," he shrugged.

"What's happened between you two?" asked Stig at last, giving me a hard look.

"Nothing, Steersman, not a thing."

"Shall I round up the lads and come with you, then?"

"By no means. This is Kalf's business and mine. We'll be back in a few days, I with my poem and he with his blessing, and both of us safe and sound. Master Ogmund, we'll find ourselves a small boat—shouldn't be hard—and row up. Bergthora, we'll need provisions. How many days rowing is it to the top of the fjord?"

"I haven't the faintest, and I doubt you'll find the place without a guide."

"We'll find it." *With luck, after the battle's over*, I added to myself. "Today's almost spent. We'll leave at sunup tomorrow?"

Ogmund nodded, puzzled but grateful. Kalf gave me a long, searching look, as did Bergthora and Stig. Not caring to have my purpose questioned anymore, I made myself scarce for the rest of that afternoon and evening.

✝

Above Nidaros, the high bluffs of Trondheimfjord give way to gentler hills and long stretches of flat land where the trees grow down to the water's edge, broken sometimes by a stretch of watery meadow or a tooth of granite thrusting up from the bones of earth.

Kalf and I pulled at the oars while Ogmund held the tiller. The day was hot and windless, and we soon shed our mail coats, laying them in the bottom of the dinghy beside our arms and rations.

Ogmund sensed the coolness between Kalf and me, and after trying for a time to keep up a conversation, lapsed into silence.

We stopped once to ask our way when we spied a woodcutter's hut by the shore. Ogmund hallooed was anyone at home and did they know where the king's army lay? The door opened a crack and a sallow-faced woman put out her head. A naked child peeped from behind her skirt. "To ficht agin 'im or wi'im?" demanded the woman in a dialect I could barely make out.

"To defend our rightful king, of course," said the merchant in his lofty way.

"Bad luck to 'ee then. My man's gone agin'im."

The door banged shut, leaving Pot-Belly fuming.

Night found us stiff and weary from rowing, and still far from our destination. To make short of it, we blundered about for two more days, stopping every so often to let Kalf scamper up a tree and look for the smoke of campfires. At last, with our food nearly gone and nightfall once more coming on, he sang out from the top of a tall pine that he could see a smudge of smoke on the horizon.

"Praise God!" cried Ogmund. "How many campfires do you make it?"

"Ten thousand!" was Kalf's ecstatic answer.

But there were far fewer campfires than that when we stood on the shore an hour later and looked across the plain of Stiklestad.

The field was shaped like a giant hoofprint pressed into the earth, the round end ringed by a wooded ridge that comes down to the water on both sides. Only one army so far was encamped there, in a disorderly sprawl of lean-tos and campfires that spread along the tree line to our left, fronted by a palisade.

In its midst a ragged banner hung from a standard, white with a golden cross: the arms of King Olaf Haraldsson. My two companions were for racing up straightway, but I insisted we first pull the dinghy into the underbrush at the edge of the field and cover it with boughs before anyone noticed it. I wanted it handy if we should need it in a hurry. Call it second sight, if you want.

That done, we crossed the grassy field to the king's camp—Kalf with his quiver and bow, Ogmund, manfully shouldering a heavy long-handled axe along with sword and shield, and I, with my new arms and armor, for no one with any sense goes to a battlefield unarmed, even if he has no intention of fighting. I toted our keg of ale, as well.

I don't know what I'd expected a royal army to look like, but something grander than what I saw. Any Iceland godi could boast better-looking warriors than these. Nor could I see a horse, a wagon, or a proper tent anywhere. Just as the galloper had reported, they looked like nothing more nor less than a band of hungry bandits on the prowl.

Where the banner stood, there was a lean-to made of pine boughs. Some spearmen lolled on the grass before it. Seeing us approach, they sprang up, and one of them ducked his head inside the shelter. Some moments later there emerged from under the boughs a big, broad-bellied man who shouted a greeting and bore down on us with arms outstretched like some amiable oak tree.

Ogmund, clutching his too-large axe, dropped to his knee and kissed the slab of a hand that was thrust at him. "King," he said, "God knows I am no fighter but, such as I am, I'm yours."

"Every man's a fighter when he fights for God!" cried Olaf in a thunderous voice, hauling Pot-Belly to his feet. "God bless you, man."

His face split into a wolfish smile, showing all his teeth.

It was a square face—battered, brown, and scarred as an old chopping block; the beard square-cut and parted in the center, and the braided yellow hair hanging nearly to his waist. But for all his ferocity, there was a pinched, hollow look around the eyes as though he hadn't slept in days. His clothes told the same story—dirty and travel-stained from weeks of hard marching and lying out at night. At least this king seemed to live no better than his men.

"Have you come up the fjord from Nidaros?"

We nodded.

"Good men! I commend you for your haste, you've left the rest of your fleet far behind."

"The rest...?" Said Ogmund faintly.

"Ask any favor of me when the war's over and, by God, you shall have it. Are you Norwegians or foreigners?"

Ogmund answered for himself.

"And you two?"

"Icelanders," said Kalf.

"Well, damn my head!" He gave a loud laugh. "Icelanders. I love you! Christ, if only my Norwegians feared God as much as your people do. D'you know that every skald in my retinue is an Icelander? Best poets in the world, too. You must meet 'em."

Then his eye lit on Kalf's bow and arrows. He took him by the shoulder, pulling him close to his face. "I need archers. Can you knock out a sparrow's eye at thirty paces? Say 'yes' and I'll love you."

Kalf stammered.

"Speak up!"

"I said, 'Yes, I can'."

"Well, then I *do* love you! I could, too, when I had a boy's sharp eye." He took Kalf in a crushing bear hug.

"King," Kalf said, "though I am a sinner, Bishop Grimkel has fired my soul to live a better life. If he is here, may I ask for his blessing?"

"He's not ten paces away. Come inside, all of you. Break bread and pray with us."

There was such a crowd under the lean-to we barely fit in. Kalf went directly to the bishop, knelt, and kissed his ring. He would have kissed his feet if the man had let him. His face shone as Grimkel made the cross over him.

Among the others, hastily introduced to us by Olaf, were Bjorn his marshal, and his six skalds. Their duty was always to be at the king's side to mark his every high deed and word and fashion them into poetry that would keep his memory green forever.

Although their clothes, like the king's, were soiled and worn, they bore themselves with such haughty dignity that I felt abashed in their presence, and glad I'd said nothing about being a poet myself. All the group huddled around Olaf. The man had an almost irresistible force of personality. I quickly gathered that one did not argue with Olaf, or contradict him. He talked and you agreed or said nothing. This frightened me, because his conversation was extraordinary.

"We're Christ's soldiers here." He threw out both arms to embrace us all. "We fight God's war. No food in the camp, they say? But didn't Our Lord multiply the loaves and fishes? He will provide. They say we're too few? How can that be when Saint Michael and his angels fight at our side? Bishop, there are plenty in Nidaros who love us, are there not?"

"Indeed, King, there are, and eager to join your cause."

What game was Grimkel playing? Was it possible he believed this? He was doing his king no service with this fable.

"Exactly what these brave men have just told me," cried Olaf, indicating us. "Rowed like demons to be first to bring me the news. Half a hundred ships or more behind you, eh?"

Believing in this fiction, I realized, he would wait here, expecting reinforcements from day to day, while his enemies concentrated their forces. When battle came, it would be a massacre.

"King," I said, "you mistook our words, perhaps. We are not the vanguard of any fleet. Some may come out to join you, but don't expect many. Perhaps the bishop heard only what he wanted to hear."

Everyone—Grimkel and Kalf, Ogmund, the skalds, and Olaf, most of all—looked at me as if I'd just pissed in a chalice. The one exception was Bjorn the Marshall. Behind Olaf's back, he nodded at me ever so slightly. He knew I was right.

"Hah!" Olaf exploded in laughter. "Bjorn, you hear that? This stranger offers to tell us our business. He informs me that my people love me not. You disappoint me, stranger, I did not expect to find weak faith in one of your nation." He came and stood face-to-face with me, his unblinking blue eyes looking deep into mine.

"I'm sorry to be the bearer of bad tidings, King, but if no one else will tell you—"

His heavy hands gripped my shoulders so that I could feel the pressure of his thumbs through my armor. Compared to Olaf, Snorri-godi was a puppy.

"Stranger, *my* tidings are brought by angels from the lips of Almighty God. They whisper in my ear as I sleep. We are three thousand strong today. In a week's time, we'll be six. I have God's word on it. If any man here thinks God's a liar, let him leave now and show me his face no more. Now, you and I ... you and I will pray later. You'll believe God's own voice, I hope? If not, you have no business with us."

None of this, mind you, was said in a violent or threatening manner. Olaf was not a common bully—though one might argue he was an uncommon one. He simply held me and looked at me, and I felt as though I'd been turned upside down and shaken. I don't know how else to say it.

"Soon," he ground his big fist into his palm, "soon, by Christ, we'll stamp these false jarls down. And these heathen farmers—we'll break their bones and grind 'em, flay 'em, and boil 'em. Soon, brothers, my banner will fly over Nidaros Town again! And before long, not a pagan will breathe in all this land of Norway. Damn my head, I will either baptize 'em or blind 'em—they can have their choice. For what right has a demon worshipper to look upon God's firmament?"

A chorus of 'Ayes' from all around.

At that moment, a messenger arrived to say that the king's half brother, Harald, was demanding again to take his place in the war council. Now Olaf's eyes turned ugly. He pulled the messenger to him by the front of his shirt. "He demands? Of *me*? That unnatural weed! I have told my half-brother once, I have told him twice, and I will tell him just once more, that I do not take counsel with runny-nosed boys. If he troubles me once again, I'll send him back to his mother. Tell him so."

The messenger vanished.

"And now, friends, on your knees before God." Olaf smoothed his features into gentleness. "I intend to kneel here all this long night through, as I have done many a night before—and I will love any man who stays with me. When tomorrow's sun rises, my friends, you will see a thousand men marching under Christ's banner to our aid. You have your king's word upon it. Does any man doubt it?"

No one doubted it. It was not their business to doubt. It was their business to die beside their king, which in all probability they would do, if the past was any guide.

Obediently, they dropped to their knees and folded their hands under their chins. Among them was Ogmund Pot-Belly and, to my sorrow, Kalf, with a look in his eye as though he were in Heaven already—a change of habitation I hoped to prevent, though damn me if I knew how.

As soon as their backs were turned, I slipped away.

There was nothing to be done for the moment. I was angry, worried, and hungry. Hunger, for the moment, took precedence. I hefted the beer keg and judged there was enough left in it to trade for a few mouthfuls of food.

With the keg on my shoulder, I followed along a muddy brook that wound through the camp, looking for a meal. Men who had only water to drink followed me with their eyes. It was strangely quiet in that camp. No one joked, few even talked over their scant dinner. This army's humor had run out with its rations long ago.

The brook led me out toward the edge of the camp, half way up the ridge, where fires glowed among the tree trunks in the gathering dusk. There, at last, I caught a whiff of roasting meat and followed my nose until I found the source. Behind some underbrush, three men crouched round a fire where a pair of scrawny fowls sizzled on a spit.

"Hello," I said, "will you have company?"

They leapt up, nearly knocking the chickens into the coals, and made ready to fight for their dinner.

"Gently, friends, gently. I have a cask of ale here to share."

With wary looks they stood back and motioned me to approach. They were an unlovely bunch—their clothes more hole than cloth, and their faces a few shades dirtier than most men's. The smallest of the three, a red, ferret-faced man with quick eyes set close together, did most of the talking for them. He was Bodolf the Noisy, he said, tapping himself on the chest, and these others were his mates, Tostig and Guthrum—all of them Swedes from Vastmanland. "Most of this army is Swedish, stranger, far from home and sorry for it," said The Noisy, "am I right, mates?"

The mates agreed.

Grateful for a fresh audience, even of one, the Noisy told me their sad history while preparations for our dinner were undertaken.

King Olaf, he said, had come through their country at the beginning of the summer, and their own king, who was some dear old mate of his, had loaned him some of his own hirdmen together with leave to sign on anyone else who cared to join up with him. "Well, I mean to say," confided the Noisy, "he promises everyone a bit of roughhouse and plenty of loot at the end of it, don't he mates? So along we come, more fools us. Fetch up those birds now, will you Tostig, before they turn black altogether; there's a good lad."

Tostig, squatting on his heels by the fire, snatched his fingers away with a yelp, and, sucking them loudly, gave his friend an angry look.

"Hasn't much brain," The Noisy apologized. "Guthrum, you do it."

Guthrum whipped a sharp, curved knife from his belt, hooked the two charred bodies safely from the flames, and set to carving them. "They don't go far for four," he grumbled, wiping the blade against his leg.

"'Deed they don't," the Noisy agreed. "But then you're lucky to eat at all in this army, ain't you, mates?"

The mates nodded.

The Noisy proceeded to serve out the portions, saving the biggest for himself. "As long as we was on the Swedish side of the Keel, why, we could plunder as we liked for all Olaf cared. But come us to the Norway side, *his* country, and suddenly we must give up looting, says he, and beg politely of the farmers for our victuals like good Christmen that we are."

"And means it, too," Guthrum added morosely. "It's worth your hands and nose to disobey him."

"Well, let me tell you, stranger, that asking politely has met with small success. Still, we must eat, mustn't we? So we take our chances and scoop up a chicken or a hare wherever we can, for not everyone can live on 'God will provide' as friend Olaf does. Mind you, there's plenty o' that—he and his bishop push it at you every morning, but it don't really fill a man up, does it?"

"No," Guthrum agreed, "you get a bit peckish by noon."

"Friends," I smiled, "you don't talk much like Christmen."

"Oh, we've been dipped," replied The Noisy, "but I tell you"—his ferret's eyes narrowed—"there's a-plenty here what haven't been and don't give half a damn for his priests and his Latin and what-not."

"None of us do," Guthrum agreed, reaching for the keg. "All we've had so far is three weeks' hard climb up one side of the Keel and down t'other, and sleeping out under our shields every night, and a lot of promises that haven't been kept. There's men deserting every day. We won't stick it much longer."

"Promises such as—?"

"Such as that his own people would flock to join him. Mighty few have. A few hundred, maybe, under his kinsman, Dag Hringsson, and a few hundred more that his half-brother—'Little Harald' as we call him—brought up from the south last week. There's a one for you, Little Harald, have you seen him yet? Well, he's hard to miss. Tall as a bleeding mast, he is—that's why we call him 'Little'. Fifteen year old but carries himself like he had twice the age on him."

"And," added Guthrum, "if you ask me, there's no love lost between him and Olaf either. Keeps separate quarters on t'other side of camp, struts around the place like he was king himself. Talk is, he fights for his brother's throne just to have it nice and warm for his own precious ass one of these days."

This fit well with what I'd already seen.

We concentrated on the food for a while. The two chickens quickly disappeared, and the keg went several times around.

"Ooh, this is prize stuff, this is!" The Noisy beamed, drawing his grimy sleeve across his lips. He was getting drunk. "Nidaros Town must be a lovely place judging by the looks of you, friend. Very handsome you are, very handsome indeed." He ran a greasy thumb over the sleeve of my scarlet tunic. "New?"

"Not anymore." I gripped his hand and bent it backward.

"Ouch! Hold on—hold on! We *are* touchy." He massaged his wrist while looking reproachfully at me. "Didn't know we was having the bleeding nobility to dinner."

"I'm not in the best of moods."

"Well—no harm done."

His two friends, who looked ready to spring at me, settled back on their haunches.

"I believe I will just have another sup of your ale, though, if I might. I do relish it."

"Keep the keg," I said, standing up, "and thanks for the conversation. Time for sleep."

"Bed down here, if you like," murmured The Noisy with a thin-lipped smile.

"No thanks." Not and have my throat cut in the night for my clothes.

"Well then, 'til tomorrow, friend."

What now? I wondered, as I picked my way down the ridge in the dark. Try to reason with Kalf? Tell him that Olaf is dreaming, that Christ himself couldn't put the spirit back in this army? At the moment I couldn't face the thought of it. And like as not, he and Ogmund were still praying with the king. Anyway, time enough tomorrow.

I chose a bit of empty ground, built myself a small fire, and rolled up in my cloak. Weary and depressed, I slept fitfully, half expecting my father might visit me in a dream, for if ever I needed help, it was now.

But he didn't.

19

CHRISTMEN, CROSSMEN, KINGSMEN

The war horn's blare, shrill as the bray of a wild ass, shattered the dawn and sent clouds of meadow birds beating up in fright from the tall grass.

All around me, men sat up, knuckling their eyes and groping in the half-light for their arms. Bjorn the Marshall, a hard-bitten old warrior, scarred with the combat of many years, ran past me up the wooded ridge, shouting orders to the Swedes to move down to a position in front of the palisade on the king's left flank.

The jarls with a great force of heathen farmers—the word traveled from mouth to mouth—were reported by our scouts to be marching through the woods from the direction of Nidaros.

No one had looked for them so soon.

"Up, you Swedish oxen, up!" cried the Marshall, racing from campfire to campfire and striking right and left with the flat of his sword.

"Ouch! Here! Mind who you're hitting with that!" Faintly in the distance, I heard my friends of last night.

"How soon will they be on us?" called someone.

"Before the sun's well over the treetops," answered the breathless Bjorn.

Less than an hour! I must find Kalf, talk to him ... do something!

I ran down the ridge, making straight for the king's banner. If Kalf had spent the night praying with Olaf, I should find him there somewhere.

All around the banner was confusion. The Norwegians running this way and that to form the shield-wall around their king, while Olaf himself stamped about, shouting orders that couldn't be heard above the general uproar.

He cut a splendid figure, though. Now, over yesterday's filthy tunic, shone a coat of mail that hung to his knees, cinched with a belt of heavy bronze rings. On his head was a gilded helmet, and from his shoulder a snow-white shield swung, embossed, like his banner, with a cross of gold. For a damned fool, he was a fine looking man, no denying it.

Calling Kalf's name, I shouldered my way through the massed ranks of spearmen until, at last, I caught sight of him and Ogmund behind the shield wall, standing in a mob of archers and stone throwers.

"Odd," he cried when he saw me running toward him. "Thank God!"

I didn't let him finish. Hardly slowing down, I seized hold of his arm and pushed him ahead of me, "Kalf, follow me out of here, we're deserting this pack of lunatics while there's still time. Pot-Belly, you can do as you please."

But Kalf wrenched himself away from me. I wasn't dismayed. I had struggled and pleaded in just the same way when he held me back from drowning myself.

"It's all right, brother, you'll soon be yourself again, just trust to me."

"Odd, I prayed to God last night to change your heart."

"Don't try my temper, brother. I know you're half mad."

"I'm Christ's soldier. If you call that mad, I ... I pity you."

"Idiot! Your king's nothing but a bloody monster, and soon to be a dead one, I'm glad to say. I won't let you waste your life for him. That's the only reason I'm here. Now do as I say, Kalf."

"No, Odd. I'll do God's will, not yours. Stand out of my way."

We were toe-to-toe, screaming at each other above the din.

I forced my anger down. "Slender-Leg, listen. Don't believe what Olaf says. He's doomed, and you with him, if you stay. Now come!"

He looked at me then with such contempt as I never hope to see again on the face of friend or enemy. "Run away, Odd. Isn't that how you treat your brothers? I should have expected it. Yes, run away and tell everyone how we died here. You're a poet. You'll tell it well. Run, Odd—run away."

All the world fell away.

A great silence seemed to engulf us for that moment while we stared into each other's eyes. It wasn't pain we saw there now, as when we'd first quarreled. No room now for pangs of sympathy. It was scorn in his eyes, hate in mine.

Oh yes. At that moment I hated him more, I think, than I have ever hated anyone—and that's saying a good deal, for I'm a lusty hater, as you know. The little psalm-singing bastard! He knew he had the power to shame me, to break me—and he used it. If he had held a dagger to my heart and thrust home, it would have been kinder.

I hardly know what words I said in answer, but they were halting, and abject. I was beaten. I owed Kalf my life twice over and he was calling in the debt. Not for me to ask, why now and why here? He had the right, that was all. Well then, so be it. Let one madness swallow us both. Let us both die for bloody Olaf and his god!

Ogmund, who had listened with great agitation to our speech, laid a hand on each of us and shouted above the uproar, "To the king's side!"

So back we pushed through the shield-castle. Its ranks were in disarray now anyway, though we could not see why until we stood within sight of the royal banner. What we saw and heard there was yet another loud and bitter clash of wills, this one of more consequence to history.

"Get you back! This is no work for boys, damn your head—not even weeds like you. Get back behind the palisade."

Olaf was in a thundering rage. Within a ring formed by the hirdmen and other warriors from the ranks, he bellowed in the face—more accurately, in the chest—of a youth who overtopped him by a full head.

There was no mistaking the family likeness. Though where Olaf's face was shaggy, this one's was smooth as a baby's. Where the king's body was thick in the waist, young Harald's—for it was surely he, whom the Noisy had described to me last night—was like a sapling. His tunic and trousers were too short on him, as though he grew faster than his mother could weave.

He was a handsome youth, his regular features marked with only one peculiarity, that one of his eyebrows sat higher on his forehead than its mate. This gave to his face a mocking expression that went well with his words.

"You think me too weak to hold a sword, brother? Then, tie it to my hand, for in God's name I will fight today, whether it please you or not. You don't command me and my men!"

"*Your* men!" The veins bulged on Olaf's neck and the square chin jutted dangerously. "Your men!"

"Let him stay, King, let him fight," the men of the hird pleaded, pressing round them both. "Hold a sword? Christ, he can bend one double with his bare hands! Don't shame your own mother's son." Anxiety showed plainly on all their faces. This quarreling among their leaders was an ill omen.

"I do it for our mother's sake," Olaf rounded on them. "That she not risk both her sons on one day's luck."

"Oh, brother of mine," said Harald with a sneer, "tell these honest warriors the truth. It's not our mother's sorrow but envy that pricks you. Must none have glory so that you can have it all?" (I should say here that I never understood what began the bitterness between these half-brothers. In later years, Harald would never speak of it, even drunk, although he kept little else from me.)

"My lords, this is neither wise nor seemly." Out of the crowd beside them stepped a man of middling age, slightly built, with a high forehead and fine features. His clothes, though worn, retained something of elegance, and his manner was easy. I recalled seeing him yesterday in the lean-to. "Come and give up this snarling like two dogs at the same dish." He looked from one to the other. "Kiss now or you will displease God and ruin our cause."

"Yes, King, kiss him—" those men who were close enough to have heard these words took up the cry, "—and God save you both!"

While Harald turned his mocking eyebrow to them, Olaf looked murder. But seeing that they would not desist, he flung up his arm at last and snarled, "Heaven forbid I should injure God's cause. Take your place in the shield-wall, Harald Sigurdarson, and thank your kinsman, Dag, for it."

"A kiss, a kiss!" clamored the men, not yet reassured.

So, the two embraced for a bare second while the Norwegians cheered, and hard-bitten warriors grew moist-eyed at this spectacle of brotherly affection. A few in the crowd, too, shouted, "Dag! Dag Hringsson!" But this made that elegant peacemaker frown, and he waved them to silence.

"Back to your ranks, you men!" shouted Bjorn the Marshall. "Only the king's hirdmen in the shield-wall, the rest of you to the front."

There came the sound of a horn faintly across the field and, while we watched, the enemy's vanguard broke from the distant trees and raced, leaping and yelling towards us, halting just little more than a bowshot away.

Behind these skirmishers rode the jarls on prancing horses with their standard bearers and their hirdmen running beside them.

A javelin rose high in the air, catching the sunlight on its quivering point. It seemed for a moment to hang there, motionless, then fell slowly back. The rider who had thrown it wheeled and galloped forward, leaning so far back in his saddle that his shoulders touched his horse's crupper. Catching the spear in an outstretched hand, flung it up again. We could hear the hurrahs of his men.

"Thorir Hound," Ogmund spat. "See the greyhound on his banner. He wears a magic shirt of reindeer hide from Lapland that no iron can pierce—and calls himself a Christman."

I thought, ruefully, of the noaidi. Could I have gotten such a shirt for myself, if I'd only thought to ask?

Ogmund pointed out more banners as they came into view—the dragon of Kalv Arnesson, the raven of Haarek of Tjotta, and many others, until the whole field was a-flutter with them.

Standing in our ranks, we watched more farmers pour onto the plain and heard the shouts of their captains as they formed them into the 'swine array'—a wedge whose point is like a pig's snout. As fast as the wedges could be formed, still more men filed from the wood. It was later said that twelve thousand warriors, from Rogaland in the south to Halogoland in the north, had gathered for this fight—the biggest army ever brought together in Norway and four times the size of ours.

Horns blew from everywhere in the field, and from our side came an answering blast.

Now it comes, I thought. Our only hope is to charge them before they're ready.

Suddenly I had to piss. I untied my breeches and did it where I stood, as others did, too—in another minute there wouldn't be time.

But no. First, Olaf must rouse us with a speech. Four strong men raised him up on his shield where he could be seen by the whole army.

"Brothers," he cried, "for this hour, God has prepared me. I mean not to leave this field unless I am the victor." This was greeted with cries of "Olaf!" and "Victory!" from the men of the shield-wall. "We are Christ's army. And every man of you is now to mark a cross on his helmet, as I have done on mine, and is to kneel and say his Paternoster, if he knows it.

And,"—he looked over our heads to where the Swedes were marshaled on the far left—"and if there are men here who are unbaptized, and I know there are some, I tell you that you must take the sacrament here and now or leave my side. God forbid a heathen should stand in the ranks of God's army on this day!"

The cheering was suddenly much thinner. On the left there was silence. The Swedes lowered their weapons and looked at one another. At that moment I began to be truly afraid.

Olaf's whole army numbered not more than three thousand men, of whom two out of every three were Swedes—and easily half of them heathen. These, now nine hundred or a thousand strong, went apart right there on the field with the enemy breathing in our faces, and proceeded to argue with each other about how they should answer this extraordinary order.

By degrees, they separated themselves into two groups—the smaller of which, four hundred or so, came back and fell into line, greeted with cheers from our side. The rest, including the wildest fighters that Olaf had, ran straight across the field to join the enemy, who waved their banners up and down when they saw them coming.

Odin help us, I thought, he's just killed us all.

For the next hour, while the sun beat on us out of a cloudless sky and the jarls' army grew larger and louder, we stood under arms as our Swedish comrades, in batches of fifty at a time, splashed uncomprehendingly in the muddy stream to the accompaniment of Bishop Grimkel's Latin spells.

The mass baptism being at last completed, we were all ordered to our knees to pray and receive a blessing. Lean-faced Grimkel, wearing his armor under his chasuble, walked up and down the ranks, flanked by acolytes, sprinkling us with holy water. I gritted my teeth when the droplets touched me. What would Olaf think if he knew that there was still one unbaptized head ready to fall for him? Then Bjorn the Marshal bawled at us to stand and look to our weapons.

At last! I tightened my grip on my shield and spear. Kalf, on my right hand, tested his bowstring while Ogmund flexed his plump and sweating fingers around the haft of his ridiculous great axe. I waited, holding my breath, for the trumpet's blast that would fling us forward.

Not yet.

Olaf had one final thing to do before he would join battle, and it made me think that he was not, perhaps, an utter fool after all.

He ordered the shield wall to part and let Thormod, the greatest of his skalds, pass through to the front. "Skald," he cried, "you are old, but your throat is silver, and your mind is clear water. I will give you a ring from my arm whose worth is the price of twenty cows, if you can sing us into battle with some ancient song of heroes."

Two hundred paces away stood the enemy in their bristling wedges, while the jarls cantered up and down before them. No time! I wanted to shout.

But Thormod, as if minutes and hours meant nothing to one whose memory stretched back time out of mind, bowed stiffly to the king and took up his place before us, carefully arranging the folds of his cloak over his left arm. He might have been a king himself to look at him, hawk-faced and straight as a spear.

The air was suddenly so still that you could hear the crickets stirring in the hot meadow grass. On the other side, too, fell a hush when they saw that he was going to sing, even though they were too far away to hear his words.

He sang the *Lay of Bjarki* (my father had taught it to me years ago), which tells how Bjarki and Hjalti, the two champions, died fighting for their king when foemen sacked his hall. No man can listen to it and not be stirred.

What a puzzle is this Olaf, I recall thinking while Thormod sang. This pious viking who won't let a heathen fight for him and yet loves the old poetry which, as everyone knows, is Odin's gift to men.

From where I stood I could see him, if I turned my head, still as a statue, only his helmeted head nodding to the cadence of the song. And well he knew that every man in the army would fight the better for hearing this song. There is no wine like poetry—holy water and Latin are thin stuff in comparison.

Soon strutting ravens rend apart our limbs (Thormod chanted)
and greedy eagles on our corpses feed,
but high-souled, hardy hero it befits
to dying, dwell by king who's rich in deeds.
The last words hung shimmering in the charged air.

"Odd, brother? Will you die for our king, rich in deeds?" murmured Kalf in a voice choked with feeling. It only made me hate him more.

"Rot your king," I said between my teeth. "I die for you, damn you, and I call the account balanced between us."

What a look of pain on his pious altar boy's face! His next words I didn't catch, they were drowned out by the war horn's bray. Once, twice, three times.

"Bowmen to the rear!" shouted Bjorn, and Kalf turned to go.

Above the scream of the horns rang Olaf's voice, "Onward Christmen, Crossmen, Kingsmen!"

And we roared back, clashing our spears against our shields. The shield-wall lurched forward. We began to walk, to trot, to race—breathless, mindless, wild with battle joy—toward death.

20

A DEADLY SECRET

All the world knows what happened at Stiklestad—or thinks it does. Some of what you hear is nonsense—the sun did not hide his face at noon—but people love to invent stories like that when a great killing happens, as if the truth were not grim enough.

Across the field we raced. A flight of arrows hit us aslant and men twisted and screamed, clutching their throats.

Our archers returned fire, sending volley after volley over our heads. Then, with a shock and a roar, we flung ourselves against their spears, like a wave breaking against rocks, recoiling on itself, dissolving into eddies and whirlpools of men who stumbled this way and that. On every side of me, armor clattered and men groaned. The press of bodies was so great that dead men stood upright with no room to fall. The foeman who faced me struck overhand with his spear, aiming for my neck. I parried with the rim of my shield and returned the blow with my spear, piercing him through the eye. Another took his place. This one raised his axe above his head with both hands, intending to split me like a stick of firewood. A bad mistake. I buried my spear in his groin. But as he fell he snapped the haft, leaving me holding a splintered stick.

Out of the tail of my eye I saw a scythe blade flash up and down, sending a head spinning into the air—a farmer mowing us down like wheat-stalks. I drew my sword and when he swung his arms back for another stroke, darted round behind him and severed his backbone.

"Up and follow me!" yelled someone ahead, hewing a hole with his axe in the enemy's line. Shouting Olaf's name, we poured in after him. But we were five ranks deep and they were twelve. To the cry of "On farmers!" they pressed us back over the blood-slick grass. Ogmund had been beside me a moment before; I couldn't see him now.

Those were the first few minutes.

We had not joined battle until the sun was high in the sky, and it was hours since we had last eaten or drunk. Now, toiling under a fierce July sun, hunger and thirst began to tell on us. We charged, fell back, charged again—but fewer each time and weaker—while our arms ached and our sweat blinded us.

My new shield was soon hacked to splinters. I threw it away and fought with my sword, two-handed. Putting myself at the front of every charge, I rushed to wherever the fighting was fiercest, reckless of my life, meaning to spite Kalf by dying. But though I faced man after man, death eluded me that day.

When the sun was well past his zenith and our dead lay upon the ground in heaps, the king's horn sounded behind us. I glanced over my shoulder to see Olaf himself, with his standard bearer and his skalds all around him, pushing through our ragged line to fight at last in the van and give us heart for one last effort. From where I stood in the crush of battle, the banners of the jarls that fluttered in different parts of the field seemed to turn, swoop, and dive on Olaf's white banner like falcons on a swan.

By this time, the battle was already lost. The Swedish freebooters on our left, who'd had no stomach for the fight to begin with, were in full retreat, while on our right the contingent of Norwegians that served under Dag Hringsson, the king's kinsman, had been outflanked and was being cut to pieces. With both flanks gone, the shield-wall was surrounded. Though we fought for every foot of ground, the farmers drove us steadily back.

A red-faced, sweating farmer charged at me, swinging a gnarled tree root, his only weapon. My shield was gone, my sword somehow entangled with another man's axe.

If he had hit me square on the head, he would have brained me. As it was, the cudgel glanced off my helmet but landed hard on my right shoulder. I sank down, dizzy with pain. I expected my deathblow in the next moment, but when I raised my eyes, the fellow had vanished in the swirling swordstorm.

I discovered that I wanted to live after all, and began to drag myself along the ground through a forest of legs. Choking and blinded by the dust, I had no notion which way I was headed. I broke through the leg-forest into a momentary clearing, where Olaf's white banner stood. Just as I wiped the dust and sweat from my eyes, the young standard-bearer who held it went down with a sword cut across his face, and Olaf himself reached out to keep his banner from falling.

At the same instant, an axe-man ran up and chopped off the king's left leg at the knee. He groaned and fell on his side. Two of his skalds—one of them that Thormod who had sung so beautifully in the morning—flung themselves on his body, but rough hands dragged them off and slew them.

The jarls and their men ringed Olaf now. He lifted his arms and called the name of Christ just as Thorir (of the magic shirt) rammed him through the belly with his spear so hard that the ring mail burst apart. Kalv Arnesson, for good measure, hewed halfway through this neck. A geyser of blood shot out, and the square, brown head fell over on his shoulder. The face, I thought, looked surprised.

There was a moment of stunned silence. Then, with a howl, both sides flung themselves on the king, desperate to possess his bleeding carcass. Thorir tried to drag it off by one foot, while the king's men hauled the other way. Harald, the 'unnatural weed', as Olaf had called him that morning, yelling mightily and swinging his long sword in humming circles around his head, drove Thorir back on his heels and stood astride his brother's body—but not for long. The enemy drove at him from every side.

The young giant fought like a boar cornered by a pack of dogs. One man he opened from breastbone to groin. He hewed the arm from another and shook a third man off his back with a twitch of his broad shoulders. But even so, he was soon overwhelmed. With the others who chose to die beside their king, he went down in a tangle of bloody arms and legs, battered shields, and broken spears.

Now the battle became a rout. With their king dead, there was no army left at all, but only a mob of beaten men desperate to save their lives.

"Into the trees!" yelled someone beside me. I needed no urging. I raced with the others back the way we had come—to the palisade, to the muddy stream, to the wooded ridge. Hundreds died with spears between their shoulder blades. The worst killing in a battle always happens that way.

The young giant fought like a boar cornered by a pack of dogs.

As I neared the tree line, I caught sight of a warrior racing before me—and here's a thing you won't find recounted in The *Lay of Bjarki*, or any heroic poem: He was going so fast that as he ran between a pair of trees his long kite-shield, which was slung cross-wise on his back, caught between the trunks and stuck fast, and there he hung, flailing his arms and crying for someone to save him. No one stopped. It is such little incidents as these that we skalds neglect to mention. As I passed the man, I saw it was Bodolf the Noisy. I don't know what became of him, nor do I care.

The farmers at our heels were shouting fit to split their lungs, but then, over the uproar, rose a scream that came from no human throat.

"Christ!" panted a man running beside me, "they're setting wolves on us!"

I looked wildly round to see what pursued us. It was a thing hardly human, a figure, naked but for a wolf pelt wrapped around its blood-smeared body, that howled and bared its teeth as it ran along.

And standing in its path, too petrified to move, was Kalf Slender-Leg! How we found ourselves together among all those fleeing men I cannot say. You Christmen will doubtless give the credit to God. I say only that the Norns love to play such tricks.

Kalf had an arrow fitted to his bowstring. At the last possible second he loosed it, but it flew high—the first time I'd ever seen him miss. An instant later, the monster swung its broadax in a flat arc, catching him in the hip with a crunch of bone, as when a butcher hacks off the leg of a steer. Kalf spun and fell on his face, his left leg splayed outward at a crazy angle to his body.

The berserker—for it must be that—staring straight ahead out of white eyes and swinging his axe from side to side, bounded forward, passing within a pace of where I cowered on the ground.

Numb with shock, I crawled to Kalf's side while fleeing men stumbled over me, got his limp body across my shoulders, and staggered up the ridge. Ahead of us, the berserker's scream rang out again. I stumbled deep into the underbrush before I finally sank down exhausted under Kalf's weight.

He lay without moving on a mat of pine needles, whey-faced, his heart fluttering in his breast like a bird's. The mail shirt he wore was buried three fingers deep in his hipbone. That was all that had kept the leg from being severed completely. I pulled the steel links away, slit open his tunic and the leg of his breeches, and laid bare a gaping bloody mouth of a wound with slivers of white bone showing through where the hip socket had been.

I wadded up his tunic and pressed it against the wound. He came to, gasping and clawing up the earth with his fingers, and crying aloud to Sancta Maria to save him. I struggled against his frantic strength while holding my hand over his mouth for fear the enemy would hear him. They were around us everywhere.

He fell into unconsciousness again after a time. I tore my cloak into strips to bind him up—over the hip, between the legs, around the waist, and over again—and twisted the knot tight with a stick.

Having done what I could, I fell back, nearly fainting myself. Only now was I conscious, again, of the pain in my right shoulder where the cudgel had struck me. I could scarcely lift my arm.

My only hope of saving us was to reach the dinghy. But it was impossible to skirt the battlefield all the way round under cover of the trees to where we had hidden it. I could never carry Kalf that far, even with two good shoulders. No. We must wait for dusk and go straight across the field in the open.

The sun inched across the lattice of pine boughs overhead for four, maybe five hours until it stopped just above the horizon. It would sink no lower. All around me the woods echoed with the shouts of farmers hunting us down and with the cries of the wounded. Gradually, these sounds grew less as the survivors crawled away or died, and the farmers gave up the chase. Finally, a deep silence covered all.

Blood still oozed from Kalf's wound, and bubbles of saliva gathered at the corners of his mouth. His skin was as cold as stone.

Why burden yourself with him? said a small voice inside me. You tried already to save his life, and for thanks, he threw Gunnar's death in your face and called you a coward. And if he dies now—as he surely will—he has only himself to blame. Save yourself while you can.

I shook my head wearily. I hadn't the strength to calculate all these rights and wrongs. I looked at him with bitterness in my heart and knew, at the same time, that I would not leave him there to die alone.

Of such contradictions are we made.

☦

Kalf groaned once as I picked him up and started with him, half walking, half sliding down the ridge onto the bloody killing ground of Stiklestad. No amount of carnage that I have witnessed since dims the memory of that sight. Everywhere were bodies—some still living, though covered by heaps of dead—and blood-reek hung heavy in the air. In place of the jarls' great host, a different army now held the field: dark figures scuttling through the violet dusk, bent low among the corpses, fingering them.

Some ancient crone came at me out of the shadows, loose-haired like a troll hag, with a knife in one bony hand and a bloodstained sack in the other in which to put finger-rings, arm-rings, ear-rings—and the flesh, too, if the rings couldn't be gotten off otherwise.

The merchants of Nidaros would have new wares to show in a few days' time! I spat at her, and she darted away.

At the stream, I flung Kalf down and plunged my head into the filthy water and drank. Cupping my hands, I tried to pour a little between his parted lips but it all ran out at the corners of his mouth. *He was dead!* No, not yet. Pressing my ear to his lips, I could still feel the faint stirring of his breath.

Here at the stream the slaughter had been fiercest. Bodies clogged the narrow channel and lay heaped two and three deep on its banks. Slippery pools of blood made the ground a quagmire where feet had churned it. More than human scavengers were busy here. The crows, with raucous conversation, had already settled to their dinner, and far off, I heard the cough of wild dogs and the distant interest of wolves.

With Kalf in my arms, I waded down into the blood-warm water, the mud sucking at my shoes, and pushed him up onto the farther bank. And there I noticed a certain body on its back, mouth gaping and dead eyes staring. His big axe lay beside him on the ground, and his soft hands clutched the broken shaft of a spear that protruded from his round potbelly—his *belly*, not his back. Ogmund *was* a fighter, after all.

The crow that perched on his chin looked up at me and spread its sable wings. Then deciding that I was nothing to be feared, it sank its beak again into his eye. How often in verses have I sung of crows and vultures feasting off some dead hero's corpse. Believe me, there is nothing heroic about it. I lay with my cheek on the sticky grass until I could swallow again.

We reached the trees, at last.

I felt my way among them, step by step on trembling legs, following the sound of the water lapping the shore.

When I thought that I must be near the spot, I leaned Kalf against a tree and began the search for our dinghy. We had pushed it down in a muddy little hollow and covered it with pine boughs. What a clever fellow I was to have thought of that! I could be standing a hand's breadth away from the cursed thing now and not know it.

In fact, I found it after some anxious minutes by stumbling over it and nearly breaking my shin.

I lay Kalf beside it, put my good shoulder against the bow and pushed. Then braced myself and shoved again with both arms, holding my breath against the pain. Panting and dizzy, I sank to my knees and lay my head against the gunnel. *I'll just rest a little,* I thought. *I'm strong enough ... I can do it.* But I couldn't do it. I hadn't moved the boat an inch.

No wonder then, that in my desperate state I heard nothing until I felt the prick of a blade on my neck and heard a hoarse voice behind me say, "In the king's name, we'll have this boat of yours."

There was an instant of pure panic before my mind began to work. "The king is dead, God help his soul," I said, crossing my breast.

"That's as may be. Stand up and turn around."

There were four of them. Three stood back where I could barely make them out against the dark trunks of the trees, but the one who had spoken lowered his point and leaned close, staring into my face. I stared back.

I got the impression of a large, rough-hewn fellow with heavy brows and a pushed-in nose, who was dressed all in sheepskins, like a farmer.

"Where were you going?" the hoarse voice asked.

"Nidaros, comrade, and—"

"Nidaros? You haven't got the Tronder speech.

"I'm an Icelander, but...."

"But you fought for our king?"

"My friend and I have nearly died for him."

"What friend is that?" His eyes darted nervously. I pointed to Kalf on the ground.

"Well, your friend may yet have to die. Our cargo is more precious than yours, and there isn't room for both. If the boat we're waiting for ever comes, tell them Thorgils said to take you where you want to go."

"And if it never comes?"

"Too bad—"

Before he could raise his blade, I had him by the arm and stepped in close with my knife, pressing just above his belt buckle.

"You must kill me first, and before you do I'll make enough noise to bring down every heathen within a mile of here."

His companions leapt forward with their swords drawn. I saw the glint of their helmets and mail coats, well-equipped warriors, all three. But then, who was this shaggy farmer to speak so bold?

With my sword arm useless for a fight, I hadn't a chance against them. I drew a breath to carry out my threat, even if it cost us all our lives. But they stopped short.

Th-Th-Thorgils," said one. "Leave him be. We c-c-can't risk it."

"Listen to your thick-tongued friend, Thorgils."

The farmer's arm muscle bunched under my fingers. He was no weakling.

I must win them over now. "Show me this precious cargo of yours," I said, standing back from him and speaking in an easy voice. "Short of leaving my comrade to die, I'm at your service."

"So," he grunted after a moment's rumination. "But you'll do our business first, damn you, before you do your own. Understood? Bring him." This, to the three companions.

They disappeared among the trees and returned in a moment, laboring under the weight of a body wrapped head and foot with blankets, obviously dead.

"This is the precious cargo—a useless corpse?"

"Shut up," Thorgils snarled. "You'll never launch this boat without our help, brave boy, and you know it. We'll put in her what we please, and you'll ask no questions."

Pushing altogether then, we got the dinghy up out of the hollow and into the water, and laid the two bodies in the bottom. With this bulky, shrouded carcass wedged in next to Kalf, it was plain that there was not room enough for all the rest of us.

Tense looks went round until the man with the stammer said, "Y-Y-You must go, Thorgils. You know the place. We'll f-find our way back."

The farmer turned on me angrily. "All right, get in and rig your sail, brave boy. Then sit forward, keep quiet, and pray."

When all was ready, the three warriors, standing thigh-deep in the water, steadied the boat as he climbed in after me and settled himself by the tiller stick. A night breeze rocked us and carried us slowly out on the dark waters of the fjord.

"G-Go with God, Thorgils," came the stammerer's voice from far away.

✝

We drifted through the grey night in the shadow of the trees with only a faint moon above us. Though I struggled to stay awake, the monotonous slap of water against the bow, the exhaustion of battle, and the giddiness of hunger soon put me in a kind of trance. But farmer Thorgils, though he must have been as tired as I, seemed immune to sleepiness. Throughout the whole long night, I never saw him yawn or shake himself—or move at all except to push the tiller stick and swing the boom around to catch the wind.

Once he spoke, when Kalf stirred and moaned—jarring me from restless sleep.

"Your friend makes too much noise. Sounds travel on the water."

"Your friend's quiet enough," I said.

"Quiet? One day, by God, you'll hear him shout."

"What sort of riddle is that, Thorgils?"

But he would say no more.

Just before dawn he brought us in to shore, dropping the sail and sculling the dinghy to a shallow place where a lightning-cleft tree leaned out over the water. Reaching up, he threw a line around one of its branches.

"Get out."

"Where are we?"

"Five miles or so above the town." Pushed by a breeze that blew steadily from the northeast, we had covered in a few hours nearly the same distance that had cost us more than two days going up. "I need you for half an hour, then go your way."

"My friend won't live another half hour."

"That matters not to me."

I made a lunge for him, but pain made me clumsy. His sword flashed out and pointed at Kalf's throat.

"Cause me trouble and I promise you, this one'll stay here till the wolves find him. That's better. Now lift my man out, while I steady us, and lay him on the bank ... gently."

Shivering in the icy water, I pulled and tugged at the lifeless thing. "He's too heavy for me. Lend a hand, can't you?"

"Oh no, brave boy, I've seen your tricks with a knife, you'll do it."

I strained again and got him halfway over the side when the blanket that covered his head and shoulders slipped, and I saw his face. I glanced away as quickly as I could and fumbled the cover back over him, but I was certain Thorgils had seen it.

With a final heave, I slung him up onto the bank.

"Well done, brave boy. Now, just you take his shoulders and I will hold him round the knees. Go where I tell you."

We trudged with our burden up a wooded slope. As we emerged from the trees, I heard the sound of water, and Thorgils said, "Lay him down."

We were on the sandy bank of the Nid, where it flows down from the hills and bends toward Nidaros.

"Why couldn't you have buried him at Stiklestad?"

"Because this bit of land is on my property. Here I can watch over him. Start digging."

"What with, dammit?"

"With your helmet, your fingernails—the sand is soft, the grave needn't be deep."

"I'll dig with my sword."

But again he was too quick for me. "Keep it in its scabbard, brave boy." He allowed himself a half-smile and thrust his own blade into the ground. "I'll dig with mine."

So we set to work—Thorgils loosening the soil and I, on hands and knees, scooping it into the river.

The man was a puzzle to me, and I can't resist a puzzle.

"I suppose you're not a popular man with your neighbors, Farmer Thorgils."

"My woman and I keep to ourselves. I've a strong arm so the others give us no trouble."

"And what makes you wiser than they?"

He looked at me in surprise. "That's a funny thing for a Christman to say. We're not wiser than the others, only more blessed."

"Of course, I only meant—"

"It was seven years ago it happened. At the midsummer sacrifice." I had set off some train of memory in him; I think he got few chances to tell his story. "We were standing in the grove where the sacrificed men hang from the trees,"—he crossed himself and spat to avert the bad luck of naming those evils— "when, all of a sudden, my woman fell down and rolled in the dirt, scratching her cheeks and puking. Later, when the fit passed off, she couldn't tell us why. After that, she never knew a peaceful day. I took her to the priest of Thor. I took her to a witch—nothing gave her ease.

"At last, I carried her in my wagon to Nidaros, she struggling all the while and biting her lips till they bled. I was at my wit's end. I marched right into his hall—he was hearing petitions that day and a great crowd had gathered—and laid her at his feet. 'King,' I said, 'some say you have the touch. Prove it on my poor woman's body.'

"He didn't want to, at first, but after he'd prayed a while, he put out his hand and touched her forehead. My woman began to scream that she was on fire—it was the demon in her that screamed, of course, burnt by his touch. She thrashed and threw herself about, but he kept his hands on her until she fainted. When she woke up she was herself again, and wondered how she came to be in a strange lord's hall. There and then I swore to repay him if ever I could. Now I keep my promise."

"King Olaf really did that, Thorgils?"

"He did."

"It's too bad then, that most of your countrymen give him no credit for it."

He shrugged. "God has his time for everything. Meantime, we wait and keep his precious body safe. Heaven forbid that that head should hang on Thorir Hound's wall and that flesh feed his dogs."

I replied with a hearty "Amen."

"But, I wonder," I said, "that the wicked heathens didn't take him when they had the chance. I saw him fall, you know, just before we ran."

"Before *you* ran. Some of us were knocked down where we stood, and some of us lay still until the enemy were past."

"But the jarls?"

"Rode off to drink each other's health. They expect to find him in the morning."

"I see. Well, you're a brave man, Thorgils, and that's the truth."

"Enough talk. It's deep enough."

Together we laid the corpse in its shallow grave, heaped up the sand, and set a heavy stone pried from the bank on top of the little mound for a marker.

"Now I will know where to find him when the day of reckoning comes," Thorgils said with satisfaction.

"So will I, you forget."

"I haven't forgotten."

If he meant to kill me he would do it now. I was as ready as I could be.

"If I knew you," he said, kneeling on the grave to scratch a cross on the marker with a bit of flint, "or, at least, your kin. But I don't."

I wasn't prepared for the handful of sand in my face. He followed with a lunge at my knees, taking me down hard. A stab of pain seared my injured shoulder. His hands closed on my throat, the thumbs pressing against my windpipe. I felt like a child in the grip of his strength—my head ready to burst, the light going black.

My knee jerked in a final spasm. He grunted and rolled away, clutching his privates. I swung my fist hard against his chin and fell on him with my knife. The blade grated against a rib going in. When he stopped moving, I pushed him off the bank and stayed long enough to see his head slip under the water.

"Go to Valhalla with your precious king, brave Thorgils," I whispered.

✝

Along the Nidaros wharf the shopkeepers were just giving each other good morning as they threw open their wooden shutters and set out their bolts of sailcloth, their ships' tackle, and their trinkets for the day's trade.

Only a handful of other folk were up and about: a fresh-faced country lass with her egg basket on her arm; a stout ship's captain hunting up his crew; a sailor, stinking of last night's beer, propped in the doorway of the tavern where he'd slept; and a solitary dog that trotted, sniffing hopefully, along a row of sacks.

When they saw me step onto the pier with Kalf's body in my arms, his head falling backward and one arm hanging down, they ran over to me—first the lass, who was nearest, then one, then two, then a dozen of the shop men and their wives.

"From the battle?"

"Yes."

"You're the first. Ain't he the first?"

"Yes, the first."

"Let me pass. My friend—" Friend no longer, but I must call him something.

"Best get another friend. That one's gone."

"Hush. What a thing to say," one of the wives chided. "Give 'im room there, he's ready to fall down himself."

"But who won? Where's the king? Come on, lad, can't you tell us?"

"Dead. The king is dead."

"Dead!" They said the word in hushed voices. "Olaf?" The sound of their voices followed me as I mounted up the winding street to the inn. "Wake up! Wake up! The king is dead!"

The inn door was still locked. I kicked it until feet scuffled within and the bolt slid back. Young Thyri, peeping out, put her fist up to her mouth. Instantly, hands surrounded me—reaching out to take Kalf from me, helping me to a bench.

They laid Kalf on a table, and Stig peeled away the crusted bandages to examine the wound with his practiced eye. Blood still oozed from it, and the flesh all around was black and swollen.

"Should have been washed with wine hours ago. Bergthora, fetch all the wine you have. Send a girl for more, and get me clean cloths and a pair of shears." She ran to get these articles.

"You there, Ketil, blow on the coals and stick a poker in 'em. The wound must be seared before he loses any more blood. Dammit, Odd Tangle-Hair, how *did* it happen?" I heard a tightness in his throat—Stig, whom nothing ever upset.

How did it happen? How had I let it come to this? I sank back on the bench and let the story run out at my lips, only leaving out our quarrel. I couldn't bring myself to speak of that, and said nothing about the business with Thorgils and his mysterious corpse. I felt too weary for that pathetic tale.

"Poor puppy," Bergthora sighed when I told about Ogmund Pot-Belly.

"A bloody shambles," said Stig, shaking his head. "You did what you could, no one could have done more."

Stig thrust the poker into Kalf's wound with a hiss and a smell of burning flesh. Kalf writhed and shrieked and began to shake in all his limbs. Snatching the flagon from Bergthora's hands, Stig splashed wine all over the wound. "Cut me a strip of bandage," he ordered, "and make it well soaked with wine."

"Oh, Stig, it's no use," said Bergthora, wiping her eyes. "Toke!" She called to Ketil's sooty grandson, who slid down from the loft where he'd been watching. "Toke, run to the church. Find *someone*. Kalf's a Christian, and he's dying."

The boy tore out the door. To me she said, hesitatingly, "You don't mind, do you, Odd? It would be a sin not to."

I shrugged and looked away.

Deacon Poppo was a brisk young man, lately arrived from Bremen to be Bishop Grimkel's secretary. Caring nothing for war and still less for the local politics, he had contrived to be absent on the day that the bishop decamped with all his clergy to Stiklestad.

The deacon came in behind Toke and gave us a sympathetic cluck. When he saw the figure on the bench, he knelt at once to begin those spells which the Christmen say for their dead. All the others there, except for Stig and Brodd, knelt beside him with their hands folded under their chins—making between me and my friend-no-more a wall of backs. But in truth, that wall had been there always, hadn't it? It had only now, at the moment of his death, become visible.

I turned and went out into the yard. There I stood, absorbed in sad and angry thoughts, while I watched the clouds roll in from seaward. A fat raindrop fell at my feet making a crater in the dust. A tear for Kalf? Why not? What use to hate him now? He'd been my friend once, the best and truest that I had. Rather hate those Christmen who had stolen him from me—that bishop and his king.

The king! I gave a start as the thought struck fully home. Shaking my head, all muddled with grief and exhaustion, I thought it through again. The body of a dead king is powerful magic, for good or ill. What a joke! How One-Eyed Odin must be laughing! That I, of all people, the unlikeliest man on earth—a stranger, a heathen, the enemy of all he stood for— should find myself now the sole guardian of that man's curious, precious, and perhaps very dangerous secret.

For I alone knew where Olaf was buried.

21

ECHOES OF BATTLE

Maybe it was the wine and the cautery, or perhaps some power in the crucifix that Deacon Poppo placed between Kalf's hands, or maybe even a little magic in the rune stave that I slipped under his bedding when no one was looking. Thanks to any or all of them, Kalf's wound did not turn black and stink. After a week had passed—days and nights filled with his screams and moans—Stig opined cautiously that he would live.

It was generally accounted a miracle.

During those anxious days, he was the constant object of my thoughts. As long as it seemed he would die, I could think that he'd been punished enough, but as his strength returned, then did all my bitterness return with it. He had said things that could never be unsaid, that would rankle in me forever. There need be no open breach, no shouted reproaches for others to hear, but there would be a coolness between us now. Our friendship, as far as I was concerned, was dead.

It was only right that I should feel this way. What man would not? Yet in my heart I felt not so much justified as diminished, as though it were I who had lost a limb.

In time, Kalf's wound healed over, but though he might cling to the nickname 'Slender-Leg' and we oblige him by using it, his swift-footed youth was gone. He would have done better to lose the leg entirely, for a man can get around nimbly enough on one leg and a crutch, but the wound was too high up to allow amputation, and so he must drag this useless limb around with him for the rest of his life. He would never be a sea rover like his father, never stride his home-field sowing barley seed. He was fit for nothing now but to be a hermit.

Eventually, they told him how I had saved his life. He remembered the monster with the axe, but nothing afterwards. He called me to his side and made the others leave us alone. His face was gray, the deep shadows under his eyes purple, like bruises. He tried to speak. I cut him short.

"Kalf Slender-Leg," I said in a low voice, "I am glad to see you alive, but give me no thanks for it. I want none. As for what passed between us, I will say nothing about it, and I hope you will not either, for it does you no credit. I think there's no more to be said."

At that he buried his face in his arm and began to blubber, mumbling the name of Christ between sobs. My father was right: what a womanish religion it is, this Christianity. I turned in disgust and left him. From that day on we seldom spoke.

✝

Bergthora's inn was soon awash with wounded men. They straggled into Nidaros by the hundreds in those first days after the fight—some piled in farmers' carts, some walking alone or leaning on a comrade's shoulder. Many from both armies found their way to her door, and she, with a good heart and a whore's impartiality, took in all alike, and did what she could for them until her hall resembled a hospital more than a pleasure house. The dragon's head from its perch above the doorway watched unblinkingly, the wounded go in and the dead go out.

With so many dead and dying, notice was hardly taken of a certain farmer Thorgils, whose body was found one morning by a fisherman, snagged in a clump of reeds along the riverbank above the town.

✝

There was a general feeling of satisfaction among the Tronders at the outcome of the battle of Stiklestad. The heathen country folk, of course, were jubilant, but even the Christian population of the town felt a quiet relief. In large numbers they had simply ignored the whole affair, not liking to fight against a Christian king, but nevertheless unwilling to support that bullying Southerner.

Their satisfaction was short-lived.

I was loafing about the harbor one morning, a week or so after the battle when the bray of a horn carried to us over the water. All along the wharf, eyes turned seaward.

At first we saw nothing, but then one dragon ship, and then another, and another, came in sight around the headland where the fjord bends, their oars rising and dipping in perfect time, their striped sails bellied in the wind, and their gilded prows flashing. Four vessels in all were racing towards us over the water. The horn rang out a second time, louder.

While we watched in silence, the dragons glided into the royal boat slips, threw out their gangplanks, and emptied their bellies of warriors. And it was no mob of viking raiders who spilled onto the wharf. Obedient to the shouts of their officers, they fell in smartly in four long ranks of sixty men each and stood to attention.

Each man wore a ringmail coat and shouldered a long-handled axe. Their hard eyes glinted through the eyeholes of their visors. Proud, disciplined, richly armed, here were the far-famed Housecarles of Canute the Rich.

From every part of the town, people gathered to the harbor, quietly and with worried looks, to see this sight. The iron faces stared them down, and the iron axes kept them at a distance.

One ship still had not given up its cargo. To the accompaniment of another raucous note of the horn, its gangplank swung out now and a dozen picked men, with swords drawn, raced down to form a double line at its foot. Behind them strode a young warrior, bearing on a staff a standard of white silk with a black raven on it: the ensign of Canute.

But the figure to step over the gunnel was not the mighty king of Denmark, England, and Norway, but rather a short, sharp-faced woman. She descended the gangplank with cautious steps, leaning on a servant's arm, while the Housecarles banged their axes rhythmically against their shields in salute.

Last, came two other persons— one, a bishop in full regalia, the other, a pasty-faced boy of about twelve who kept his eyes on his shoes.

The sharp-faced woman, we very soon learned, was the Lady Alfifa, a minor concubine of Canute's, and the boy, her son, Svein, one of the king's numerous and little-valued bastards. The bishop was one Sigurd, a Danish cleric from England. To these three, we soon learned, the realm of Norway was entrusted. Canute himself could not be bothered to set foot in it.

Out of the crowd bustled Deacon Poppo with energetic clasping of hands to receive our masters. The deacon, I should mention, still represented the Church in Nidaros. Bishop Grimkel, it was reported, was alive but had fled with his clergy to the south to take refuge with Olaf's mother.

Flanked by the Housecarles then, and with Poppo dancing attendance, Alfifa, Svein, and Sigurd marched in state up the winding street from the harbor, while the Tronders fell back to give them way. They did not smile at the Tronders, and the Tronders did not cheer. Squatting on its hill above the town, Olaf's empty hall seemed especially to glower at its unwelcome new tenants.

✝

Within a week of their arrival, our new masters put an end to any doubts about how things now stood between Norwegians and Danes. One wet morning, the ringing of the church bell summoned us to the square where a Danish herald read out to a stunned populace a decree, whose gist was as follows:

New taxes henceforth to be levied on fishing catches and harborage. All Tronder men to be subject to forced labor on the royal estates. In legal disputes the word of one Dane to be counted as equal to that of ten Norwegians. At Yuletide, every household to deliver to the king—the boy Svein was meant—a measure of malt, the leg of an ox, and a pail of butter. And on, and on.

Of course, the people turned angrily to their jarls. And soon the jarls came riding into town. Not for this had they driven the Fat Man from his throne. They would send this hatchet-faced bitch home on the next tide.

The people waited.

But the jarls came out of the king's hall tight-lipped and grim, mounted their horses, kicked them savagely, and rode back to their estates, beaten. Canute, it turned out, held a hostage of every one of them as his 'guest' in England. Alfifa had only to lift her finger....

Soon after that, a surprising thing happened. Or not so surprising, when you thought about it. These same men who had just reddened their hands in Olaf's blood began to whisper to their friends that he had been, after all, a pious man. Indeed, one could go so far as to say he was a holy man, a saint, in fact. Thorir of the magic shirt, who had run his spear through Olaf's body, began it. Kalv Arnesson, who had sawed Olaf's neck, followed suit. Then, almost overnight, one heard it everywhere: a blind man cured with a few drops of the water in which Olaf's wounds had been washed, prayers addressed to him in Heaven promptly answered. He secured health for this man, a safe journey for that one. The testimony multiplied day by day.

In every shop and on every corner, people gathered to recall his saintly life, telling each other in solemn tones—just as Thorgils had told to me—about demons he had exorcised and trolls he had wrestled, and how, wherever he laid his head at night, the elves fled the place, burned by his prayers.

Soon it was hard to find anyone among the Christian population of Nidaros who would admit to ever having been his enemy. Even hard-headed Bergthora finally succumbed, though grudgingly, to the general persuasion.

Our new bishop, Sigurd, so I was told, ranted long and loud against this talk until most of his parishioners refused to hear him and left him alone in his church. If the bishop was any indication, the Danes were worried. Olaf dead was becoming more dangerous to them than Olaf living had ever been.

Kalf, who day and night lay helpless on his back in a dusky corner of the hall, nourished his madness on these stories, which the girls brought back from the marketplace and recited to him by the hour. They were his meat and drink. Certainly, he took little else besides. It astonished me that he could survive on the pitiful ration of water, bread, and vegetables that he allowed himself. Bergthora tried every way she could to feed him manly food, but he was unshakable in this. Plainly, he had set himself to become one of those starveling hermits whom he had heard praised by Bishop Grimkel.

But he was a very popular hermit, and soon became a local hero. The inn was always a place congenial to gossip, and now each night the pious Tronders, and the more pious of my crew as well, would coax the shining tale from him once again. Though he could scarcely speak above a whisper, he made them sigh when he told how saintly Olaf had baptized the heathens in his army, and how he had led them in the charge (which he had not), and how he had died—especially that part.

No doubt Kalf had been somewhere near the scene and witnessed the same events as I. Only he saw them through the eyes of zeal and passion, which made them glow in quite a different light.

Now and again, someone who remembered that I, too, had been there would trouble me for my version, but I gave them shrugs and vague answers, and they soon turned back to Kalf to hear it yet again from his pale lips, until Bergthora would scold them for tiring the boy and chase them away.

"And the king's body?" they would always ask when he had finished. "Never found?"

"No, never found."

"Ahh."

It was commonly known that Olaf's body had vanished from the field—likewise, strangely enough, the body of his giant half-brother Harald. And this mystery only added a further proof to the arguments for his saintliness.

"Angels—God's Valkyries—" they would say, nodding sagely, "have carried him off to Heaven's mead hall where he eats and drinks with Charlemagne, brave Saint George, and all the rest of Christ's warriors."

I listened to this drivel with my secret locked tight behind my teeth. 'Confide in one', the old saying goes, 'never in two. Confide in three and the whole world knows.' I decided to confide in none. A king's body is a dread thing, heavy with magic. If good men like Thorgils could kill to keep it hidden, what might the Danes not do to find it and destroy it? As long as I alone knew Olaf's secret, it could harm no one else. And there was another thing, too, that helped to seal my lips. I feared Thorgils' ghost if I should betray him. That man had been almost too much for me in the flesh.

But all the same the secret weighed heavily on me.

✝

Though he continued to live in a brothel, Kalf made his corner of it into a place that was his alone—where visitors found themselves speaking softly. When the girls offered to sleep with him (this was when the hip had healed as much as it ever would), he only shook his head and smiled kindly. They went away feeling that he had somehow favored them more than if he had taken them to his bed.

He and I, as I have said, rarely spoke, though sometimes he cast long, sorrowful looks at me. They made me so uncomfortable I would leave the room to escape them. Stig, Bergthora, Starkad, and some others asked me what was wrong between us. I told them they were only imagining things.

✝

Winter came on. We passed the brief twilight days and long nights huddled close to the hearth, while the wind roared along the roof and hammered at the walls. Kalf took his first steps, dragging himself up and down the hall, on a crutch that Stig made him, until the sweat, even in that ice-cold room, ran down his face. He was also learning to read. Not runes, but the Latin of the Christmen. Deacon Poppo became a regular visitor to the inn—generally, as I observed, around supper time—and they would crouch together mumbling over their page for an hour or more each night.

I, with nothing to do but eat and drink, felt restless and out of sorts. And more and more, as the days went by, I wondered what I ought to do with myself come spring. I and my crew had made no plans beyond the winter. Should we be honest merchants or should we turn viking? Sail north, south, east, or west? I knew little of what lay beyond the horizon in any direction. Only one thing was fixed in my mind: I would not go home again just to be an outlaw in my own land. The time to settle accounts with Hrut and Snorri was not yet. But in my heart, I began to fear it would never come.

✝

Midwinter's Day arrived, which the Christmen, just as we 'heathen' do, celebrate with bonfires, dancing, and games. They call it Saint Lucy's Day. Stuf and Otkel roused me early in the morning and asked me if I would go with them to the banks of the Nid, where a game of ball was starting up. My shoulder by now, had repaired itself; there were no broken bones, and I was happy to accompany them.

The air was snapping cold and the townspeople, all bundled to the eyes in fur robes and hats, had built fires along the riverbank and set up benches in front of them where they sat, holding mugs of hot ale in mittened hands and cheering the young men out on the ice.

"If only we had skates and clubs," Stuf complained, "we'd show them how Iceland boys play the game."

It wasn't long, though, before the benches began to fill up with injured players, as always happens in a game of ball, and we were able to borrow what we needed to join the game. We tied on the horse bone skates, winding the leather thongs tight around our ankles, and, gripping our clubs like battle-axes, skated out to enlist on the side that seemed to be getting the worst of it.

Crack! The wooden ball skittered across the ice with all of us after it. Bodies collided in bone-crunching melees, and blows were aimed at heads and knees as often as at the ball. I blocked for Otkel, sending two fellows careening off the ice, and he put the ball neatly across their line for a goal. The spectators cheered, and our teammates clapped us on the back. My muscles grew warm, my face glowed, and for a time, I emptied my mind of home, of Kalf, of everything except the whizzing ball and the pounding of my blood.

Before long, though—so soft and lazy had I grown during these idle weeks—I wanted a rest. Leaving my two friends to carry on, I glided off the ice toward one of the bonfires, where I saw a bench that was nearly empty.

Only after I'd sat for a bit, catching my breath and feeling the fire toast my back, did I give attention to the solitary figure who sat, wrapped in an enormous blanket, at the farther end.

"I see you have no skates or club, friend," I said. "Use these if you like, I've had enough exercise for a while."

He turned slowly towards me, showing a great flat moon of a face in which drooping eyes, a nose like a knob, and a round pink mouth seemed all too small and arranged too closely together. His eyebrows met in the middle. He was bareheaded, and his shaggy hair caught my eye, for it was entirely gray, although his face was not old. I also had the impression that his neck was about as thick as my thigh.

He gave me a doleful look and shook his head.

"Have you hurt yourself, then?" I asked. "They play rough here, for a fact."

No, he replied, he wasn't injured. When he spoke, his voice was as soft as if a baby lay sleeping between us.

"Then why not join in? You look sturdy enough for the rough and tumble."

His face reddened and he hesitated before he said, "Neither side will let the other choose me. It's always like this."

"Why," I laughed, "do you cheat?"

"I kill."

"Beg pardon?"

Another pause. Then with a shrug he unfolded his arms, letting the blanket fall open, exposing his chest to me.

"You see how it is," he murmured. "I wear the wolf skin shirt."

I didn't see. "Good-looking pelt," I said, at a loss. "Skin 'im yourself?"

His little bow mouth now curved into a shy smile. "Where do you hail from, friend, that you've never heard tell of the berserkers?"

Suddenly, I had trouble breathing.

"Don't stare at me, stranger, it makes me uneasy."

Dropping my eyes at once, I made a sign with my fingers behind my back to ward off evil.

Pulling the blanket back around his shoulders, he said in his mild voice, "It's how I'm made. Not so different from other men, except—you know—when it's all blood and confusion."

"As in a game of ball?"

"Yes."

"Or a battle?"

"Oh, yes, always in a battle. Then I do feel the prick of Odin's spear, and—I kill," he said simply, "anything in my path."

And so saying, he turned on me a look full of puzzlement, as though every time he considered the thing, he felt lost again in wonder at the mystery of himself.

Curiosity, as usual with me, got the upper hand. Despite his warning, I stared hard at him—at his brows, his cheekbones, the curve of his jaw—trying to discover beneath the skin, other brows and bones and other teeth. Oh, it isn't possible, I thought, not this mild fellow.

Seeing him grow restless under my gaze, I said quickly, "Forgive me, friend, but I thought the wild warriors of Odin had vanished years ago. I remember that my father, who knew many things, mentioned them once as creatures of the distant past."

He looked grieved to have to contradict my father, who knew many things. "You will find a few of us still, in Sweden."

Sweden! "Tell me your history, friend," I said tight-voiced, "it's no idle question."

"If you like. I was born on the shores of Lake Malar and my parents named me Glum. My childhood was nothing special until I reached the age of thirteen. It was then that I began to suffer from headache and to be troubled by dreams in which I ran through woods and fields all the night long, and in the morning I would wake up exhausted. One day, it happened that a neighbor boy wanted to fight me, as boys will. I broke his neck and slaughtered his friends as well. They say I cried Odin's name. And so my father, taking it for a sign, brought me to Uppsala, where the great temple is. There the priest touched me with the sacred spear, Gungnir, and I chose the wolf to be my animal because it seemed to me that I entered the wolf's body when I slept."

"In real truth, are you a varg, a shape-shifter, as old stories tell of?"

Again that puzzled look.

"Oh, yes. I have eaten the wolf's heart, I wear the wolf's shirt. I am a wolf. Most of us are wolves, though some," he added in the same thoughtful manner, "are bears. In olden times, we were honored for it. Kings, you may know, kept troops of berserkers, treating them to the best of everything, and placing them in the front rank of their armies. Oh, to have lived in those days! Our present king worships the White Christ and like your Olaf, has no love for men like me."

"And so," I said, "you thought to try your luck on this side of the Keel?" I knew the answer before he spoke.

Yes, he confessed, he had joined Olaf's ragtag army and was one of that mob of heathens who went over to the enemy rather than be touched by the priests' water. This creature alone, I supposed, could have been worth fifty men to us. One question remained. I feared to ask it.

"I wonder," I said carelessly, looking away from him, "what you recall of the battle. I mean after you became a ... you know ... a..."

"A wolf?"

"Yes."

"Nothing."

"Not a face, perhaps?"

"No, nothing. That's the way of it."

"Ah."

We were silent for a bit until he gave a little cough and asked with a voice full of concern, "You were there?"

"Yes, actually, I was."

"And did you ... Did I...?"

"It's no matter. Please forget I asked. Now," I said to change the subject, "what keeps you still in Norway?"

"Oh, well," he looked shamefaced, "after the battle, I joined Jarl Thorir's hird. He was pleased to have me, for all that he's a Christman. But his men, when they learned what I was, refused to eat or sleep with me, and so I was discharged. It's too late in the year now to walk home. There's nothing to do but sit here and wait for the snow to melt in the passes."

"And how are you living meanwhile?"

Ake, the shipwright, he replied, was letting him sleep in his ship shed in return for cutting trees and trimming them up into masts. It served to keep his axe arm limber but was no proper work for such a man as himself. "It's hard," he finished with a sigh, "to be shunned only for being what fate has made you."

Meanwhile, not far from where we sat, a brawl had erupted on the ice and the lads were going at it with clubs and fists while the spectators shouted encouragement from the sidelines. I was just going to speak again when I saw the berserker hunch forward on the bench, his eyes riveted on the struggling figures and his thick fingers gripping his knees.

"Odd Tangle-Hair, there you are!" I whirled round to see Stig and Bergthora crunching toward me through the snow. "Hullo," she sang out. "We're off to the square for the dancing. Everyone's there. Will you come?"

"Uh, Bergthora don't—"

She halted a few steps away to warm herself at the fire. Stig, beside her, cast an inquiring eye on Glum's broad back, which even under the blanket wrap was visibly heaving.

"Friend of yours?"

"Not exactly."

"Let him come, too, if he likes," said Bergthora.

The berserker gave no sign that he even heard us. On the ice, the spectators now had joined in the brawl. A couple of injured men were running our way holding bloodied heads. I had to do *something*. Without giving myself time for second thoughts, I jumped up and planted myself squarely in front of Glum, blocking his view of the river. Face to face with him, I saw his appearance undergo an indescribable change.

Like a man straining to lift a boulder, his skin was purplish, his nostrils flared, and the veins stood out like ropes in his neck. His lower jaw was thrust forward and the lips drawn down and back, exposing long teeth. Worst of all were his eyes, which a minute ago had been so mild and sad. They were wide, white, and bulging, and they stared with a desperate ferocity.

There could be no more doubt. It was him—the monster of Stiklestad. I swallowed hard. "Friend Glum," I said, "I've lost interest in watching a game where such babies play that they can't make room for a man like you. Now, what do you say to going along with these friends of mine?"

I was ready to run screaming onto the ice if he made a grab for me.

"Yes, come along Glub, or whatever your name is," urged Bergthora behind him, stamping her feet impatiently. "We can't stop here all day."

The berserker blinked.

The muscles of his face went suddenly slack, the brow unfurrowed, the lips crept back into the semblance of a pink bow. In a matter of seconds he was a wolf no more.

"Glum," I said, taking a deep breath, "these are my friends. Glum, here, is a woodcutter by trade."

Standing up and turning, he gave them his apologetic smile. "Friends," he murmured.

The size of him at full stretch, even though he stooped and hung his head, gave me a turn. He was enormous.

"Stig," I warned, "he doesn't much care for being stared at." Stig was giving him a cool going over, as only Stig could.

"I imagine he doesn't," he replied thoughtfully, lifting an eyebrow at me. "Well, let's go."

†

The Lucy festival that year lacked its customary gaiety. Although the pipes and fiddles played, and couples ran up to throw a pinch of incense on the bonfire for health in the coming year, the presence of the Danish Housecarles, helping themselves to the ale and fondling the women, produced a sullen anger you could feel. There were muttered words and hard looks, and here and there scuffles broke out which might have turned at any moment into a general bloodletting. Even Stig was not inclined to cut any wild capers.

We departed the square before long and walked with dampened spirits, arm in arm, back to the inn.

Along the way, Stig chaffed Bergthora about the Danes, making her admit that Ogmund had prophesied truly about them, and that Nidaros would never know peace as long as they stayed. To change the subject, she snapped, "Will one of you brave men be so good as to tell that hulking creature to leave us alone?" For Glum, unasked, padded silently behind us, keeping a distance of about ten paces.

If I *had* been brave enough, I would certainly have done as she asked, for I did not relish the thought of Kalf coming face to face with the monster that had crippled him. If he should somehow discover Glum's identity, I would be bound in sworn brotherhood to seek vengeance for him. Not to do so would disgrace me before my men.

Nor, it seemed, was Stig brave enough. With a knowing glance at me, he advised Bergthora gruffly that our new friend was peaceful as a pig—so long as he was well fed and talked to gently. "Knew a man like him once," he confided to us in a low voice. "It's something in the eyes, you know. You never forget it, once you've seen it. Good man in a fight, too—when he could remember whose side he was on."

Bergthora asked him sharply what in the world he meant by that, but he would say no more.

✝

During the month of Yule, the ale flowed freer at the inn than at other seasons of the year. The midwinter dancing and the chances it offered of getting their arms around some lassie's waist brought many men in from the countryside who one never saw at other times of the year, and quite a few of these had found their way to *Karl's Doom*.

By evening, forty pairs of skis leaned against the icicled wall outside, while inside the hall a merry crowd, most of them strangers to me, called for meat and beer and drank endless toasts to Saint Lucy on her day, and to Bergthora, their generous provider, and to the sun, to cheer him through this longest night of the year.

After dinner, while the Yule log smoked on the hearth, we chose our drinking partners for the evening and stretched our legs to the fire, sitting in pairs of man and woman, as the custom is; each pair sharing a big horn of the warm, thick ale, and each partner railing good-naturedly at the other for drinking too much or too little, too quickly or too slowly. I sat with Thyri, Stig, of course, with Bergthora.

Then Kalf hobbled over from his corner to join us, and was only a few steps away when one of the dogs ran between his legs, upsetting him. Before any of us could make a move, Glum bounded from the bench, caught Kalf in his arms, and set him down gently beside him. My heart shrank within me as they looked straight into one another's eyes. Yet not a flicker of recognition passed between them, not a sign that they had ever met before in less agreeable circumstances.

On the contrary, there seemed to spring between them a kind of instantaneous sympathy. I never understood it, but it was there from the first moment, and it endured. Whether Kalf's frailty struck a spark of tenderness in Glum, or whether the sorrowful look in the berserker's eye touched Kalf—they gazed at each other like fond friends before a word had passed between them. And soon Kalf was showing Glum his whistle, and Glum was trying to fit his huge fingers to the holes and chuckling. I almost laughed myself.

As the evening wore on, I could not keep from stealing sidelong glances at Glum, the werewolf, the berserker. Not in fear, but in fascination. During the whole night's conversation, which ranged from curses on the damned bloody Danes, to the weather, to the scarcity of provender and the price of cod, Glum never once opened his mouth, and yet accompanied our talk with an extraordinary dumb show.

If a man reported that his cow had sickened and heaven only knew what they would do now for milk, Glum frowned and shook his head. If another boasted of a shrewd bit of trading that had turned him a profit, Glum beamed and slapped his knees, and so on through an amazing repertoire of grimaces, shrugs, raised eyebrows, and head-wagging. It was as though, at the center of this strange creature, was a void which could be filled only by an arrangement of bits and pieces borrowed from those around him—an expression, a posture, a tone of voice, a mood—and all of them registered, in their subtlest changes, with an animal's sensitivity.

Soon, all eyes were secretly on him and it became a sort of game with us, from which only Kalf refrained, to catch him in these grimaces and wink at one another.

Naturally, he was asked once or twice who he was and where he hailed from, but the story he had told me only that morning, he would not repeat now in front of a dozen men, until I almost began to think I must have imagined the whole thing.

✝

At last, the hour grew late. Most of our group dispersed to their sleeping places, Bergthora went off to see to her other guests, and Kalf, too, rose stiffly and said goodnight. Stig started up to help him, but once again, Glum was quicker. Resting on that murderous right arm, Kalf retired to his corner.

Out of nowhere a great longing, tinged with melancholy, came over me. "Stig?" He had stayed by me, gazing into the fire, comfortably drunk and humming some tuneless melody. "Stig, if only I could see a little of my fate, only so much as to know where I will be this night a year from now, and what I'll have done that is worth anyone's remembering. My heart aches to know it." It hadn't been in my mind at all to make this speech.

He stopped his humming and studied me over the rim of his ale horn. "Because you imagine you have a future. No end of heartache comes from that. Look at me. I've no future save what the morning breeze blows in. I come here, I go there. I make no plans, no promises, and I'm the happiest man alive."

"But I have made a promise, Stig, to my Dead Ones, and I must keep it, somehow. But the how of it troubles me in the night."

"A fool, Tangle-Hair, lies awake all night pondering his troubles. When morning comes he's worn out—and whatever was, still is. Give up trying to see so far. It can't be done."

"I suppose," I sighed. "You know, my father had second sight, or

213

claimed he did. He said that if he put his hand on his hip and someone looked through the crook of his arm, that person would see his fate before him as clear as day."

"And did you do it?"

"No. Somehow we never did. Now I think of it, I don't suppose he knew his own fate either, or he might have managed things better. I imagine it was all just conceit, like the rubbish they talk about Olaf."

"Captain." Stig looked suddenly sober and gazed past my head at his distant horizon, as he always did when he had something important to deliver. "Captain, be careful what you say about that dead king. Mind you, I care nothing for him myself, but I say it for your own good. Don't be known as his enemy. Wherever his ghost is, I think he hasn't done with us yet. I feel it whenever I listen to these Tronders talk—that somehow we'll hear that dead man shout again."

I was drunk and sleepy and for a moment, while he talked, had fallen into a reverie. *Hear him shout again?* I was drifting in the dinghy on the dark bosom of the fjord, half way between waking and sleep.

"One day, by God, you'll hear his shout..."

"Thorgils!" I said with a start.

"Who?" Stig watched me curiously.

"What? Oh, no one. No one you know." I shook myself and stood up. "It's late, Stig. I'll say goodnight."

"Good night, Captain."

The coals glowed dully on the hearth and the smoke hole overhead was a faint circle of gray. Somewhere a cock crowed. Threading my way across the room—for the floor was littered with sleeping bodies in every position, as though they had been shaken out of a giant's hand—I peered into Kalf's dark corner. He was asleep, and next to him lay Glum, curled on his side, with his knees drawn up to his chest, like some monstrous baby. Or, was it only his husk that I saw and his spirit, at this very moment, was loping across the snowfields, a swift shadow against the moon? Who could conceive what thoughts whispered in that wolfish brain?

Bergthora was still up. Her boast was that she never slept so long as any of her guests was right side up. She sat at a table at the back with half a dozen sleepy-eyed farmers playing at draughts by the guttering light of a lamp.

As I passed them by, searching among the sleeping bodies for Thyri, who had wandered off some while ago, the men pushed the gaming board away, scooped up their silver, yawned, and began to look round for their hats and mittens.

I found my girl in the larder, curled around the butter churn fast asleep. I gathered her up and slung her across my shoulder. She was more child than woman and slept like a child, profoundly. I went back through the hall to the ladder that led up to the loft and saw Bergthora's sleepy guests in the gray rectangle of the open doorway, winding their scarves around their heads. The cold draft on my back made me shiver as I put my foot on the rung.

"It's a chill morning, boys, and a long way home," she was saying in the way she always bantered with her customers. "I've plump girls here aplenty to warm your bones...."

I hauled myself up through the trapdoor and lay Thyri down on the straw. Through the floorboards I could still hear Bergthora's voice and the shuffling of the men's feet.

"Everyone of 'em a beauty, or I wouldn't have 'em in the place. See if they aren't."

And then a man's voice that answered her just before the door banged shut: "N-n-not tonight, thank you. Maybe an-n-n-nother time."

22

MY SECRET DISCOVERED

"Wake up, Odd Tangle-Hair. Wake up!"

Ketil's grandson shook me until my eyes opened. The loft was dark except for the feeble light of his candle.

"Eh? What do you want, Toke? What hour is it?"

"Not yet cockcrow, sir, but you're to run down to the wharf just as quick as you can." He said it particular, 'as quick as you can.' He gave me another shake for good measure.

"Who says?"

"Man what was just here, sir. Rouses me with rappin' on the door and gives me this message for you from One-Legged Gorm. It's your ship, Master Tangle-Hair. There's been a fire in the ship shed. You're to go and see for yourself what's to be done."

"Hel's Hall!" I was up in a second and fumbling in the dark for my clothes. "Damn the man! He has six silver ounces from me to keep her dry over the winter and what does he do but burn her! Toke, fetch me a light."

Throwing a sealskin coat over my shoulders, I scrambled after him down the ladder.

"When Stig wakes up, send him after me."

"But can't I go along?"

"Do as I tell you."

I lit a torch from the hearth and stepped out, shivering, into the starry night. The snow, which lay thick all around, was crisscrossed by deep trodden pathways. I followed one that took me past rows of houses down to the square, where a black circle on the ground was all that remained of the Lucy fire that had burned itself out three nights before. Another path led around by the side of the cathedral and brought me to the waterfront.

By the time I reached it, a ribbon of gray lay along the horizon and the huddled shapes of sheds and warehouses were just creeping out of the darkness.

"Gorm!" I roared, as I slid and splashed ankle-deep through the salty slush that covered the wharf. "Gorm, you son-of-a-bitch, if my ship is ruined, I'll tear the other leg off you!"

One-Legged Gorm's shed, which was nothing but a broad shingled roof supported on squat posts, loomed ahead in the gloom, from under its eaves a glow of firelight. I rushed inside.

"Over here," said a low voice. A torch flared in the dark, splashing its light against the curved hull of my ship and one of the props that supported it. The man who spoke stood with his back to me.

"Gorm, what's it all about? The shed's not afire—"

"N-no indeed."

He spun and landed me a blow in the face that staggered me. At the same time, a pair of arms circled me from behind. He hit me a second time, and a third, until I sank down, unconscious.

A helmetful of icy slush in my face brought me to. I lay on the deck of my ship with my hands tied behind me and my eyes blindfolded. My jaw ached and my mouth was full of blood. What a fool I was to have walked into this childish trap—to have thought that the stammering man hadn't seen me at Bergthora's.

"S-s-sit him up."

Rough hands rolled me over and shoved me up against the bulwark.

In the conversation that followed, I distinguished three men—the same who had been with farmer Thorgils that night at Stiklestad. Unable to see them, I named them to myself according to their voices. Stammer had done the talking so far. The second I imagined to be a fat man, because his voice was deep and he breathed heavily, and so I called him Rumble-Guts. The last one, from the way he talked high up in his head, I pictured with a good deal of nose on his face, and so named him.

"You know us, don't you?" whined Nose close to my ear.

"What d'you want with me?"

"Oho, we want a good deal. Yes, a great deal."

His fist struck the side of my face, slamming my head against the gunnel, nearly making me black out again.

"That for Thorgils!"

"Hold off," Stammer commanded, "he's n-no use to us dead."

Nose whined again, "That farmer was worth a hundred of you, you heathen scum! When his corpse was found with knife wounds on the breast, we knew who was to blame."

"Would it matter if I said he tried to kill me?"

"Shut up! What matters is the body we trusted him with. Shall I tell you whose body it was?"

"I know whose it was."

"I expected you would. And did you bury it, heathen, or just fling it to the wolves when you murdered our friend?"

"We buried him."

"So. For weeks we've tramped Thorgils' property searching for the grave, while his widow took us in and fed us, for we're Southerners and have no kin here. When the snow came and covered everything, we lost hope. But God sees all, and look what he has sent us"—he banged my head against the gunnel again—"you!"

"My friends will be here soon."

"Your friends are hard d-d-drinkers and late sleepers," said Stammer. "You see, we know all about you—who you are and w-what you are. It only took a f-f-few questions asked in the right places. And now you will tell us where to find our k-k-king."

"So you can make magic with his rotting carcass? Splendid idea—and good luck to you. Now let me go."

"Scum!" cried Nose again, trying to get at me with his fingers, but the other two, with scuffling and grunting, held him back.

Rumble-Guts leaned close to me and growled in an urgent bass, "Hear the truth, heathen, and try to understand. Magic is of Satan—far be it from us. But when we possess the king's bones and good Bishop Grimkel, touching them, prays for our deliverance from the Danes, and Olaf himself pleads our cause at Heaven's Throne, how then will God refuse us?"

"Even C-c-canute," added Stammer, "cannot prevail against God. In the Spring, when Grimkel can journey up country, we will unc-c-cover the king's precious body in front of all. Then the false priest, Sigurd, and Alfifa and her brat will quake and c-c-cringe, and our jarls will take new c-c-courage, and we will throw the foreigners out."

In my mind's eye I saw their faces—plain, rough faces, honest and earnest, like the face of farmer Thorgils or, for that matter, of Kalf Slender-Leg.

"We're wasting time," Nose struck in. "Tell us where his body is and you can go your way."

"No, friend, I'm a fool, but not a big enough one as to believe that. I'm a dead man as soon as I've told you what you want, and so I will tell you nothing. It's the end of your little scheme."

"Oh," replied Stammer softly, "n-not quite. Suppose you don't mind having p-pieces of flesh cut from your body. There are still the others— that c-cripple whose life you were so anxious to save, the old whore at the inn who c-coddles you. And remember that we know their faces, but you don't know ours. You can't protect them. We are not c-c-cruel men, but we mean to have our way."

Oh, no, I thought, never say 'cruel'—not when the cause is so noble! "Look, I don't know where your bloody Olaf is. It was dark, it was four months ago." I fought down the fear that rose inside me and tried to think. "Maybe when the snow is gone ..., yes, I could find him then. You won't want him until spring anyway. We'll look then."

"And by that time," sneered Nose, where will you and your friends be, eh? And maybe in the meantime you decide to tell the Danes, eh? We are shrewder men than that, my friend. No, just you show us the spot now and we will dig—enough to know that it *is* the spot. Then we'll cover him up again."

"Dig in two feet of snow and the ground as hard as iron?"

"Nothing is impossible with God," sounded Rumble-Guts' bass. "You can't have buried him deep."

"All right, then but let's have more men to lighten the task. My crew—"

Nose laughed unpleasantly. "You underestimate us again. Your crew isn't worth discussing. Even among loyal Tronders, we've kept our business to ourselves. Men talk; their wives talk even more."

"Now," said Stammer. "Enough. We'll look for the k-king tonight. And this, my argumentative friend, is what you will do...."

When he had done talking, they untied my hands, dropped silently over the side and scuttled away. In a moment, there was nothing to be heard but the shrilling of the wind and the crash of the sea on the desolate beach outside.

In a fury, I cursed Olaf and all his wretched countrymen, who had caused me nothing but sorrows since coming to this place. But cursing only made my head hurt worse, and I needed it clear. I let myself down from the gunnel and stumbled out into the gray morning.

Just outside the shed Stig caught me in his arms. Looking into his questioning face, I nearly told him all—but thought better of it and didn't. My crew would arm themselves to the teeth, bluster about the town, and accomplish nothing except to drive these pious assassins deeper into the shadows. And every day thereafter we would have to fear a quick knife thrust in the crowded street, an arrow through the open door, a torch tossed onto the roof at night. For I never doubted that they would carry out their threat to harm Kalf and Bergthora, who were the hostages for my good behavior. I put Stig off with some story about thieves ambushing me.

But, Odin All-Father, what was I going to do?

✝

That night, when the moon rose, I mumbled an excuse for going out, and skied to a stand of pines that lay beyond the north wall of the town. After I had stood there for some minutes, my jaws rattling with cold, I heard a hiss of skis and saw three shadows glide out from the trees to surround me.

"I'm half frozen."

"Just making sure you came alone," Nose answered.

I peered at their faces in the moonlight. None had the features and bodies that I had given them: Noses's nose was nothing exceptional. Rumble-Guts turned out to be a slight, narrow-waisted man. And Stammer, as well as I could make him out, was one of the handsomest men I'd ever seen.

Without more conversation, we struck out, two abreast, through the silvery wood. My captors wore their swords slung on their backs, but on my back they had tied a heavy bundle of picks and spades, so that soon, despite the bitter cold, my shirt was soaked with sweat.

It was not exertion alone that raised this sweat on me. Since coming to Norway, I had discovered that I suffer from a peculiar uneasiness in the deep woods. I know other Icelanders, too, who feel it. At home we grow up able to see for miles across our naked, wind-swept barrens, so that an Iceland child actually does not know what it means to be lost. The forest is alien to us; it hems us in, suffocates us like the fog at sea. I never willingly went into the woods. Of course, my preferences were not being consulted at the moment.

"How will you k-k-know the spot?" asked Stammer, running on his skis beside me.

"There's an excellent chance I *won't* know it. Somewhere along the bank of the fjord, about five miles from here is a blackened tree, not different from a thousand other black trees, except that it's lightning-struck and has one branch hanging over the water. That's the task you've set yourselves."

"We'll f-f-find it," was his determined answer.

We skied for a long time in silence, winding in and out of the pines and birches that grew down to the water's edge, keeping the fjord on our left, while to the right of us the ground rose gently to a line of distant hills. Somewhere in the space between, hidden beneath the snow, lay the icy ribbon of the Nid.

But nothing in this bleak landscape offered a sign.

We were working our way up a long stretch of rising ground, when Nose began to complain, "It's too far. He's taken us clean past Thorgils' land and he knows it. Devil skin him! He's leading us a chase."

Stammer halted and the three of them stood around me, with angry looks. Their leader brought his ice-bearded face close to mine. "Are you tr-tr-tr-," the word stuck in his teeth. He shook himself in vexation and squeezed it out, "tricking us?"

"For what possible reason?"

"You worship the demon, Odin, the Father of Lies. That's reason enough for you," whined Nose, reaching back his hand to grasp the hilt of his sword. "I say we kill you now and go home—this was a fool's errand to begin with." He took a menacing step towards me.

In the distance a wolf cried. No one in the forest hears that sound without shivering.

"Listen!" Nose again, his high-pitched twang sounding higher than before. "The brute's got our scent. The whole pack'll be on us soon."

"Control yourself," Rumble-Guts snapped.

But Nose was plainly frightened. "Kill him and leave him for the wolves. They won't chase running men where there's easier meat."

"We need him, you i-imbecile!" said Stammer.

"Damn you all, I'll do it myself!" Nose took another step toward me with his sword upraised while I retreated so as to get Rumble-Guts between us. To the surprise of us all—I disappeared.

We were standing, without knowing it, on the brink of a deep hollow. I slid backwards, making windmills with my arms, until my skis flew out from under me and I hurtled down the slope in a spray of snow, sometimes head first, sometimes tail, and afraid I would meet my death in collision with a tree before my murderous companions had time to overtake me.

The tree did come first, catching me flush on the forehead and leaving me stunned.

On my face in the snow, with my legs sticking up at queer angles, I returned to my senses as Stammer and Nose resumed their argument over my fate—an argument which Nose seemed to be on the point of winning. Luckily, Rumble-Guts shouted just then, from a little ways away, to come and have a look at what he'd found.

"It's very like, isn't it?" I heard him say to them.

"Like enough. F-fetch him over here to see it."

Nose came back for me, yanking me upright and setting me down hard on my legs, which, I am sure, he hoped were broken. We pushed through a thicket of branches down to the water's edge.

"W-W-Well?" Stammer asked, slapping his hand against a blasted trunk whose single crooked branch hung over the water.

I started to say that Yes, it did seem....

"It *is* the one," he said with finality. God does not p-p-play jokes. So. And you will f-f-find our king."

"I'll find him when I'm damned good and ready!" I'd had enough of being ordered about by these three. With slow deliberation I brushed the snow from my clothes, adjusted the bindings of my skis, and felt my various bumps and bruises while they watched impatiently. "All right," I said at length, "follow me."

Where we came to a ribbon of snow that divided the wood, I stopped and pointed to my feet.

"You're s-s-sure?" asked Stammer sharply.

"A few paces right or left, I can't remember. There's a stone over it about as big around as a plate."

So Stammer and his friends began a slow march up and down the bank, stooping and thrusting their swords into the snow at every step. After a few minutes of this, Rumble-Guts' sword struck the stone. From the farther side of the stream—louder than before—the wolf howled again. Nose stifled a groan.

"Wants his dinner," I remarked pleasantly.

"Just you get to work," he spat out.

After some minutes' steady digging, we cleared a rectangle of three paces by two down to the sandy crust of the riverbank and rolled aside the stone marker.

"It is my fate," I sighed, "to dig and un-dig this king."

"How d-deep," Stammer asked.

"Less than a foot."

"Good. Pray first, comrades, and G-God will guide our hands."

So they prayed, and God, it seemed, did.

Stammer pushed his spade into the ground, working the handle from side to side, prying the sandy soil away. Steel glinted dully in the moonlight—a patch of mailed coat.

"Gently," urged Rumble-Guts. "God forbid that we injure this sacred flesh."

Two more spadesful and the moon shone upon Olaf's face.

I squeaked with fright, I admit it, and jumped backward. My captors let go of their spades, dropped to their knees, and commenced to pray in earnest—all three of them stammering now, they were in such a state.

It is one thing to believe that the dead live in their tombs, another thing to see it. The face seemed longer and thinner, the flesh had sunk in around the bones, making dark hollows of the eye sockets and the cheeks, and the ruddy skin had paled to the color of old ivory. But it was Olaf's face—whole and uncorrupted, I will swear to it. To see him, he might have been asleep. And if asleep, dreaming bloody dreams—for even the moonlight could not soften that hard mouth and that jutting jaw.

It occurred to me later, when I had my wits again, that the sandy soil, the shallowness of the grave, and the hard frost that autumn might

223

have been enough to save him from decay. Who knows?

"See his beard," whispered Nose. "Is it not longer than it was?"

"Aye, it is," came Rumble-Guts' hushed reply. "He lives. He's only waiting."

The wolf wail that sounded again seemed fitting music for this sight.

They crossed themselves and, unsheathing their swords, turned on me.

"Naturally, we c-c-can't l-let you leave."

"Naturally."

"Your friends will c-c-come to no harm."

"Good of you to say so."

"And now, we will slay you by his grave. A heathen's blood will g-gladden him."

Yes, I agreed, I was sure it would.

"And leave your corpse for the wolves," Nose laughed evilly, with a nervous glance into the dark.

"I will be missed."

"Oh, but don't you have the same belief as Norwegians," said Rumble-Guts, "about the Yulerei? The ghosts who roam the countryside in the month of Yule, carrying off folk who are foolish enough to go out alone at night? That is what your friends will think."

A growl rattled in the throat of something very near. Where we looked, two luminous eyes shone in the dark. Nose let out a strangled scream and flung himself into the snow, churning it with his legs. His friends stood their ground for only a heartbeat longer. The Thing bounded forward, brushing me with its matted coat as it shot past. It caught them before they had gone a dozen steps, lifted them screaming one by one into the air, and cracked their backs on its knee.

Afterwards, it crouched over them, moving from one to another, making wet mouth sounds. Then, standing to its full height, the growl still in its throat, it's face smeared with blood, it started toward me.

For a swift instant I stood again on Stiklestad plain, paralyzed with fear. Does he know me? I had worried about that when I made my plan with him, but what choice did I have? The werewolf's steaming breath, sweet with blood, licked at my face. If I ran, he would kill me for sure. I stood, not moving a muscle, my eyes lowered in an animal's gesture of submission, and repeating, "Odin—Odin—Odin—" to myself, filling my mind with the magic name. The creature's jaws gaped open, showing red teeth, he shook his huge head from side to side—and with an enormous yawn sank on his knees before me.

I let out my breath very slowly. "Wash your face in the snow, friend Glum," I said, "and then lend me a hand with this lot."

"Sleepy," he answered with a weary groan. "Always after I change shape."

"Well, you can't sleep here. Come along now."

Reluctantly, he helped me drag the bodies over to the trunk of a pine where we threw snow over them. They should stay well hidden until the spring thaw. In the meantime, Thorgils' widow, or anyone else who missed them, could mutter darkly about the Yulerei all they pleased.

I looked at them one last time and wondered at the force of the passion that had driven them. Was it conceivable that Kalf, as drunk on religion as any of them, could have done to someone what they had tried to do to me? I didn't like to think of it.

"Friend Glum," I said, "I find no joy in these killings."

The berserker only shrugged, as if joy or the absence of it had simply no meaning for him.

You will ask me if he really was a shape-shifter. The berserkers have all gone now, and people begin to doubt that there ever were such men. They never met Glum. He howled, ran, killed as a wolf does. He smelled like a wolf, and he dreamed a wolf's dreams. What more is required? And haven't we all some drops of the wolf's blood in us? Glum, at least, could put a name to his frenzy that carried some honor once. And that is something.

I turned my face toward Olaf in his grave.

"King," I addressed him in a solemn voice, "you've only yourself to blame, you know. If you hadn't driven the heathens from your army that day, my friend Kalf would still be walking on two good legs and we would have launched our dinghy by ourselves and gone away, never meeting farmer Thorgils and these others, and your secret would still be safe. Something to think about during the long night, King. And farewell to you."

When we had closed up his grave and spread the snow around, I put on my skis again and said, "Now you can rest, friend Glum. Stand up behind me and hold tight to my belt."

Bruce Macbain

With only the whisper of my skis hissing in the silent forest, we glided back to town.

23

I GO A-VIKING

The rest of that winter passed uneventfully.

I decided, for the time being, to say nothing about my adventure in the forest, and swore Glum to secrecy as well. And the three Norwegians, it seemed, had kept their mission a secret. No one else came to trouble me about King Olaf's sweet-smelling corpse.

The weeks wore on without bringing any change in our circumstances. Between Kalf and me there was still that coolness, those awkward looks and silences, which had continued for so long now that they went uncommented on.

Month after weary month, I nursed and cherished my anger. "Run away, Odd," he had said. "Isn't that how you treat your brothers?" *Devil* and *coward!* he had called me. Whenever I felt myself weaken, I called it all up again as fresh as if it had happened yesterday.

As for Kalf, he spent all his time now conning Latin. He was laboriously translating a book lent him by Deacon Poppo about the Life of Saint Anskar, who had been a missionary to the Danes two centuries ago.

At night, Kalf would recite his translation to a circle of listeners, which at different times included Bergthora and her girls, and several of my crew, but always Glum. Long after the rest had drifted away, the berserker would still be found sitting at Kalf's elbow in rapt attention, with what sort of understanding, who could say? He was content just to be distracted, I think, from the puzzle of his existence.

It was bound to happen sooner or later that Kalf learned who and what Glum was—and did the most astonishing thing: kissed him on the cheek, forgave him, and renounced any act of vengeance to be taken in requital for his wound! Which puzzled the berserker mightily, but he took it in good part, even agreeing to wear a crucifix which Kalf hung around his neck.

There was even talk of preparing Glum for baptism, but when he was made to understand that this meant a dousing with the magic water, the same that Olaf had tried to force on him and his comrades at Stiklestad, he ran howling from the inn and stayed hidden for two days. Thereafter, it was pretty well agreed between Deacon Poppo and Bishop Sigurd that Glum's conversion, while being a victory for the Church greatly to be wished for, must be allowed to happen in God's own time, which might be a very long time indeed.

✝

Through it all, the town of Nidaros, under its blanket of snow, seethed with rumor and report and smoldering hatred of the Danes.

It was on a bright morning early in the month of sowing that two boys out hunting noticed a sparkle of metal at the top of a snowdrift that had begun to shrink in the sun, and going over to have a look, discovered the crown of a helmet, and scooping away the snow with their hands, uncovered three fresh pink faces with beards as brittle as gingerbread and black ragged holes in their throats.

Time to be going, said I to myself, when the news of this got around. For I had settled in my mind that I would turn viking for a while.

Calling my crew together, I opened my plans to them. Stuf, Otkel, Starkad, and Brodd agreed to ship with me for another year and try their luck at the viking life. But Stig shook his spiky head, no.

"Looting's a young man's game," said he, "and I've grown fat and comfortable here, I won't bother to deny it. I'm content to be a tavern-keeper."

"But Stig, it was only last year you looked forward to buying a farm in Iceland—you said as much to Hoskuld."

"Did I really? No, not the thing at all for old Stig. Too hard on the back. No, this is the life for me."

Bergthora, standing behind him with her hand on his shoulder, allowed herself a smile of triumph. Her wandering bird was safe in the nest at last!

"But I'll tell you boys something," he went on, "if you'll take an old thief's advice. You want a sleeker ship to sail in than Hrut's fat-bellied tub. A sow can't be a fox, try as it may, and you're liable to end up as the dinner on someone else's plate. Now, if I was you, I'd pay a visit to Ake the shipwright and see what he has on hand."

"Steersman," I urged, trying him one more time, "what good will a ship like that do me without you to hold the tiller?"

"Pah! In all my thieving days I never handled a dragon like the one you want. What there is to steering one of those, old Stig can't teach you." He looked at me severely. "That you must learn where the spears and arrows fly."

✝

A little ways beyond the wharf, the music of hammers and the odor of pitch and pine proclaimed Ake's shipyard.

Here Glum labored. I spied him at once, standing a-straddle of a pine trunk, working along it with his axe. I hallooed and went toward him over a carpet of shavings.

"How goes it today, friend Glum?"

"Not so badly," he sighed, peeling off a long curlicue of bark with a swipe of the half-moon blade, "but not so very well, either." His face wore a particularly woebegone expression. "It's soon time that I walked home to Sweden, and yet here I am with my fortune still unmade. I expect a scolding from my aged father and nothing but raillery from my brothers."

"Well, Glum, this *is* a coincidence. You see, I've made up my mind to go a-viking this summer. Now, I think our victims would shower us with their wealth if only you were to growl at 'em. What d'you think? And afterwards, if you like, we'll set you down on the coast of Sweden and you'll go home a far richer man than you left. Would that suit you?"

His little bow mouth stretched itself into a wolfish smile.

"It might suit."

"Agreed then! We'll talk more about it later. Right now I'm in search of a ship for us—a sleek one and fast. Show me to your master."

Nearby, a dozen men swarmed over the skeleton of a ship while the master builder stood back, cocking his head first to one side, then the other, measuring the curve of her hull down to a finger's breadth with only his sharp eye.

He was a rope of a man, with knotted muscles on his long arms and big knuckles on his fingers. We talked over the clack of axes and the chink of hammers.

"A ship?" said Ake. "A ship is like a tool, they come in every shape and size, each right for its purpose—and what might yours be?"

I told him.

"Aha! Then cast your eye over this very one we're building." And taking me by the arm, with Glum following behind, he led me 'round her.

"She's a karfi—a small dragon, seventy-six feet from stem to stern, seventeen in the beam, and mounts sixteen pair of oars. Add a steersman and you can sail her with a crew of just thirty-three, though you could cram a dozen more in her if need be.

"Now, a trim little craft like this one, while she's got the fast lines of a big dragon-ship, can hold her own in rough water better than one of those, for they're all too narrow in the beam for the length of 'em. She handles better, too. In a pinch, a good steersman could spin this ship around on the head of a pin. And she'll draw but three feet of water. You can run her up on a beach, strike, and be off again before they ever know what's hit 'em."

He reached a long arm up to the gunnel, hauled himself up and over, and dropped down into the hollow of the hull, where the deck planking had not yet been laid. Glum and I followed.

"Solid oak," he said, thumping the mast block with his fist. "Oak won't grow this far north, as you know, but this ship was a special commission— no expenses to be spared. We had timber brought up from the south for mast-block, keel, stem, stern, and ribs."

Dropping to his haunches alongside the keel, he ran his fingers over the smooth-planed strakes.

"I'll show you something else. Only a landlubber thinks that a ship floats on the water. A well-joined ship swims in the water like a fish. Look here." He tugged at a length of pliant root that was knotted over one of the ribs where it passed in front of a strake. "All nine strakes below the water line are tied to the ribs with these. Without nails, they're free to move, and when you stand on her deck in a rolling sea you'll feel her ripple under you as she fits herself to the waves.

"The upper strakes we nail, as you see the lads doing now, then we caulk her with braids of horsehair dipped in pitch, give her bottom a coat of tar—and she's ready for the water."

"She hasn't got her figurehead yet," I said.

"Ah, that comes last. When we give her her head and tail, we say goodbye to her because she's alive then and wants to swim. The heads are carved separate. I've a shed full of 'em and any one you like can be fitted on."

"Hold on, Master Ake, you talk as if I'm to buy this ship, and I wish I were, but you said she was promised to another."

"Died of the cough this winter, poor man. But I will finish her just the same. She won't go looking long for an owner."

"And how much might you be asking for her?"

"What—with sail and tackle and oars and all?" He stared into space for a while, moving his lips, then named a price that fairly knocked me over the side. I shook my head sadly.

"Not so fast," he said. "You've a sea-worthy merchantman, haven't you? I know where I can sell one of those and no questions asked about where she came from." He said this with a wink, for it was pretty well known around the harbor that we'd lifted the ship. "That'll take a good bit off the price, and for the rest—why, I'll give you until we finish her to find it. Young pirate like you shouldn't have any trouble grubbing up a bit of silver."

And how long, I asked, until he finished her?

"Oh—I should say two weeks if we don't have a lot of rain."

"Do it in one and you'll have your price."

"Heh? You're an eager one. All right. Done."

We sealed the bargain with a handshake. As I left the shipyard, I turned back for one more look, seeing her in my mind's eye slicing through an ocean swell or nosing up a wooded creek, hunting for a village. Oar-Steed ... Surf-Dragon ... Fjord-Elk. I recalled all the timeworn kennings by which we poets signify a ship, trying each one on my tongue. But this newborn creature deserved a new-minted name. I thought some more and finally hit upon the name of Sea-Viper, because the viper's a small creature, but she has a wicked sharp tooth.

†

That afternoon, I brought the lads down to have a look at her, for I calculated that it would take all the silver we had left amongst us to buy her. The rest of that day we spent in going out to our caches, and in the evening we came together at the inn to count our wealth—each one spilling his hoard of coin and hack-silver onto the table. Starkad, his moustache twitching with excitement, weighed it out on Ogmund's little scales and I notched the sums on a stick.

And when we had tallied it all up, we looked at each other dumbly across the table, not knowing what to say. Where had it gone? Was it possible we had drunk and whored and eaten so much, spent so much on cloaks and swords and girls?

"Odin!" I struck the table with my fist, making the coins jump.

There was a long silence and then—

"But you haven't asked me for my contribution yet." Kalf had been watching all this time from his corner. He dragged himself towards me on his crutch. "My life has been less costly than yours. I think you'll find enough in my cache to make up the difference."

"No thank you, Kalf," I answered sharply, not looking at him. But when the others protested, I added, "You must save something for yourself to live on."

"He'll live here for nothing as long as ever he likes," Bergthora spoke up.

"All the same, I will not take his money."

"Odd Tangle-Hair, have pity on me! No, don't look away this time, brother, don't leave. I've tried a hundred times to say this and each time you've cut me off. Now I will speak—and in front of all."

"Kalf, don't."

"You are cruel, Odd. Like the Hebrew children in the Scriptures, you are a proud and stiff-necked man. Unbend. Don't drive me away. Let me make my poor amends. Brother, as I forgave Glum, forgive me. And take, at least, my money—for what else can I give you but my prayers, and those you scorn."

He stood with tears shining in his eyes. There was a deep hush in the room.

"Kalf Slender-Leg," I replied in a low voice, "what can I do but hate you? Why did you say to me things that no man can forgive—coward, run-away, betrayer?"

He looked at me helplessly. "My reasons will make no sense to you. When you first decided to go to battle with me and Ogmund, I didn't want you to. I suspected your real reason. But then I thought it might be my last chance to save your soul, and so I agreed to it.

"All that night in Olaf's lean-to, I prayed for just one thing—not victory, not the restoration of the king—but for God to open your heart and make you a Christman. Only that. And by the first light of dawn, after so many hours of prayer, I believed it would come to pass. Then, out of nowhere you threw yourself on me, calling the king a monster and a lunatic, me an idiot. And I felt as if God had spit in my face. And you kept on and on, until, to make you stop, I said the cruelest thing I could think of.

"I knew then that you would have to stay and fight. We'll go to our death together, I thought, and together fly up to Heaven, to God's mead hall. For it seemed to me God must pardon you, if you died for him. But if you turned your back on Him this time, your soul would be lost forever."

I shook my head in disbelief.

"It was a stupid and wicked thing I did. And to punish me, God has given me this." He touched his shattered hip. "Every day of my life, I do penance for those words I spoke in a desperate moment. But I fear I will never earn God's forgiveness until I first earn yours. I don't deserve it but I do humbly ask for it."

All those weary months of misery ended in an instant.

"Kalf, if only all the Christmen were as good as you!" I jumped up and embraced him, holding him tight to me. "I've never forgiven anyone for anything in my life, but I forgive you a thousand times over, and I beg the same of you. I accept your silver gratefully, and—wait!" A thought had just struck me. "All right, I accept your gift, but only on one condition—that you accept a gift from me. Come, lean on my arm and walk with me out to the yard where we can be private, for my gift is a deep secret."

We spent a long time talking. The grass had grown high between us, as the saying goes. We cut it down. Not all of it, that could never be, but enough that when we came back to the house we were brothers again.

That night I slept peacefully.

✝

Kalf's calculations were exact. The next day we brought our silver to Ake and weighed it out for him to the last ounce, and with enough to spare for awnings, a tent, and other gear that we would need for a summer's cruise.

Next, I set about recruiting. Having no word-fame or victory-luck to boast of, I made do with swagger, bluff, and the promise of generous shares. The Danes helped, too, by making life in Nidaros so unpleasant that I soon signed on twenty-nine new hands, some tough and experienced men among them. In just over a week I had my ship and my crew.

One night during that time I had a dream. It seemed to me that I stood on the edge of a towering cliff overlooking the sea, and so high up that my head touched the bowl of the sky. A wind blew, frothing the water below me and dashing it against the rocks. I wanted to cross the water but could see no way to do it in the teeth of that wind.

My father appeared beside me—my father, except that he was strangely clothed in shreds of deerskin and blue cloth that flapped in the wind like flags, and that he had but one eye. Touching me on the shoulder, he pointed to a dead tree, cleft by lighting, which I had not noticed before, and, tearing off a crooked branch, thrust it at me. In my hands the branch became a spear, and I understood in some fashion that this was Gungnir, the spear of Odin All-Father himself.

"Throw!" my father commanded.

I did so with all my might, and he, smiling at me—which in life I don't remember him ever to have done—said over and over in a sort of singsong, "Fly to all your heart's desire, silver, blood, and Hekla fire."

The spear flew from my hand into the glare of the rising sun—which had not been there a moment before—so that I could not see where it fell.

I awoke with a warm feeling in my breast. My father had spoken to me, as the noaidi said he would, and I guessed at once the meaning of my dream. My name—Odd—is, of course, also the ordinary word in our language for 'spear point', and Odin All-Father, like my father in the dream, has but a single eye. So, I reasoned, by flying wherever Odin should send me, I would gain everything I desired—wealth, the death of my enemies, and a return to my home under fiery Hekla.

I told my dream that morning to Bergthora, for in the matter of dreams one should always seek the opinion of women. At first, she complained that I thought a good deal too highly of Odin, but in the end she came round to admitting that it was a most excellent sign.

And it *was*—as far as it went. It's only that dreams have a way of never telling all the truth.

✝

Bergthora sat across the table from me now on my last night in Nidaros. She and Stig had insisted on giving us all a farewell feast.

Long-beaked and long-necked, she nuzzled like an affectionate crane up against Stig, who sat beside her on the bench. She filled up both their mugs with an excellent wine that she had bought for the occasion, and pushed the flagon towards me.

"Odd Tangle-Hair," she began, "a woman in my line of trade meets every sort of man sooner or later. You're not the handsomest of 'em, that must be admitted, and as for your soul, well, it don't bear thinking about—but I am fond of you all the same. It was a fair wind that brought you and Stig to me, and I'm only sorry that the two of you must be parted. He does think the world of you, you know, though he'd rather die than say so."

Stig found something of interest to study at the bottom of his mug.

"I never had little'uns, as you know." A tear started unexpectedly, which she erased with an angry swipe. "Well, Devil skin you, what I mean to say is that you must think of us as mother and father, being as you've none of your own. There, I've said it." She closed her lips tight and looked fierce.

What a good woman she was.

"Bergthora Grimsdottir," I replied, "I could wish you better luck than to be kin of mine, for they've all fared poorly. But I will call you mother if it pleases you. My own mother would have been proud to know you." I leaned across and kissed her cheek.

Stig, having had his fill of this soft talk, changed the subject with a loud slap of his hand on the table. An old sailor, said he, beached and stranded as he was, could still delight in the names of foreign ports. And where then, did I aim to sail?

"England," I answered off-hand. The fact was, I had given the matter practically no thought.

Ye-es—he nodded, his eyes scanning that far horizon of his—but had I considered how the English coast was thick with soldiers now that Canute reigned there?

"Ireland, I mean."

Ahh, but wasn't it a marvel how bold the Irish had grown lately, and how it was Norsemen that asked for quarter now?

"Well, you're mighty full of news, Stig, for a beached whale or whatever!"

"Only the waterfront gossip," he answered mildly, with a twinkle in his eye. "Probably half lies."

Stuf and Otkel, listening nearby, were making snorting noises behind their hands. Kalf was laughing, too.

"So, Steersman," I said in my sternest captain's voice, "I suppose there is some part of the ocean you like better."

"You mean, if any young sea rover was to ask me?"

"Yes, confound you."

Up and down the table they stopped to listen.

"Well, since you ask, I'll tell you. This bit of the world is played out, don't you know. What was worth taking was taken long ago, and the natives are damned if they'll part with the rest.

"But there is a sea, far away to the rising sun,"—the moment he said that, the picture in my dream flashed like an arrow through my mind— "where the water is warm and nearly fresh enough to drink, and they say the ships are heavy-laden with cargo, and the people bury their kings under mountains of gold! Vikings who harry there either come home rich, or like it so well that they never come home at all."

"Stig, you've seen this sea?"

"Pah! Do I look rich? But I've been told that she lies somewhere between Sweden and the land of the Wends. If you follow the coast southwards and eastwards you must come there sooner or later. Here—you may as well have this, too, just in case." Slipping his hand into the wallet at his belt, he brought out the precious sun-stone and laid it in my palm.

"Stig, thank you. It's a far journey you send me on."

"Wasn't too far for Olaf in his viking days," said Bergthora. "The sea Stig means is called by some the Varangian Sea, and there's many a tale of how he harried there as a youth."

"Did he indeed! Then the Varangian Sea it is," I cried, "and by One-Eyed Odin, we will harry her as she never was before!"

From thirty throats burst a roar, accompanied by pounding of the boards and pounding of backs, tipping back of heads, and pouring of drink into mouths, into beards, down chins, and down chests. Then, one after another, the men leapt to their feet, purple-faced and wild-eyed, to vow in thundering voices that *this* and *this* many heads they'd take, and so and so many weeping girls they'd have, and so many—oh, so many— sacks of gold they'd lift, or else, damn them, be ashamed ever to see their fathers' faces again!

Meanwhile, Bergthora's girls ran from barrel to table and back again keeping the drinking horns full, but always, of course, stopping long enough for squeezes and wet kisses in between.

Warm with wine and expectation, I leaned back comfortably and looked along the table at the flushed and happy faces of my crew: at Stuf and Otkel, the two friends; at rough-tongued Brodd; at steady, careful Starkad; at Glum, whose speaking face, never resting, mirrored all the others; at the new men whose faces I scarcely yet knew. Some of them will feed the crows and leave their bones to bleach on the shore of this eastern sea, I thought, and *they know it*. There came to my mind that old viking verse:

Cattle die, kinsmen die,
You die yourself one day,
But word-fame, when you've won it, boys,
That never dies away.

✝

As day broke, I breakfasted on salt-fish and butter, and went down with my men to the shipyard. Bergthora and Stig, old Ketil and his grandson, all of Bergthora's girls, and Kalf came down to see us off, as well as a crowd of womenfolk—the mothers, wives, and sweethearts of the local boys in my crew.

The Sea-Viper, splendid with her new serpent's head and tail, lay on rollers at the water's edge, while we trundled our chests, water barrels, arms, and provisions aboard her.

"Oh!" said Toke, pointing to the sky. "The geese!"

We looked up. Fleets and squadrons of them, flying out of the sun, passed over us in long slanting lines, sounding their war-horns like armies of the air.

"A good sign," said Stig. "All brave creatures are astir today."

"Aye," Ake agreed, as he squinted to measure his handiwork one last time, "the Viper wants to go, too."

Truly, she was a beauty—eager and impatient, searching the sky's edge with her bright painted eyes. Only my stallion, Grani, had ever filled me with so much pride.

Gear stowed away, tackle all in order—it was time to say goodbye. From the water's edge, I gazed back beyond the wharf to the huddled roofs of thatch, to the winding streets, to the cathedral spire, set there by a troll, to the king's hall on the hill—and tried to recall that first morning so many months ago. That day, Stig had missed the smoke that should have risen from the royal hearth. Smoke was rising from it now. The Housecarles' women were cooking fish and venison for their men's breakfast.

Enjoy it, Danes, I thought. Something tells me you won't dine much longer off the fat of Nidaros.

Hours earlier, a rider had set off for the south to fetch back Bishop Grimkel. And when the Bishop came, it would be Kalf—Kalf the cripple, dragging himself in pain and joy, Kalf the Christman, singing hymns and giving thanks, Kalf Slender-Leg, my friend and brother, who would lead bishop and jarls and all the good Christian folk of Nidaros to that spot by the river. He would touch it with the tip of his crutch and say, "Dig here," and so restore her saintly king to longing Norway.

That was my gift to him: the only thing of value I possessed, and far more precious to him than gold. What might happen after that was no affair of mine.

One last time, the men embraced their women, and some tossed their little'uns in the air, warning them sternly to mind their mams.

"Take care, Odd," Bergthora sniffed and dabbed at her eye with the corner of her apron. "Whenever I think of the way poor Karl went down, why, it gives me a flutter."

"Don't fear, Old Mother, I'm hard to kill."

"Odd Tangle-Hair," said Kalf, "I have lit candles for your safe homecoming to every saint I know." Seeing something in my face, he said softly, "You aren't coming back, are you?"

"I expect not."

Bergthora stiffened.

"Mother, I leave you Kalf Slender-Leg, a better son than you would ever have had in me."

"God knows when we'll meet again," said Kalf.

"They say an Icelander always goes home at last."

"Someday in Iceland then, Odd."

"Someday soon." I clasped his arm. "Don't forget me."

Glum joined us. "Friend Kalf, if you'd come with us, I would carry you on my back and never let you come to harm."

"I know you would, my friend, but a warship is no place for someone like me. Now Glum, you won't forget what I told you—that you have an immortal soul, or, I should say, half of one anyway, and that I pray for it every day."

"It's kind of you," the wolf-gray head bobbed up and down. "Between Jesus and Odin I shall be well watched over, I'm sure." Leaving Kalf bemused, he shambled away to the ship.

I kissed Bergthora and Thyri, shook old Ketil's hand and looked round for Stig.

"Devil skin him, he was just here," Bergthora scowled. "I swear he sneaks around like a cat."

"Which is why he always knows so much," I replied. "I'm sorry to miss him at my leave-taking, but he doesn't like goodbyes, does he?"

"We're all ready, Captain," sang out Stuf from the fo'c'sle, "let's be off."

"Good-bye Kalf, Bergthora!"

Heaving altogether, we pushed the Sea-Viper out into the shallow water and swarmed up her sides. Mounting to the stern and taking the tiller in my hand, I gave the order to take down the oars from their racks and put them through the oar ports.

"Ready, boys."

I looked down the double line of rowers—thirty-two men, each on his sea chest with his oar poised to strike the water. And thirty-two pairs of eyes gazed back, in every eye the same question: would I steer them to riches or to doom?

Just short of a year had gone by since the trial at the Althing, the house-burning, my near death, and my bout of madness. A year is a long time in the life of a boy—long enough to become a man. I was ready to be their captain.

"Now, you big-bellied boys," I cried. "I'll row the winter's fat off you.

At the double beat—pull for warmer waters!"

A roar went up as oars churned the water white—again and again—the men's shoulders cracking, the veins standing out in their necks and the blood coming up in their faces. The Sea-Viper shot forward, skating on the sunlit surface of the sea.

"Not so fast!" came a cry from shore.

"Stig!"

"Red-faced and puffing, his sword and bedroll on his back, the steersman raced along the wharf. He passed Bergthora with a wave of his arm.

"Stig, you whore's son'!" she wailed. "You troll! You black-hearted, lying bastard!"

"Back in the autumn, old girl—"

"You said that the last time!"

"Back water!" I shouted.

As she made a grab for him, he dove and came up sputtering. Tossing the water from his bristly head, he struck out for us.

"Starkad, throw him a line," I laughed, "before he drowns."

Eager hands reached down to help him.

"Mother Bergthora," I called, "I'll send him back to you, I promise."

She buried her face in her apron and shook her head.

Stig stood dripping on the deck and grinning.

"Old girl," he yelled, "I've left you half my silver—you've earned it."

A corner of the apron came down.

"Steersman," said I, "I've never been so glad to see anyone. Will you take the helm?"

"Thank you, Captain. I will."

Again, the water churned and the Viper shot forward. I wanted to see, and wanted *them* to see, what a quick and lively snake she was. I kept them at it for a good long time before I let them slow down.

By that time Nidaros was far away.

THE
VARANGIAN SEA
AD 1031

24

VICTORY AND DEFEAT

We hadn't been long at sea when the men began to complain because Glum was refusing to take his turn at the oar. They took it hard—especially the Christmen—that he thought it beneath his station to row like any other man. I did try reasoning with him, but he was immovable, literally. He would settle himself on the deck with his broad back up against the mast, tug his sheepskin around his shoulders, and fall asleep at once. Shape-shifters, as I had already had occasion to learn, were great sleepers. As I didn't care much for the idea of pushing Glum around, I turned on the grumblers instead, and told them to leave off. Soon enough, I promised, they would have reason to think better of the "great lazy heathen."

Thirty-five men, mostly strangers to one another, on a new ship with a new captain, are a mob—not a crew. It needs days and nights of gossiping and tale-telling, bragging, complaining, and more than anything else, of rowing—hour after long hour of it, when the wind is down—before they grow together into a single body with one heart, one head, and many arms. Even then something more is needed: they must face death together.

✝

Day followed day, while the wooded coast of Norway slid past, running like a ribbon along the foot of the giant mountains, broken now and then by a grassy river mouth or sandy bay, or by a great fjord, its cavernous walls hung with rags of mist and sometimes, clinging high up on its shoulder, an impossible sloping farm, with a sloping house and a sloping cow, tethered lest she drop into the sea.

Our second week out we rounded the southern tip of Norway and sailed out into a wide gulf which they call the Skaggerak. Here, where the sea pours into Oslofjord, we came upon the bustling harbor town of Skiringsaal, the home of Ogmund Pot-Belly, as I recalled, and lay to for a few days while we took on provisions.

From Oslofjord, we turned east and then south again into a gulf called the Kattegat, keeping the coast of Sweden on our left, while to starboard we had only the open sea for three whole days before the flat coast of Jutland came into view.

We were drawing near now, said some of my crew, to that eastern sea of Stig's, whose entrance is barred by a string of islands that stretch between the long tongue of Jutland and Sweden's southern coast. The narrow sounds between these islands, they warned, were a favorite haunt of pirates.

"Tight as a virgin's furrow," Stig observed, as we lay off shore and surveyed the mouth of the sound that divides the island of Sjaelland from Scania. "Catch you fore and aft between two ships and cut you to pieces. Best run her at night, Captain, unless you care to fight on unequal terms."

I took his advice, though it meant a seven-hour row in the dark, battling a headwind all the way.

The sun was an hour high when, stiff-backed and weary, we passed the point of Trelleborg and saw spread out before us, the bright expanse of a brand new sea. We lowered a bucket and tasted the water: as promised, it was nearly fresh. All the ocean's salt is left, for some reason, on the farther side of the Sounds.

A freshening breeze sprang up behind us, ruffling the water and filling our sail. I whispered a prayer of thanks to Njord, god of the sea, and giving Stig the helm and telling the others to rest while they could, stretched out on the deck and was instantly asleep.

It seemed only a moment later—though the position of the sun told me it was hours, really—that Stig woke me to report that we'd come in sight of an island. Looking where he pointed, I saw a chalk cliff, dazzling in the sun, off our starboard quarter.

"Bring us in closer, Steersman, and spy out a snug cove. We'll lay up for a bit and rest."

I started to turn away, but a warning word brought me back. A black sliver had darted out from behind the curve of the cliff less than a mile away, crossing athwart of us and standing out to sea. We squinted at her in the sun's glare.

"Hawk or pigeon, Captain?" said Stig.

A shiver of excitement ran through me. "Rouse the lads, Steersman."

They woke grumbling, until I showed them our prize. Then how they jumped to—scrambling to fetch the oars down from the rack, slinging their shields on their backs, and spitting into their hands. And Glum, with a feral growl, took his place in the prow, where a berserker always stands in battle.

Meanwhile our quarry was drawing farther away. In my mind's eye I saw some flabby merchant, bearing a strong resemblance to Ogmund Pot-Belly, with his bags of silver piled all around him and his sweating face pale with fright, running for the open as fast as he could go.

This pleasant notion vanished almost at once.

"He's changing course," said Stig. "He's doubling back."

He was indeed, and as he came about, he dropped his sail and put out his oars—twenty-five, maybe thirty pair!

"Stig, he's foxed us. He has us up against the cliff and nowhere to go."

Gone was that quaking merchant: in his place a wily viking in a damned big ship.

"Strike sail!" I ordered.

The yard came rattling down the mast, landing heavily across the gunwales.

"Heads up! Bengt, watch your head! Get her up onto the crutches. Kraki, lash your end."

Fighting a ship is a steersman's art. He needs a sure hand on the tiller, and he can't be encumbered with a sail that may catch a breeze and throw him off his aim. But more than all else, he needs the trust of his rowers. Thirty men race backward towards death; he alone can see the enemy. They see only him, and from him they must take their courage—from his eyes, his voice, the way he stands.

I took the tiller from Stig. This must be *my* victory—or my death.

"Easy lads," I coaxed, "easy strokes—let them do the hard rowing."

I held our course steady as he closed on us—near enough now to see the fighters crowding his deck, and to see that his ship was both longer and higher in the water than ours. Size would give him the advantage when it came to boarding, but would also, I reckoned, make him sluggish at turning.

"Odd!" Starkad dashed back from the fo'c'sle with my helmet, clapped it on my head and tossed my shield at my feet, then stood with his own shield over me. Once within bowshot, their archers would be marking me.

"Stig, if I'm hit the tiller's yours."

He nodded without looking.

All the night's weariness was gone. The blood sang in my ears and a great happiness, just salted with fear, filled me up.

The wound-bees began to buzz about our heads. Bui rolled from his seat with an arrow in the angle of his neck and shoulder, and Helgi screamed a curse seeing his hand pinned by a shaft to the handle of his oar. Soon Starkad's shield bristled like a boar's back with arrows. One shaft flew past him and struck me between the eyes, rebounding with a *whang* from the nosepiece of my helmet.

Our enemy bore down on us, his warriors leaning out from the prow, screaming and shaking their weapons.

"Boys," I shouted, "listen sharp now, and we'll play this sea-ox a trick."

Perhaps it was Odin who whispered it in my ear. Or was it my father, for I sensed him close? I take no credit for myself.

"Steady ... steady now ... watch me."

It was plain from their course that they meant to grapple to us on the port side, so their port rowers would be alert for the command to ship oars at the last instant before they struck us, while the men on the starboard side would be at ease.

"Steady—steady—*pull!*"

The water churned as the Viper leapt forward—three ship's lengths ... two ... Now! I threw myself against the tiller, and the Viper slewed around, darting across their bow. "Pull again!" I hauled the tiller hard over and she danced on the water like a dolphin, turning on her tail and springing ahead again. "Oars in!"

Before our enemy could help himself, we were on his starboard side, running up on his oars and snapping them like twigs, and knocking his rowers, tip over ass, all over the deck. Out snaked our grappling hooks and, with a groan of wood on wood, the two hulls slid together.

Glum hopped from foot to foot in a fine madness, howling and biting the rim of his shield, his breast laid bare. As the ships touched, he flung the shield away, took their gunnel at a bound, and landed in the their midst, whirling his long-hafted axe around his head.

Seeing him, the battle joy rose in all our throats and shouting the name of Odin—for not one of us was a Christman now!—we went screaming over the side.

It was a wild brawl of a battle. I remember they had a big fellow on their side who wielded a halberd with both hands. His style of fighting was to ram a man in the belly hard enough to burst his ring-mail and then, just as if he were pitching hay, swing him up and hurl him overboard.

He had done this to two or three when Glum, who had already cleared off one side of their deck, cut a path to him. One look at that face was enough: the haymaker threw himself into the sea.

As for me, I shoved and was shoved all over the rolling deck, chopping away at legs and necks and "bathing my blade in the red wound-dew" (as we poets say), when at last I came within reach of their captain. He was a big, shaggy man with a broad face as pink as a ham and a red beard braided into pigtails.

Finding me before him, he struck his thigh and roared out that Red Kol would yield his ship to no ugly young pup such as I or, by God's guts, they could take and feed him to the eels! And, so saying, he charged me with his sword.

He had the advantage of size, but I was quicker. I kept him in play, dodging his lunges and swipes and leading him round in circles, 'til before long he was blowing like a whale, and his color had darkened from ham to roast beef. Desperate to end our duel while he could still stand, he aimed an especially hard blow at me and bent his blade double on Wound-Snake's tempered Frankish edge.

"Hold," he puffed, "while I straighten her." And leaning against the bulwark, he put his knee up to his sword to bend it back.

When a man's luck is out, nothing is to be gained by helping him put off his doom. When he dropped his eyes to his sword, I swung up with a backhanded stroke that caught him in the mouth, slicing off his lip and chin and spilling his teeth on the deck. He went down, choking on his blood.

249

"Red Kol won't kiss his wife again," said one of his crew, tossing his own sword at my feet.

As the word passed that their chieftain was done for, the rest of his crew broke off and asked for quarter.

My victory was so sudden I couldn't for a moment take it in—until Stig's crooked grin showed itself to me, and the flushed faces of Stuf and Otkel, laughing because they had had their first blooding and were still alive; and Glum, filthy with gore and his howl reduced to a hoarse croak—until, in short, I saw them all around me and heard them cry: "Tangle-Hair! Tangle-Hair! Tangle-Hair!"

I have been saluted by troops many times since, but the first time, like a boy's first woman, is surely the sweetest.

"D'you hear, Black Thorvald?" I whispered. "D'you hear it, Father?"

It soon appeared, however, that glory would be our only reward. Kol and his men had gone all spring without taking a prize and there was little aboard worth stealing.

We turned instead to sorting out the dead and wounded. Seven of my new Norwegians had been killed and two others so badly hurt that they died within the day. And all the rest of us were cut up some way or another. For my part, I found I had lost just the tip of my right little finger, I don't know how. A ridiculous sort of wound but painful once the heat of battle was past.

As we were throwing the dead overboard, Red Kol did a fine thing. Not caring to live with his shame—or without his chin—he dragged himself to the gunnel, indicated by some pathetic gestures that he wished to hold his sword in his hand, and clutching it, toppled into the sea.

His men looked sullenly at me. "See how a Dane dies!" one of them said in a loud voice. They were all Danes, they said, sailing out of Hedeby Town in Jutland—and not accustomed to taking orders from other men.

"Butcher the lot," snarled Brodd to me, "and take the ship, she's worth a bit, ain't she? It's a shame to fight so hard for so little."

But for one thing, we hadn't the men to put a crew aboard her, and for another, who would be left to tell our deeds in Denmark if we killed them all?

"I'll choose out fifteen of their best," I said. "We can guard that many, and at the first market town we come to, we'll put them on the block and share the profits. Meantime, we'll hobble them with ropes around their ankles, sit them at the oars, and make them do the rowing."

For this I was cheered a second time long and loud. Oh, what a shrewd and far-sighted captain I was!

When we were ready to sail away, "Danes," I cried, with a wave of my hand, "tell them in Hedeby Town that Odd—that *Black* Odd Thorvaldsson is the man who beat you!"

✝

My plan was to make for some port on the Wendish coast where, besides selling our slaves, I could leave my wounded and enlist more crew. One of the prisoners, a man called Ottar, volunteered in a whisper—hoping, no doubt, to earn my gratitude—to guide us to Jumne, which, he said, was the greatest town of the Wends, where men gathered to buy and sell from every country in the East, and where good sailors could always be found.

And so for Jumne I set our course.

We sailed by easy stages, making landfall twice at little islands on the way to rest and fill our water barrels. Our prisoners gave us no trouble, for I set Glum to watch over them day and night. They were so docile, in fact, that we soon stopped bothering to tie their feet.

The sun had set on the fifth day from the sea fight and the sickle of a new moon was rising when we spied a light on the dark horizon.

"Jumne?" I asked Ottar.

In spite of his mates groaning and cursing him, he nodded that it was.

As we drew closer, what had appeared as a single point of light divided in two—each a beacon fire burning on the top of a square stone tower. And what had seemed to be only a stretch of dark coast between them, became a pair of vast stone arms that reached into the sea to encircle a wide harbor. The beacon towers stood at the two ends of these arms and were joined together by an archway that was high and wide enough to let a dragon ship pass under it, mast, oars, and all. The passage, however, was barred against us by a massive iron chain.

Coming within hailing distance, and seeing no signs of life anywhere, I cupped my hands and hallooed. No answer came back from the black wall that loomed above us.

"We're a peaceful ship," I called again, pronouncing my words carefully to make these foreign sentries understand, "seeking Jumne Town."

Above us, a laugh, and the silhouettes of heads appeared on the parapet. Suddenly, I had a bad feeling about this place. But before I could change my mind, a thrum sounded from a loophole in the wall and a point of fire flashed out, boring a smoking hole in our sail. We dove for our shields.

"Veer off!" shouted a voice from the wall. "You've nothing to do with the Jomsvikings, nor they with you!"

"Braggi! Hi, Braggi!"—a different voice—"Ingjald wagers a silver ounce you don't hit a man before he does!"

"Back water!" I cried as a second fire-dart streaked toward us. One of my Norwegians twisted and dropped to the deck with the thing flaming in his chest.

"Pay me, Ingjald!" crowed the one called Braggi.

More voices took up the challenge, and from all along the wall catapults thrummed, raking our deck with fire. A tongue of flame licked up the sail where a fire-dart pinned it to the mast. From somewhere amidships Stig was bawling, "Push, damn you—push on the oars!" And from the bow I heard the scream of my baffled berserker.

Then another voice: "Up, Danes!"

In an instant they were over the side and splashing toward the chain—half our rowing strength—while my own men cowered behind their sea chests! I thought I would go mad then and there, with helpless fury.

The sail was now a sheet of flame and the timbers smoked in a dozen places. Deep within me, memories stirred of that other fire, while the smell of burning flesh filled my throat. I stood for an instant paralyzed with fear.

Stig broke the spell, shaking me and crying, "Odd, the sail. Help me!"

Bending low, we dashed through the hail of darts and together hacked at the shrouds until the yardarm fell in a shower of sparks. We stamped out the smoldering rags of sail, then plunging our helmets in the water barrel, dashed out the smaller fires on deck, and all the while screamed at the men to row.

Taking an oar myself, we pushed for our lives, moving the Viper slowly away from the wall. The darts began to fall wide, hissing into the water off to our left. With our fires put out, their gunners had lost us in the dark. The whole bloody shambles probably hadn't lasted three minutes.

Stunned and spent, we drifted out of range.

"Everyone call out his name," I ordered, "and say if he's hurt."

Voices answered in the dark:

"Stig—nothing much, burnt my fingers."

"Kraki—not hurt."

"Bengt—not hurt, thanks to God and Blessed Olaf."

"Halfdan—I think my leg's broke."

I counted twenty-one.

"Stuf?" came Otkel's voice in a whisper. "Stuf?" He groped along the deck, throwing himself on one smoking corpse after another, until he touched one that slumped over its oar—"Ahhh, Stuf!"

We Icelanders stood around him as he cradled his dead friend in his arms. Looking closely, I could see where the dart had pierced the back of Stuf's skull, gone clear through the helmet, driving the metal into his head, and come halfway out through his mouth.

"Say a Paternoster for him, Otkel, if you can," Starkad said gently, "and then quickest out of sight is best."

The boy wrenched out some words while we lifted Stuf up and slipped him over the side. He was the first of my Icelanders to die.

We felt in the dark for other bodies.

"Here's something," called Brodd from the fo'c'sle, dragging a figure to its feet. "One of Red Kol's." Twisting his arms behind him, he thrust his face at me. I beat it with my fists until I had exhausted my rage enough to speak. And then I pricked him in the throat with the point of my knife.

"You cowardly bastard, what *was* that place?"

"Call' Jom'bor'," mumbled the face through bleeding lips.

"Called what?" I pressed harder with my knife.

"Jomsbor'—Jomsborg."

"Not Jumne?"

"Please—not my idea," the fellow began to sniffle, "Ottar's idea—he passed us the word."

"And those—what did they call themselves, Jomsvikings?—they're friends of yours?"

Not friends exactly. His story came out in quavering fragments of speech. The warriors who held that harbor were greedy, grim, and pitiless men. Still, they were Danes, and maybe inclined to reward some countrymen for delivering into their hands a well-made ship and its crew. At worst, it was nearer home than the slave pens of Jumne.

"And you—why didn't you jump with the others?"

"Can't swim," the bruised lips mumbled.

And, finally, did this scum, this maggot, know where Jumne really was? And would he show us the way in hopes that I might forget to cut his throat?

He would.

25

the Last viking

We found Jumne later that same night on an island hidden in a maze of channels and lagoons at the mouth of the River Oder. I kept my promise strictly to the maggot—about not cutting his throat, I mean. When we were sure of our bearings, I let Otkel tie his hands and push him overboard.

As we brought the Sea Viper in toward the sheltered roadstead, a sea of lights spread out before us—the cook fires of merchants encamped along the beach next to their ships. Around their fires they sat, jabbering in Frisian and Saxon, Wendish, Arabic, Greek, and still stranger tongues (although I couldn't have told you then what any of them were). Here we too would camp, but first our rumbling bellies needed filling.

We beached the Viper, removed her figurehead out of respect for the spirits of the place, hung out our shields on the gunwales, and plunged greedily into the confusion of taverns and cook shops that sprawled helter-skelter along the waterfront. But as it happened, no place was roomy enough for us all, and so some stopped here and some there until finally there remained only Stig, Glum, Brodd, and myself, together with Kraki and Bengt of the Nidaros boys.

Beyond the beach, the lights of the town shone everywhere from doors and windows thrown open to the heavy night air. The place was huge—many times bigger than Nidaros—and it stayed up later at night. Putting aside hunger for a while, I led our party up one lane and down another, deeper into the town, just to take in the size of it, until before long we had left the hubbub of the waterfront far behind.

"Listen!" said Stig. There was a murmur of shouting from somewhere far in the distance. "There's no end to the place," said Brodd. "If you told 'em at home, they'd call you a liar."

"Icelanders?" sneered Bengt. Lank-haired and dumpling-faced, at fifteen he was the youngest of our crew. "Why, I guess Icelanders would call you a liar if you was to tell 'em dogs have fleas! Eh, Captain? Ha, ha!"

Norwegians love to pretend that we are bumpkins because we have no towns.

"It's hard if we're to be mocked by babies," said Brodd, and knocked Bengt down with his fist. Immediately, Kraki went for his knife. He was Bengt's second cousin and big enough to tackle Brodd. I jumped between them, swearing at all three with a rougher tongue than I had used before to any man in the crew.

It's what we've just come through, I thought, being shamed and beaten by those Jomsvikings and not a thing we can do about it, and so we turn on each other.

Stig and I held them apart until they cooled off.

"Enough of this wandering then," grumbled Kraki, "I want to drink."

So we set about to retrace our steps. After blundering a while down streets too dark and quiet, it was plain that we were lost.

"Let these shrewd town-dwellers find us the way out," muttered Brodd.

But Bengt and Kraki kept quiet.

As we rounded a corner into still another unfamiliar lane, Stig grimaced and said, "What is that stench?"

From the front of nearly every house, long poles leaned out over the footway, from whose ends hung the rotting carcasses of fowls and cats and other small things—offerings, I guessed, to the city's gods. In this region of the world, the White Christ still trod lightly.

At the bottom of the lane we chose a branching path, and presently found ourselves in a dark little street that was fenced along one side by a row of palings higher than our heads. Baffled again, we were just turning back when the shouting that Stig had heard before sounded suddenly closer.

Out of the shadows ahead of us, burst a mob of running men, their faces garish in the light of torches. We stood back to let them pass, but before they reached us, a gate in the palisade flew open, and paying us no heed at all, they halted and milled around it, all shoving at once to get through. In the midst of them, a figure thrashed and struggled, letting go a string of curses in a fine, fiery Norse that rose above the foreign babble.

Now, here's a chance, thought I, to wash away the taste of defeat.

And so I cried, "Boys, does it seem to you too many foreigners for one lone Northman? We must make him share!"

With a whoop, we charged them.

Their rear rank turned in surprise to face us. They were armed mostly with stones and cudgels, though a few brandished swords. Meanwhile the rest, with their prisoner, hurried on through the narrow gate, banging it shut and bolting it behind them.

We made short work of the defenders and five blows of Glum's axe brought down the gate. We stumbled through it just in time to see the mob disappearing inside a steeply-roofed building that stood some hundred paces back from the fence. On either side of the doorway, poles, like those that lined the streets outside, receded into the shadows. A breeze carried the smell of decay to our nostrils. All this I took in in less time than it takes to tell it.

Glum was first to the door and held it open for us with his shoulder. With swords drawn, we burst inside—and stopped short. The narrow chamber was packed with men and women: short, broad-headed, mostly fair; the men's heads, which were shaved back to the ears, presented a great surface of scalp to reflect the glow of the torches that lined the walls. The look on those faces was murderous. But that wasn't what stopped us.

Against the farther wall, there squatted, huge and heavy, on feet crusted with blood, a god, whose oaken body was cracked and black with the smoke of centuries. It stared out of white saucer eyes set in four misshapen heads. I hadn't the squeamish nature of a Christman, but this was not an easy god to look at all the same.

And stretched on the ground with his head between two of the god's black feet, was their prisoner, writhing under the weight of three or four of his captors, one of whom held a wicked-looking short sword to his throat.

"Wendfolk business. Go away, you!"

A thick-set man glowered at us from under bushy eyebrows. Behind him, his people raised their clubs and stones menacingly. I guessed there were upwards of fifty of them to our five.

But Glum replied with a terrific howl that made them all gasp and shrink back though there was little room in the packed chamber for them to move. All, that is, but the bushy-browed man, who bravely stood his ground.

Seizing the moment, I cried in a ringing voice, "That man's our friend, let him go!"

Bushy-brows scowled and gave me back just as loud, "That one steal. You look—"

Turning, he pushed his way to the side wall of the temple, bent over a low stand, and came up with a great wooden bowl cradled in his bulging arms. "You look!" he commanded again.

I looked and saw enough copper and silver there to have paid for my ship twice over.

"Steal," he repeated.

"Is *that* what this is about? I shook my head and smiled. "Up to his old tricks again, is he? Well, we are heartily ashamed of him. Look, you tell me what he took and I'll make it up to you—no, no, I insist."

The subject of our talk stopped struggling and lay quite still, too startled, no doubt, to move.

"Now, how much did you say?" I asked in my friendliest tone while reaching into my purse and pulling out a handful of coins—the last ones that I possessed in the world.

The Wends began to whisper among themselves. Bushy-brows just stared and looked perplexed. Finally, balancing the heavy bowl in one arm, he held up a square hand with three blunt fingers showing. "This many ounce."

"Only that?" I smiled.

Before he could think again, I handed my sword to Bengt who was beside me, and stepped forward with my palm out-stretched.

Cautiously, bushy-brows moved the bowl towards me—the whole room leaned forward—and with a kick I sent it flying into the air.

Pandemonium. I flung myself on the man with the short sword, the lads leapt in around me, slashing right and left, Glum howled and the Wends fell over each other, scrambling for their treasure and bolting for the door.

"Man, get me on my feet and be quick!" snarled the figure on the floor.

Not long on gratitude, I thought, and started to say, "Find your own feet," when I took a closer look at him.

He was nearly as dirty, cracked, and seamed as the wooden idol that crouched over him. But while that god was oversupplied with eyes, hands, and feet, this poor fellow lacked one of each.

"Odd, half the damn town's out there!" called Stig from the doorway.

"Right, old fellow, up you get." I gathered him and slung him onto Glum's shoulders piggyback. "Form a wedge, boys," I ordered.

But the boys, aside from Glum and Stig, were on their hands and knees, scrabbling in the dark for the coins and stuffing them down their shirts and in their shoes and caps as fast as they could scoop them up.

"Brodd, damn you! Kraki, Bengt!"

They pretended not to hear me.

A spear thudded against the doorpost, making Stig jump back for cover. Beyond the open door stretched a fiery sea of torches. *If they light the roof—!*

"As you hope to live," I shouted, "stand to!" And finding my sword on the floor, where Bengt had tossed it, I applied the flat of it to their backsides. They looked mutinous, but they got to their feet.

Behind Glum, who cleared the way with more stupendous howls, we charged into the crowd.

"Where away, old man?" I shouted to the bundle on Glum's back.

"Out the gate and hard to starboard!"

With the mob hot on our heels, we raced through dark streets. About the time I thought I could run no more, our pursuers fell back and let us go. We had reached the waterfront, where the foreigners outnumbered the natives, and they feared to raise a riot here. Gasping and laughing, we staggered about, while from the taverns that lined the street, a crowd poured out to see what all the commotion was, and buzzed with curiosity at the sight of Glum and his passenger.

We chose a place and went in. It was full of the usual waterfront riff-raff, jostling each other on the benches, gambling noisily, and dousing themselves with ale. On closer inspection, a half dozen of the riff-raff turned out to be my men. Starkad caught my eye and waved us over.

"Bit of fun with the locals," I explained breathlessly.

"Who's that wreck of a man?"

259

Out the gate and hard to starboard!

"Can't say—we've just met."

Glum bent down and the old man slid lightly to the floor, steadying himself with a bony hand on the berserker's arm. Then, giving himself a shake, he peered narrowly at us and in a rasping voice, announced himself as, "Einar Tree-Foot"—simultaneously thumping the floor with his peg leg by way of explanation of the name—"who would stand you to a round of drink, for he knows how to behave politely, but that he hasn't got the silver for it. Lacking that, he'll say good night to you."

He let go of Glum, but immediately stumbled against the table, catching himself as best he could with his one hand and his round knob of a wrist. He tried another step, gripping the table's edge, but keeping his face turned away from us, as though ashamed of his infirmity. I caught him under the arms before he fell again and sat him on the bench next to Otkel. We crowded in beside him.

"Bloody Wend bastards took away my crutch," he growled.

Starkad, sitting down opposite, pushed a trencher of boiled venison and a pile of flatbread toward him. "Sink your fang in this, old man. Put some flesh on those bones—what ones you have left."

We laughed, and the old man smiled, saying that he would take just a bite for politeness, since he had dined already that day and wasn't very hungry. But from the way he fell on the meat, giving it light treatment with his few stumps of teeth and swallowing as fast as he could put it in his mouth, I guessed that he had not eaten in days.

While we watched him, I told the others what little I knew, and when at last he pushed the trencher away and belched contentedly, I asked him to tell us his story.

He was a while making up his mind to speak, tugging on his beard, which resembled a Billy goat's, and frowning to himself. Then he said abruptly, "You've stood me to a supper, and so I will sing for it. Einar Tree-Foot knows what's fair. I live as I must, being too old to fight and too young to beg."

As to his age, he must have been seventy or more. He was leather-skinned and lean as a bone. His shirt hung from his pointed shoulders like the faded sail from a yardarm on a windless day. Of his eyes, the left was a socket, barely hidden behind a bit of filthy rag, but the right one was needle-sharp, black and quick, like the eye of a bird.

"Come every new moon night, these Wends like to throw a coin in four-headed Svantevit's bowl—him being the chief bogey hereabouts—and I do likewise, except that I have a trick, don't you see, of taking out more 'n what I put in—with these."

He held up his left hand, flexing the skinny fingers and running a supple thumb over the tips of them. Stig, who claimed to be a thief of some pretensions, looked on with interest.

"The blind old hag that guards the place never caught me at it once in all these many years. Only tonight they had a different old woman mounting guard, and doesn't she let out a yowl when she sees me pop a coin into my mouth—that's where I hide 'em. Well, I lay her out with my crutch and make off hot-foot with the lot of 'em at my heels. Was a time, when I was a younger man, that I could run faster on one pin than any of you on two, but this time they overtook me, and the rest you know. I'm obliged to you"—he noticed me with a nod—"you're a trickster. I like tricksters. And I'll say 'Thank you', which you may know that Einar Tree-Foot doesn't say to many."

I thought, here's a stiff-necked old codger, for a petty thief. But I returned the nod and told him there was no need of thanks, since we were men who craved adventure, as he could see for himself, and who owned a sleek dragon and were bound for the viking life.

"The viking life!" He half rose from his seat and pounded the table with his one good hand—astonished, bowled over, ambushed, and routed by this huge absurdity. "Vikings!" He threw back his head in a cackling laugh that ended in a fit of coughing.

"You're too late! Go home to your mother, moon-calf. There are no vikings anymore."

Now I was out of patience. "Tell that to Red Kol," I shot back. And my men joined in with a chorus of angry grunts.

"Red Kol?" The black needle eye pricked me. "What've you got to do with Red Kol?"

"We met him at sea a few days ago," I answered coolly. "And he looked like a viking to us."

"Yes, well, there is him"—he screwed up his mouth as though tasting something nasty—"and one or two more like to call themselves vikings and scare folks. But it don't signify. How'd you get away from him?"

"We didn't get away from him," I weighed out my words slowly. I wasn't going to let this evil old ruffian make light of us. "We took him."

"Because," Starkad broke in angrily, "we've a captain who knows his business."

"And because," I added, with my arm on Glum's massive shoulder, "we are so lucky as to have in our band a genuine Swedish berserker."

The old fellow, who was just putting the ale horn to his lips, swallowed fast and looked up in wonder. "By the One-Eyed Odin, I should have known! The real thing? D'you bite your shield, man? D'you bare your breast to iron?"

Glum gave a deprecating smile and in his husky voice replied, "You can say you have ridden on the wolf's back, old man."

"Indeed, I'll say it." He looked from one to another of us as though only now seeing us for the first time. "And I'll say that sometimes Einar Tree-Foot speaks too quick."

Satisfied with the impression I had made on him, I poured him more drink and asked carelessly, "Have you been a viking in your own day, then?"

He was silent for some moments while he fingered his beard and frowned. I was about to shrug and let my question pass, not wanting to embarrass him, when he said,

"There's a fortress on this coast not far away, stone walls around its harbor. You'd have passed it sailing in."

All the warmth went out of me. "We did, old man. We found them rude."

"Oh, young friend," he chuckled, "men have found them rude these hundred years. What, have you never heard of the Jomsvikings?"

That word seemed to cut through all the other hubbub in the room. Faces everywhere looked up. Perhaps this old man's story had been heard here before, perhaps was worth hearing again. He aimed his voice high and began.

"Some still live—drunk most of the time and gone to fat, skulking behind their wall. But most of us are dead, or as good as. Time was, though, when we could put sixty dragons in the water.

"Palna Toki the Dane, foster-father to King Svein Forkbeard of Denmark, built that fortress and put in her the best of the Danish fighters— blood brothers all, none younger than eighteen nor older than fifty. Inside her gates no female ever passed, nor was any slander kindled twixt one man and another, nor any word of fear ever spoke. We shared our booty, obeyed our jarl, and the bond between us was stronger than the bond of kin.

"And every summer we sailed out to plunder—from Bjarmaland to Ireland. Men wailed and prayed when they saw our sails coming."

Kraki snorted, as much as to call the old man a liar, looking round belligerently at the rest of us.

Einar, without noticing Kraki's existence by so much as a look, continued.

"It so happened one night, though, that Jarl Sigvalt—he was our chieftain in those days—drank deep at a feast and swore a powerful oath that he would hunt and harry his old enemy Jarl Haakon out of Norway, wipe his ass on Haakon's best cloak, drink up all Haakon's ale, and lie with Haakon's wife. In the morning when he sobered, it seemed like a poor idea, but he had said it out loud and so he was bound."

In spite of my irritation with the old man, I leaned forward, enthralled. Here was word music!

"We sailed for Norway in our sixty dragons, thinking to take Haakon by surprise. But don't the Norns love a joke. We found him laying for us in the Jorundfjord with a hundred and eighty sail at his back, all the hulls lashed together and crammed to the gunwales with fighters. Even so, he found us a tough mouthful to chew. We gave him blow for blow until in his fear he sacrificed his very own son, his youngest son, to Odin! No sooner done but a hailstorm come out of nowhere and beat against our faces."

Here, Glum, his face more than ever a living mirror, laughed out loud as if to say, Yes, that's friend Odin—that's his style.

"Then it was Jarl Sigvalt's turn to be afraid," Einar continued. "He turned tail with his own squadron—it shames me to say it—and left the rest of us to perish.

"I was a warrior aboard Vagn Akesson's ship, and just about your age, my young captain. Scarce had my beard yet, but I was as fierce as any. Now came Haakon's oldest son alongside and grappled to us. We gave him good play at Odin's game, but he beat us down at last and took us prisoner—thirty of us in all with our captain. They brought us ashore and sat us down on a log with our feet tied together, and then, just to mock us, asked us if we minded dying. 'Not a bit', says we with a smile. So they commence to chop off our heads. One man of us says, 'Strike me in the face so you may see that I don't go pale.' Another one says how he had always wondered if the body lived on for a bit with its head off and might he hold a dagger in his hand, to raise it as a sign if he could still form the thought.

"Well, they chopped and they chopped, each man making some joke or other as they took him—until they come to the eleventh man—which was this man that sits here before you.

"Now, I had a fine, handsome head of golden hair in those days, and I pulled it for'ard, like *this*." He raked his hand up the back of his head and stirred up a few white strands "And I ask politely wouldn't someone hold it away from the blood, being as I was vain about it. So up steps a Norwegian and takes hold of it with both his hands and—I can't help but laugh when I think of it—as the axe comes down, I jerk back my head, and I pull that man for'ards—" Einar hunched and tossed himself around, "like this. And doesn't that axe lop off both his hands! You should've seen his face!

"Then up jumps I, crying, 'Who has his hands in my hair?' and 'Not all the Jomsvikings are dead!'

"To make short of it, Haakon gave us our freedom out of admiration. Admiration! But only a score of us out of that whole ship's company lived to tell of it. And many a brave boy was left behind to feed the crabs in Jorunga Bay."

There was silence in the room as he finished—broken finally, by someone's loud laugh. Someone else, sitting at the next bench, tossed a copper onto the table in front of the old man, which he caught with a quick movement of his fingers and dropped into his bosom, never looking where it came from. A few more pennies followed.

But to me, my victory over Red Kol was beginning to seem like nothing but a piddling skirmish.

Then Stig asked, "Einar Tree-Foot, what became of you after that day?"

"Oh, it wasn't quite the end of us," he sighed. "Not quite the end. There were more fights, and I was in 'em. I left this hand in Sweden"—he flourished the knob in our faces—"and this leg in England, and this eye—well, I forget where this eye went. But when I got too old and trimmed of my parts, they put me out to end my days where you find me."

I looked ruefully at my bandaged little finger that was shorter by a joint. Only a small beginning, but still—how many parts would I be trimmed of, I wondered, when half a century was gone.

Otkel remarked bitterly, "Fine brothers, these, to cast you off." His heart still ached for his cousin, Stuf.

"Stick to what you know, boy. It's our way, and Einar Tree-Foot don't complain of it. But that's why I laugh, don't you see, when you tell me that you crave to be vikings. Because *we* were vikings, my young friends, and the world won't soon see our like again." He took another pull at the horn and a ferocious bite of bread. "And so, to business."

"Eh? What business is that, old man?"

"Your business, of course. D'you mean to go a-viking or do you not?" I said we did.

"Then, you'll want a pilot."

"No, old man," I answered quickly. "The odor of the Jomsvikings is too strong on you."

"You needn't sniff me."

"So say you," said Starkad. "But if we should ever run into these blood-brothers of yours outside their walls, would you not choose their side?"

"Pah!" The knobby wrist waved his question away. "You've more profitable things to think about than that."

"There's Otkel," I said. "He has more reason than any of us to hate you. They killed his kinsman, and he may want to kill you in return."

Einar raised an eyebrow at this and turned to the shy youth. "Is that true?" he asked, as one might inquire about the weather. "And will you stab me in my sleep or how will you do it?" He looked long and searchingly into Otkel's face until the boy dropped his eyes and shifted on his seat.

"Otkel and I will get on," said Einar smoothly.

"Tree-Foot," spoke Stig, gazing up and away. "Men can put away their hatred for good enough reasons, and no one should think the worse of them for it. What reason might we have?"

"Sense at last," Einar snorted. "What reason? Because I was spawned on this coast, and she has been mother, father, and sweetheart to me since babyhood. Because I know every shoal and current, every creek and cove of her from Hedeby to Ladoga. I know where the fat villages are hid, and I know the mounds where old kings lie moldering with their gold!"

He leaned across the table, bringing his head close to Stig's and mine— patchy-scalped, white-bearded, loose-skinned, maimed, toothless, and decayed—the whole of its life force concentrated in an eye. I tried to see there another face, of a youth about my age, ruddy-cheeked and yellow-haired....

His hand reached out and gripped my arm. There was more strength in the fingers than I would have believed.

"Einar Tree-Foot wants one more viking summer, Captain, before the crows have his carcass. He'll make you rich for it." For a long moment, the eye held me. "Now," he said, "I am going out in the street to piss." He let me go and heaved himself up, tottering on his ill-assorted legs. "And when I come back, tell me your decision." He accepted Glum's long-handled axe to steady himself with and turning, clumped away to the door.

"He's all gristle, that one," said Stig.

"Aye, and what a story," said Starkad with a shake of his head. "You think he's fooling us, Odd?"

"I don't know. I'm inclined to put him to the proof. Otkel, could you bear to ship with him?"

Otkel kept his eyes down and shrugged.

"Stig? You others?"

They nodded one by one.

"Then it's settled."

I found him just beyond the tavern door, standing straight as a stick with his back up against the wall and Glum's axe on his shoulder as though he had been set there to guard the place. I touched his shoulder and led him back through the door. He went without looking to right or left, with his chin thrust out and his mouth set in a warrior's scowl. And if, where the firelight caught his eye, it glistened—just possibly—with wetness, I was careful not to see.

26

CAPTURED

Four weeks later.

A startled deer burst from the underbrush ahead of me—I jumped back with fright and then cursed myself silently. As the day died and a ghostly gray crept down through the tangled branches overhead, that uneasiness that many an Icelander feels in the deep woods grew stronger. Soon it would be too dark to see the path we were following, or the marks we had notched on trees along the way.

And it was getting colder, too. In these northern regions, a damp chill steals into the nights even in high summer, and after a day of rain the forest reeks with a clammy steam that curls around your feet and legs like the fog at sea.

The order to turn back was on my lips when one-legged Einar, who always somehow outstripped us on the march, gave a shout. We ran forward, pushing through the dripping pine boughs that swept our faces and soaked our sleeves, and caught up with him where the path skirted a little clearing.

"Heh? Heh?" Gripping my shoulder, he jabbed the air with his crutch. "Heh? Has Einar Tree-Foot lied?"

We pressed around him and looked where he pointed.

After all the long toilsome weeks, here finally was the thing he had promised us. Within a low ring of stones, the rounded grassy hump of a mound, shoulder-high and wide enough to hold a prince and all his treasure. In barrows like this, Einar had said, the chieftains of Finland lay sleeping in earth that was salted with silver and gold.

"By the Raven, we're rich men!" His bright eye glittered.

"Well, maybe he's told us the truth at last, the old fraud," said Starkad.

We stepped into the clearing, circling the tomb, probing it with our spear-points, looking for the way in. Except for the sound of our breathing and the soughing of the wind in the branches, a deep silence lay over everything. How could we know that Kammo eyed us from those dark treetops?

The summer, until now, had been disappointing. After taking on a dozen new hands and paying out the last of our silver for the Viper's refitting, we had spent nearly a month in coasting east and north along the marshy shore of the Varangian Sea.

To pass the time, I plied Einar with questions about the tribes who lived beside those stagnant pools and creeks: the long-haired Prussians with tattooed bodies, who inhabited the dismal swamps; the warlike Kurlanders whose ringforts held the wooded coast beyond the Vistula; and still farther north, the Ests, who worshiped birds and dragons and sacrificed men to unpronounceable gods.

"When a great one among 'em dies," said Einar, "they'll leave him to lie out for months sometimes, even in the summer while they mourn him. The body never rots, for their sorcerers know the trick of making cold, don't you see. Why, one time I saw a wizard of theirs freeze a pitcher of water with only the look of his eye."

"Tree-Foot, you *saw* this?"

"Well a brother Jomsviking saw it, then. You do vex me with your questions, Odd Tangle-Hair."

There was more in the same vein—fascinating, but no substitute for the bright gold we all craved.

From time to time we stopped to put off landing parties, but either the forts were too strong for us, or, when we attacked a lonely farmstead, it was only to find the inhabitants had fled deeper into the wood with their livestock and their women. We burned their houses in disgust and took what little they had left behind in the way of honey, wax, or pelts, but even these prizes we had to surrender to the greedy merchants of Gotland and Truso in exchange for just enough ale and meat to live on.

Once we caught some women, which raised our spirits for a while, and got a decent price for them, too, from a passing slaver, though they

269

were the worse for wear by then, and not particularly good looking to begin with.

But riches eluded us. As we drifted up into waters less and less traveled, the men grew unhappy and talked of turning back.

Still, Einar was undismayed. Farther to the north, said he, beyond a great gulf, lay the country of the Finns. "Witches there are, and monsters, as I've heard tell. But loot! You'll not see the like of it anywhere—*if* you're bold enough to look."

So on we sailed. And if any man was frightened he would not say so.

✝

So we came to be in that darksome wood; the Viper, a good hour's walk behind, moored to the bank of a creek with Stig and ten men to guard her, while the rest of us explored a path that must bring us at last, we thought, to some farm or village. It had brought us to this lonely barrow instead. By the All-Father, we were due for a change of luck!

Glum stepped forward and swung his axe, making the dirt fly up, and a little gold coin fell glittering at his feet, as shiny as the day it was put there.

"I'll chop all day for these wages," Glum smiled. Then we threw ourselves upon the barrow with knives, with fingers, like hungry men let loose on a haunch of meat, prying out the clods of turf, tearing them apart for their treasure.

Brodd drove his spear in at one end of the barrow striking wood, and we dug away the sods there to lay bare the timber frame beneath—too busy to notice how the shadows of the trees inched across the clearing.

"Pry 'er open!" cried Einar, dancing on his one leg, "Smash 'er in!"

As the wooden staves gave way under Glum's axe, a foul exhalation knocked us back. But the odor of gold was stronger. We squeezed inside, as many as could fit, to see our prize.

Not that you could see much—my memory of it comes through my fingertips. The corpse had not altogether dissolved and I had to touch it more than I cared to as I groped among the grave-goods heaped beside it.

Desperate for breath, we worked like frenzied moles, flinging the pieces of treasure out behind us—buckles and rings of silver, a casket of coins, a pair of well-wrought swords, a helmet richly embossed, a lump of amber the size of a fist with a piece of the sun inside it.

But while we plundered this old warrior of his wealth, each of us knew in a secret corner of his mind that the dead live on in their tombs.

Twilight found us still bundling our loot, and I began suddenly to fear that we could not get back to the ship before night fell.

"Why not camp here, then?" said young Bengt with a careless air.

"You'll stay alone if you do, you young fool," Brodd growled. But Bengt answered back, saying how Blessed Olaf had kissed him at his christening and how for that reason his mother had always taught him he had nothing to fear in this world or the next.

"Bengt," said I, "if we'd all been kissed by Olaf or even by your old mother, maybe we'd be braver men than what we are. Pick up your load and let's be off."

So off we went. But we had hardly gained the trees when Einar must run back for one more look around in case we had missed a ring or a button. By the Raven, he hadn't come this far to leave anything for another's pickings!

Once again then, with our shields on our backs and clutching our booty in our arms, we plunged into the forest. We hadn't gone half a mile before we realized we were lost. It had begun to rain again, too, and suddenly it was very dark. While we stood quarreling whether to go forward or back, we heard the first low note far away behind us.

"Eh?" said Starkad in a hushed voice. "Wolves?"

"Never," replied Einar firmly. "It's a moose or some such."

"Moose? No moose ever called like that."

"No, nor any wolf neither. Now, I tell you...."

It came again, off to our left this time—three wild and mournful notes close together.

"It's him, isn't it?" croaked Ivar, one of the new hands. "He wants his own back!"

"Well, he won't get it back from me!" swore Einar. But there was a catch in his voice.

I began to taste fear like steel on my tongue. "Enough talk. Keep close and follow me. Glum. Glum! Where are you? I need your sharp eyes."

"Glum's gone strange," came someone's voice from the rear. "He's mewling like a sick cat and won't take his hands off his ears."

"Before I could reply to this, the grisly cries sounded again from left, right, and rear of us.

Bruce Macbain

"It *is* him and all his dead mates," Ivar groaned. "Here! Have it back." He flung down the few pieces of treasure he had bundled in his cloak and shoved past the men around him.

I gripped my portion all the tighter and struck off through the trees, Einar swinging on his crutch beside me, and the others pressing on our heels—and none of us knowing where we went, only that we couldn't stay.

Still, the ghost voices pursued us, gained on us, drove us faster until we were trotting, running, losing each other in the dark, while a wind swept through the trees, hurling the rain at our backs and making the forest tremble.

Then Kammo's cold fingers squeezed our hearts. Flinging down our treasure and our shields, we crashed through the branches, slipping on moss-slick rocks and gray, rotted wood, careening against black tree trunks—fleeing in mortal terror while the ghost voices howled all around.

Scratched and battered and sobbing for breath, I tripped and pitched forward into a black ooze that sucked at my hands and feet. Around me others splashed and struggled in the muck. I heard their voices crying to Odin and Jesus.

"Back! Turn back!" I screamed, twisting around and heaving myself at a tussock of marsh grass. The ghost voices shrieked on every side of us now, unbearably loud, but mingled with them were other sounds as well—barking dogs and humming arrows.

Shadows darted among the trees by the margin of the swamp. I drew Wound-Snake from its scabbard and slashed about me wildly, striking only empty air—until a snarling form hurtled out of the dark and bore me down. Instantly, hands held me, wrenching my arms behind my back and binding them with a bowstring.

They were hunting us down and herding us together at the edge of the bog. There they pushed us to our knees and strung us together on a rope, like fish on a line.

Meantime the howling kept up in distant parts of the forest, until one of our captors lifted a long funnel of birch bark to his lips and gave an answering blast.

This was the ghost voice—a birch bark horn! I groaned aloud for shame. If I had only kept us in a circle with our shields locked together, we could have withstood these men, whoever they were, all night long. Instead, I had run with the fleetest. For, as I have said, Kammo lurked in

272

the trees that night: that is the name the Finns give to the sudden terror that falls on men and beasts in the wildwood, sending them flying in mindless panic until they drop.

It was he who had beaten us, and I would feel his cold finger on my heart again before I ever left this land.

Their leader came to inspect us where we huddled in the wet grass, taking each of us in turn by the hair and forcing back our heads to peer at us by the light of a torch.

His own face was long and narrow, the lips thin, and the eyes sunk in deep shadow as though they looked out from caves. He moved amongst us with the silent step of a cat. In the days to come we would know him well. His name was Joukahainen. And he was cruel as only cats are.

"Viikingit," I heard him say in a low voice to one of his men.

Hauling us to our feet, they began to drive us at sword's point through the black and dripping woods, setting their dogs to bite our heels when we stumbled. How long we walked I have no notion. The smell of pine alternated with the stench of the fens until, at last, we emerged into a wide stretch of meadow and I smelled all at once the fragrance of hay and a faint whiff of the sea.

All the while my brain seethed with half-formed schemes of escape. Thank the gods I had left Stig in charge of the Viper. Some way or another his cool head would find us.

Beyond the meadow an earthen rampart rose out of the black, and at the sound of a low whistle, a massive timber gate swung out on creaking hinges. Through it we were driven into a shadowy yard.

In the center of this yard the shape of a hall could just be made out, timber-sided and thatch-roofed, of such a size that a hundred men might sleep in it without touching elbows. Not far from this stood a little square building made of tightly fitted logs, a shed or a storeroom of some sort, as it seemed. It was here they halted us while a door was slid noisily to the side, and then drove us, still strung together, into the black and airless room.

At once we stumbled over bodies trussed up in the same way as ourselves and, as the door slid shut again, the muffled voice of Stig, from somewhere beneath my rump, bade me a good evening.

"Ambushed us ashore whilst we were cooking our dinner," he said bitterly when we had sorted ourselves out a little. "Shot us down with arrows before ever we saw them. Some of us are hurt, three they left for dead."

The Viper, as far as he knew, was still moored in the creek, and they had done her no harm. What direction that creek lay from the stinking hole in which we presently found ourselves, he had no more idea than the rest of us.

By counting off, I numbered us nineteen; six in a bad way from wounds. Sixteen were missing. One of those was Einar Tree-Foot. Still, we told each other, we would take the measure of this place come morning and show these Finns what sort of men they had to deal with.

Glum put an end to that brave talk. "Mates, I—I have never before tonight felt fear," he began in a voice so small we barely heard him. "Never felt Odin—gone. Friend Odd—" his voice trembled and broke, "friend Odd—I have lost the rage!"

We did our best to reassure him: "Glum, don't think about it," I said earnestly. "Anyone's nature can fail him now and then, you'll soon be your wolfish self again."

"Why, even Odin," urged Stig, "must sleep sometimes."

"And besides," added Starkad, "who could be at his best waist-deep in muck with a dog hanging on each arm and the wailing of god-knows-what in his ears?"

But Glum only moaned.

He could sense things in his animal soul—presences, powers, dangers—where we saw nothing. What did he sense now? We lapsed into silence. Wedged side by side with our knees under our chins, our backs sore, and our hands numb from the cutting bowstrings that bound us, we whiled away the long hours in gloomy thought, with nothing to do but wait for what the morning might bring.

✝

It came soon enough.

Slivers of gray seeped through chinks in the wall, and we caught the familiar sounds of a farm waking up. Still, no one came near us, and we began to wonder if we were forgotten, so we pounded the walls with our feet and shouted to be let out.

Footsteps came our way. The door slid open on its track with a screech, letting in the gray day, and I saw with a shock what a wretched-looking bunch we were—dirty, bloody, haggard, and tangled like crabs in a sack.

Blond, bearded men—they could have been our countrymen but for their outlandish speech—dragged us out and stood us on our feet by the shed. Outside, the sky was the color of iron and a cold drizzle was falling. I saw that most of our captors were armed with crossbows. These deadly devices were their favorite weapons and they coated the tips of the darts with poison.

With shouts and blows they marched us from the shed around the corner of the great hall into the yard that lay before it. My heart sank as I took in the size of the place: it was both farm and fortress. Its tall rampart of earth and sharpened logs enclosed easily a dozen acres, with stables and granaries and all the usual outbuildings, and living quarters for several hundred.

My guess about the sea had been right. It seemed we were at the head of a narrow bay or inlet, for the tops of some wooded hills showed beyond the rampart on all sides but one. Set in the wall on that side was a wide gate of rough-hewn planks, bolted with a heavy crossbeam. On a parapet above it, sentries stood watch. Surely, I thought, there must be boats of some kind beached on the other side, if only we can get to them.

To my left, southwards more or less, another sturdy gate opened towards the fields. It was through this that we had passed the night before. It was the only gate they would ever open for us.

In the opposite direction, some few hundred paces away, the ground rose sharply and the rampart was extended outward and upward to enclose the foot of a peculiar cone-shaped hill of bare, dun-colored earth, which dominated the whole settlement. No feature of the place was of greater importance to us than this hill, but I was not to understand that for some time to come—if I can truly claim to understand it even now.

I had no more time for gazing, for a more worrisome sight forced itself upon me. I now saw the source of a smell that had assailed my nostrils the night before as they marched us along in the dark. I thought perhaps a dog had died and no one had taken it away. The yard in which we stood was sown with sharpened stakes of about the height of a man, and on most of them, in every stage of decomposition, were human heads.

Odin All-Father, I prayed, *let me not show fear*. Aloud, I said with a smile, that I didn't much care for the flowers they grew in this garden, and my men laughed loudly. Let no one say we weren't true vikings now!

Then, coming toward us through the gruesome thicket, I recognized that man with the silent cat's step. My impression of his features, I saw now, had been no trick of the firelight. His age was about five and twenty, his build extraordinarily thin. He was smooth-shaven, and his face, framed by straight blond hair, was nearly as fleshless as the whitened skulls atop their stakes.

Joukahainen. I felt the hairs stir on the back of my neck.

At a word from him, his men began to cut us loose from the ropes that passed under our arms. Four of the lads, unsupported, sank to the ground. In a swift instant his sword was out, and one, two, three, four, he struck off their heads—like turnips off a stalk. We hardly knew what we were watching before it was over.

I thought he would kill us all, but it was only the wounded, the useless ones. Two more poor lads were pulled out of line, forced to their knees, and slaughtered in the same way. One was Otkel.

When he stopped in front of Stig, whose hair on one side of his face was caked with blood, my heart froze. But Stig roared an oath and aimed a kick at him. Joukahainen smiled coolly and passed on. Clever Stig. Strong enough to fight, strong enough to work.

We watched the butchery of our mates with a careless air, as brave men should. And the lads died well—Einar the Jomsviking would have approved. Then, crowing like a cock, the Headsman, as we came to call him, did a little dance around his new trophies while whirling his sword around his head.

This weird performance might have gone on longer, but he stopped in mid-step at the sound of a voice that issued from the hall behind our backs. I turned to see who was there, but the only impression I got was of an untidy bundle of old clothes and wisps of white hair, half-hidden in the shadows well back of the open door. This puzzled me because I was sure I had heard the simpering voice of a little girl.

The Headsman, his thin lips curved into a smile, sauntered to the door, speaking some gibberish to his men with a final glance at us as he went by. I caught 'Viikingit' again, and another word that we would learn well in the days ahead—'orjat'. Slaves.

✝

We were slaves plain and simple. Like the thralls on my father's farm; only we were not treated like animals, for farmers treat their animals well enough. These men took pleasure in abusing us.

We all came in for our share, but Joukahainen made it his special business to torment Glum as soon as he discovered that the giant would not defend himself. A dozen times a day he would cut him with a sleigh whip until the blood ran, and jeer when Glum cringed and threw up his scarred arms in front of his face. The pain and confusion in the berserker's eyes then was almost more than I could bear to see.

The work they set us to, I need hardly describe: forking hay, mucking out the stables, tending the stock—things I had done all my life without minding much. What was hard were the constant threats and beatings; the confinement at night in our airless wooden box, not ten paces square, that stank of urine-soaked straw and unwashed bodies; the vile grub of spoiled greens and gristle; and always the pall of dismal weather and the stench of decay that overhung this place.

The one spot of brightness was that Einar Tree-Foot was not lost to us after all. Late in the afternoon on the third day after our capture, a hunting party brought him in, crutch and all, caked with mud and reeking to the sky. He'd been hiding all the while in the swamp where we were captured.

"Gave m'self up—for Einar Tree-Foot doesn't desert his mates," he said scowling when we were alone with him. "Young vikings want looking after."

Well, that was his story, and I won't dispute it. Certainly, those few days saved his life. Maimed as he was, he surely would have lost his head with the others that first morning. But when they brought him in Joukahainen was enjoying his daily sauna, and no one dared disturb him. The next day, the Headsman spent hunting, and by the time he finally noticed Einar, the old man had assigned himself the care of the chicken coop and appeared to be useful enough to let live.

In fact, with those nimble fingers of his, he pilfered eggs for us, which was all that saved us from starving utterly.

✝

After each weary day, we lay, huddled body against body on the cold earthen floor of our prison and dreamed of escape.

"Trolls take the place!" Kraki swore one night early in our captivity, down on his hands and knees, scratching in the dirt with his fingernails.

"Give it up," sighed Starkad wearily. "Haven't we tried? Without some sort of tool..."

Kraki turned on him savagely, "We'll steal a tool—a hatchet, a knife. Thor's Billy goat, we could steal a knife, couldn't we?"

"Not until our jailers grow more careless than they have been."

"Too late for me, I can't stick it. Captain," he turned his anger on me, "I'm not made like you and these others. I won't be a dog in chains! I mean to run away tomorrow when we're in the fields, and if there's a brave man here, let him come with me!"

"Run where?" Ivar laughed bitterly. We might as well be on an island in the ocean, except that it's an ocean of trees. The Finns know their way in it, and we don't. They'd catch us before we went half a mile. And if we did reach another settlement, who's to say they would treat us any better? It isn't this shed that's our prison—it's the whole damned country!"

"But the sea," cried Kraki, "that's *our* ocean. We've only to steal a boat..."

"Only that?" said Stig wearily. "Have you noticed, friend Kraki, how they guard the sea-gate day and night? And as for wriggling through the marsh that lies between the meadow and the shore, why, the sedge grows so thick you couldn't part it with a sword, and you'll meet some pretty snakes there, too."

"Heh?" struck in Eystein Crickneck. He was an addle-brained youth whose head lolled permanently to one side as the result of his having fallen out of a tree as a baby. I had taken him on in Jumne for the sake of his uncle, who was an experienced hand.

"Heh? Snakes is it? A snake won't bite you, friend Stig, if you rub up your toes with butter and ashes, you know. Bless me, I never go a-walking but that I rub up my toes—and I've not been bitten yet."

"Eystein Crickneck," Stig answered dryly, "a man may be thought wise if he never speaks and comes inside when it rains. Take it to heart."

There was a little laughter—most of it Eystein's, who always laughed the loudest at his own foolishness. And after that, silence.

At last young Bengt said, "Well, then, my God, what are we going to do?"

"You'll do what your captain tells you!" Einar snapped at him. "You and Kraki and all. You'll bide your time and save your lives for a better day."

I was glad to see that the Jomsviking, for all his talk of brave viking deaths, had a cannier side to his nature. Men who are determined to die like vikings usually succeed before they reach his ripe age. Einar Tree-Foot was a survivor. I liked him the better for it.

But Kraki answered him in a surly tone. "I want no wise words from the old fool who brought us to this." He flung himself past Eystein and his fingers reached for Einar's throat.

"Enough of that!" I ordered, putting myself between them. "Kraki sit down and listen to me. We are a crew. What one does, all must do. Sooner or later they will make a slip, and we will strike. Until then watch and wait."

I put as much conviction into this speech as I could manage, but truly, I hardly believed it myself. I could see despair growing in us, a little more every day. Soon it would turn to melancholy, in time to madness. More than a year had passed since my escape from Iceland. If this was to be the end of my adventure, I would have been better off to burn at home. "Wake up, Father Odin," I spoke to the dark, "please, wake up and see us."

Next morning, while we were working in the hay, Kraki made a dash for the trees. The guard who had been set to watch us saw him go, but made no hurry about sounding the alarm.

That evening they carried Kraki back. His head went up on a stake. His body they threw into the shed with us. From the looks of it a bear had gotten to him first.

To a man, we were frightened.

✝

Then one day, when we had been prisoners for two weeks or three, we made a discovery: we were not alone in our captivity.

It was evening, and we were being fed our slops and sour beer, as usual, on the ground in front of our cell, before being shut up for the night. Even in the rain—it had been raining all day—we would not willingly go inside that stifling box. As we squatted there, picking the stuff over, a figure came squelching through the mud in our direction—not on a straight course but in a series of looping tangents, like a boat tacking against the breeze. He came to rest, at last, in front of us, with a look of vague surprise on his face as though this were not at all the destination he had planned. Then, with a sudden twitch of his shoulders, he dropped down beside us.

"Turnips," he said. "Not so rotted as they might be."

Our heads snapped up as if yanked by invisible cords. We stared at him blankly.

"Like your quarters?" He smiled and winked as though this were some private joke that we all shared. "Know the inside of her like the palm of my hand. Used to be this was the sauna—what they call a steam bath here—until they built the bigger one closer to the new well. That's why she's put together tight as a boat's bottom—to keep in the heat, don't you see. Now it serves 'em for a lock-up."

We burst out in a rush of speech—which seemed to alarm him so much that I thought he would run away. "No, no, friends, not so eager, not so eager." He waved a skinny finger in our faces. "You know they aren't half pleased about me talking to you. Just you sit quiet. There, that's better."

"But who are you?" I whispered.

"It *is* good to hear the old speech again, damned if it ain't." He grinned, showing bad teeth. "You know, I feared I had lost it with no one to talk it to these thirteen years."

"Thirteen," murmured Bengt weakly.

The poor fellow lowered his watery eyes to the ground, while his narrow shoulders worked up and down in a constant motion—for this was a peculiarity of his that he seemed quite unable to control. His head, too, would take violent jumps to one side or the other as shudders ran through him. In fact, now I remembered seeing him before, trotting here and there about the place with his queer shakes and a lost look on his pinched and dirty, young-old face. Bits of straw in his hair, tattered clothes, and birch bark shoes as big as boats at the ends of his skinny legs, made him seem just another one of the peasants whose huts clustered within the wall.

"Maybe fourteen—maybe more," he chuckled, settling himself on the ground with his legs tucked under him. "Name is Hrapp, though the Finns call me hullu—'fool,' as you might say in our words."

That brought me up sharp. "You understand their speech?"

"Oh, yes. Talk it, too. The first few months I just kept my mouth shut and my ears open and pretty soon, why, damned if she didn't start making sense to me. After that it come quick." He laughed again and tapped his forehead with a skinny finger.

"And why do they call you fool?" said Stig, studying him with a careful look. "You aren't a fool, are you, Hrapp?"

"Ha, ha! Maybe yes and maybe no—but I must start my story at the beginning if you want to know all.

"There was fifty-six of us when they caught us. Brave lads, from Sodermanland in Sweden, off for a summer's harrying—like yourselves, as it might be? Well, you've seen how things go here. After a while there wasn't a one of us left alive but me. Shall I tell you why? It was learning their gabble kept me alive. Because the old woman—you haven't met the Mistress yet, old Louhi—she loves stories, just dotes on 'em. Any sort—stories about trolls and giants, kings and battles, just anything at all. They never sail far from home, these folk, and they know naught of the world outside. And I got to be a fair hand at putting stories into their words. Done it all these years—told every story I know a hundred times if I've told it once. But she never seems to tire of 'em, and she lets me live."

"If you call this life," muttered Ivar.

"Well, damn it, I like it better than watching the world go by from the top of a sharp stick. Though there was the time that I got fed up—for it is a grim place here."

"We know," I said.

"Oh no, friend, you don't know—you don't know...." His voice trailed off, and he stared vacantly, as though we had all suddenly vanished. Another great twitch of his head and shoulders brought him back to attention.

"It is a grim place here—and so I ran off to the woods one time. After a few days, though, wandering about, cold and starving, I come back. Didn't mind by then if they did whack my head off. Joukahainen was for doing it, too, but Louhi wouldn't let him. Instead he gave me a beating that near killed me—left me this dent on my forehead here, do you see it?

"Then they throw me down the dry well that's a trash pit now, over inside the old well house, cram me down in it with a skin of water and a bit of moldy cheese, throw a dead goat in after me and shut the trap. And there I sit, just me and the worms and the rats—big'uns, too, and as hungry as me.

"I don't know when it was that I begun to wail and throw myself about—feeling the vermin all over me, if you see what I mean. Even tried to kill myself by holding my breath, but you can't, you know. And it was a long, long time before they pulled me out.

"I've been shaky in my ways ever since then, and they take me for a crazy man. But I don't complain. I've got the run of the place, sleep where I like, and nothing to do all day but tell my stories whenever Louhi takes the fancy. I'm luckier than most!"

It was she who ruled here, then—the bundle of rag and hair I had glimpsed that first morning and never seen again. I begged Hrapp to tell us more of her, though he was plainly unwilling to, glancing uneasily around him while a whole series of minor tremors ran through his body.

"She's a witch, I can tell you," he said softly. "There's death in her mouth. She can sing herself into an eagle or a hawk, call down sun and moon, send the killing frost...."

Stig, who took such things lightly, snorted.

Hrapp shot him a frightened look. "It's the truth! Day and night she sits in the hall with her wizards, and they sing and sing till the place stinks with taika—what they call magic. Times like that she sends me away, and I wouldn't stay there if she was to beg me."

While Hrapp talked, I stole a look at Glum. His face was in his hands, and he rocked back and forth, groaning. He had known it that first night, had felt the crippling magic all around that was deeper and blacker even than One-eyed Odin's.

"And she rules wide," he went on. "This place they call Pohjola—North Farm, as we should say. It's the strong-place of her tribe. But she takes tribute from others too, all up and down the coast."

"Alone?" I asked, "No husband?"

"There she is unlucky. He went a-hunting one day last winter and never come back. They found him in the woods, shorter by a head. But he was hardly worth the killing. Even while he lived, it was only her they feared. She did carry on, though, and buried him handsome."

Stig looked up and caught my eye. "The barrow—"

"What? Oh, no, no, no," Hrapp sounded almost offended. "No, they wouldn't treat you near so kind as they do if you'd rifled *his* tomb. No, Louhi put him where no man's hand will ever touch him."

From where we sat, we could see over the roof of the hall to the barren, cone-shaped hill that had impressed me on our first morning here.

I followed Hrapp's gaze to it.

"All that for him?"

"Ask *nothing* about that." He tore his eyes from it and glared at me with desperate anger.

"As you like." I put up my hands and smiled until he seemed easier.

"And the Headsman, Joukahainen?" asked Einar. "He's her son, is he?"

"Of sons she hasn't any, though she loves him like a son. And some say," he added slyly, "better than a son."

"Friend Hrapp," I broke in suddenly, for in my deadened brain a thought had begun to stir. "Hrapp, teach *me* to speak. I am a story-teller too."

"What d'you say?" He eyed me narrowly. "My Old Woman wants no other story-teller." He tried to draw away, but I held him fast by his ragged shirtfront.

"Stop, stop it!" he cried. "They'll see." Now his eyes bulged with fear.

I gripped him tighter and commenced to shake him, while Stig and Einar and the others stared at me as though I had lost my wits.

"Now, mind me, Hrapp the Fool. I don't want your wretched office. I want freedom for my men and me and I'm powerless until I can speak. Help me and come with us—or else, rot here for thirteen years more."

"You're the fool!" he cried. Spittle gathered at the corners of his mouth. "How will it serve you to talk to Louhi, eh? You think she'll let you go for that? Or Joukahainen? He has precious little conversation, has poor Joukahainen, except in the matter of heads!"

My other hand closed on his throat. "Say yes, Hrapp." Across the stable yard, a guard stared at us. "Hrapp, they're watching. Say yes."

"Yes—alright, yes."

I pushed him back on his heels. The guard, unslinging his crossbow, started toward us.

"Now, Hrapp, quickly"—I smiled into the twitching face—"what shall we say to this curious sentry? Begin my lessons."

27

OLD LOUHI

Try as we might, we could not ignore our former shipmates, who were a mute audience to the daily round of our lives. At first they had regarded us from the tops of their wooden stakes with expressions of sleepy indifference or only mild surprise. But as the days passed into weeks, other emotions seemed to possess them. Their mouths drew back at the corners so that some appeared to be smiling in secret amusement, while others frowned or even screamed in silence. But this, too, changed in time, as the rain and the crows and the vermin cleaned them up, until, when a month had passed, there was not enough flesh left on them to interest a fly; and they had ceased to be our friends.

Meantime we, the living, came more and more to resemble the dead. Glum, who was still sunk in his special despair, toiled through the day like a dumb beast of burden. Stig grew morose and irritable. Though he never said so aloud, into his eyes oftentimes came a look that told me his mind was on Nidaros and Bergthora and how he might have been there now, sitting by a warm fire with food in his belly. Even Einar turned moody, baffled by the silent resentment of the others. They needed someone to blame for their sorrows and he was the outsider, the hated Jomsviking.

For us all, the days dragged by in ceaseless toil and growing despair. Added to our other miseries, we soon began to notice the black bruises on our arms and legs, the bleeding gums, and faintness which herald the dreaded scurvy. So at night, when we sank down on our cold floor that hadn't even the comfort of a bit of straw on it, we slept the restless sleep of sick and exhausted men.

Nevertheless, I continued to work at learning the speech of our captors. I couldn't have said why. I had no plan really. Stig and one or two others who had caught my enthusiasm for it in the first days had long since given it up, but sheer perverseness kept me at it. I must do *something*. And so I willed myself to believe that somehow my effort would bear fruit in the end.

I should say something more here about my teacher, Hrapp the Fool. As to his age, I had guessed him to be near fifty. It was a shock to learn he was only thirty-two. He had lived nearly half his life in this wretched hole. For all I knew, he was a cheerful and generous youth when he and his mates set out on that unlucky voyage that ended here, but fear had taken him over like a leprous wound, deforming him beyond recognition. He trembled as easily as he breathed; cringed as naturally as he shat himself; was fawning, greedy, sly, and suspicious. When I asked him once if he suffered much from nightmares (as I did myself), he only laughed. I suppose he meant that this life was all one nightmare.

He was certainly not stupid. To have survived here at all bespoke quick wits. But he grudged each little bit of knowledge that I dragged from him, whether about the speech, customs or history of Pohjola, as if it diminished by so much the precious hoard of knowledge that was literally his life's blood.

Why, feeling as he did, had he agreed to teach me at all? Though I had taken him by surprise with a bluff at our first meeting, I had no real hold over him. Nevertheless, he quickly fell into the habit of following me to my work every day, and even of spending the nights with us in our foul little cell, although my crew mistrusted him.

I doubted he was a spy. Where was the need? I decided finally that while he might fear me as a rival for his Mistress' favor, he also dreaded the thought that we might go off without him. And so he balanced on a knife blade of doubt whether he should risk the little that he had for the much he might gain.

I pitied Hrapp easily, liked him with difficulty, and never for a moment trusted him.

In any case, though, I put him to good use; always making him speak to me in Finnish, asking him the name of each thing, and saying it over until I had it right. And soon, what had sounded like nothing more than the twittering of birds, began to separate itself into words I could roll around on my tongue.

I have more wit for this than most men. From my earliest childhood I possessed a great memory for words, which is the reason my young head was as well stocked with tales and poems as many a man twice my age.

Soon I could hold simple conversations with the peasants who toiled alongside us in the fields, though they had little to say.

What their rank in the society of Pohjola was, I never understood. They were angry when I called them orjat, and yet they seemed no better off than slaves, being as dirty, dumb, and starved as the rest of us. It was only the children who were sometimes merry, and vastly entertained by my efforts to speak their language. Whenever I made a mistake they would put their hands in front of their faces, shriek with laughter, and guess wildly at my meaning until the approach of some sour-faced elder put an end to the game.

Sometimes I would try to overhear these peasants talking among themselves. Mostly they spoke too quickly for me, and I didn't get much, but there was one word that I would catch now and again that intrigued me—sampo, as nearly as I could make it out. When they said it, they would lift their eyes quickly to the hill, then look away and bend their heads again to their tasks. And this they did more frequently as the first month of our captivity drew to an end.

That hill began to haunt my dreams. Nothing grew on it, nothing near it. Our work never took us there, and I could make no one talk to me about it. And yet its shadow, in every sense, hung over us. In some lights, as when the setting sun threw a bloody haze over the landscape, its dun-colored earth seemed to glow like molten copper. At those times it reminded me of my own Hekla—and stirred troubling memories in me.

✝

The warriors of Pohjola, who lived with their women in the great hall, were a class apart. They did no work of any kind, but passed their days sweating in the sauna, carousing, and swaggering about the place dressed in their finery and armed to the teeth.

One day, though, Joukahainen assembled three score of them together, more than half his total force, and led them out, shrieking their war cries, through the sea-gate to their boats.

Following that, we spent one joyous week without beatings, until, on a gray morning, the sentries blew long blasts on their birch bark trumpets and presently the gate swung open and the warriors pranced through again—fierce scowls on their faces, crowing and leaping and whirling their swords around their heads as the whole farm ran down to greet them.

I happened to be standing at the woodpile by the hall, where I had been sent to split firewood. From there I had a clear view down to the sea-gate, and through it, for the first time since our captivity began, glimpsed a sliver of sea. I could see the prow of a boat, crammed to the gunwales with hides, sacks of meal, and other stuff as might be looted from a rich settlement. Unnoticed, I joined the crowd and drew closer.

While his warriors carried this cargo in and heaped it up in the yard, Joukahainen displayed before us his special prizes—the inevitable heads, eleven of them, which he unwrapped one at a time. He held each one up by its hair and encouraged the Pohjolans to scream abuse at it before handing it over to one of his men to set on a stake. Several were the heads of women, five were children, one an infant.

His best prize he saved for last—a girl, pushed through the gate by two warriors. She was slim as a willow and dressed in a red shift that was sewn all over with little bells and golden disks. Two yellow braids hung down to her waist. With a sudden pang I thought of my dead sister. Joukahainen shouted up to the hall for his Mistress to show herself and accept the gift he had brought her.

By and by, Louhi answered his call. Pulling her head down into her shoulders tortoise-wise, she advanced with a quick shuffling gait over the dusty ground between us. The crowd drew aside for her, warriors and peasants alike, touching their foreheads and dropping their gaze as she passed by—this stumpy, halting old woman, swaddled to her ears, as though she feared the touch of what little sunlight there was. In a month, I still had not had a good look at her face.

Standing in front of the girl, she thrust a finger at her and spoke some words, but too low and quick for me to catch. Then, in an instant, the girl spat in the old woman's face. Louhi, recoiling, dove into the folds of her clothing and came up with a knife. She would have ripped the girl from belly to breastbone if Joukahainen had not made a lightning grab for her wrist. It astonished me that he dared this, such fear did she inspire in everyone. But he had his way. She retreated a step and the knife went back inside her rags.

In return, he made her a very low bow, while touching his fingertips to his forehead, and said something to the effect that she must be patient just a little while longer. To this she made some piping reply, and turning from him, scuttled back to the seclusion of her dark hall.

The Headsman followed her there, dragging the girl behind him. With fair Louhi and gentle Joukahainen gone, the crowd dissolved and drifted back to its labors.

✝

My curiosity about that morning's business was soon to be satisfied. Hrapp found me some hours later in the stables and informed me coolly that a feast was ordered that night to celebrate Joukahainen's victorious return. I was to present myself to Louhi, who was aware of my progress in the language, and entertain her with whatever poor effort I was capable of. I swallowed hard and thanked him.

The rest of that day I spent in a sweat of preparation, cudgeling my brains for some simple story that I could manage in their tongue and feeling my little store of words leaking away by the minute.

The feast was already under way when Hrapp and I crept into the high-raftered hall and took seats at the farthest table from where Louhi, black and shriveled as an old spider, sat amidst her warriors and wizards.

The smoky fire-lit interior hardly differed from that of any chieftain's hall at home. Six broad tables lay end to end on trestles and the warriors and their women sat together on benches, leaning their elbows on the sand-scoured tops and carving their meat with their knives. Above them, rush lights in brackets cast a fitful light across the rows of painted shields and arms that hung on the walls. And down the middle of the hall, women and barefoot girls carried mugs of ale and bowls of stew, ladled from two great cauldrons that swung above the hearth, while dogs and children ran in and out of their legs. The din was enormous.

By no means did the best of the fare find its way to where we humbler guests sat. Still, it was enough to make my head swim and I ate greedily, knowing that tomorrow it would be fish heads and turnip tops again.

I noticed at once—for it was my habit always to keep a wary eye out for him—that the object of our celebration had not yet made his appearance. And it was some little while before the door, near which I sat, flew open with a bang and revealed Joukahainen, drunken-eyed, framed in the doorway.

In one hand he held a flaring pine branch, while the other arm was thrown round the shoulders of the girl that I'd seen that morning. When he was sure that every eye was on him, he pushed her roughly before him and stepped inside. In the light of the torch his white skin glowed red and glistened with sweat, and his hair stuck damply to his neck. The girl was wet-haired too, her cheeks were burning, and her shift clung to her small breasts.

"Joukahainen comes late from the sauna!" a warrior called out, laughing.

The Headsman acknowledged this with an icy smile. He was a handsome man, no doubt, in a chilling sort of way. His tunic and breeches were of gray wool trimmed in blue and fastened at the wrists and ankles, in Finnish fashion, with buttons of bone. From his shoulder swung a cloak of spotted lynx skins that he always wore, and his silver bracelets and the hilt of his sword glinted in the firelight.

Other warriors took up the refrain from the first one, calling out—a shade too heartily, I thought, as though even they were not really easy with him—"Is the girl well trained, Joukahainen? Has she learned sauna skill from her mother? Does she know how to strike with the birch twigs to rouse a man's passion? Does she make it hot enough for you, eh?"

Ignoring their leers and gestures, he stalked past them with his quiet cat's step, like a beast that knows it is master in its lair, until he reached the seat of honor. With a shove he sent the girl to the cauldron to fetch him his food, and took his place at Louhi's side.

I applied myself to my own food and paid them no more attention for a while. Only when I had satisfied the cravings of my belly, did I question Hrapp about Joukahainen's victory.

"A slave's got no business to be so curious," he answered in his customary sullen tone.

"I know," I said, smiling, "it's my one fault. Tell me or I'll let slip to the guards that you're planning another escape."

That brought on the quakes and tremors. "Ease off! What a bloody scarer you are! I only know a little anyway. They say he's come back from Kalevala—a place that lies on the coast, to the south somewhere. During all the time I've lived here the two folk have been enemies. Don't ask why, for I don't know. Pohjola is the stronger, but the Kalevalans are rebellious dogs, and they strike back whenever they dare. One of their warriors, especially, a sly fox named Lemminkainen, gives us trouble. He haunts the forest and the islands offshore, never staying long in one place, but aiming quick blows at our farmsteads and ambushing our hunting parties." It amused me how Hrapp always spoke of "our" this and "our" that, when he meant his enslavers. "'Twas in one of those skirmishes that Louhi's husband lost his life, or so goes the talk."

"Come to the girl, Hrapp, who is she?"

"Now, how am I to know that? Joukahainen sometimes neglects to tell me all his business, you know—rude of him, but there it is."

"Come on, Hrapp, do better than that."

"All I know, dammit, is that the house servants called her—"

"Ainikki!"

It was Joukahainen who shouted it, jumping up from his place and dragging the girl into the middle space between the benches. Having eaten and drunk, he was now ready to trumpet his deeds in Kalevala.

Holding the girl by her chin, turning her face this way and that so they could see her, he began his speech. I give the sense of it here as best I can, for many words I didn't understand:

How they sailed down along the coast and fell like a thunderbolt on Lemminkainen's farm, catching them all asleep except for the man himself, who was nowhere to be found. But that was all right, for it was all a part of Joukahainen's plan. They had burned the place to the ground, he crowed, slaughtered the animals and set fire to the fields, and every soul they found they tortured and killed, save two—the old mother, who was half dead anyway, and this pretty one, the outlaw's little sister. Now the mother would give her son no peace until he tried to save the girl—"and then we pluck him!" Joukahainen grabbed a handful of air as if it were Lemminkainen's throat and shook his fist. "And by Death's ugly daughter, we'll tickle him. Hai! Flay him and spit him! And pretty Ainikki and I will watch, won't we, little sister? Hai! And then make him watch when

I lay you on the ground and open your legs, as I have done to you seven times already in three days and mean to do every day. Yes, I promise myself that pleasure. Finally your brother will beg me to kill him. I will do him that favor. Hai! There is a stake already sharpened, higher than all the rest, that waits for Lemminainen's handsome head." He drew his sword and slashed the air to show how he would sever the neck of his enemy. "Hai! Hai!"

All along the benches men and women imitated his cry and pounded the tables with their wooden cups, while old Louhi, tilting up her chin and raising her arms above her head with the palms outstretched, gave out half a dozen piercing notes, like the screech of a hunting bird.

Joukahainen pulled the girl to him, kissed her, then struck her across the face with his open hand. "Fetch more ale, little sister, quench my thirst."

Her knees sagged and a trickle of blood ran from her nose, but she kept her head up and stood her ground—longer than I think I would have done if I'd been her—before she turned and went slowly to the ale vat.

The feasting resumed amid shouting and clatter and strains of song, and I attended to my plate and cup again. It had been long since decent ale had wet my lips. I would happily sit there the whole night through. But I was growing nervous about my performance.

Presently Hrapp left me and crept to Louhi's elbow. She squinted in my direction and sent him back to fetch me. Quaking inside and cursing myself for every kind of a fool, I shuffled the length of the hall. What, in my folly, had I hoped to gain by this? I would be laughed at and beaten for my trouble—or worse—and that would be the end of it. Hrapp was doubtless preparing to enjoy the sight.

Louhi's features, when I got near enough finally to see them, did nothing to raise my spirits. I noticed three things: the eyes, jet black slivers buried in folds of wrinkled skin; the teeth, small and brown and set with wide gaps between them like old tombstones in a row; and the hands, blue-veined with knobby fingers, curved and nailed at the ends like the toes of a bird. Hadn't Hrapp said that she could sing herself into the shape of an eagle?

And she stank. It was the stink of dirt, of death, of magic. I was afraid for a minute I might lose my dinner.

Touching my forehead, I stammered through some little speech of salutation that Hrapp had rehearsed me in, although Joukahainen and the others around her continued to talk and eat without a glance at me. When I hesitated, uncertain whether to go on, she waved her hand impatiently for silence and, as the murmur of voices died, tilted her old face up to me, folded her hands in her lap, and indicated that I should begin my story.

Looking from that hideous countenance to the unfriendly stares of the others, I felt my throat constrict. But I called to my aid a common trick of storytellers for overcoming nervousness.

At the far end of the hall, behind Louhi's back, was a loft high up under the rafters where the house-slaves slept. Tonight, however, the warriors' children had scampered up to find their own amusements in its dark recesses. Looking up, I could see only bare legs and black-soled feet dangling down, but to their imagined faces I would tell my story.

With pantomime, grimaces and comic voices to eke out my meager store of words, I told how once upon a time, long, long ago, Thor and his two companions, Loki and Thialfi, had traveled to the land of the giants and offered to compete with them in trials of strength. But, to their chagrin, the gods were bested in every single contest, and it was only when they were on the point of leaving, feeling thoroughly ashamed of themselves, that the giants' king confessed how he had tricked them. For, he said, the man who could eat faster than Loki was Fire, and the youth who outran Thialfi was fleet-footed Thought, and the decrepit hag who had wrestled Thor to the ground was none other than Old Age itself.

"Then," cried I, "Red-Beard flew into a rage and swung his hammer up, intending to destroy these great jokesters. But as he lifted it to strike"—I waved my fist above my head—"the giants' kingdom vanished! Leaving him and his friends bewildered, as you may imagine, in the middle of an empty field." I spread my fingers on either side of my face and peered about with my eyes wide and my mouth in the shape of an O.

As I spun the story out, there were giggles from the loft, so I knew I was succeeding on that front. And with the Mistress, too, it seemed. Louhi sat with a dreamy look in her half-closed eyes, munching with her jaws and winding and unwinding a bit of ribbon around one finger. When I was done, she clapped her hands. The filthy old woman was childish!

There were other sounds of approval around the room as well, and now that it was over, I was seized by a rush of elation. How easily I had charmed these simple souls, how quickly I would win their trust!

But Joukahainen threw out an arm, sweeping cups and platters off the table, and lurched to his feet.

"This Thor of yours, Viikinki," he sneered, "is a very great fool."

He stood so close that I could feel his breath on my face. "We, too, have a god who thunders in the sky, his name is Ukko, and he is not so easily deceived."

Angering the Headsman was no part of my plan. "Thor is oftentimes a fool, sir," I answered mildly, "but he strikes hard blows for all that."

"Does he? In your country, perhaps. But you know who strikes the hard blows here, Viikinki, don't you? Hai!" He drew his sword half way from its scabbard and laughed.

But Louhi pouted, looking reproachfully at him, and complained in her piping voice that he was a surly man and forever wanting to spoil her fun, and maybe she was tiring of his haughty ways—that was the drift of it.

Tight-lipped, Joukahainen touched his forehead and bowed before his Mistress.

"He won't frighten you again, boy," she chirruped. "Louhi is pleased with you. Now, go away."

I mumbled my thanks and was turning to go when I found myself caught by a pair of green eyes that, half-hidden behind a post, watched me intently. The taut, brown face around them was all angles—the cheekbones high and sharp, the jaw square and ending in a pointed chin. For an instant I met Ainikki's stare, then dropped my gaze and passed her by.

Back at my bench I found that Hrapp hadn't much to say in praise of my effort. Was the man really so stupid as to be jealous of me? *No matter*, I thought. *I've made a beginning. Somewhere here is an advantage to be pressed—time will show it to me.*

I poured myself ale, leaned back, and sighed deeply.

✝

The hour grew late. Many of the feasters had staggered off to bed or snored noisily where they sat. From time to time I looked down the row of tables and observed Louhi. She appeared not to be a great feeder, but she downed her ale, cup for cup, with the men.

Just as I was falling into a doze myself, a commotion began at that end of the hall. With a scraping of benches, they got to their feet—Louhi, the Headsman, and a half dozen of the men near them, men with rippling beards and filets around their temples, whom Hrapp had called her sorcerers.

Standing apart from them, Louhi lifted her arms and gave out with another series of piercing cries, wild and shrill with a high little sob at the end. Then, dropping her voice, she sang a sinuous line that repeated again and again while the bass voices of her magicians throbbed under it. The effect of it was weird and beautiful.

Hrapp awoke with a start and gave a mighty shudder. Ainikki heard it too. With a scream of hate she flung herself at Louhi, and would have knocked the old woman down if Joukahainen hadn't stopped her with a blow on the chin that sent her to the floor. What a fighter this girl was!

The Mistress paid no attention, but started down the hall in our direction—dancing on her short legs in a sort of hopping, dipping, stamping gait. Behind her, bearing torches lit from the hearth, followed the sorcerers, imitating her step, their shadows leaping ahead of them on the floor. I shrank back lest the shadows touch me.

As they went by and out through the door, Joukahainen, marching a few steps behind, turned his head back and, looking me full in the face, cocked an eyebrow and smiled, for all the world as though we were friends passing in the road.

The great hall emptied quickly as the other guests, bench by bench, fell into step with the procession. Beside me Hrapp croaked, "It's back to the shed with us, my popular friend. Our welcome's over. We'll tell your mates what an evening you've had while they lay listening to their bellies growl."

I pushed him away and joined the tail of the procession as it went out the door.

Outside, a full moon lit the scene in flashes between wracks of scudding cloud. A raw wind blew from the sea in gusts. We wound 'round the corner of the hall to the side where the hill loomed, and approached to the foot of it. There we halted and formed ourselves into a wide semi-circle. I saw now, for the first time, a flight of narrow steps crudely hacked into the dirt, which curved up and around the belly of the hill.

On the lowest step, within a ring of torches, stood Louhi, piping the same few monotonous verses of her song. I strained to catch the words and could make no sense of them except that I heard again that word which I had overheard the peasants use.

Sampo.

A trembling hand touched my shoulder, making me start. It was Hrapp again, fairly gibbering with fear. "Come away!"

I made no answer.

Then, a scream. Not from the hill, but behind us—a man's voice, but so tortured it sounded barely human. A pair of warriors, dragging a bound figure between them, raced past us and flung down their burden at Louhi's feet.

Hrapp's shaking fingers tightened on my arm, for coming toward us was the Headsman himself.

"Viikinki," he purred, "you have saved me the trouble of fetching you. I wanted you to see this thing—to see great Louhi's power. I fear you dread her too little. The hullu will tell you—he has seen it before, haven't you, hullu?" Hrapp, moaning, tried to hide behind me. "Louhi wished for pretty Ainikki to see it, too, but the little fool made me strike her—too hard, perhaps—and now the hour can't be put off."

The screams of the terrified figure on the ground nearly drowned his words.

"Joukahainen, what poor devil has deserved this?"

"What? You don't know the voice? It is the one named Eystein Crickneck. I chose him myself."

Eystein! The simpleton who liked to give away his possessions to others and who would always throw back his head and laugh louder than the rest at his own nonsense. Hrapp's arms locked around my chest. His shaking voice repeated in my ear, "You can't save him—you can't save him—you can't—"

"Why him, Joukahainen?"

"Why, because he is young and full of juice—and he's an idiot, is he not? An idiot's thing is always of great size. The Bridegroom grows small on the thin juices of the peasants but this one will make him frisky again. Hai!"

They ripped Eystein's trousers away and Louhi knelt down between his legs with her little, bright-bladed knife. What had he done wrong? Eystein asked between his sobs, and if they told him, he would never,

never do it again. Then he made a sound that I still hear in my dreams—that pulls me from my sleep, sweating and trembling.

The hag held up his severed manhood in her dripping hands while the body jerked and shuddered at her feet, pouring out its foaming blood onto the barren earth. Hrapp's fingernails dug into my muscle.

Eystein Crickneck, I swore silently, to your ghost and to the others, by Odin and by Christ and by every other spirit of Heaven or Hel, I promise you these lives.

Then one of the magicians handed her a bowl for the thing, and another gave her a small lamp. With these in her hands she began the ascent of the hill, her body bent nearly double, her arms outstretched before her to balance herself. And all the while she kept up the shrill singsong, which became with every step, more distant, more breathless, and more urgent.

Up and up rose the twinkling lamp flame until it reached the summit—of Louhi herself, wrapped in her black shawls, one could see nothing—and there it continued to glow while the strains of her song drifted down to us.

"Now—" breathed Joukahainen at my side, and just as he said it, the light winked out.

There was silence on the hilltop. Like the giants in my story, Louhi had simply vanished. A long exhalation of breath hissed from a hundred throats.

"So," said the Headsman to me. "you have seen great Louhi go to the Bridegroom, who is our wealth and strength. No one can see more, not even I. These men will lock you up now. Sleep well."

Guards appeared and began to push Hrapp and me through the crowd. I felt sick inside and made no struggle.

"And Viikinki," he called after me, "I did like your story."

28

Little Ainikki

On the day following Louhi's feast, we were sent to the meadow to gather the last of the hay. All morning long in the thick and hazy air, we worked along the meadow side where the forest runs. We were strung out in pairs, one to pitch and one to bundle.

I had hardly slept. Eystein's killing left us all shaken. As I sweated and choked in the hay, throwing forkfuls of it up to the rick where young Bengt sat drowsing, my eyes burned with tiredness, and my limbs were as heavy as my heart.

I was bending for another forkful when something, a stone or a clod of earth, struck me on the back. In a flash of anger I spun around, thinking it was some stupid joke of Bengt's, ready to kill him—my temper was that worn— but his fright on seeing the pitchfork upraised in my hands seemed genuine, and I faltered.

"Bengt, the, uh, handle is coming loose," I stammered to cover my confusion, "go ask for another fork, will you?"

He looked at me strangely, but jumped down from the rick and disappeared among the haymows.

When he had gone, I glanced around, puzzled at seeing no one nearby who could have thrown at me. I shrugged and sat down in the straw to steal a minute's rest.

"Viikinki! Viikinki, over here!"

Without bothering to wonder who called me or why, I ran toward a nearby stand of trees from where the voice seemed to come.

She crouched in a hollow just beyond the tree line, hidden by a screen of pine boughs. I recognized the corn-colored hair in its long plait and the angular jaw, swollen where Joukahainen had hit her.

"Viikinki, at last!" She reached out a small hand and pulled me down beside her. Through the skin of her fingertips I felt her fear—like a hare hiding from the fox: quivering, alert, ready to streak away at the first rustling of a leaf.

"Ainikki? What are you doing here?"

"Please—just listen—there isn't much time." Her words tumbled out in such a breathless rush that I was lost at once and shook my head.

"Yes, yes, slower, I'll try." She took a deep breath and began again, pronouncing the words carefully. "Joukahainen is hunting. Louhi is still asleep. She came back late from—from where you saw her go last night. Yes, I know about it. I slipped out the gate early this morning. I've been circling the fields for an hour looking for you. Last night I heard you speak our language. And the other outlander, the one who shakes, says you have a dozen brave men."

"I have one fewer than I had yesterday," I replied grimly.

"I know. I'm sorry."

"Why? It's nothing to do with you."

"No, you're wrong. I don't know where to start. You know I'm the sister of Lemminkainen the Rover. You know I was taken from Kalevala, and—oh, Viikinki, it's a beautiful land. Sunny. Not like this awful place. Here we are so near the Dark River of Tuonela, where Death's Ugly Daughter washes the clothes—it makes me shiver."

I half smiled, "People put Death's country in many places."

"Look around you—can you doubt Death's iron fingertips touch us here? He lives only a few days' walk to the north. Lemminkainen could show you, he went to the land of the dead and came back to tell of it."

"I'd like to meet this brother of yours."

"But you will! You will meet him. And together you and he will kill and kill—until this graveyard of Pohjola is more heaped with dead than ever it was before, and Kalevala has the sampo again." Cold hate glittered in her eyes.

"The sampo!"

She must have read my face for she lowered her gaze at once. "I don't know what you saw, or what they told you..."

"You tell me. Tell me everything."

"Not to an outlander. I can't—"

"Then you've gone to some trouble for nothing, my girl," I said, quickly standing up.

"No, please, don't..." She screwed up her face with thinking. "All right, I must trust you. Listen then. The Kalevalans were rich once, because we possessed a ... a secret thing. It's very old, very powerful. We called it sampo. That was before I was born. In those days, Kalevala and Pohjola were friends, and the people visited each other often, until one day Louhi stole our sampo from us. I can't say how, for the old'uns don't talk about it. I think because it makes them look like fools. But she never means to let it go, for it's her source of strength, and she keeps it buried in that hill yonder, 'bolted with nine bolts, locked with ten locks, and its root sunk nine fathoms in the ground.' At least, that's what Ilmarinen the Smith says. Our sampo, buried like a corpse in a tomb."

"But what is it, Ainikki? What does it do? And why does it need poor Eystein's juices?"

"Stop shouting, they'll hear you! I don't know. I told you I've never even seen it. But it was a good thing, Viikinki, when it was ours. How could it not be? Imagine a mill, which no hand turns, that grinds out grain on one side, salt on the second side, and silver on the third, all day long: a bushel of each every day! The old'uns say it's like that."

I shook my head in disbelief.

"It's true. Long, long ago a blacksmith, who was a great magician as well, pumped his bellows for three days and three nights, and when he looked into the heart of his forge, there was the sampo being born. Into the making of it went the tip of a swan's feather, the milk of a farrow cow, an ear of barley, and the fleece of a summer ewe." She counted these items off on her fingers, as though reciting something carefully learned. "Compared to its value, gold pieces are playthings, and silver pieces are jingling bells. That's how the old'uns tell it, and that's all I know. For years and years we've tried to get it back, but this wall that she has built around it mocks us. Even Lemminkainen failed, though he slew her husband— and for that, they have laid this trap for him and baited it with me."

I seized upon her thought, feeling my pulse quicken. "And if your brother were to try again—and we opened the gate for him?"

"Yes, Viikinki!" Her face was eager. "Could you do it?"

"Hel's High Hall! Yes—if we have to fight them with our teeth. How soon can you find your people?"

"Oh, no, not me," she said quickly. "It's you who must go to Kalevala. If they miss me an hour from now, they'll know exactly where I've gone. But you? Why should you run south and not some other direction? And being only a slave of no importance, they won't chase you far."

I doubted that, remembering what they had done to Kraki, but I let it go.

"And if you can find my brother, you know our tongue well enough to tell him what he must do. And Viikinki," she looked at me steadily, "how else will you and your friends ever escape from here?"

Once again, Kammo's cold breath tickled my neck. "I'm no forester, Ainikki."

"I will teach you, Viikinki—everything. I know all the forest's secrets. And I will ask Ukko, who talks through the sky, to watch over you. He always does what I ask him. Will you go?"

"Of course I will."

She clasped my hand in both of hers and touched it to her lips—and in that instant an arrow of desire shot through me. My sex stirred like an old forgotten friend, and I realized with a shock that I hadn't wanted a woman in weeks. Suddenly, I ached for this one.

"Ainikki, pretty one..." With my heart in my throat I wound one hand in her plait and lay the other on her small breast. "I want you." She stiffened and twisted her head away when I tried to kiss her. "Let me ... I want you." I pushed her down and fell on her, burying my face in her hair, clawing her skirt up, forcing my knee between her legs while her heart pounded against my chest. "Ainikki, don't fight." But she kept squirming and trying with all her strength to push me away until suddenly all my desire turned to fury. "I *will* have you." I got my trousers down and pressed hard against her thigh. "Ach! Damn you!" She sank her teeth in my neck, held me by the hair, and raked her fingernails down my cheek. As I threw up my hands to guard my eyes, she wriggled away.

We knelt on the ground, both of us trembling and panting. Her teeth were bared, two flaming spots burned in her cheeks. My desire seeped away. I fumbled with my trousers to cover myself.

Her voice was choked with anger. "I am a warrior's sister—not your whore!"

"And no virgin, either," I shot back scornfully. "Not anymore."

"You throw that at me? Then you deserve to be Joukahainen's slave. You're no better than he."

"You let him have you. Must I have less because I can't chop off your head?"

"*Let* him!" She covered her face with one hand, clenched the other in a small white fist and struck her thigh.

And it wasn't even the words she spoke, but some little thing—that helpless fist perhaps, or the sudden catching of her breath against a sob—some small thing, over in an instant. But it pierced me to the bones. In that instant, I began to love her.

"Ainikki, don't," I stammered. "I wouldn't hurt you, not you. It isn't me, it's this place that has scraped me down to the bones and left me rough." I reached for her clumsily, held her, smoothing her hair while sobs shook her. "Don't cry—don't cry."

After a time she ceased to weep, but still hid her face.

"Little Ainikki, how old are you?"

"Fourteen summers," she whispered. "Why do you ask me?"

"Because you are the bravest girl I know."

"I'm not. I'm frightened all the day long."

"I am too. Only fools are fearless here. Dry your eyes now and look at me—please."

"Are we still—still allies even though I wouldn't—?"

"To the last drop of my blood."

With that she looked up, touched her fingertips gently to my bleeding cheek and tried to smile a little. "We mustn't waste it, then."

I kissed her forehead and vowed to myself, *I will marry you or die for you, one or the other.* "When do I start for Kalevala?" I asked—sounding braver than I felt.

"Oh, not yet. There's so much still to tell you. I have to go now. They'll be looking for me. I'll find you again—tomorrow, if I can."

She rose and glided away as silent as a shadow, hardly stirring the leaves under her feet. At the edge of the trees she turned back. "Viikinki," she said shyly, "What is your name?"

I told her.

This time she laughed and wrinkled up her nose. "What a funny name."

Young Bengt was leaning against the hayrick when I came back, looking petulant, with a pitchfork in either hand.

"Nothing's the matter with this'un. Here, what's happened to you, then?"

"Went to shit and fell into a thorn bush."

"What, head first? Ha, ha!"

Bengt was so entertained by this that he laughed over it all day long, stopping every so often to say, "Head first?" and setting himself off again.

I decided for the time being to say nothing about Ainikki to anyone.

†

I didn't see her the next day or the day after that. Joukahainen had returned from the hunt with a prize of elk and deer, and the house-slaves, among whom she was made to work, were kept busy scouring the hall and making beer and butter for another feast.

Meantime, the Headsman lounged about the farm. He seemed never to be out of sight and his eye missed nothing—especially nothing Ainikki did. He handled her openly when he felt like it and struck her when she didn't please him, took her into the sauna with him every evening, and, Hrapp told me, slept with her at night.

I hardly slept at all for thinking about it.

†

At last, when nearly a week had passed, Hrapp and I were again summoned to the hall to wait on Louhi while she dined, and this time we were brought to her table straightaway. As before, Joukahainen was at her side—her hand rested on his knee—and behind them stood Ainikki, looking thin and sick. One of her eyes was blackened.

They're driving her to her death! I thought. I forced myself to look past her as though she were nothing to me.

We waited in silence to be noticed.

"Hullu," Louhi said, scarcely looking at him, "have you a new story for me?"

Hrapp shuffled his feet but said nothing.

"I thought not, you crazy man, you fool." She laughed at him—"chee,

chee, chee"—a sound like the chattering of a rat. "But Viikinki, you have a new one for old Louhi, haven't you? Hai! You're a good'un, Viikinki, old Louhi likes you. And Hullu, you listen, eh? And learn something. Make a place at the bench for Hullu, there."

Hrapp, his whole body quaking, squeezed himself onto a corner of the bench and glared at me with dumb hatred.

The Mistress of Pohjola gave me a gap-toothed smile, folded her hands in her lap, and cocked her head.

Forcing my mind to the task, I gave them the saga of Ragnar Hairy-Breeks: telling first how he came by his name when his wife made him trousers of fur, coated with pitch and sand to protect him from the fiery breath of a dragon. And following that with other deeds of that ancient king. I ended with his death, when, bent with age, he was hurled by his enemies into a snake pit, and there, to his everlasting fame, sang his death-song as long as the breath was in him. I sang a verse of Ragnar's song in the Norse language—quite movingly, if I say so myself—and received the applause of the whole table.

"Viikinki." It was Joukahainen who spoke, gazing at me over the rim of his ale cup. "What an interesting story. What an apt story."

"Master?"

"The snake pit, I mean. It has put me in mind of something. Do you suppose there really lived a man so brave as could sing in a place like that—and as beautifully as you sang just now?"

Louhi shot him a questioning look, which he acknowledged by raising his cup again with an easy gesture and toasting her. I began to feel a prickling down my back.

"Do you remember, Mistress," he purred, "how once we put the hullu in a pit—and not a snake pit, either, for who could have thought of such a thing? The song he sang wasn't the least bit tuneful. These viikingit puzzle me, for they are all so brave in their own mouths, but when you put them to the test...."

"Skinny Man," she replied—this was her love-name for him—"what is in your mind?"

His eyelids in their deep recesses almost closed. "The hullu, it so happens, Mistress, has a story to tell you. He told it to me yesterday. Unlike his others, it is a true one. Hullu, tell the Mistress your story."

Hrapp twitched, rolled his eyes, and made gargling sounds in his throat. No intelligible words came forth, but he raised a shaking finger and pointed it straight at me.

"The hullu," Joukahainen said smoothly, "seems to be having one of his fits. I can recite his story for him. It concerns our new friend here. It seems he is planning to betray us to the bandit, Lemminkainen." He was on his feet suddenly, his voice ringing down the length of the hall. "Seize him!"

A half dozen of his warriors leapt from their places and laid hold of me, twisting my arms behind my back and forcing my head down until I felt my neck would snap.

"No!" Louhi flew at her lover, her shriveled face contorted in anger. "The hullu's only jealous because I delight in this one. His story is all lies."

"No, Mistress, I don't think so. Anyway, you'll take no such risks as long as I defend you."

"Skinny Man, my handsome young lynx... " Now suddenly she was all softness, taking his arm and drawing him down to her on the bench, simpering in her little girl's voice.

"You do care for me. Lucky woman that I am to have such a defender! But I am vexed when we quarrel. Please, lovely Skinny Man, don't kill my storyteller." One taloned hand stroked his shoulder while the other touched his lips—which twitched and curled as though an insect were walking on them. It was suddenly obvious that he loathed her.

"It is not my intention to kill him," the Headsman replied. "Only to lock him up until the bandit is in our hands. To put him in that same pit where we put the hullu—for a few days only."

Louhi pouted. "But then he will shake like the hullu when he comes out. I don't want two shakers."

"Oh, not this brave young fellow—and so fortified with poetry?" The Headsman could scarcely disguise his smile.

Louhi looked doubtful. "If you think so. But he is not to be beaten, I won't have it—and no snakes."

"Certainly not," Joukahainen murmured, touching his forehead. At his signal I was jerked to my feet.

Hrapp had betrayed me after all. He had run out of hope that I could save him. Now in his crazed mind I was simply the hated rival, out to steal the pitiful crumbs of his existence. And this was his revenge. He must have wormed our plan out of Ainikki. And what new tortures would

Joukahainen invent for her now? I stole a glance at her. She stood white-lipped and still as a post, seeming to see nothing.

"Take him out," ordered the Headsman.

As they turned me around, Louhi piped encouragingly, "Remember, Viikinki, Hairy-Breeks' brave song..."

The last face I saw was Hrapp's, contorted with malice. I promised myself to kill him, if I lived long enough.

✝

I lay in pitch darkness on a putrid bed of refuse, slimy with decay and crawling with life, in a space no wider than my outstretched arms nor higher than my head. My foot touched the sticky carcass of some dead animal. This was the abandoned well, now a trash pit, inside its sagging well-house, where once they had buried Hrapp; a grave now, covered by a wooden lid weighted with a stone.

Insects swarmed over me, running up my shirt and pants' legs. A rat's tail brushed my face. I flung myself away, striking out in a frenzy, feeling the scream come up in my throat. How long had Hrapp held out before he began to quake? Was he listening for my screams now? I ground my teeth and fought it down. "You'll wait long, damn you!"

Squatting against the wall, I hugged my knees and began to rock back and forth, back and forth—slower and slower, until I sank at last into a drifting mindlessness.

Ages passed.

A scratching above me roused me from my stupor. Looking up, I saw a sliver of yellow appear in the black and grow wider.

Too soon to let me go, I thought. Joukahainen's come to kill me after all.

I tensed for my last fight.

"Viikinki? Odd?"

"Ainikki!"

I was out of the hole in an instant and huddling beside her on the dirt floor of the shed. In the light of her lamp, the shadows appeared deep under her eyes and in the hollows of her cheeks.

"You're bleeding," she said, touching my forehead. "He promised not to beat you."

"I must have done it to myself when I was dancing with the rats."

"I'll sing a charm to Pain Girl to ease it for you."

"Ainikki, how did you get away? If you're in danger—"

"Not for a while yet. Joukahainen is bedded with Louhi tonight in her closet. She insisted on it—it seems he hasn't done his duty in a long time."

"If he were anyone but Joukahainen he'd have my sympathy."

"And everyone else is asleep, it's nearly dawn."

"I was afraid they'd chain you up after filthy, bloody Hrapp..."

"Oh, don't curse him, the poor man, this was all his idea. Didn't you see him wink? There was no other way to get you alone, with Joukahainen always underfoot. And the best thing about it is that they won't bother with you for days now."

"It was *planned*? But Joukahainen could have killed me!"

"We had to take the chance. Here. I've brought food scraps from the tables,"—she thrust a rucksack at me—"and here's a tinderbox and a knife. I wanted to bring you proper weapons, but I couldn't manage. I know where some are, though—in the loft where I sleep sometimes when ... when Joukahainen is finished with me. There's a whole pile of swords and spears there."

"Clever girl! They must be ours. Now then, how to find your home?"

"Even an ugly viikinki like you could find it." She pulled her eyebrows down and pushed out her lips to imitate my face, and grinned mischievously. It was the first time I'd seen her smile. Suddenly, we were both merry, holding on to each other and giggling like a couple of sillies. Because it was all right now. In just a few days we would be free of this horror.

"Stop now, my girl, be serious."

"Yes—seriously—" she swallowed her laughter. "All right. Four days' walk, no more, with the sea on your right. It's not a fortress like this. Everyone keeps to his own farm. Whomever you meet, ask them to take you to Slack Water Farm, to see Old Vainamoinen. Remember the name, Vainamoinen. He'll see to the rest."

"Well, then," said I, hoisting the rucksack to my shoulder. "I'm ready."

"Of course you aren't ready!" I haven't taught you the charms. Now listen closely and say them after me until you know them by heart."

"But Ainikki..."

"Hush! It's just your good luck that I'm an expert in these matters.

She wrinkled her forehead in concentration, a careful mother instructing her child. "Where to begin? Yes ... the charm for calming snakes—the fens are full of them. It goes like this. Say it after me."

"Ainikki..."

"Say it after me."

I gave up and did my best to repeat the jingling words, which hardly made any sense.

"You *are* quick—for an outlander. You must learn the charm for admonishing bears—we always speak politely to the bear, and the one for setting out on a journey."

"Ainikki, enough."

"Stop arguing. The one for averting wood demons starts..."

We were in the middle of the one to drive away Fog Girl, when I heard a cock crow and, a moment later, an anxious tapping on the wall.

"Oh, great Ukko," she gasped, "we're not half through."

"Ainikki, I'm going. It's now or never. I won't spend another day in the pit."

"Oh, I hope I've told you the right things. If you get lost, pray to keen-eyed Tapio, who guides hunters on their way."

"That I will, and to Odin, and Thor, and the White Christ, and Blessed Olaf, and anyone else who comes to mind."

Outside the door stood Hrapp, with his arms jiggling, shoulders jumping, and head rolling as though he were a jointed doll on a string.

"Friend Hrapp," I put my arm around his shoulder and looked into his blinking eyes, "I'm at a loss how to thank you for risking my life in a witless, hare-brained scheme that could have gone wrong in a hundred ways—but you've risked your own life, too, and I won't forget it. You may pull an oar on my ship for as long as you like to—and that day isn't far off now."

"I won't pretend I always meant you well," he stammered. "Thank this little'un here for making me heel over and change course. Jesu, try and argue with her!"

"I know what you mean."

"But Odd—or Captain, if I'm to call you that—I must tell you something now that won't please you."

We had been speaking in Finnish out of habit. Now he switched to Norse. "The barley is nearly ripe. When the last of it is cut, they will kill all your men—all. I saw 'em do it to my mates and many another. Once a year, after the barley is in, they bring the sampo out of the hill and the wizards carry it round the stubble. And whatever prisoners they have on hand they wrap 'em up in straw and slit their throats so that their blood runs over the sampo and onto the ground. They reckon it strong magic—and it saves them the feeding of idle mouths all winter."

I sank back against the wall. "Must everything conspire against us? Damn their bloody superstition!"

He gave me a quizzical look. "If I hadn't been told the contrary, Captain, why, I'd take you for a Christman, the way you talk."

I was in no fit condition to answer that one.

"Does Ainikki know this?"

"I think so."

Bending low, Hrapp, Ainikki, and I dashed across the open yard, making for a stretch of the rampart, on the side opposite the meadowgate, where the forest curved nearest to the farm.

Under the wall, I hoisted my rucksack, climbed onto Hrapp's unsteady shoulders, and stretched for a handhold—the top was an arm's length beyond my reach!

"Ahhh, no," Ainikki cried. She had been strong enough for everything but this.

We stared blankly at each other. In only minutes Pohjola would come awake.

"Hrapp, do we dare try a gate?"

"All guarded through the night."

"Wait a minute, I have it. The woodpile by the hall—there's an axe there."

He nodded and disappeared.

Minutes crept by. The palisade's sharp teeth showed black against the lightening sky. Ainikki, shivering in the chill of dawn, crouched beside me. I circled her with my arm and held her to me. She found my hand and put her small hand in it, just as if I were—what? a comrade? a brother in arms? a lover? Surely not.

Somewhere a baby woke, crying.

More than likely I will die out there, I thought, and never have told her that I love her.

"Ainikki"—my mouth was sticky—"darling Ainikki, listen—"

Footsteps. Clutching the axe, Hrapp scuttled out of the dark.

"No time to lose," he panted, "they're stirring in the hall."

With a wrench I let her go, standing up quickly. "Good-bye, my friends. Hrapp, not a word of where I've gone to anyone but Stig. He's in command now."

"Odd." She came close to me, taking my hair in her hands, pressing her slim body to mine, and kissed me—one shy kiss that landed on my chin, and one long lingering kiss, a woman's kiss, that drew my soul inside her. "Come back, Viikinki."

"That I will, brave girl," I answered her with a smile. "Believe it."

Once again mounting Hrapp's unsteady shoulders, I hooked the axe head over the top of the wall and pulled myself up hand over hand.

"Good luck," Hrapp whispered.

"It's what I'm known for."

I dropped down heavily into the ditch on the other side, scrambled up over the lip, and raced for the trees.

29

το καλεναλα

Once again, I found myself in the deep woods—ancient, close, impenetrable, and vast as the sea. The great pines touched heads so high above me that they nearly shut out the sky, while around their feet sprawled lesser tribes of birch and willow, and ferns as high as my waist.

And everywhere there was water—in oily pools, black with peat, in vast lakes, and in the treacherous fens that could swallow a cow at a gulp. I swam as often as I walked. Day or night, my clothes were never dry. I skirted one great swamp so far inland that I lost my way and wandered for two days, desperate over the lost time, before I found the coast again.

I nursed a hope, too, of stumbling upon that creek we had sailed up in the Viper, and finding her still where we had left her. One stream I followed for miles, positive that I recognized landmarks we had passed, only to give up finally in fury and confusion.

The scraps of food Ainikki had given me lasted three days. When they were gone I began to starve. The woods teemed with beaver, otter, and squirrel, the fens with teal and goldeneye, and the lakes with pike. All of them mocked me. I chased animals on foot till I dropped, flung my knife uselessly, and cursed Ainikki for not equipping me with something so simple as a fishhook and a bit of string.

And then there were the things that wanted to eat me. One whole day I spent up a tree, mumbling Ainikki's charm with all the politeness I could muster, while a she-bear and her cub prowled below. And the nights I spent by my fire, hearing wolves in the wailing of the wind. It was often that I prayed to kindly Tapio, but it was Kammo the panic-maker who dogged my footsteps.

I had eaten nothing in five days when I stumbled out of the trees one morning into a field of grain. I can recall the women, who were bundling sheaves, running and shouting for their men, and the bright, blue sky revolving slowly around my head as I sank to my knees and rocked back on my heels. And then came blackness as I pitched over on my face in the grass.

✝

I struggled up from a deep well of sleep, plucking idly at drifting shreds of speech: "forest ... the filth ... yes, your name, very clear ... he's stirring, Vainamoinen."

Memory rushed back. I blinked away a cloud of black dots that swam and popped before my eyes, and slowly there came into focus a mountain avalanche of snow-white brows and hair and beard, with two bright blue eyes peering out.

"They thought you spoke my name, stranger, and so they sent for me. What do you want with Old Vainamoinen?"

I managed to croak that before anything else, I wanted food. He made way for the farmwife on whose floor I lay, and she spooned broth and beer into me. When I could feel a little strength returning, I began the speech that I'd rehearsed for days.

The old patriarch, Vainamoinen, looked on as I spoke, giving no sign of surprise at anything I said. When my tale was done, he heaved himself up, and, turning to a slim youth who hovered behind him, said quietly, "Find the Rover."

The beer was making me light-headed and I wanted to sleep some more. As the farmwife piled coverlets over me, I thought I might never willingly move again. And, in fact, I didn't until the next day's sun was high in the sky.

✝

Lemminkainen the Rover came in the afternoon, slipping silently out of the woods with twenty crossbowmen at his back. He was a handsome man, not yet thirty, lithe and slender, with his sister's straight nose and strong jaw. His equipment was more elegant than I would have expected of a homeless renegade, with ornamented shoes turned up at the toes, a belt of silver and amber over his leather jacket, a ring in his ear, and fine looking weapons.

With him came another whom Vainamoinen had summoned—Ilmarinen the Smith—a short man, squarely built and strong, with a shock of grizzled hair and sad eyes.

"Viikinki," said this blacksmith, as we sat on the grass within a whispering circle of onlookers, "what do you know of our treasure?"

"Nothing," I lied, "except what Ainikki told me—pretty-sounding words, but they left me no wiser. You could tell me more, I think."

"I could, if I chose. I made it."

"You? But she said it was ages old."

"Children. If a thing happened before they were born it's as good as a thousand years ago."

"She also said Louhi got it from you by some trickery."

"Yes, Louhi." What a sorrowful look in those eyes. "She was not always as you saw her, you know, not always a monster. She was a handsome woman once, sweet-voiced, white-armed, small-footed, deep-minded, and skilled in mysteries. Her husband was a sorry man."

"Old friend, there's no need to tell a stranger this," urged Vainamoinen gently.

"And the short of it is, I loved her. And to please her, I told her a secret. She loved secrets the way a child does; she had that quality about her. I showed her the sampo, still hot from the forge and heavy with magic. She looked, and she put her arms around my neck, wheedling and smiling, and said, 'Handsome Ilmarinen, strong Ilmarinen, clever Ilmarinen, let me have the use of it for just a little while.' My friends, if anyone can be made wiser by the misfortune of another, then I am bound to tell this story, though it shames me. Put no faith in sweet words from witches!

"And so, she keeps it now. So much of my breath was consumed in the making of it, there can never be another one. It was meant to be a good thing, Viikinki—to serve us and make our lives easy. What it has become...." He broke off and spread his hands wide.

We were all quite still during the telling of this sad history, except for

Lemminkainen. He fidgeted and dug at the ground with the point of his hunting knife, and as soon as the smith had finished, gave a lowering look around him and said:

"Ilmarinen, with respect, I am tired of hearing about this thing. Its days were long ago, and too many men have died already for its sake. Let the old'uns pine for it if they like to. I doubt we'll ever see it again—nor do I much care. I care for nothing but to bring my sister home alive, for I have no other living kin. Now, tell me, you—what are you called?"

" Odd Tangle-Hair by some. Odd Thorvaldsson is my..."

"Viikinki will do. Tell me a plan, Viikinki, that doesn't promise her death before we ever get close enough to the sampo to spit at it. This is what gnaws at me."

"Lemminkainen," said one of his men, a dour fellow who reminded me of Brodd, "she could be dead already for all we know. Is it likely Joukahainen let her live for even one hour after he discovered the Viikinki gone? He only needs you to hope she's alive in order for his trap to work."

"No," I broke in, "I don't think so. I heard him vow in front of everyone what he would do to her while you looked on." I repeated the Headsman's words as I had heard them that night at the feast.

Lemminkainen's face was a mask of stone. "What is your plan, then, Viikinki?" he asked, harsh-voiced.

I'd had plenty of time to think over my plan, and I knew how it could be done—provided my men were still alive. But when I told them what Hrapp had said to me, Vainamoinen and the others exchanged worried looks.

"Here, we're nearly through harvesting the barley already," said Lemminkainen. "You were a long time getting here, Viikinki."

"He is not to blame," rumbled Vainamoinen. "Today we gather our fighters, and on tomorrow's dawn we will sail for Pohjola. If luck is with us, we will win back both the sampo and little Ainikki. If not—well, we will have drunk the beer of war, and that is no bad thing."

"Spoken like a viking!" cried I—and instantly wished I hadn't. There were dark looks all around. They knew the viikingit—knew that we came to rob their graves and steal their women. I and my men had only been careless enough to get caught at it. If it were not that I held the key to Pohjola for them, they would happily have made a present of me to Louhi.

Lemminkainen looked me over with especial venom. "If we succeed,

Viikinki, what reward will you ask for your part in this?"

"To feed Joukahainen and his Mistress to the crows one piece at a time, friend Lemminkainen, and lift as much silver as we can carry away—that much we are owed for our pains. The rest is yours. And I'll ask you to find us our ship if it can be found, or give us another, and we'll part friends." I said nothing about Ainikki.

This met with nods and murmurs of "well spoken," but not from the Rover.

"Friends, you mean, until you come raiding us next summer." He rose on one knee, and I saw his fingers tighten on the hilt of his hunting knife.

"Gently, now, gently." Vainamoinen brought him down with his eyes. "I think we will be safe in trusting this young man's word, for if I had been as unlucky in his country as he has been in ours, I vow I would never go near it again." His eye twinkled and a laugh rumbled up from deep in his chest.

Then, out of bits of bread, a cap and a belt, I built Pohjola in miniature for them on the grass, and laid out my plan.

We were interrupted presently by the shouts of more warriors coming across the meadow. They'd been trickling in all morning. These brought with them, slung on a pole, a fine, big bear, which they had killed along the way.

Everyone ran up to see, and greetings were shouted—to the bear as much as to the men, for a bear is the son of the god Tapio and nothing must be overlooked in making him welcome.

A chorus gathered round the men who carried him, singing:
Hail, honey-paws,
Shaggy one, golden one.
Come under our ridge-pole,
Chubby-one, handsome one...

Stretching him on the grass, they skinned him carefully, then folded the pelt and put it away. They cut the meat in chunks and put them to boil with lumps of salt in copper cauldrons.

Meantime, Vainamoinen, who, among other things, was a wizard, sang a spell over the bear's head to claim his powers for the folk, while he pulled its teeth and put them aside for safekeeping. Finally, the head was set high in the branches of an evergreen tree at the edge of the woods and the people sang farewell to Tapio's son and thanked him again.

It was a fine feast. Women and children from the nearer farms had come along with their men, and because the air was warm, we sat outdoors and dined on gobbets of bear meat with salmon and bread and plenty of ale to wash it down.

When we had eaten and drunk, Vainamoinen placed on his head a tall peaked cap, and sat down on a low stone in the midst of us. The last slanting rays of the autumn sun streamed through the branches of an ancient rowan that arched above him. Mothers hushed their children while he tucked his flowing beard in his belt and took up his kantele—so fragile a thing that he could have crushed it in his hands.

He brushed the horse-hair strings with his fingers and it sounded like birds and little bells. I had never imagined music so beautiful.

After a time, he handed over the instrument to another man and turned towards the slim youth sitting beside him, who was his apprentice in the art of yoiking. For this is their custom that, while one man plays, two men will sing together, sitting face to face, with knee pressed against knee and right hand holding right hand.

They sang for an hour or more—singing the seas to honey, as the Finn folk say, the hills to sweet cakes, and the rocks to hens' eggs. I wished it had been me sitting there. Could my father, I found myself wondering, could Black Thorvald have been to me as Old Vainamoinen was to that youth, if only the Christmen had not driven him mad? I found my eyes suddenly filled with tears.

A little girl crawled into my lap and fell asleep with her head against my chest. In the grass, crickets creaked. The sun went down.

Here in Ainikki's world, among the people she loved, watched over by her kindly gods, I felt myself, for the first time that I could remember, deeply at peace. What a spell the old magician cast.

Lemminkainen came and squatted beside me, looking gentler than before, for the music had that power even over him.

"How old is he?" I whispered.

He shook his head, "No one remembers when Old Vainamoinen wasn't old."

"He must have a fine brood of grandsons."

"It's strange, that. He's never had a child of his loins, though he's lusty enough. In a way, I suppose, we are all his children."

"And I'm puzzled, Lemminkainen."

"How is that?"

"The sampo. Why do they want it back so badly? For its magic is filth and dust compared to the magic in Vainamoinen's song. And what if they learn too late that its only power is the power to turn Kalevala into Pohjola?"

He looked up sideways and searched my face for a long moment, "What a peculiar sort of viikinki you are." Then sighed and shook his head, "The wise are never quite wise enough, are they?"

It was nearly dark when the singing ended. Men and women moved away, to bed down where they could, and I returned the sleeping child to its mother. Vainamoinen stood and stretched himself and straightway grabbed at a lassie who flitted by—she could have been Ainikki's twin. He gave her a woolly kiss, but she escaped from his arms and ran away laughing, "You're too old, Vainamoinen!"

"Too old," he sighed after her, "too old." He turned and shambled to the house.

The thought stirred in me that if I were not 'the viikinki'—or maybe even if I were—here, with a sweet little wife to warm me and this wizard to teach me all his wit, here might be a place to rest a while from wandering.

Inside, while the lamps still burned, I stayed up with the young men, sharpening weapons and boasting how many of Pohjola's folk we would send down the Dark River.

"But their magicians are fearsome," said one.

"Bah!" said another. "We'll leave them with grass growing through their heads."

By the All-Father, I hoped so.

30

ᴄhᴇ BEER OF ᴡAR

The sun was over the treetops when I awoke. A young Kalevalan, armed with crossbow and sword, was prodding me with his toe.

I tried to get up but sank back with a groan, knowing I was going to be sick again. It was all that lovely fat bear meat I had loaded my shrunken stomach with. I'd spent most of the night clutching my belly and shitting, and only near daybreak had gotten to sleep at last; a sleep filled with rushing, crashing dreams.

Making my way shakily to the water bucket, which stood in a corner of the big empty room, I plunged my whole head in, which made me feel a little better. I dressed myself in Finnish clothes lent me by the farmer's oldest son and buckled on a borrowed sword and dagger.

Weak-kneed and hollow-bellied, I emerged into the glare of a bright fall morning just as Vainamoinen's rumbling voice rang out across the yard. He was marshaling his troops and calling each man up by name to present his weapons for inspection. The singer was in fine feather, with his tall cap on his head and a leather jerkin studded with brass nails over his leaf green tunic. His snowy beard rippled down his chest to the buckle of his sword belt. Waving his sword to one side and the other, he sorted the men into batches of a dozen, the complement for each war-sloop.

It came as a surprise to me, seeing him now, to observe that he wasn't actually a very big man. But he had a way of filling all the space around him with his presence, so that you remembered him bigger than he was.

Even that may not be the whole truth of it. Against all sense and reason, it seemed to me that at a certain moment of high feeling—as I will tell below— he actually *got* bigger. Absurd, of course.

"Hai, Lemminkainen," I heard him call to the Rover, "you grim fellow! Shouldn't a man laugh when he drinks the beer of war?"

But Lemminkainen was not to be cheered. He stood with his men, apart, looking morose. I, too, hailed the brother of the girl I loved—and got only a curt nod in reply.

All the smoldering anger that he harbored against the viikingit had returned with double force, it seemed, as soon as the gentling effects of Vainamoinen's music had worn off.

Not a good beginning.

I had worked it all out in my mind during the night, in between bouts of nausea. With their father dead, I figured it was Lemminkainen's right to give his sister in marriage. Of course, it was too soon to speak of that—I feared to anger him when Ainikki's life depended on our working together. First I must make him my friend. I didn't expect it to be easy.

With a smile on my lips, I strolled over to where he stood.

"Here, Viikinki." Frowning, he thrust a crossbow into my hands like the one he himself carried. "Don't play with the darts, they're dipped in adder's venom."

Like your tongue, I nearly said, but muttered thanks instead.

These pleasantries were interrupted by the women of the farm, who brought out bowls of curds for our breakfast. We ate in haste, sitting all together on the ground. As soon as we finished, we started down the path to the beach. There the singer sang over us a charm to make us proof against the iron of our enemies and then, with wild war cries, we ran to launch the boats.

The Finns have no long-ships such as we have. Their largest craft is a sloop, not much bigger than a large rowboat and holding a dozen men if they hug their knees and hang half over the side. In five of these, with Vainamoinen's own red-painted one in the lead, we set sail for Pohjola.

Out of our whole force only Lemminkainen's twenty crossbowmen looked like tested fighters, and even they didn't possess one helmet or ring-shirt between them. The remaining forty or so were indifferently armed, some only with cudgels and scythes. To fill out our strength, we counted on my twelve half-starved men and on an unknown number of

Kalevalans who were said to be gathering in their own boats to join us farther up the coast. Unless these amounted to half a hundred at least I didn't give much for our chances.

The weather was fine our first day out, and Vainamoinen steered a brisk course in amongst the tiny skerries that fringe the shore. But in the afternoon of the second day, the sky turned black and sheets of rain swept the gray water.

We bailed for our lives. Lemminkainen, in whose sloop I sat, made us take the sinew bowstrings off of our crossbows, roll them up in our caps and stuff them in our shirts to keep them dry. But it hardly helped.

And with the rain beating against our faces, we never saw the boats that had been supposed to meet us. Perhaps they were never there.

Late that night, hours later than we had planned, we dropped our sails and rowed silently to the far side of a little wooded isle that lay in the bay of Pohjola.

I counted it the eleventh night since my escape.

The rain had passed on by then, leaving behind a cold drizzle that hung in the air and penetrated our bones. Despite the damp, we got a few wet twigs to burn and soon had a smoky fire going, down behind a hummock where it could not be seen from the shore. There we dried our bowstrings and crowded round to warm ourselves, as many as could. Still, our teeth chattered and our spirits were low.

Since that first evening when his singing had charmed me, I had wanted a chance to know Vainamoinen better, but there was never the opportunity. And now, again, he was in ceaseless motion, everywhere at once among the grumbling men. He trotted from group to group where they sat hunched on the cold stones, praising, encouraging, joking. In truth, this man was everything to them.

And so I decided to pass the time with Ilmarinen the Smith, for I thought that he, too, must know many interesting things. I found him sitting some distance from the others, on the trunk of a fallen tree, with his chin on his fist, and seeming deep in thought.

I sat down beside him.

"My father was proud of his blacksmith's skill," I began. "He was a sorcerer, too. He's dead now, though he visits me sometimes in dreams ... He was a gloomy man."

The smith grunted.

"This sampo of yours," I began again, "it wants a lot of blood, doesn't it, and fattens on men's pricks. I suppose there was no other way?"

"It eats what it wants and wants what it's been taught," he said angrily. "Do a man's children always turn out as he would like?"

"Ah ... well, I hadn't thought of it just that way. So, when you bring it back, you'll train it to other food?"

He lifted his head from his hand and looked curiously at me. "How should that possibly concern you?"

I didn't intend to answer that question just yet, and so I shrugged it off and we sat for a time in silence.

"Your father," he said after a while, "he ... ah ... taught you things?"

"What—magic? No, not much. It's against the law, actually, in my country. They're liable to put you to death for it."

"You don't say so."

"And what he did teach me—rune-spells and such—well, I hardly know what to think of it. It did him little good."

"Oh," he said gravely, "it never does the sorcerer, you know. That's the price we pay."

I thought he sounded very sad.

Lemminkainen called to me just then. Leaving Ilmarinen on his log, I went to where the foresters were gathering round their chief. We readied our gear and one more time rehearsed our plan.

The drizzle had thinned now to let a few pale stars shine through between the scudding clouds. The moon had already set. Time to start.

Into the bottom of his sloop we threw our lassos, crossbows, a sack containing tinderboxes, candle stubs, a pot of bear grease, and four extra swords. Then, with whispered farewells all around, two of the Rover's men rowed us to the far side of the inlet where the trees grew down to the water's edge.

These two complained of leaving their chief and asked to be allowed to face death at his side. But he refused them. This was a mission for the two of us alone. We watched the black night swallow them up and waited till the creak of their oars had faded.

"Now, Viikinki," he said in his biting tone, "let's find some plunder for you."

Keeping just out of sight of the rampart, we crept through the dripping trees around the curve of the inlet to the spot where I had made my escape, and, catching the tops of the palings with our lassos, pulled ourselves up and over. Together we huddled at the foot of the wall.

"You hear?" he whispered. "Where's it coming from?"

Distant voices drifted to us.

"Louhi's hall, I think. But it's seldom they carouse so late."

"Celebrating maybe?"

Celebrating what? I wondered. The end of harvest and the slaughter of my men? He must have been asking himself the same thing. Neither of us dared say it aloud.

Then a dog barked, loud as thunder in the still night, and out of the dark a snarling black form shot at us. Before I could react, Lemminkainen swung his bow around and fired at the glowing eyes, which was all of the beast we could see. The poison worked swiftly.

"Night patrols?" he hissed. "Curse you, Viikinki, why didn't you say so?"

"I didn't know!"

We crouched against the wall, listening with all our ears. Far away, a second dog barked in answer to the first. After that, nothing.

"All right, we go on," he said at last. "Stick close."

But first we needed to get our bearings.

"Remember the model I made, Lemminkainen. The hill is ahead of us to the left, a good bowshot away. The sea-gate is off to the right about the same distance. Between them is Louhi's hall. Beyond that you come to the brew-house, the sauna, some other buildings. Then up by the meadow-gate on the far side are the peasants' cottages, barns and stables."

"And the prison of your men?"

"About fifteen paces this side of Louhi's hall. From its door you can see their door—and, if they look, they can see us."

"So. The sea-gate first."

Over the gate a short parapet projected from the inside of the rampart, supported on posts and reached by two ladders, one at either end. Day and night, a pair of sentries stood here looking out to sea. Hrapp had said that Joukahainen was fanatical about this precaution.

Pressing close to the wall and moving by inches, we crept to the foot of the nearer ladder. Lemminkainen tiptoed beneath the parapet and crouched at the other end.

"Now!"

We took the rungs two at a time, leaping onto the parapet with our bows leveled—and nearly shot each other. There were no guards.

The drawbridge, which should have been hauled up at sunset, still lay in place across the ditch below.

We exchanged worried looks. Could it be only carelessness? Or were we being drawn into a trap?

"Load the fire dart, Lemminkainen."

I bent over the tinderbox and struck a spark to light the oiled rag that he had tied around one of his arrows. With a snap of the string, it streaked low over the black water, toward the island where Vainamoinen had a man watching in a tree-top.

Back on the ground again, we lifted the great oaken cross-beam out of its iron brackets and set it down softly by the wall.

Half our mission was done. Soon the Kalevalan war-sloops would be rounding the island, rowing with muffled oars up the inlet. They would cluster silently, poised to burst through the gate. We had Vainamoinen's promise to wait for the last possible moment before dawn—until, with my arm stretched out before me, I could count my fingers, he had said— to give us time to find Ainikki and get her safely away.

My plan was simply to fire the out-buildings by the meadow-gate— that being the farthest point to which we could lure them—and wait for Joukahainen and his ninety warriors to run in that direction. Then, I with Lemminkainen and my vikings, would rush into the hall, gather up Ainikki and run with her to the sea-gate. There I would have men posted, to hold it open until the Kalevalans landed on the beach. They would attack when they saw the glow of fire from the burning out-buildings.

How simple it had sounded two days ago in the war-council at Kalevala. But now, how foolhardy and desperate! Were my men even alive? Back we slipped along the rampart to where the little prison house screened us from the view from Louhi's door, then, bending low, dashed to its side.

I pressed my ear to the planks. No sound. There was ice in the pit of my stomach.

"Hand me the bear grease," I whispered.

Holding my breath, I stepped round the corner. If anyone should walk out of Louhi's hall now he would see me. Lemminkainen, with the lassos and crossbows, pressed close behind.

I dipped two fingers in the grease and worked it into the tracks, top and bottom, over which the door screeched when it was slid open. Then I groped for the lock—a contraption of leather loops with a pin that went through them—and fumbled with it.

"Can't you hurry?"

"I've never worked the thing before—I can't see to do it."

"Let me."

"Get away!"

Throwing down all our gear, he thrust his hands in among mine and we struggled with the lock and each other. From the hall came a snatch of song and the sound of a bench scraping. Every nerve in my body screamed, "Run!"

At last the pin came away in my hand.

" Now, pull, Lemminkainen, while I push ... gently...."

"It doesn't move.

"A little harder...."

There came a screech like the yowl of a scalded cat. My heart somersaulted into my mouth.

"Wide enough ... get in." He shoved at my back.

We stepped into complete and total blackness.

They're dead!

Next moment, a fist crashed into the side of my head and another into my stomach. Hands gripped my arms and legs and flung me on my back. Stinking, naked bodies held me down and a foul breath blew in my face. Nearby, the Rover also thrashed in the straw, cursing.

A hard hand covered my mouth and the sharpened end of a broken stick pressed against my throat.

"This for you, whoreson!"

"Ahh—ahh! Stig, it's me!"

In the glow of our candles their faces hovered like phantoms, dark-circled eyes screwed up against the light. Skeletal ribs and breastbones showed through the holes in their rags. Their skins were black with grime, and coils of matted hair and beard hung from their heads like hunks of rope. Were we this bad? I had to leave and come back to see us as we really looked.

"Odd, it's you?"

They put out their hands to touch me. Stig, with his crumpled nose jutting out of a fleshless face, and Glum, with the skin sagging on his huge bones. Einar Tree-foot's neck was nothing but tendons, I could close my hand around it. And young Bengt's face, black as a lump of coal and streaked with tears ... and Starkad, and Brodd, and all of them....

I swallowed until my voice would work.

"Well, I will pick my next crew for looks," I said, and they laughed a little. "This is Lemminkainen." He was picking straws from his clothes and watching us with a gimlet eye. "And outside the sea-gate is a band of warriors waiting. Are you fit for sword play?"

Thor's blazing beard, yes, they were fit!

"How have you been, old friends?"

"Joukahainen said you were dead," answered Stig in a low voice. "'Twasn't but two days after we last saw you that he learned you'd slipped him. Hrapp said the old witch just kept at him to let you out of the pit. Imagine his surprise when he found it empty.

"He came straight to us in a blazing fury, with Hrapp along to translate, and said he knew where you'd gone to, that that little girl was behind it, and he'd have you back in short order and skin the both of you together. After that, they spent the next five days sending out parties to look for you. I didn't know they cared so much about you."

"Not me," I replied, "my friend here. Forewarned, he would be hard to trap—as we're about to prove."

"Well anyway, Joukahainen comes back at last, sneering and crowing, to tell us that you're dead—just like that—your bones found picked clean by wolves. I guess he had to say that, didn't he, and hope it was true. Of course, we didn't believe him without a piece of you to prove it, but we didn't know what to think. How did they miss finding you?"

"I suppose because they knew where I was going."

"How's that?"

"They knew the way to Kalevala better than I did. While they were watching it, I was wandering around lost, miles from where I should have been."

Stig's ugly face cracked into a smile, and I considered to myself that Tapio, god of hunters, had done right by me after all.

Starkad took up their story. "After the Headsman called off his search, it was back to the fields for us. Hrapp had gotten to us by then and told what was in store for us. We didn't let on that we knew—just said our prayers and worked mighty slow."

"Where is the hullu?"

He shrugged, "Never saw him again."

"We saw that little girl though," Einar struck in, "two, three days ago. Joukahainen was marching her to the sauna as we were coming back from the fields. Him strutting along, cock o' the walk, with his arm on her neck and she with her bundle of birch twigs to stroke him with. She didn't look at us, nor we at her—just a little flick of an eyelid as we passed. She looked as white as if she hadn't a drop of blood in her body."

"But alive!"

I translated for Lemminkainen.

He gave the merest nod and never changed his expression.

"And that was the same day we finished the harvest," said Stig. "And the funny thing is that no one's come near us since. Three days, by the crowing of the cock. No Joukahainen, no anyone, except for an old woman and her boy once to bring us a bucket of water and some slops. That was yesterday."

"And us near to perishing," Einar added, "and so, says I, 'better to go like wolves than lambs.' Broke off a sliver of my crutch for a weapon, and we made a pact to jump the first Finn bastard who stuck his head in the door—kill him, and make a run for it. Hah! Turned out to be you!"

"But then what *are* they waiting for?" I shook my head in puzzlement. "Why haven't they killed you by now?"

"Working themselves up to it, maybe? It's for certain something's been going on. We've heard wailing and horn-blowing like to stand your hair on end."

"Lemminkainen, what do you make of it?"

"We waste time," he said shortly. "Dawn's coming."

Quickly, then, I explained our plan—not forgetting to mention that our weapons, according to Ainikki, lay in a heap up in the hall's loft.

"Bengt, take my tinderbox and run to the meadow-gate. Fire the barn, the stables, everything. I'm depending on your speed and wits." (The boy was completely useless in a hand-to-hand fight.)

"And Stig, these are for you."

Lemminkainen and I shrugged out of the two sword belts apiece that we had slung around us. "I wish we could have managed more. Take Glum with you, and Halfdan and Ivar, and go to the sea-gate. You must hold it for the Kalevalans."

"Viikinki," Lemminkainen hissed from near the door, "I have thought of an improvement to your plan. I will go first."

Before I could stop him, he had slipped noiselessly out through the narrow opening, carrying his lasso. We watched him disappear around the corner of the hall. A moment later a low shadow crept along the ridgepole, to about the mid-point of the roof, and there compressed itself to nothingness.

"Nimble fellow, your friend," said Stig. "Not a great talker. I like that in a man."

I blew out my bit of candle, plunging us into darkness again. "Right—Bengt, get ready."

He was halfway out when the door of Louhi's hall flew open, letting out a momentary flood of light, and a man stepped through. Bengt jumped backward so fast he bowled me over.

Footsteps crunched in the darkness, coming straight towards us. Though the night was cold, the sweat dripped from my armpits and trickled down my sides. Grunting peacefully, the man pissed against our sliding door not a foot from where we crouched, then turned and crunched back the few steps to the hall.

"Now, Bengt!" I propelled him with a shove. "And now Stig's bunch—one at a time, and keep low."

The rest of us huddled by the opening to watch for the flare of burning buildings.

We saw only blackness.

"What's he doing, damn him?" muttered one of the men. "He has to be there by now."

"Be patient," I said. "Everything's sodden from the rain."

I stretched out my arm in front of me and opened my hand. The fingers were still indistinct.

With aching knees and backs, we waited and watched, while the stars in the eastern sky grew paler. If the Kalevalans stormed the gate at dawn, before we had lured the Pohjolans from the hall, Ainikki was as good as dead.

"Einar, how many fingers am I holding up?"

"Three. Why?"

"I'm going after him."

"Odd, wait!" Starkad's hand pulled me back. "What's your friend doing?"

The outline of Lemminkainen rose, balancing on the peak of the roof and gesturing with a shadowy arm. An instant later the sky above the hall showed red. From his vantage point he'd seen it first. And suddenly the night was shattered by the bray of birch bark horns.

"Bengt's done it!"

Then out poured the men of Pohjola, like angry ants from an anthill, buckling on their swords as they ran, with their dogs yapping at their heels. Most headed for the meadow-gate, but some veered away and raced toward the sea—it was too much to hope that Joukahainen would neglect that precaution. Now it was up to Stig's tiny force to keep them at bay.

As the shouts of the Pohjolans grew fainter, I threw my shoulder against our prison door—not caring how much noise it made now—and out we tumbled. Then, with a shout, we burst through the open door of Louhi's hall. At the same moment there came a shout from overhead, and down from the shadowed rafters flew Lemminkainen like some winged demon. He had tied one end of his lasso around the ridge-beam and squeezed himself through the smoke hole. Landing on the raised platform of the hearth in an explosion of sparks, he whirled his red-flashing sword around his head and bounded to the ground before the coals could singe his shoes.

The effect of it was amazing.

Standing in the doorway, I scanned the length of the hall. Everywhere was wreckage and disorder. Benches were overturned, bedclothes spilled onto the floor.

A moment's panic hadn't done all this.

From the wall benches peered the faces of women and children. Frightened faces—for what sight is more chilling than slaves who have burst their bonds? Still, there was not a single scream or whimper. These women outnumbered us several times over and, even unarmed, could have given us a fight.

But the men, at least, had all gone—except for three of Louhi's magicians. We found them cowering in the shadows by the door. One I recognized as Juvani, a dried up grasshopper of a man with a mean twist to his mouth. He was the chief of her seers.

Lemminkainen shook him by the neck.

"Where is the girl, Ainikki?"

"What—the Kalevalan kitten?" he sneered. "All this for her? She isn't here, look for yourself. Still she's not lonely where she is—oh no, plenty of good company where she is!" A dry laugh rattled in his chest.

Lemminkainen drew back his fist to strike Juvani, but the magician's hand went swiftly to his belt where his power stick hung. He thrust the thing, with its bones and feathers tied to it, in the Rover's face. That one jumped back and my finger closed on the trigger of my crossbow. The dart hit the wizard just below the breastbone and sank in him up to the vanes. He turned startled eyes on me, then dropped to his hands and knees and rolled over on his side, dead.

Then Lemminkainen's sword whistled in the air and the heads of the other two fell between their feet. Joukahainen himself couldn't have done it neater.

We turned from this to search the hall, calling Ainikki's name, looking everywhere, while the Pohjolan women followed us with their eyes.

At the farthest end of the hall was Louhi's own bed-closet, its door tight shut. I put my shoulder to it and burst through, prepared to skewer the old hag. But there was nothing of the Mistress there save her sour smell—and no Ainikki either.

"Liar," snarled Lemminkainen behind me. "You said she'd be here."

I spun around to face him. "Shut up! I want her as much as you do. You hear me? *As much as you do.*"

That brought a hard and narrow-eyed stare.

Lowering my voice, I said, "I've told you already, they won't kill her until they've got you, too. The magician told the truth—they've put her somewhere else."

Meanwhile, my men had scrambled up to the loft, found our arms and begun tossing them down.

We pawed through them eagerly, each man knowing his own pieces even in the near darkness by the heft and the feel of a well-worn grip. Holding them in their thin hands they straightened their backs and stood like men again.

"Yours, Captain," Starkad called out me, holding up my brass-studded belt with the sword, dagger, and purse dangling from it.

I drew Wound-Snake, ran my thumb lightly over its edge and brushed the runes on its blade with my fingertips.

"You've wept in the dark too long, old friend," I whispered.

From the direction of the sea, shouts began to reach our ears, faint but growing louder. The Kalevalans! From the open doorway we saw their torches moving along the rising path from the sea-gate, while to our left the sky was now lit by the flames of the burning out-buildings. But from that side, too, came the pounding of footsteps drawing nearer. Joukahainen had discovered by now that he'd been tricked, and was doubling back.

The two armies clashed in the Garden of Heads in a pushing, shoving melee to which the skulls were a silent audience. Vainamoinen's voice carried above the din, shouting his people on, and Lemminkainen, with a shrill cry, rushed past me into the heaving mass to rally his foresters to him.

My men, too, pressed and clamored to be let loose on their enemy, but I stood in the doorway and held them back.

The Kalevalans were brave, but bravery was not enough. Already, their charge was faltering in the face of the more numerous and better armed Pohjolans. They hadn't a chance of winning.

Why had no one wanted to admit it when there might still have been time to make a better plan? Why did we think that this ragtag band of sixty, even with the aid of Vainamoinen's magic, would be able to fight its way from the sea-gate to the Copper Mountain and back again against the Headsman's well-drilled warriors?

The blame was more mine than anyone's, but seeing the folly of it now, I was damned if I would sacrifice the last remnant of my crew in a lost cause.

Not when there was a better way.

"Inside all of you and bolt the door!"

"Aren't we to fight?"

"Einar, Starkad—no one goes out, you understand?"

With puzzled looks they nodded, yes.

Lemminkainen's lasso still hung from the smoke hole. Slinging a shield on my back and jumping lightly over the coals, I caught hold of the end of it and pulled for the sky.

Up on the roof, I scrambled to the gable, which overlooked the garden and holding my shield in front of me, cried, "Pohjolans, throw down your arms or never see your women and children again!"

Instantly crossbows snapped and half a dozen darts struck my shield. "I mean it! Throw down your weapons or they'll die before you can save them. You know what sort of men we viikingit are."

The noise of battle died. Faces stared up at me. Then one warrior pushed his way to the door, tried it with his shoulder, put his lips against it, and called, "Maila! Who is guarding you?"

"Whipped dogs," the answer came back.

"Armed?"

"What difference to Pohjolan women—aiii!"

And Einar's cheery voice sang out, "One throat cut. Who'll be another?"

I had their attention now.

"What do you want from us, Viikinki?" shouted the Pohjolan.

"I talk to no one but Louhi or Joukahainen. Where are they?"

"Where? In the Mountain, where else? Talk to 'em all you want." He laughed bitterly.

In the Mountain, I thought. Then Ainikki's there, too.

"Listen, Pohjolans. I and the chiefs of Kalevala will go to the mountain to parlay. In the meantime my men stay in the hall. One move from you and they will rape your daughters and murder all the rest."

The Pohjolans threw down their arms. The Kalevalans, with crossbows leveled, moved swiftly to surround them.

Inside the hall again, Einar Tree-Foot leered evilly at me. "Raping is it, then, Captain?"

"That was for their benefit, old man. I'll kill anyone who lays a hand on these women without my order. Once we harm them, they cease to be hostages."

Turning to Lemminkainen, I said, "Come along now and fetch your sister, she's as good as saved. No matter how much Joukahainen longs to kill her, he can't sacrifice every woman and child in the tribe for her, his men wouldn't stand for it."

I threw an arm round his shoulder and walked him out the door, still determined somehow to win the good will of this future kinsman of mine.

Outside, we clasped hands with the Singer and the Blacksmith. In the light of torches their sweaty faces were aglow.

"To the Mountain," I said, striding past them. But Vainamoinen laid a heavy hand on my shoulder and pulled me back.

"You presume too much, Viikinki. Ilmarinen and I must make that trip alone. You and the Rover will stay here."

Lemminkainen sputtered in anger but the Singer was firm. "Your job is to watch these Pohjolans—I trust no one else to do it. If little Ainikki is in the Copper Mountain, be sure that we will bring her out to you."

The Rover looked mutinous, but he obeyed.

I looked obedient and disobeyed. That was the difference between us.

"Vainamoinen, you'll never find the steps by yourself, even in broad daylight they're nearly invisible. But I, it so happens, have seen Louhi mount them to the top—though where she vanished to when she got there is a mystery. Let me guide you as far as the bottom step."

Just as reasonable as could be. What could he do but agree?

It was dawn in the east, but the hill was still only a dark shape against the sky.

A shiver ran along my spine. At long last to see this thing that had wanted to drink my blood, to see Louhi and Joukahainen on their bellies, most of all to see Ainikki's wise, sweet face and hold her to my heart!

At the foot of the stairs Vainamoinen said in a stern voice, "Go no further, Viikinki."

"As you say."

When his torch was half way to the top, I started after.

31

THE SAMPO

Pressing my left shoulder against the hill's cold flank, I felt my way up the narrow steps. The climb was even steeper than it looked from the ground. What could have nerved that old woman, what could have given her the strength to climb this pile, not once but again and again? And how had she driven her people to raise it up in the first place? The labor of it!

Then at last, I was at the summit and peering into the black mouth of a tunnel. Vainamoinen's torch, far below me, cast up a faint, retreating light. Easing myself down, I groped for the first step with my toe.

It was like descending into a grave. The air smelt of dank earth tainted with decay, and the sweating walls glistened with the phosphorescent tracks of snails. The stairway plunged so steeply downward I began to fear that it would lead me to Hel's own kingdom. I made a sign with my fingers to ward off evil.

But the steps ended only in a puddle of rainwater.

Vainamoinen's light and the sound of his and Ilmarinen's footsteps came back from far down a long gallery. Keeping well back of them, I followed. Branching off both sides of this gallery were the dark mouths of other tunnels and chambers. In one of them, as I'd been told, the old hag's nameless husband lay. What lay in the others I couldn't even guess.

Then I began to hear Louhi's voice—the same warbling cries as on that other night. Only now her voice was ragged and cracked.

The gallery ended in a narrow, low-ceilinged chamber. Tallow candles burned in niches in its walls, filling the air with a greasy smoke that had nowhere to go. I could hardly breathe.

Along one side of the chamber stood five or six rough posts about the height of my waist, their tops carved into flat, round-eyed faces: Pohjola's gods. On the clay floor at their feet a body lay, stretched on its back and covered with a linen shroud, all but the face. The bone-white skin of that face was even whiter and the sunken eyes even deeper than they had been when Joukahainen lived.

I looked into the yellow haze, standing on tiptoe to see over the heads of the two Kalevalans who stood just inside the entrance. With a sinking heart, I saw that besides ourselves and the Headsman's corpse, there was only Louhi in the room.

Stark naked. The withered flaps of her breasts, the purplish skin, the sagging belly—revolting enough. But what she was doing was still more so.

I had imagined the sampo to be a grindstone of some sort, for Ainikki had compared it to a mill that endlessly ground out barley, salt, and silver.

But those were only poets' words. Around the base of it, indeed, three open casks were placed, each one overflowing with one of those treasures—whether put there by the Pohjolans themselves or magically produced by the sampo, I cannot say.

But the sampo was no mill.

It was a pillar of black iron, from base to tip about three feet and a half high, and the thickness of a man's thigh. The tip was plastered with strips of gold foil, bits of colored cloth, and ribbons, and over all was looped a cord to which were tied little shreds of parchment—or so I thought at first—all shriveled up and hard. But I looked again and my skin went cold. Poor Eystein Crickneck. One of those shriveled remnants was surely his, squeezed of its juice to feed the iron prick.

What is it about gods, I thought with sudden revulsion, that brings out the worst in us all—not only the Christmen, as I once believed, but all? What crimes we commit for their sakes!

Louhi crouched with her arms wrapped around the thing, running her hands up and down the cold metal, while she threw back her head and wailed her shrill song.

Just as I came up behind the Kalevalans, she must have sensed that she was not alone. Her cry died in her throat. She turned and peered at us through the tangle of greasy hair that had fallen half over her face.

One look at those eyes told me she was quite mad.

"Ilmarinen? Is it you? Ah, I knew you would come. I cast rowan twigs in the fire and saw you in the smoke." The voice was small, the words trailing off into sighs.

"You love me still, don't you, my strong-armed blacksmith? Oh, I know you do. Help me, then. Help your poor Louhi."

She formed her lips into a simpering smile such as a little girl might put on to entice some favor from a gruff father. On her face the effect was ghastly.

"I have been here so long. I have sung to it, pleasured it, only to make it bring back his life. But it won't. Ilmarinen, you command it, make it give Skinny Man back to me." Her body shook with sobs.

The Smith put his hands to his face and sagged against the wall.

"Mistress." Vainamoinen addressed her in a hard voice. "We've come for the sampo—and for the girl. What have you done with her?"

"Eh? Done with her? But you've seen her, Vainamoinen, unless old age has blinded you at last! Or is it night outside? Yes, of course, and you passed her in the dark. Little Ainikki, that sweet child—the prettiest flower in my garden!"

"No," I breathed.

"She murdered *him*," Louhi screamed. "Murdered my Skinny Man. In the sauna—with a knife hidden inside her bunch of twigs, inside the whisk of passion. She stabbed him—let out his blood through his lovely white skin. Then she locked the door and piled more and more wood on the fire, kept pouring water on the glowing stones until the steam took her breath away. The cunning bitch! She knew what I would do to her. Oh, she knew. But I have had my revenge all the same. For three days and nights, while we sang the death song over Joukahainen, I cut and I carved. She isn't pretty Ainikki anymore. Can a girl be called pretty without eyes—heh? Without a nose? Without lips?"

"I'll have your life!" Not knowing how I got there, I stood in the middle of the chamber with my sword in my fist and black hate in my heart.

But Louhi was too far-gone in madness to be frightened.

"Viikinki? You? Have even my slaves come to mock me?"

A spasm seized her, and she let out an animal scream, shaking her head back and forth in a frenzy, flinging foam from her lips.

The scream ended as I struck her in the face with all my strength. Her head snapped back and she slumped against the sampo. I aimed my sword at her heart and drew back my arm.

"I forbid it!" Vainamoinen's voice exploded in the tiny chamber. He took my wrist in a crushing grip and held it until my fingers opened and my sword clattered to the floor.

His face was terrible—red, round-eyed, as different from his accustomed one as mud from milk. But his size terrified me the most. It seemed to me that he towered above me, filling the chamber, that his voice was a thundering waterfall, that he held over my head a fist as big as a barrel.

I waited for the blow that would kill me—my eyes shut like a frightened child. When it didn't come, I dared look again. There was only Vainamoinen the man.

"Why did you disobey me?"

I couldn't find my voice, but the Singer seemed to read my face, my mind.

"The girl? It's to do with her? So."

His fingers relaxed a little on my wrist. "Listen to me, Viikinki. It's not for any plain man like you to kill the Mistress of Pohjola. Leave that to Ilmarinen and me. But let this thought console you. You cried out for Louhi's life? We have it. Ainikki has taken the lover, and we will take the sampo—these are her life. If you hate her, Viikinki, wish her many long years of life to come."

"But Ainikki—"

"Died in her anger with her enemy at her feet, as it's good to die. She needs no pity from us. Now, seeing that you're here, you may stay. Ilmarinen tells me that you know a little of magic. Stand in the corner and be quiet. You may learn more."

He turned back to Louhi, who crouched by the sampo, her shoulders working up and down, and strings of blood and spittle hanging from her mouth.

"Now Mistress," he said, "Let it go. We want it."

"Heh? What do you say? Want what?"

"You understand me. Undo the binding spells or Ilmarinen will break them—and break you."

"The sampo? You've come for the sampo? Fools!"

"Come, come, Louhi," Vainamoinen's voice was soothing. "Are we not old friends? For friendship's sake...."

With a sob she wrapped her arms around the thing, clamped her knees to it, hugged it to her withered breasts.

"Feel the hot blood beating in it," she moaned. "How it throbs and burns my cheek! Give up this? The power that quickens the seed in my fields, that makes my rams and bulls and warriors lusty, that makes me rich!"

The Singer looked hard at his friend. Ilmarinen's rough face was pale and pinched, but he drew a long breath and began his chant—bass notes that echoed in the little chamber like the rumble of boulders on a hillside.

Louhi answered with her own weird birdsong. Beginning faintly while she still clung to the sampo, then gathering strength and tempo until she was on her feet, with her head back and her mouth wide open to show the flickering tip of her tongue between her teeth. And with their singing the air was so filled with taika, with magic, that I scarce dared breathe, and feared the crypt would burst with it like a putrid egg.

Ilmarinen's bass swelled and grew deeper, until he struck a note that I could feel through the soles of my shoes. The candle flames shuddered in their niches.

But Louhi's overtaxed voice was like a saw ripping wood, like a sled dragged over stones, then, finally, like nothing at all.

She swayed and Vainamoinen caught her under the arms and pulled her away. Ilmarinen regarded her with liquid eyes full of pity and fondness. Then planting his stout legs wide apart, laid hold of the sampo. His muscles cracked—he strained and grunted.

"He fails," she hissed. "His song was too weak."

But with a roar, he wrenched it up and swung it to his shoulder, nearly toppling backward under the weight of it. And at the same moment, Louhi uttered a sound like the sigh of a tired child and closed her eyes.

In the shallow depression where the sampo had stood, a white grub, discovering itself in the light, made haste to escape.

Louhi's undershift and shawls were lying all about where she had thrown them. Vainamoinen gathered them up and hastily dressed her. Then tossing her over his shoulder as though she were a bundle of twigs, and grasping his torch with his free hand, he ducked through the low entrance way and started up the gallery. Behind him followed Ilmarinen, staggering under the weight of his burden.

Which left me.

Throwing my own burden onto my shoulder, I hastened to follow—my burden being one of the sampo's three gifts—and not the barley or the salt. This much, by the Raven, was due me, and I meant to have it.

Coming out into the air again, I was bathed in the red light of morning. From the top of the Copper Mountain I could see all of Pohjola beneath me now, and beyond it the endless forest on one hand and the endless sea on the other.

Going down, the steps were even more slippery than before. With the heavy casket of silver clutched to my chest, I covered most of the distance on my backside.

At the foot I found Bengt waiting for me with none other than Hrapp the Fool beside him.

"Your mates said you'd come this way," Hrapp said. "You went—inside there?" He lowered his voice and glanced up sidelong at the hill.

I said I had and asked him where he'd been hiding all this time.

"In the hay-barn that this rascal set on fire. I haven't felt any too safe these last days and figured to lie low there. But I guessed what was afoot when I heard Bengt here hollering 'Help, fire!' The damned fool was shouting it in Norse!"

Bengt sputtered and wanted to know what in God's name he was supposed to shout it in, not having addled *his* wits with learning the filthy lingo of this place!

I silenced him. "What's been going on here?"

Hrapp squeezed his forehead between the palms of his hands, as if trying to push his thoughts into some order.

"Well, first they put off the harvest while they looked for you, even though the ears were ripe as could be."

"Captain knows that," Bengt taunted.

"And when they did finally put your boys to work again, and the crop was all in, the night before they was— was to have the sacrifice—well, that young'un—I mean to say—Ainikki, she—" he broke off and covered his eyes with his hand. "I mean to say, like someone in a poem—like a damned hero in a poem—and I never—wouldn't have let her—" He stopped again, unable to speak.

He loved her, too, I thought. Well, and why not?

"I know what she did, friend. But why, when she'd held on for so long?"

"She bought you time with her life!" Hrapp's shoulders leaped out of control. "She never doubted you'd come. Oh no, her gods wouldn't play her such a trick. But when she found out that they were getting ready to slaughter your men, she did the only thing she could think of that would bring all Pohjola to a standstill. And damn all, wasn't she right! No sooner did they break down the door to the sauna and find Joukahainen's body than the place went all to pieces. The warriors and the magicians fought over what to do with your crew—the warriors wanting to kill 'em at the Headsman's funeral and the other bunch holding out for the sacrifice in the fields for the sake of the crops. And only Louhi could have decided between 'em, but she'd gone clean off her head, tearing her hair and raving to where no one was anxious to go near her. Finally she made 'em carry her Skinny Man's stinking corpse up the hill where she's kept it and herself ever since. Three days ago, that was. And all the while these proud Pohjolans, without their Mistress and their Headchopper to order 'em about, have been acting like the idle dogs they are."

Thirteen years of terror was finding its voice at last.

With Hrapp and Bengt at my heels, I ran to catch up with Vainamoinen. He had rejoined his warriors in front of the hall. He had his sword at Louhi's throat. She had revived a little by now and was weeping and shrieking by turns. He told the Pohjolans that he would let her go only when he and his men were safely away with the sampo.

They heard him in silence, standing all in a bunch with Kalevalan crossbows trained on them from every side. In the dawn's light you could see their faces, baffled and sullen, staring at their Mistress, but staring even harder at that locked door behind which their women and children were imprisoned.

Catching sight of Glum, who had returned from the sea-gate, I gave him the treasure chest to hold and asked where Lemminkainen was. He pointed with his chin to the Garden.

I suppose Vainamoinen had told him how she died and he was looking for her. I went and walked with him.

We found her on the ground where a stake had been uprooted in the fighting. It was only by the hair that we knew her. Of her face there was not much left. What a bitter sight. We turned our eyes away.

"She is a warrior and deserves a warrior's honors," I said between my teeth, "to pass through the fire to Valhalla. Instead of a blazing ship let's give her Louhi's hall!"

Lemminkainen's cold eyes flashed. "Hai, Viikinki, it's a good thought. And the women of Pohjola will be her handmaids, their screams will be her dirge, when their skins burst in the twisting fire."

"Torches here!" I cried.

We wrapped the savaged head in a cloak and, holding torches above our heads, ran to the hall. The Finns of both tribes followed us with wary looks. My men inside unbarred the door for us, then shut it again and held the women at bay while we prepared Ainikki's pyre.

We laid her head on Louhi's bed and around it heaped necklaces, rings, and brooches ripped from the hostages. Then setting fire to the bedclothes, we ran around the hall torching everything—hangings, rushes, thatch, woodwork.

When the Pohjolan women saw what we intended, their courage gave way and they commenced to wail, holding up their babies to us and pleading for their lives. We drove them back and slammed the door shut behind us, fastening it from the outside with a spear shaft passed through the wooden handle and wedged against the jamb.

The Pohjolan warriors groaned and the Kalevalans, with their weapons at the ready, shifted their feet uneasily. In an instant flames licked up through the thatch and billows of black smoke poured into the sky. The women shrieked and pounded on the door.

Hrapp appeared at my elbow, trembling in every muscle of his body. To see that hall burn, its savage guards helpless, its Mistress made pitiful! Not until this moment had he dared to think, to truly believe, that he was a free man.

His features twisted in hate, he leapt up and began to prance around Louhi, waving his arms and crying, "What'll you do for a house, old witch, old dog's vomit, old dog shit! Heh? What'll you do for a storyteller, old pig's slop, old puke!"

Disgust at this unseemly tantrum showed in Ilmarinen's honest face. His blade flashed up and down. Hrapp's shoulders gave one last, seismic shudder and delivered his head at Louhi's feet.

Meanwhile the women kept screaming and battering at the door. The roof was a mass of flame. The heat drove us back.

One Pohjolan warrior, unable to bear it any longer, broke from the others and ran at the door. A couple of Kalevalan arrows flew wide of him but Lemminkainen slashed at his legs as he went by, cutting his hamstrings and felling him. The Rover dropped on him and had the man's head off in an instant. Lemminkainen began a dance before the burning hall. In one hand holding up the Pohjolan's head by its yellow hair, and whirling his sword in the other, he leapt and twisted, and shouted, "Hai! Hai!"

Perhaps if he had not done that, I wouldn't have done what I then did.

In my mind's eye I saw Joukahainen dancing that same dance on the first morning of our enslavement, when he had cut down my six friends. And I saw also other men, who leapt and howled around a burning farmhouse far away on Rangriver-under-Hekla. In my nostrils was the stink of things burning that ought never to burn.

Glum stood nearby me with his broad-axe hooked over his shoulder. I snatched it from him and, leaning against the fierce heat, dashed in and swung at the spear shaft. The door burst open and bodies tumbled out in a cloud of smoke and cinders; choking, weeping, some crawling, some reeling and falling with their little 'uns in their arms.

"Traitor!" Lemminkainen howled, shrill as a woman, and rushed at me from the side with his sword upraised. I watched him come like a figure in a dream, and I, the dreamer who wants to run but can't. I would not be alive now if Ilmarinen had not shot out an arm and caught him by the sleeve of his tunic, jerking him off his feet.

"Oh, proud one," snarled the Smith, pulling the Rover to him by a fistful of shirt. "Oh, clever one. The viikinki's got more sense, by the gods, than you have. Burning the women! Not even for sweet Louhi's sake would these Pohjolans have stood still another minute, and then we should have had to fight our way out and lost everything."

Lemminkainen was white with anger, but the Smith overmastered him as firmly as the Singer had done me.

Meanwhile, Louhi's fighters ran in to help their women get clear of the burning building.

"Quick," cried Vainamoinen, "away to the boats!"

Ilmarinen hastened Lemminkainen in that direction with a firm hand between his shoulder blades, then again heaved the sampo to his shoulder and staggered toward the sea gate. Vainamoinen and Louhi followed. The

Kalevalan warriors closed around them, keeping their crossbows cocked and watching their enemies over their shoulders.

My lads started off, too, but halted and looked back at me puzzled. For I stood stock still, distracted by reproachful thoughts. *Sense or soft heart, Odd Thorvaldsson? When will you ever put on the hardness of a man? 'Kill and kill,' Ainikki said—and meant it. And what have you done now but rob her poor ghost of the blood that was owed it?*

Einar Tree-Foot roused me with a jab in the ribs. Stig was calling to us from the sea-gate to hurry.

"Right," I said, giving myself a shake to clear my head, "let's go before the Kalevalans leave without us."

When we reached Stig, I threw an arm around his shoulder and said, "Well done, Steersman. I had a bad moment when I saw Pohjolans running to the sea-gate. Did they press you hard?"

"Not a bit. Where you and your Finnish friend dropped the crossbeam, a blind man couldn't have missed it. So we carried it down the beach a little ways and threw it in the water where the tide took it out. Then we just laid low and listened to them run around looking for it until the Kalevalans were on top of 'em." The corner of his mouth turned up. "Saw something else out there—on the beach. Care much for surprises, do you, Captain?"

The others who had been with him nudged each other and snorted.

"I'd say I've had my ration for the day—what now?"

"Guess."

"Damn it, Stig, as you hope to live, what is it?"

"Just step this way, Captain, out the gate."

"The Sea Viper!"

Beached at the far end of the strand, where we never could have glimpsed her from inside the walls or from the fields.

"All this time!" I cried, thumping my forehead with my fist. "The bloody bastards sailed her here and had her all along."

Laughing and crying, we ran—thirteen scarecrows, with our clothes flapping on us like flags, limping, hobbling, holding one another—down the beach.

We stood close around and drank in the sight of her. It was like wine and willing women to our spirits.

Stig said, "We went aboard her for a quick look-see. The chests and stores are all broken into but the oars and tackle look right enough. We can put to sea in her."

But could we? She was high and dry on the beach and the tide ebbing fast. We flung ourselves against her and pushed until we sank gasping on our knees. Meantime the Kalevalan boats were putting out, with never a backward glance at us, and the Pohjolans with wild cries were streaming out the gate behind them.

"Odin," I cried, "Christ and King Olaf!" (I was ashamed of myself later, of course.)

Then Starkad said, "Look there! The filthy whore's sons—they've crippled her. She'll never go like this."

We followed his gaze up to her serpent's head: each of her white eyes bristled with poisoned darts. They had blinded her because they feared the spirit in her.

"Bengt, can you shinny up from the fo'c'sle?"

He was up in no time, with his legs hooked around her neck, leaning far out to reach the darts.

"Once again boys, with all your might!"

Slowly, slowly she rocked and slid, scraping and grating, over the mossy stones, gathering speed, moving with her own will. Her stern floated free, then her bows. We swarmed aboard her and, standing on her deck again, grinned like fools.

"Run out a dozen oars," I ordered. "Einar, you take the helm and put her alongside the Kalevalans." The Jomsviking could manage the tiller well enough with his one hand. Stig and I were of more use at the oars.

I looked back along the beach.

The Pohjolans, men and women, were crowded down to the water's edge, watching the five Kalevalan boats pull away. In one sloop, Ilmarinen and Vainamoinen stood together, gripping the sampo and Louhi, their hostage.

For us, it was hard work at the oars, being only a third of our full rowing strength, but we made way slowly to intercept the Kalevalans. We were a good bow-shot out from shore by the time we came alongside them.

What happened next I cannot well describe. I, myself, rowing on the far side, saw only the aftermath of it. As for what others claim to have seen, I leave it open. But we all heard the piercing cry, and it *was* like the scream of a bird. And Vainamoinen, when seconds later I saw him standing empty-handed in the stern of his sloop, bore telltale marks upon him—his beard spattered with blood and red gashes on his face and hands.

Some of my crew swear they saw black wings beating around his head and talons ripping at him. On the other hand, I remember that wicked knife that she carried concealed under her shawl. Who can say?

By the time we came alongside, they were dragging Ilmarinen back in. And Louhi, her thin hair plastered against her face and her shawls floating out behind her, was making frantic motions toward the shore, where already the Pohjolans were racing to their boats.

In the boats of Kalevala there was silence and blank despair. Because, sunk in the sandy bottom of the bay, deeper than an oar's length beneath their keels, was the sampo. I suppose that Ilmarinen made a grab for Louhi—whether in bird form or human—and lost his grip on the thing, nearly capsizing the sloop and spilling him into the water.

They stared dumbly at the spot where it had disappeared. Gone without hope of recovery. The sampo might spread its wondrous seed in the fields of the sea, but nevermore in theirs.

Presently one of the Pohjolan boats came close and fished Louhi from the water. She lay in the bottom like a heap of wet wash while her warriors stared stone-faced. They had lost all, and they knew it.

The same loss was written on Kalevalan faces, but to my mind, wrongly. What did they want with that foul thing? Vainamoinen singing them to sleep at dusk should have been magic enough for them—but of course they would not have heard this kindly from the lips of the viikinki.

Floating to the surface of the water as the glue that held them dissolved, were bits of the colored cloth and gold foil that had decorated the sampo's tip; and these the Kalevalans, reaching out with oars and hands, were trying to salvage. Vainamoinen directed the operation while gruffly fending off those who wanted to bandage his gashes and wash the blood from his face.

Old Vainamoinen. What was it Lemminkainen had said? *No one remembers when he wasn't old.* I suspected he would be old for many years—for many ages—still to come. He was everything to them.

And not like you and me.

I wanted a word of parting with him and, leaning over the gunnel, called his name three or four times. But he made no sign that he heard me, nor Ilmarinen either.

The Rover heard, though.

He stood stiffly in the prow of his tossing boat, surrounded by his foresters, many of them wounded and bleeding. He turned his hard face to me. Our eyes met and held each other.

Between us, most of all—between us two, who loved the same dear girl—there should have been some word. But for a long moment neither of us spoke.

At last he clapped his right fist to his heart, held it a moment, and let it drop.

"Hyvasti, Odd."

I had grown so used to being always called 'Viikinki' by them, that the sound of my own name came strangely to my ears—stranger still, in the mouth of that man.

"Hyvasti, Lemminkainen," I answered. "May we meet again in happier times."

Vainamoinen's voice rang out just then, bidding them make haste for home. And so they turned their prows to the south and their little boats melted into the mist.

Behind us, Louhi's house fell in with a crack and a roar, sending clouds of embers whirling up into the air. And with them Ainikki's little shade, flying from its pyre. I hoped she would think kindly of me sometimes and forgive me for releasing the Pohjolan women. Surely Pohjola's ground was blood-soaked enough already.

And dimly through the haze of smoke beyond the hall, the Copper Mountain squatted, its cold womb ripped and empty.

Vengeance was satisfied.

"Pull!" I cried, bending to my oar, suddenly desperate to be away. "Einar, take her out among the skerries."

Was I a fool to have thought I could ever have a home among the Finns or to have believed that Ainikki could love me? Well, it made no difference now. Of one thing, though, I was certain. Just as Vainamoinen had said, it would be a fair length of time before ever I sailed these waters again.

On the poop, by Einar's feet, sat the casket of silver. And being Einar, he couldn't wait. Dropping the tiller, he fell on his knees, fumbled open the lid and dug his hand deep into the heap of coins and rings, scooping them up and watching them fall between his fingers.

"Heh, look 'ee! Ha, ha!" he crowed. "Did Einar Tree-Foot say he would make you rich or did he not? Come on—who have you got to thank for it all, heh? Who's to be thanked?" Cackling, he looked from one of us to another—then frowned and gave a peevish tug to his beard. "Well, I mean to say, why do you look at me so?"

I glanced at Stig and he at me, shaking his bristly head and wearily smiling.

32

OUR LUCK PURSUES US

Running before a smacking breeze, we skimmed the wave-tops and put miles of green sea between us and Pohjola. I stood at the helm once more, my hand upon the tiller, and felt the Viper's lithe body roll under my feet.

Skerries lay all around us—many just barren rocks, humped and gray like whales' backs, where sea-birds flocked in their thousands, others shaggy with fir, birch and alder. On the leeward side of one of these we found a sheltered inlet and went ashore, making our camp where a rivulet of cold water ran down from a cleft rock.

What a sad remnant we were.

Thirty-three men sailed out of Jumne Town on a spring morning. It was now the end of autumn and we were thirteen. Besides myself, Stig, Starkad and Brodd were all that remained of the Iceland crew. From Nidaros came Glum, young Bengt, and three others—Halfdan, Ivar, and Svein—all brave and capable men. And from Jumne, besides Einar, were Bolli, Lambi, and Swarozyc, of whom the first were a pair of brothers who quarreled constantly, and the last was a Wend who was never, during the whole time he served with us, overheard to say a single word.

Taking stock of our supplies, we found that the Finns had helped themselves to whatever was worth stealing. Both anchor and chain, made of precious iron, were gone; likewise a set of hammers and chisels that had belonged to Kraki. All of our sea chests had been ransacked of anything in the way of coins, buckles, or brooches.

Looking under the loose deck planks, where our bulkier gear was stowed, we found the ship's awning untouched, though they had lifted all our sleeping sacks of oiled sealskin. Of ship's stores, the water barrel was dry, the ale cask gone, and the oats and biscuit maggoty.

But no matter, we were alive. Free.

We peeled off our rags and splashed in the sea, washing away forever the smell of Pohjola. We picked lice from each other's heads, trimmed our hair and beards with our knives, and cleaned our teeth and our fingernails. And that night we feasted on fresh-killed roebuck until we rolled on our backs and groaned.

We lacked only ale and women. But those at least we had the means to buy as soon as we were among men again. For we had Pohjola's treasure—stowed carefully away under the Viper's deck.

And so passed some dozen golden autumn days in hunting and playing, bathing, sleeping, and eating until our bellies filled our skins again, and all our spirits rejoiced.

All except Glum's.

The berserker looked more woebegone than ever and had no more to say than if his mouth were full of water. He worried me.

I had gone off one morning to shoot at game with my Finnish crossbow and had bagged some hares. Bringing them back to camp, I tossed them down where Glum sat moodily under a tree and began to skin them.

"We'll soon be dining in Jumne Town, old friend, and telling our tales to bright-eyed lassies, eh?"

He mumbled some reply.

"What is it then, Glum? Can't you shake off this black mood, now that we're free of Louhi's spells?"

Frowning at the big hands that lay useless in his lap, he said in a mournful voice, "Friend Odin has lost me, Odd, or I him—I don't know which. Ever since I was a lad of thirteen I've felt him here under my hide"—he indicated the general region of his belly—"and knew that I was his. But now?"

"By the Raven, can't you see what ails the man?" Einar Tree-Foot had hobbled up while Glum was speaking and eased himself down beside us.

Einar had been a very mother to Glum during our captivity; cheering him by day, sleeping near him at night, even, when he could manage it, stealing an extra egg or two for him, because a warrior of Odin needs more food than ordinary men. And even now that we were free, he seldom let the berserker out of his sight.

"They stole his spirit in Pohjola with their filthy tricks," Einar fumed, "and he hasn't got it back, and so of course, Odin don't know where to find him. Any fool can see that."

"As it happens," I replied, "this is a subject I know something about." And I told them about how I had lost my own soul and how the ancient noaidi had fetched it back for me. "Ask Stig, he was there. He can tell you what a different man I was before and after."

Stig, who sat nearby mending his breeches with needle and thread, looked up and smiled, agreeing that I had indeed been mad before and only half-mad since.

"Odd Tangle-Hair," said Glum, brightening, "could he find my soul, this wizard? Do you think he could?" He appealed to me with his eyes.

"Glum, it's ever so far to the north, I honestly don't know where. Perhaps next summer we could try...."

The spark of hope died, his eyes went dull again. Not knowing what else to say I turned back to cleaning the hares, when suddenly Einar snapped his fingers.

"Glum, my lad, you don't ken the rune-signs, do you?"

No, Glum sighed, such things were not for his head.

"Ah, but Odd, you have the craft, have you not?"

"I have, Tree-Foot. Why?"

"Well mates, now Einar Tree-Foot is going to tell you something that he don't tell to many—and he don't want it repeated neither, for when folks find out that a man has the craft, why they won't leave him alone with their nonsense."

"Einar, what are you talking about?"

"I mean to say," he dropped his voice to a conspiratorial whisper, "that I have the wit to talk with Odin All-Father through the runes."

"You never—"

"The runes come from Odin, don't they? Why, even as simple a fellow as Glum knows that much."

The berserker gave a wan smile and allowed as how the whole world probably knew that much.

"Well then, and there you have it. We don't need to be running after some foreign magician—not that he wasn't a lucky find for you, Captain, in your time of need. But it's not for Glum. All we have to do is carve Glum's name on a rune stave and burn 'er, don't you see? Send 'er to Odin in the smoke. And by Ymir's Eyebrows, the All-Father will know what to do then. Glum, my boy, your troubles are just about over."

I shook my head, disbelieving. "Einar, this isn't—"

"And, Odd," he went on quickly, "this is where you come in. The cruelest blow that that scoundrel dealt me, who parted me from my right hand so long ago, was to put an end to my rune carving. I've never got the hang of it with this other. And so, Odd, my friend, if you'd be so kind"—reaching across Glum he took me by the shoulder and looked steadily into my eyes—"as to do that for us?"

"Einar, for one thing, it must be carved on a rowan slip," I protested, "and there's none about."

"Rubbish! Must I be lectured by a stripling? The wise-woman who taught me had the craft from Odin's own lips, and she never said aught about rowan. Carve from this here." He handed me a scrap of driftwood.

I did as he asked, wondering what foolishness he was up to. With the point of my knife I scratched the four signs of Glum's name: *kaun*, the torch ... *logr*, the water ... *ur*, the wild ox ... *madr*, the man.

Bengt sidled up and eyed us suspiciously. "More deviltry?" he sniffed. "We might as well have stayed in Pohjola!"

"Hold your tongue!" snapped Einar. "When I want a sniveling Christman's opinion I will ask for it. Now then, Odd, give it here."

He brought the slip close to his good eye and tipped it back and forth. "You were taught fair, I'll say that. Mind you, not as well as I was m'self." (He was holding it upside down.) "Now, a helmet, if you please, and the use of your tinderbox."

As a wisp of white smoke rose from the upturned helmet, Einar uttered a string of unintelligible words in singsong fashion. Bengt crossed himself and beat a retreat while the others stood around and watched us from a safe distance. Glum stared at the piece of wood smoldering in the bottom of the helmet as though his eyes would pop out of his head.

When it was done, Einar beamed with satisfaction, stirred the ash once with his finger, spat into the helmet, and clapped it, ashes and all, on Glum's wondering head.

"Done! He's found you and he'll have your spirit back under your hide in double-quick time. You'll howl with the wolves again!"

Glum's little O of a mouth curved into a smile and his eyes lit up. "Then I'd best sharpen my old axe," he chuckled.

✝

That evening I drew Einar aside.

"I know, I know. You're a smart'un, Odd Tangle-Hair, I never thought to fool you."

"But have you thought that fooling with Odin might be a little dangerous? The All-Father isn't particularly known for his sense of humor."

"Bah! Odin and I are old friends. He'll not complain. By the Raven, man, should he let one of his own berserkers just pine away to nothing?"

"I suppose it could have worked."

"If it did or if it didn't, Glum's feeling his old self again and it warms my heart to see it. And just bear in mind that Friend Odin is, among other things, the god of liars." He gave his beard a decisive tug and winked.

✝

Next morning early, Stig sniffed the air. There was a bite in it and the damp feel of snow.

"I'd feel happier if we were snug in Jumne harbor right now," he said.

And so it was decided. We filled the barrel with fresh water, brought on board the deer meat we had dried, and were soon at sea.

All day we sailed along the Finnish coast, and just at dusk, approached that gulf of the Varangian Sea that separates Finland from the country of the Ests. There we took a bearing on the setting sun and made our course south-southwest for Jumne.

We were in good spirits and just thinking about putting food in our bellies when the sky fell.

The day, which began cool, had by midday turned hot and close. The wind died to a whisper, yet something unseen was in the air that made us feel ill at ease. Then very quickly that sensation, whatever it was, increased a hundred-fold and we saw that the hairs on our forearms stood up and crackled when we touched them.

The sky turned green, and all along the horizon, a wall of black cloud gathered and rolled toward us. From it, quivering tongues of lightning leapt down, marching across the water.

"Put her nose about," said Einar tensely. "Run for the coast."

A bolt struck so near us that we leapt straight up at the *crack*.

"Secure oars," I cried, "take in sail. We'll ride her out!"

While we rushed about the deck, the black wall rolled in, and a wind lashed us with volleys of hailstones as big as pigeons' eggs. The sea rose and the deck dropped under me. The Viper pitched and plunged like a hooked salmon. It was only Ake the shipwright's skill in making her so loose-jointed that saved her from breaking up. Still, she labored fearfully hard in that confusion of pounding waves.

As for ourselves, we clung grimly to our handholds and begged Thor or Christ to save us.

It was then that I caught sight of Glum. Through a film of streaming seawater, I glimpsed him standing amidships with one arm round the mast and the other brandishing his long-handled axe. Flashes of lightning lit his face—Great Odin, his wolf's face! The mouth open, lips drawn back over the teeth, nostrils flared, eyes white and round. He shook his wolf-gray head in a fury from side to side and screamed, joining his howl to the howling of the wind in one indistinguishable roar.

The All-Father had found him! In the midst of this crashing chaos he was the god's berserker again, crazy for battle.

Still the lightning licked around us, and at the top of the mast, where the shreds of our sail stood straight out in the wind, hung a crackling blue halo of light.

"Glum, get away!" I cried, but the wind took my words. I started to crawl towards him over the tilting deck. Too late! A light more dazzling than day burst around me. There came a *crack* like the splitting of a mountain asunder, and a searing heat. I cowered with my hands over my face while black flowers bloomed behind my lids. The noise of the storm sounded as faint to my ringing ears as an echo in a shell.

When I looked again, the stump of our mast was riven to the deck.

And of Glum there was left—not a scrap.

But the storm left us no time for wonderment. Rain pounded the deck and towering seas broke over us. The Viper shipped water and began to

Flashes of lightning lit his face—Great Odin, his wolf's face!

founder. Still dazed and clumsy from the shock of the blast, we struggled to lift out the deck planks to open up a place to bail.

Looking down at the water roiling in the hold, we despaired. Our treasure! The chest, had burst and all the precious silver tumbled everywhere in glinting streaks and eddies as the Viper rolled and pitched.

We could try to save our riches, or we could bail and save our lives. To do both was impossible.

We bailed—hour after hour, flinging helmets of water back into the face of the storm. And every foaming wave that swept over us went away with more of our silver in its pockets. Until, by the time the wind died late that night and the stars came out, it was gone, all but a handful of coins trapped in the folds of the awning and a length of silver chain that had gotten wedged between two strakes.

Like the poor Kalevalans with their sampo, we stood in dripping clothes and gazed bitterly at the black water.

Don't mock us for our greed. Possessing that treasure, whether its worth was great or small, signified that our long pains and sorrows in the country of the Finns had gone for *something*. With that treasure we might have taken our ease in some cozy tavern, thumb in belt and feet to the fire, tipping a wink to the yokels sitting round, jingling our purse, and saying, "Finland, my friends, if its loot you're after. Queer sort of place, though, thick with witches...." We would've spun the wretched straw of slavery into golden coins of stories.

But without the treasure, we were dogs. Runaway slaves without fortune or fame.

✝

As day broke, clear and serene, we took stock. Half the deck planking was lost, a part of the aft bulwark was stove in, and most of the sea chests had gone overboard—not that they had much in them, but they served us for rowing benches. The oars, at least, had been tightly lashed down; of those we had many more than we needed: with Glum now gone, we were only twelve.

Spying a low coastline some miles distant, we made slowly for it. While we rowed, Einar Tree-Foot held up his thumb to the rising sun, tasted the water, which was hardly salt, and guessed that we had been blown far into the gulf and were somewhere along its southern shore, near the place where the waters of Lake Ladoga pour into it through the swift-flowing Neva. If he was right, then our nearest refuge was Aldeigjuborg, a prosperous town just beyond the farther shore of that lake. With winter closing in fast, it was foolhardy to try for Jumne now. I put it to the others.

"Why not?" Stig laughed without mirth, "Einar Tree-Foot's advice has been nothing but a blessing to us so far."

The old Jomsviking ignored him.

But first we must try to rig a makeshift sail. This coast was a desolate place where nothing grew but grasses and shrubs, with here and there a slender pine tree sticking up. Vanished with Glum was his long-hafted broadax, the only axe we had. So, it was the work of a full day, hacking and sawing with our swords, to bring down a tree of the right girth and trim it up. Another day went to shaping a yardarm, rigging the awning on it, and fitting it to the mast-block. During those two days we had nothing to eat but raw plovers' eggs, and only brackish water to drink.

"Just like home," said Stig, making a wry face.

The night we spent on that shore was a miserable one, with nothing between us and a raw sea wind but our ragged shirts. We hadn't even the comfort of a fire, for our tinderbox was lost.

As I lay on the ground shivering, who should come creeping to my side but Einar.

"Odd Tangle-Hair?" It was a halting voice, quite unlike his usual one.

"Yes, Tree-Foot?"

"I do miss him ... I never thought...."

"I know. I miss him too. It's all right. The gods are deep-minded and lay their own plans. Don't blame yourself."

"There weren't so many of his kind left in the world, you know. What do you think's become of him?"

"Ah, there's a puzzle. When that old sorcerer of the Lapps fetched back my soul, he went downwards to a place he called Jab ... Jaba ... well, I can't pronounce it, but anyway. But then, Ainikki told me that the dead of Finland dwell in Tuonela, which lies beyond a dark river near by Pohjola. Her brother once visited the place, she said. While we Norse say that the dead land is up, in Valhalla, where Odin keeps his mead hall with feasting and fighting for the heroes all day long—or else in Hel's cold hall beneath the ground for those who die in their beds.

"The Christmen, too, I think, place it both up and down—up for themselves, that is, and down for the rest of us. But then again, it's plain that the dead live on in their graves or, like my kin, in a mountain—and then, of course, there are the draugs that won't stay put at all, but hang about their former homes injuring folk.

"I've given some hard thought to it and come to the conclusion that everyone goes to the dead-place of his own nation and then returns at night to this world to sleep or walk. Because, otherwise, I can make no sense of it at all."

Einar was quiet for a while, mulling this over—it being more answer than he'd bargained for.

"You know," he said at last, "I never wanted to live as long as I have. Death always skipped me and took another. But there's a thing I do fear: that sloping road to Hel where the old and sick go, the ones that die without any word-fame. It's not the way for a Jomsviking."

"No," I agreed.

"They say you must die with steel in your guts to be carried off by the Valkyries to Odin's Hall. Dammit, I've had a hundred chances to die that way and missed every one. And so I was thinking that, ah, maybe I will just turn Christman, for I hear it said that their god keeps a fine table, too, and makes no bother about how a fellow dies."

"Tree-Foot," I answered, smiling in spite of myself, "the Christmen wouldn't have you, you're the very Devil himself. You know what I think. I think Glum's in Valhalla this very minute, drinking Odin's ale and boasting how he matched Red-bearded Thor blow for blow until the great hammer carried him off—and they'll love him all the more for it."

"You think so?"

"I do. And I'll tell you another thing, old friend. You'll drink with him again one day, for I undertake to see that you die with a sword in your belly, if I have to put it there myself."

"Heh?"

"Which may be sooner than you think, if this Aldeigjuborg of yours proves to be as jolly a place as Pohjola was."

"Never fear, Captain," he chuckled.

33

RAGE AND PRIDE

Driven by an icy wind that tore at our makeshift sail, we worked along the barren shore and soon came within sight of the mouth of the River Neva. The length of this river, said Einar, was ninety miles, and its current so strong that it could be seen far out in the water.

"Lay on the oars, boys," I cried. "This next stretch will put iron in our muscles."

"More likely kill us," muttered Bengt.

"Why don't you just walk it then, little flea," said Brodd, cuffing him on the ear.

Bengt looked alarmed. For it was a melancholy landscape that lay before us: everywhere stagnation, mud and mist. We tore strips from our ragged clothes and tied them around our hands for warmth. Then, as we had done before, I took an oar behind Stig while Einar worked the tiller.

We had been toiling for hours and barely making headway against the current, when Stig's eagle eye picked out a glint of gold in the haze behind us.

"Tangle-Hair, look yonder."

It was the bronze prow ornament of a dragon ship. As we watched, a hull took shape behind it. She was big, with sixty oars or more and two men on each, and her broad sail strained at the shrouds. She bucketed through the water, throwing up great sheets of spray, riding in our wake and gaining fast.

I saw myself viewing Aldeigjuborg from the top of a slave block—Pohjola all over again! My fingers itched for Einar's throat.

"We'll die here if we must!" I shouted to the others.

She was nearly upon us now, but hadn't yet dropped her sail as a ship would do that intended to grapple.

"She wants to overtake us is all," called Einar to me from the poop.

"Well, damn him, isn't there enough river for the both of us!"

A figure stood up in her prow, clad in silvered helmet and armor, with a scarlet cloak whipping around his shoulders. As they closed on us, this fellow hooted and waved us out of his way as though we were just some wretched fishermen!

When one single drop is added to a brimming pail, the water spills over. So weeks of building anger spilled over in me: the gall of slavery, sweet Ainikki's death, shipwreck and lost treasure, so many comrades gone.

"I'll not turn aside for this glittering ass," I screamed into the wind, "I give way to no man! Einar, hold her steady!"

"Odd, give way," Stig said between his teeth, turning half round to me. "He'll break us to splinters."

"Let him!"

"Odd!"

"Row, I say!"

Not trusting Einar to obey me, I dashed to his side and took the tiller in my own hands.

The other ship was so close to us now that I could plainly see that man in her prow. Tall as a tree—and yet beardless. *Great gods,* I had just time to think, *don't I know that face? Olaf's young brother Harald, the unnatural weed? But he died at Stiklestad!*

"Give way there, you dogs!" he bellowed again through cupped hands.

He meant to ram us—I could see it in his face. Well, let him see as much in mine! I'd send us all to the bottom before I'd move aside for this bully.

Then Stig, the steadiest friend I had in all the world, betrayed me.

"Port oars up!" he cried. "Back water, the starboard! Do it!"

Instantly they obeyed him, and though I strained to force the tiller in the opposite direction, the Viper swung narrowly out of the big ship's path. She missed us by feet. And as she shot past, rocking us and drenching us

357

with her spray, the giant laughed and jerked his thumb.

I drew my sword and went for Stig.

It had nothing to do with will or wish. It was that busy, muttering madman in my brain. Rage.

"Whoreson! Pig-fucking bastard!"

I swung, splintering the oar handle that he held up in front of him. For the first time ever, I saw fear in his eyes.

"Coward!" I screamed.

He retreated until his back was to the mast. Again I swung. He leaned away. My blade stuck quivering an inch deep in wood. Before I could pull it free, he stepped in and hit me a short, sharp blow with his fist under the breastbone. I went down gasping.

Now the others rushed in between us, some holding Stig and some me, as I struggled to my feet.

"Damn all!" Brodd swore. "Here we are lost in some filthy corner of the world and you two want to kill each other!"

The others grunted and Starkad, his moustache twitching rat-like under his long nose, said, "Make it up, the both of you, while no blood's yet been spilt." And turning on me, he pleaded, "We had to follow Stig this time, Odd—you do see that?"

Anxiously they watched us. But Stig and I stood mute, avoiding each other's eyes. I wonder to this day what was in his mind.

I know what was in mine.

A year earlier, being the boy that I was then, I would have asked his pardon in a minute. Or he might have laughed and asked me mine, as when we were among the Lapps and he pledged to follow me although my sword-point was at his throat. Where only one is a man, there is no shame in yielding. But in the year since then I had changed. I had become the captain of my ship, not just in name, but truly. What he had done was mutiny and no captain can forgive a mutiny. Ever.

Any more than he can be forgiven for uselessly risking his men's lives. There was no room here on either side for pardon.

Einar broke the silence to observe that while we stood idly about, the current was wiping out our hard won gains.

"Tree-Foot's right, back to your oars." I made my face a mask and my voice low. I must seem, must *be*, in command again.

We toiled again in silence, but I felt their eyes on me. Eyes that held that same veiled and sullen look as when last I went mad and they had wanted to drown me in the sea—the very same men, some of them. Oh, I hadn't forgotten! And but for me, every one of them would have lost his head in Finland. The scum! Is a man's credit so quickly exhausted?

Those were my thoughts at first, and I was fierce with my oar, chopping the water as though it were Stig's neck.

But gradually my anger spent itself, and I began to feel ashamed. A hundred times I was on the point of jumping up and embracing him. My face grew hot and my heart quickened as I was going to ... was going to ... *No!* My legs, my arms, my tongue would not obey me, no matter how I willed it.

No captain forgives mutiny.

On the bench in front of me, Stig bent and straightened, bent and straightened over his oar.

Stig, ask my pardon, I silently entreated, *and we'll be friends again. Of course I was wrong to do what I did, and you were right to stop me. Just let it go and beg my pardon. Speak first, Stig. Damn you, Stig No-One's-Son, you crow's meat without even a father's name, what is shame to you?*

But his back only bent and straightened, bent and straightened, without cease. And with every stroke, I felt us sink deeper into a pit from which there could be no escape.

✝

Towards evening of that day we broke out of the Neva into Lake Ladoga, a vast sheet of water that stretches to the horizon like a sea, and coasted along its marshy shore until again we felt the rush of a current coming to meet us. This was the Volkhov, on whose bank, some eighteen miles upstream, Aldeigjuborg lay, surrounded by forest and fen. But the sun being low in the sky and ourselves exhausted with rowing, it seemed best to camp for the night before tackling this last stretch of our journey.

Nothing felt right. Sitting wearily on the wet ground, I sneaked a look at Stig, caught him watching me, and quickly looked away.

The next morning, under low, dirty clouds we boarded ship again and threw ourselves groaning into the mouth of the Volkhov. Past midday, after seven weary hours at the oar, we rounded a bend and saw Aldeigjuborg's earthen rampart high up on the steep left bank of the river, and ranged along the quay beneath, a forest of masts rocking at anchor. I stood beside Einar at the tiller and searched the quayside for an empty stanchion to tie up to.

"Next to Jumne I do love this place best!" he chuckled, showing me his toothless grin. "A man can find delight here—delight, I say! Oh, don't it make me wish I had my parts! Though I've a one still, mind you, works as well as ever!"

"Spare me that, old man."

He looked crestfallen and shut his jaws with a snap.

I hadn't meant to be sharp with him, but words must be sour with so sour a taste in my mouth.

I was remembering myself a year ago on the morning that I sailed, warm with wonder and expectation, into the harbor at Nidaros—with the whole world before me and true friends at my side—trusty Kalf, resourceful Stig. How much had happened since that day, and how little of it good.

I surveyed us cheerlessly: ragged and dirty, our clothes and hair crusted with salt, skins burnt brown from the wind; and, except for Einar, strangely silent and subdued for men making port after a long haul. We were a crew no longer, and the fault was mine. What I had created over weeks and months, I had blasted in an instant, and had no idea how to repair it.

I clapped a hand on Einar's shoulder to reassure him, and the old man started up again at once. "Look'ee there now, captain, on the bluff above the town. You haven't seen the likes of that—a hall built of solid stone? Jarl Ragnvald Ulfsson lives in that hall and holds the town for the Rus prince of Novgorod."

"The Rus?"

"The folk who rule here. They were Northmen once, just like us, but you'd hardly think it now to hear 'em jabber away at each other. Their country, which is a big one, goes by the name of Gardariki. Now, Novgorod is the…"

I stopped listening when I spied the ship.

No mistaking the gleaming bronze vane on her prow. She lay rocking peacefully at the pier with none aboard her as far as I could make out. From her masthead a banner hung, white with a cross of gold.

I knew where I'd seen that before.

A few berths farther on, we found space where a merchantman had just departed. Moving like sleepwalkers, we went through the rituals of docking.

"We need food," I said, "and drink, and women. And for the Viper, timber and new tackle, though how we'll pay for it is more than I know. Tree-Foot will come with me to scout the town. The rest of you stay close here. Stig..." Stig is in charge, I had nearly said from long habit. "I won't be long."

Einar and I made our way up from the quayside and through the town gate, pressing through the crowds of sailors, hawkers, and bustling citizens who pursued their noisy business along the narrow, plank-paved streets. We bent our steps toward a tavern that he knew, where he hoped that his credit might still be good.

We hadn't gone a hundred paces when we met the giant.

He burst on us out of a side street where two lanes crossed, he and a score of armed men, all talking loudly and laughing. With never a backward look he brushed Einar with his shoulder as he strode past, knocking the old man off his peg-leg and sending him into the mud. The fellow's manners were no better on land than on the water.

"Hi, you!" I shouted at his back. "Half-Troll! You've too much body for my likes—come back and I'll shorten you by a head!"

They turned.

I hauled Einar to his feet and, with hands on our hilts, we stood to face them.

"Jomsviking," I said under my breath, "I've a feeling you may get to Valhalla sooner than you thought. Are you game?"

"You needn't insult me with asking," he growled.

I studied the young tree-trunk as he came toward us. He had grown even taller in a year, nearer seven feet than six I guessed, and broader in the chest and shoulders. His face, too, had taken on the lines of manhood, although the beard was still just a silky down. What was he now— sixteen? A year younger than myself.

He stopped at sword's reach and looked at us with hard eyes. "Heh? By Christ, isn't it those beggars who nearly took a bath in the Neva! Well, you'll die unbathed now!" This joke was greeted with laughter from the hirdmen at his back.

"You know who this is?" asked one of them with a sneer.

"I do believe it's the Unnatural Weed," I answered, "Olaf of Norway's kinsman. Yet I thought I saw him die."

Still vivid was that scene of a year ago: King Olaf's bloody corpse with its head hacked nearly off, dragged back and forth in the dirt as Tronder jarls fought with the king's hirdmen for possession of it; and from the king's side this boy—Harald, the slighted half-brother—standing astraddle of the corpse until the enemy overwhelmed him and he disappeared under a heap of bodies.

I recalled also the rumor that Harald's corpse, just like the king's, could not be found afterwards. At the time, compared to the mystery surrounding Olaf, this had seemed a thing of small importance.

"Saw me dead?" Harald laughed harshly, tightening his grip on his hilt. "Not as dead as you'll soon wish me—draw your sword!"

Behind him a gathering crowd of onlookers who had stopped to watch the fun, retreated to a safe distance.

"That he will not!" Out of the knot of men beside Harald stepped a short, square-built man of about fifty. His square head, jowled like a bulldog's, sat upon square shoulders with no neck between. "He'll not draw his sword in the streets of my city nor you either, Harald Sigurdarson—not while I have the charge of delivering you to your benefactor." The tone was quarrelsome and overbearing.

Naturally, Harald's reply was to draw his sword and raise his arm to strike. Einar and I fell back a step with our weapons up.

"But you're right, of course, Jarl Ragnvald!"

The speaker of these words emerged from around Harald's other flank. "It's a thing of no consequence—an accident on the Neva two days ago, tempers flared. Now, Harald, there's no cause for bloodshed here."

This one, too, I had seen before. That handsome, elegantly dressed man who had patched up a truce between Harald and Olaf before the battle, and was cheered by the army for it. I remembered the ironic smile and the observant eyes.

He turned them on me now. "You were in that fight? On the king's side?"

I nodded.

"Well now, Harald, our cause hasn't got so many friends that we can afford to kill them off for sport!" It was said with an easy off-hand manner.

I was on the point of telling them what I truly thought of their cause and king when I saw that his words were having an effect on the Unnatural Weed. His brows unbent and his blade came slowly down.

The elegant one addressed me in the same easy tone: Was I a Norwegian?

"Icelander."

"You're a long way from home."

"I have my reasons, they needn't concern you."

"Come, come, my short-tempered friend. I am Dag Hringsson." He touched his fingertips to his heart. And you? Surely you owe us that much before you and your alarming companion carve us meat from bone. Will you name yourself?"

The words worked on me even while I sensed the method behind them. I have known plenty of silken-tongued courtiers since, but that breed was new to me then. I dropped my sword point and motioned Einar to do the same.

"I am Odd Thorvaldsson of Rang River-by-Hekla. My father was Thorvald-godi, his father was Odd Snout…"

Dag Hringsson gazed at me in astonishment. "Thorvald Oddsson was your father? The same one who sailed among the Orkney Isles thirty years ago and more? By God, of course it is! You have those wild black brows of his. Black Thorvald! Why, he was often a guest in my foster-father's hall when I was a child. He always had a brave word for me and would let me hold his drinking horn at dinner. Black Thorvald's son! Well, if you're half the fighter he was, I'd say we're all lucky to be alive!"

I was struck dumb. A man who knew my father from his long ago viking days? And liked him!

Turning to Harald he said, "Prince, you and this young man must be friends for my sake. I won't have it otherwise." The tone, as before, was light, insinuating, purposeful.

Reluctantly the long sword crept back into its scabbard and Harald extended to me a huge open hand.

"I can deny nothing to my brother's hirdman," he said. "Please blame my behavior on the hotheadedness of youth."

Stilted and awkward, this speech, as though he had been made to learn it off by heart—probably by this smooth-tongued counselor of his. Dag's words had their effect on me, too. Best, I decided, to let it pass. My troubles were heaped high enough already without adding a new one.

Besides, I wanted to live long enough to hear more about my father.

"All right, then," I replied, "but my friend is owed the same apology."

Harald looked rebellious again for a moment, but finally extended his hand to Einar too. "Will you join us?" he asked. "Jarl Ragnvald, our host, is leading us on a tour of his market place. We're exiles and travel light, yet we mustn't arrive in Novgorod empty-handed."

I said that we had errands of our own, but Dag leapt in before the last words were out of my mouth.

"You and your crew will dine with us tonight!" And in the same breath, to Ragnvald: "We tax your hospitality already, Jarl—but as a favor?"

The jarl frowned and grunted his assent.

So that was settled, and we drew apart.

"How many are you and where do you stay meantime?" called Dag over his shoulder.

I answered, not bothering to add that we were penniless. Our rags told him that much.

He answered with a smile, "I never knew an Icelander to stay poor for long. Till tonight."

The crowd of townsfolk, disappointed that there was to be no bloodshed, turned back to its own pursuits.

"What do you make of them, Tree-Foot?" I asked when we were alone again.

"What—the rough jarl and the smooth-tongued one? Two dogs eyeing the same bone, I'd say."

"My thought too. And a damned big bone, at that."

34

the uses of poetry

The approach of evening found us back at the Viper, footsore and discouraged. No inn would have us, no shipwright or timber merchant would even talk to us without hard cash down. My crew, who lay about on the deck, only grunted as if they had expected no more.

"And where is Stig?" I asked carelessly, for he was not among them.

"Out and about," Starkad shrugged. "You know him."

"Well, I've one piece of good news at any rate," I said, and told them how we would feast at the jarl's hall that night. Which bucked them up considerably, until Bald Brodd complained that he, for one, was ashamed to visit a noble hall in the rags he had on. And though the others protested that they would go stark naked through the middle of town for a horn of beer, I knew that secretly they felt the same way.

Just then we were hailed by a voice from the dock.

Peering from under the flap of the awning, I saw a youth holding the reins of a pony cart in which, with some other baggage, was one large bundle tied up in a red cloak.

"You, in the dismasted ship—are you Odd Thorvaldsson's crew?"

"We are."

"Well, Harald of Norway sends you this."

I went down to him and undoing a corner of the cloak, saw that it held articles of clothing.

"Take these back to your master," I said angrily, "and tell him that

I'm his guest, not his man, and it's not my custom to take gifts I can't repay."

"Oh, now don't come the great lord with me," answered the youth. "I'm ordered to tell you from Dag Hringsson, if you should start in to ranting just as you are, that he begs you to accept it from Harald as amends for something or other, and from himself, too, out of respect for your pa which was the dear friend of his childhood. Now take it and have done, for I've more chores than this to do before I get my supper. The fancy dress is for you," he added over his shoulder as he cracked his whip and wheeled his cart around.

On the deck we spread the bundle out and saw it consisted of eleven white linen tunics, neatly stitched, with collar and cuffs of blue—one for each of my men. But for me, a costume the likes of which I had never before set eyes on, except that very day in the streets of the town. While the others looked on, I applied myself to its mysteries.

First, I exchanged my tattered breeches for the trousers. These were of white linen, striped with blue, and cut so full you could have hidden a bushel in each leg. With them came a pair of red-dyed leather boots of amazing softness. I tucked the trousers in, letting them hang over at the knees.

Next I approached the coat. It was of fine blue wool, with a high collar, long close-fitting sleeves, and a very full skirt. The puzzling feature was that it was entirely unfastened down the front.

Were there pins somewhere?

"By the Raven!" howled Einar, "What a bumpkin! D'you see the little knobs? These here, on the edge. Now d'you see those little slits opposite 'em. Well? Don't stand a-gaping at me, just push the knobs into the slits—it's all the fashion out here!"

My fingers were sausages. The little knobs escaped me as I grasped them, the little slits winked at me. By dint of much cursing, I succeeded at last in connecting one knob with one slit, and after a deal more cursing, showed myself finally to Einar.

"No ... no...." he rubbed his chin, "you've gone wrong somewhere. She's crooked. Have at 'er again."

"By the gods, Tree-Foot, d'you mean to say men do this every day?"

"Stand still," said Starkad, chuckling, "ten bumpkins may succeed where one failed—we'll put you to rights."

They set upon me all together, turning me this way and that, encouraging each other with shouts, fumbling and fastening and unfastening, and all of us laughing so hard that the tears rolled down our cheeks.

"What a pretty sight."

Stig stood swaying on the gangplank, a wine jug under his arm and his face fiery red.

Their hands drew back from me.

"Oh boys, isn't it an elegant, isn't it a popular captain that we have!" His voice was thick and ugly.

"Steersman, you were told to stay by the ship."

"Was I now? Not my way, Captain—not old Stig's way at all."

Stig, don't do this! I pleaded silently, but said aloud, "There's a clean shirt for you, a present from the boy on the Neva. It seems he's King Olaf's half-brother. We're dining with him tonight."

He looked at the shirt and he looked at me. "Well, damn all," he breathed, "you do work fast. I've never seen the likes of you. A nobleman's rig for you, who would have sunk him if you could, and this bit of stuff for me who saved him from it!" He moved the shirt with his toe. "Am I ordered to this feast?"

"No, of course not."

"Then excuse me to King-bloody-Olaf's half-brother and just tell him that old Stig has lost his appetite in recent days—has had it taken clean away, so to speak—with disappointment." He tipped up the jug and the red wine ran down his chin and throat.

"I'll tell him you were too drunk to walk! Follow me the rest of you."

For a long moment they stood frozen where they were. Then the Nidaros and Jumne men slouched to the gangway. Brodd went with them. "Empty belly wins the argument," he growled as he passed in front of Stig.

But Starkad stood by his friend, unmoving.

I turned on my heel and left them.

✝

As the sun was setting, we arrived at the gate of Jarl Ragnvald's stone hall. Inside, the dining room was ablaze with torches and a great throng was assembled, with all the merry noise of feasting. Ragnvald was not, at any rate, a stingy host. I told the men to find places where they could, and catching sight of Harald's head above all the rest, steered for it.

Dag saw me coming and made room beside him at the long table. He, like Harald and the jarl and most of the other men there, was wearing the same outlandish costume as I, though theirs were more adorned with fur trim and jewelry.

Jarl Ragnvald sat on Dag's other side with his wife and his younger son, and opposite them, Harald, with a number of others, including a priest. Ragnvald, without putting down the bone he was gnawing, mumbled introductions while making a point of not remembering my name.

The Unnatural Weed was looking pleased with himself. After I had thanked him for his generosity to my men and me, he said, "I trust your luck was as good as ours today, Odd Thorvaldsson. With the jarl's help, we have purchased excellent gifts for Prince Yaroslav and his wife."

He waved an arm at a couple of servants who stood along one tapestried wall. They approached, one holding a box and one a cage.

"For the Princess," he said, "a silver reliquary. She's a lady of great piety, I'm told, and collects relics with a passion. And this for Yaroslav." In its wicker cage, a young snow-white gyrfalcon strutted and mantled, shaking the silver bells of its jesses. "She's a fine specimen, isn't she! Come all the way from Greenland, I think."

"Or Iceland," I replied. "We breed them, too, and sell them far and wide."

"Are you a falconer then?"

"No, not I."

"But your father could fly a bird," Dag struck in. "I wonder he never taught you."

"Could he? I didn't know. My father in his later years—gave up many of his interests."

"Gave?"

"He's recently dead."

"Well, I'm sorry to hear it. I expect he's sorely missed."

Then, of course, it was necessary to tell the story— though not quite the whole of it. I doubted they would care to hear how the Christmen's religion had unmanned him; how Black Thorvald had turned blacker still in anger until the heart in him was as dead as an old coal. Not for this pious hall that bitter tale. But as shortly as I could, I told of the feud with Hrut, my outlawry at the Althing, my father's sudden death, and the slaughter of my family.

Dag looked distressed. "Icelanders," he sighed. "You're a quick and lively people. I've always had a fondness for you. But by God, you're prickly, litigious, and bloody-minded. Feuding will be the ruin of you all one day."

"So now you lead a viking's life!" said Harald with enthusiasm. "Christ, don't I envy you! My brother Olaf was a viking before he decided to be King of Norway. It calls to me, too, I can tell you. Might you have an adventure for us? We would gladly hear it."

I had made up my mind that a man among strangers should listen much and say little, and I had said more than I meant to already. But Harald would not be put off, and so I told them how we had fared to Finland and what befell us there. All along the table, conversation died down as people paused to listen to my tale of Louhi and her garden of heads.

"Bravo!" cried Harald, when I had done. "A capital story! And nearly came away rich—bad luck! If I'd been there, I'd not have let that silver slip through my fingers, storm or no. For it's money, after all, that matters most, friend Odd, isn't it? Money makes a man's fame. I tell you someday I will be rich, Devil skin me, I will!" He began to glance around him with an intensity that seemed extraordinary and his voice got steadily louder. "Mark me, the day will come when Canute the Rich, Prince Yaroslav, even old Charlemagne in his grave, will gnaw their knuckles for envy when Harald's name is spoke!"

He was no longer talking to me but to the whole room, and he was answered with a thunderous pounding on the tables and shouts of "Aye!" and "Brave Harald!" from every Norwegian throat. With his face screwed into a warrior's scowl, he stood up and showed himself to them while they cheered and cheered.

But Jarl Ragnvald, I noticed, seemed about as comfortable as a man shitting a stone, while Dag—and this intrigued me most—looked as though he might at any moment make an ungraceful leap for the door. What was he afraid of?

Harald, taking his seat again finally, turned back to me. His face was flushed. "You hear that—how they cheer me? They love me! For how many have done what I've done already at my age? If you were there, Odd Thorvaldsson, then you saw it for yourself—a boy of fifteen, but I hewed the legs off a dozen warriors before some troll caught me with a spear through the lungs. Hah!"

"Indeed, I saw it," I replied, "and am still wondering how you come to be here now."

It was none other than his elegant kinsman, Dag, he explained, who had saved his life by pulling him from under the heap of bodies and dragging him from the field. Commandeering a farmer's cart, Dag had taken him, more dead than alive, to a cottage deep in the woods and left him with the family there to be nursed. And there he had lain, too weak to move all winter long, while the remnant of Olaf's faction was hunted down by Canute's Danish warriors, who now occupied the king's Hall in Nidaros.

"At last, with the coming of summer, my strength returned and, guided by the cottager's son, I got across the Keel into Sweden, where Dag had gone before me. Then it was just a matter of rounding up our scattered friends, finding a ship, and here you see me!—You there, pour, damn your eyes..." He held out his empty horn to the young cupbearer who stood behind him.

Aye, I thought, I see you. But there were two youths carried half-dead from that field, and the better of them must drag out his life a cripple while you prance and posture. It's a true saying that "fated and fair keep poor company."

But I told him it was a brave story, returning his praise of mine, and added for good measure, "More Tronders than you might guess will rejoice to hear it, for it didn't take them long to decide that the Danes weren't to their liking. By the time I left Nidaros this spring, they were missing your half-brother and telling each other of his miracles."

"Ah, of course!" exclaimed Dag. "Being enslaved in Finland all these months you've not heard the most recent news. The king's body is found! We learned of it some weeks ago. And I myself sent word ahead to the jarl here, and to Prince Yaroslav. They say a young cripple, inspired by God in a dream, led Bishop Grimkel right to the spot. And the body was uncorrupted! Can you imagine what that means?"

It means, I smiled to myself, that friend Kalf has played his part well, and they shall hear nothing from me about what really happened.

"It means," Dag answered himself, "that he is a saint—Rome is bound to confirm it—the first from our country!"

This remark produced a solemn moment, as Harald, followed by everyone within hearing of us, blessed themselves and mumbled prayers—myself included, I hasten to say, for it's sound advice, when you're thrown among wolves, to howl like one.

But I did just steal a glance at young Harald. What thoughts ran around that head so piously bowed? Surely he had hated Olaf—that much was common knowledge in the camp. But his future rested in the hands of Olaf's hirdmen now, and he knew it. He was playing his part well.

"But if you were safe in Sweden, Harald," I asked, "what brings you now to the country of the Rus?"

"You know surprisingly little of King Olaf for one who claims to have fought for him." It was not Harald but Jarl Ragnvald who spoke, turning on me sharply. He had been deep in conversation with his wife and the priest, and I hadn't thought he was even listening. I promised myself not to make that mistake again.

"Do they never mention the Lady Ingigerd's name in Norway?"

"Never that I heard, Jarl."

He affected a smile of pity, like one speaking to a half-wit. "Know, then, that she is the sister of the present king of Sweden and daughter of the old one, wife to Yaroslav, Prince of Novgorod, and my own cousin."

"My dear Jarl," said Dag in his most ingratiating manner, "tell my friend her history, and don't be modest about your own part in it."

Ragnvald did not strike me as a modest man, and he had taken on a quantity of drink besides, which is generally a loosener of tongues. Still, for my benefit, he took the trouble to look put-upon.

The story he told was a complicated one. I will give it as simply as I can. The gist of it was that some ten years ago King Olaf, hearing of Ingigerd's beauty, had asked the Swedish king for her hand, despite the fact the two countries had long been at war. Olaf sent his skalds to press his suit and they praised the king so highly that Ingigerd fell in love with him sight unseen. They also gained the support of Ingigerd's cousin Ragnvald. But Ingigerd's father flew into a rage and said he would never consent to the marriage of his daughter to his hated enemy. At about the same time, an offer for her hand came from Yaroslav, Prince of Novgorod. Now Ragnvald did a rather daring thing. He took it on himself, without the

Swedish king's knowledge, to arrange a marriage for Olaf with Ingigerd's younger sister, Astrid. When the king found out, he threatened to hang Ragnvald. But Ingigerd saved him. She would consent to marry Yaroslav, she said, only if she could take her cousin with her and install him as jarl of Ladoga. And that is what happened.

Then a year ago who should appear on their doorstep but Olaf—older and stouter, but still a handsome man. He had been driven from his throne by the mighty King Canute of England and fled to the court of Yaroslav and Ingigerd. His only claim on their hospitality was his marriage to Ingigerd's sister, although interestingly, he had neglected to bring the Lady Astrid with him. Was it perhaps a more intimate connection with Ingigerd that he sought to trade on? The rekindling of an old flame?

I interrupted Ragnvald to pose that innocent suggestion.

The Jarl's expression congealed; even Dag's pleasant face hardened. Only on Harald's lips was there, perhaps, the faintest flicker of a smile.

"You do not take my point," Ragnvald said icily. "My cousin is a most religious woman, while Olaf was a man who had already shown marks of Our Lord's favor. It was only natural they should admire one another. The testimonials to Olaf's piety during the few months he was with us at court are an inspiration to all of our Faith. One time, I recall, at Princess Ingigerd's personal request, he cured a child of a boil by the laying on of his hands. Another time when, on the Sabbath he had absent-mindedly picked up a stick to whittle, seeing with horror what he had done, he burnt the wood shavings in the palm of his hand for a penance."

"Having met the man myself," I said gravely, "I can well believe it of him." Indeed, I could believe it of that brutal fanatic. Ragnvald, assuming that I had meant it in praise, favored me with a bleak smile.

Poor Yaroslav, I thought. His wife, seeing at long last the man she once had loved, finds him still to her liking—and who could believe that it was only Olaf's piety that fluttered the heart of this willful woman? What to do? The first thing he did was offer to make Olaf king of the Bulgars—at quite some distance from Novgorod. But when Olaf decided finally to try to regain his throne instead, Yaroslav was delighted to shower him with money, give him leave to raise troops, and wish him Godspeed back to Norway.

"Needless to say," the Jarl continued, "the court went into deep mourning when word reached us of the tragic outcome of Stiklestad.

Indeed, the Princess took it—" He looked away blinking, allowing us to picture this dismal scene for ourselves.

"Well, at any rate," I said, "they must be cheered to know that his brother still lives."

The compression of Ragnvald's bloodless lips suggested otherwise. "We were delighted," said he, fixing me with a very chilly stare, "delighted to learn that there was a *half*-brother,"—(I noted the emphasis)—"though his existence, I must say, took us all by surprise. No one has been able to recall Olaf ever mentioning the young man." He looked wickedly at Harald. "Of course, the Prince and Princess look forward to receiving him, knowing how anxious he must be to embrace again his little nephew, Magnus, King Olaf's son and heir—"

Came the eruption.

"Magnus!" Harald flung out an arm, sending cups and candlesticks flying. "My brother's bastard, you mean! Whelped under the stair by some concubine. Sickly little Magnus, who pukes in his nurse's bosom? 'Nephew' is not one of the words I call him!" He finished up leaning across the table and bellowing this in Ragnvald's face.

A crashing silence followed, while the jarl, teeth clenched and jowls aquiver, stared straight ahead of him. With an effort, he forced a little dry laugh.

"Self-control's a hard lesson for the young, is it not, friend Dag? I will do you the favor of not repeating his remarks to my cousin—they would only distress her. Olaf, as of course you know, left his son—his *acknowledged* son—in her care when he returned to Norway, and she and Yaroslav love the boy like one of their own, he being the only thing that remains to them to remember the father by."

Well, well, I thought, our proud young Harald isn't quite what he seems. Not important enough to have accompanied Olaf to Yaroslav's court, and distinctly not his heir. What then, are he and Dag after?

"Ragnvald, my dear friend," Dag spoke urgently, pressing his host's arm. "I will not permit us to quarrel like this. Harald and I have come to Gardariki seeking only refuge and a chance to serve those who served our king so well. Nothing more. When the princess has had an opportunity to know him, she will esteem Harald, too. He is an accomplished young man—"

"I can ride," the Unnatural Weed burst out in a truculent tone, "I can sail, ski, shoot a bow, harp, and rhyme. And I take second place in these to no runny-nosed baby!"

I saw Dag's fist, lying in his lap, clench, and the knuckles turn white. I imagined I could hear him screaming to the young fool to shut up.

"Can you rhyme, then?" I asked pleasantly. I hadn't grown up in my father's house without learning how to manage those intimate family occasions that veered toward mayhem.

He looked at me sharply. "I said so."

"Let me hear something."

"Hear this then. I made it last winter, while I lay half-dead on that cottage floor." He turned his eyes again on Ragnvald, and looking his fiercest, began:

There was I where shields were shattered,
Blood ran red from murd'rous blows;
Now in holes I hide me, hunted,
without honor—yet, who knows
what wide word-fame my Luck will bring me,
what pale terror to my foes?

"It's well-turned," I said truthfully.

"You're skilled in such things?"

"As it happens, I am. My father, in his day—"

He shot out a line of verse and commanded, "Give it back using none of the same kennings."

It was a line composed ages ago by Bragi the Old, where he refers to a warrior as 'mast of the sail of the sword' because, as a mast holds up the sail, so a warrior holds his shield. Without hesitating, I gave him the line back, substituting a kenning made famous by Olaf's own skald, Thormod: "feeder of the swan of the crashing wave of wounds," by which he means to say "feeder of the raven of the battlefield."

"Not bad," he conceded, cocking that one eyebrow of his which was higher than the other and casting his mocking expression my way.

"And shall I try you in turn?" I asked.

"If you like."

I decided to give him a verse of my own—the knottiest I had ever composed. (My brother, Gunnar, had gotten in such a muddle when I tested him with it that he stamped off in a temper.) "Listen, then: the slinger of the fire of the storm of the troll of the protecting moon of the boat house's steed! Interpret it."

"Heh? You think I can't?" A smile spread over his face and he rocked backwards on the bench, his eyelids half closed in pleasurable thought, the anger of a moment ago apparently all forgotten. "The 'boat-house's steed' is a ship—that much is obvious." He touched one finger. "The 'protecting moon,' that's the shield hanging on the gunnel, no? Now, the 'troll of the shield' must be a sword—that's original, I like that—and, of course, the 'storm of the sword' is battle. Then, the 'fire of battle' is sword again, and the 'slinger' is a warrior. Done!" He threw back his head and laughed.

After that we settled down to test each other in good earnest, and for a full ten minutes capped lines: 'Sun of the deep' for 'fire of the wave,' 'corpse-sea' for 'wound-dew,' 'necklace tree' for 'sewing Valkyrie,' 'fjord-elk' for 'sea king's ski'...

The room watched us in silence. Men who knew their poetry nodded and smiled. Dag was one of these. But the jarl, it seemed, was not. His eye swung back and forth between us, catching none of the fire.

Harald was good—he put me on my mettle—and as he warmed to the contest, I wondered if I could be looking at the same bragging bully who had sat there a moment before. In his place was only a boy, eager, quick-witted, and in love with the dance of the word-music.

Dag saw it, too, and looked at me thoughtfully along his eyes.

After a time, Harald said, "Enough of this playing at poetry, friend skald. Have you ever composed a poem for a high-born person?"

"No," I replied, "for I've never met one."

"You have tonight. Will you shape a verse in my honor?"

"Shall it tell how skillfully you guided the 'Sea-king's ski' on the Neva two days ago?" I kept my eyes on his and waited.

His shoulders tensed. So did mine. And then he slapped the table with the flat of his hand. "Ha! Ha, ha! Christ, that's blunt enough! They say an Icelander will tell you the truth! So you've nothing to praise me for, eh? All right, fair enough. But one day, my friend," he brought his face close to mine, "one day it might happen that you'll compose an ode that will honor us both."

"It might," I answered carelessly.

"What do they call you familiarly, Odd Thorvaldsson?"

"Tangle-Hair, and you?"

"Nothing. Not yet. When the time comes I'll choose a name that suits me."

(And, of course, in time he did, for the world knows him as Harald the Ruthless.) Then he surprised me. "Odd Tangle-Hair, come with me to Novgorod!"

"Novgorod—what for?"

"Why d'you think? To be my skald, of course. A nobleman must have one and I have none. My brother had half a dozen. They all died at Stiklestad, singing his fame. How shall I have honor when no one sings mine. Will you come, Tangle-Hair? For I swear, you're the best fellow in all the world!"

I stared at him—longer than I should have—perplexed how to say that I would as soon lay my head on a chopping block as go off to Gardariki in the retinue of this noisy beggar boy.

"Well—? Is it every day you're offered the friendship of a king's brother?" His color began to darken. I dared not shame him here.

"Harald, I am by nature a fellow who chews things slowly, and this is too great a matter to decide on a moment's whim." He's drunk, I thought. By tomorrow it will all be forgotten. "Let me call on you in the morning with my answer."

But here Ragnvald broke in: "Tomorrow you will find us gone hunting. I would offer you a horse, but my stables are not large and, as you see..." His hand took in the room.

"But surely, Ragnvald," Harald began angrily.

"Thank you, Jarl," I said quickly. "I've had more than enough exercise lately. I'll find quieter amusement in the town."

"I am sure you will," he murmured. The voice was noncommittal, the words might have meant anything.

"In the evening, then," said Harald to me, sounding none too pleased at being thwarted even in the smallest thing.

"In the evening. Jarl Ragnvald, Lady," I said, standing up, "I thank you for my dinner. My time is never wasted when I learn some new thing, and tonight I have learned many."

Ragnvald smiled sourly. "I'll send a man with you to light your way."

But Dag was on his feet already. "Don't trouble your people, Jarl, I'll see him back. His father, you know...."

With a firm hand on my arm, he steered me toward the door.

35

A HARD CHOICE

The ground glittered with a dusting of snow as we walked through the icy night air. The sounds of feasting grew fainter as Dag and I picked our way down the path to the harbor.

"Odd, you never said how you came to be in Olaf's army."

I was prepared for that question. For the most part I told him the truth—why shouldn't I? Except that I spared him my true opinion of his dead king, nor did I say anything about my accidental role in smuggling the saintly corpse away from the battlefield.

"And you saw Harald there? And me, too? By Christ, I wish I had known it, I would have invited you to fight at our side."

I made a vague sound of agreement.

"Odd, how do you find Harald, now that you know him a little? Would you make him your friend?"

"I make friends only to lose them. I'm resolved to make no more."

"Good God," he laughed, "what a thing for a young fellow to say! And you sound as though you meant it, too. But make an exception of me, at least. I'm your friend, as your father was mine."

We spoke a little then about Black Thorvald the viking. But he soon brought the conversation back round to Harald.

"I've known him from a baby, you know. He and Olaf had the same mother, Asta, my kinswoman, though she bore them twenty years apart. She's a strong woman and bred strong sons, but only Olaf was connected, through his father, to the Ynglings, the old royal line of Norway, descended from the god Frey."

"With the result that Harald was pushed into the background?"

"Quite. His own father, Sigurd Sow, cared little for him. He was raised with Olaf's brood of concubines' children and bastards. It drove him wild being lumped with the likes of them. I can remember once seeing him— he was just a little thing, if you can imagine that—playing with wood chips in the pond and pretending they were so many dragon-ships under his command. Olaf and Asta happened by and Olaf laughingly remarked to her that she was raising up another king. No doubt he soon forgot the incident. Harald never did. It has made him—hard to deal with."

"And not helped any by his extraordinary size."

"Yes, that too. It's forced him to play a man's part too soon. It makes him less sure of himself, not more, feeling that older and shrewder eyes are always on him. And so he must always be proving something."

I replied that I'd had a taste of that already.

"That silly business! I'm sorry—if I had been there—"

"Weren't you?"

"No indeed. I came over from Sweden a month ago to— ah—sniff the air, so to speak, before Harald's arrival. One can learn only so much from informants."

"And what have you learned?"

"That we must step lightly—but let's say no more about that just now. Harald, of course, bragged to me about what happened between you two in the river. Odd, there's a kind of person who is willing to die to prove a point—even a very small point. Harald is one. He fought at Stiklestad, you know, because Olaf ordered him back. Trying to run you down when you wouldn't make room for him was just more of the same."

"Meaning that because he comes to Gardariki with his cap in his hand we must all clear out of his way?"

"Something like that."

"Men like that are dangerous, if they don't kill themselves first."

"Aye," he answered, "they are that. They may also grow to greatness. Do you know that the crewmen talk of nothing else. They idolize him for the sheer reckless stupidity of it, even though he might have stove in his own hull as easily as yours and sent some of them to the bottom."

Why, I thought with a pang, can't my men idolize me for being equally a fool? I said, "That's what worries you, Dag Hringsson, isn't it? That he's too much for you. That you can't govern him."

He gave out a laugh and threw a friendly arm round my shoulders. "You're quick to seize the point, Odd Tangle-Hair, I knew you would be. Let us say that it gets daily more difficult."

"Well, I wish you luck with him."

"But that's what you and I must talk about." He was instantly serious. "Won't you take his offer of a place in the hird? To be a royal skald, Odd! A skald does more than just praise his lord. He shares his perils, performs missions in his name, and most important of all, advises him. He is his lord's right hand. The skald of a great king is a great man himself, and his words live forever on the lips of poets. That must excite you!"

"Maybe. Why me?"

"Because he likes you. Dammit, *I* like you. I confess I had my doubts when you challenged us this morning—that was reckless. But the way you handled him tonight! There would have been murder done in another minute and ruin for us all. I couldn't see how to stop it, but you did. Not many have that gift. Be his advisor, Odd. I and all the older heads were Olaf's men before now, not his. He resents us. But his own man, someone nearer his own age—he'd listen to you."

"I'm no courtier. He'd profit little from my advice."

"The advice would, of course, be—weighed ahead of time."

"Ah. Then I wouldn't be precisely *his* man...?"

"We needn't press the point too hard."

"I see. I'm sorry Dag Hringsson, your offer is kind but my present life—"

"Don't be an idiot!" he rounded on me with a violence that startled me. "I do nothing from kindness. The stakes are very high. I mean the crown of Norway."

"Norway belongs to the Danes."

"For the moment. You said yourself that they're hated, while Olaf's fame grows. The only question is who will pick up Olaf's banner and drive them out—little Magnus the bastard, or Harald the half-brother? It must be one or the other, for Olaf fathered no sons with his queen. I've chosen to bet on Harald and I advise you to do the same. Don't underestimate him just because he boasts—that's the boy talking. There's solid stuff underneath. He's got Olaf's energy without Olaf's scruples.

Where he begs today, tomorrow he'll command—if, as you say, he lives long enough."

"All right, let it be so. Why should an Icelander care who rules Norway?"

"Because you hope to go home someday with your outlawry lifted and your lands restored."

That brought me up short.

"Odd, do you know what year this is as Christmen count them?"

I thought for a minute. "One thousand and thirty?"

"Thirty-one, actually. Time passes, Odd, by little and little, though we don't notice it all at once. We live no more in the world of lawless chieftains and freebooters that your father and mine grew up in."

"So I've heard," I said, remembering how Einar had laughed at us the night we told him that we wanted to be vikings.

"All that is passing. This new world is a world of kings, and Christian ones at that—the Church being a friend to kings for good reasons of Her own. I spent years enough at Olaf's court, as hirdman and friend, to learn that lesson. Ragnvald understands it, too, and the rest will learn it sooner or later."

I looked at him slyly and said it was a pity no one had explained that to the Tronder jarls.

"Don't be stupid on purpose! Every nobleman on that field was fastened to a leash whose other end was, and is still, in London. Olaf was beaten by Canute—another king. Now consider your country—torn by feuds, unable to grow enough grain to feed itself or enough timber to build its own ships. How many years' grace do you think it has left? Depend upon it, Odd, the man who rules Norway will rule Iceland, too, one day. Only make sure that man is your friend and your enemies will crawl under fiery Hekla to escape you."

I began not to like this argument and said coolly that I would know how to deal with my enemies when the time came. "In the meantime my life suits me. I've a ship and a crew and I sail where I please,"—I said this with more ease than I felt—"and what would I be trading that for in Novgorod?"

He shook his head and replaced the arm on my shoulder, for I had thrust it off. "How can I make you understand? You were lucky this time. You got away from the Finns with your life and a rousing good story, if nothing else. Fine. A boyish ambition fulfilled. But that sort of thing will never get you what you really want. If you want that, you must learn to take it from the hands of a king."

We had been standing for some time now on the dock where the Viper was moored. I turned to go up the plank but stopped and came back when a new thought struck me.

"Friend Dag, a minute ago you said Harald was so stubborn a fellow that he was willing to die to prove even a trifling point. What makes you think I'm not one, too?"

He looked embarrassed. "Well, Odd—I mean to say—on the Neva— someone had to have the sense to give way. And dammit, any sane captain would have done the same in your place."

So that was it. No one on Harald's ship had heard Stig order my men to change course. They thought it was I who had blinked, who would, no doubt, blink again when given my marching orders. A safe, pliable sort of fellow to have for a cat's paw. Well. Let that be my secret.

"Good night, Dag Hringsson."

"Will you think about what I've said?"

I lay awake for a long time that night.

36

A NEW START

The skulls on their stakes chatter all around me: "Too late ... too late...."
As fast as I push them down, more spring up—all chattering and whispering
together: "He's too late ... Oh, too late...." Nearby, Ainikki runs this way and
that, searching for me among the heads, crying my name. When I try to
answer her, I choke and no sound comes. Tears run down my cheeks.

Now Joukahainen leans against the doorway of Louhi's Hall, silently
laughing, and now he springs at my darling, catching her in his skeleton
hands, which move like white spiders' across her body. And now he is
leading her to the sauna and she, hardly resisting, follows. Then suddenly,
here is Lemminkainen, his mouth twisted in anger. "Traitor!" he screams at
me, "You were too late!" And strikes my neck with his sword....

"Odd Tangle-Hair! Wake up, now, wake up! There's someone here to
see you and says it can't wait." Einar jabbed me hard in the neck with his
crutch.

I moaned, still half in my dream, and with a great effort wrenched open
my eyes.

"Captain, it's a woman."

I tried moving and found my limbs were stiff with cold, tried swallowing
and found my mouth dry and my throat very sore. Sitting up on the deck,
I shook off the last shreds of dreaming, pulled my cloak about me, and
glowered at my visitor.

"Khaptain Ott Thorvaldsson, called Tangle-Khair?"

"Who are you?"

"You khom wid me, please."

She was wrapped in a hooded caftan of gray wool that hid her face and covered her to her feet. Whoever sent her had taken pains that she not be molested along the way. She lifted the hood just enough to show why. Her skin was the color of honey, her eyes jet black with heavy lashes.

"Khom, please."

"Pity the lass," cackled Einar. "Likely, she's seen you in the street and been smitten—young stallion such as you are! And Einar Tree-Foot'll come along for company—"

"No," said the girl firmly, "only dis one."

"Heh?" He yanked his beard and scowled.

I felt weak. Still, I got shakily to my feet, slapped the wrinkles from my clothes, and with a wink at Einar, bade my visitor lead on.

A few steps away, Stig huddled under his cloak, watching me.

Walking briskly ahead of me, the girl threaded a course through the jungle of pens and tents and open-faced shops where, even early on a wintry morning, the waterfront merchants of Aldeigjuborg were conducting their noisy trade.

We came at last to a spreading tent, far larger than any of the others, in front of which a man sat on a low stool. Seeing me, he waved and called out, "Here I am sir, over here!"

He was dressed in the local fashion, with billowing trousers over his boot tops, a long-skirted coat with shiny buttons, and on his head a shaggy fur hat.

As the girl slipped past him into the tent, he trotted towards me, arms thrown wide, and pounced upon me with a wet embrace.

"I am Stavko—Stavko Ulanovich, merchant, dealer in fine wares. I rejoice to see you, Odd Thorvaldsson, or Tangle-Hair—I may call you so?"

"The invitation was hard to resist," I answered, wrestling free of him. "Do you always entice your customers this way?"

"What? Oh, no, no, no. No, you very special customer, very special. But come in, come inside where is comfortable, ah-ha-ha."

He had a trick of chuckling as he talked, ending every phrase with a string of little wheezes. I saw, too, that his hair hung down to his shoulders in greasy braids, weighted at the tips with lead balls, and that his face was round and sparsely bearded, with bulging eyes, upturned nose, and full lips. He licked them with the pink tip of his tongue.

"Come into tent of Stavko and see—ah, what shall I call them? What makes young men old and old men young? Eh? Ha, ha!."

Grinning and chuckling, he propelled me through the open tent-flap. The entrance gave onto an antechamber, screened by a curtain from the larger space beyond. Pushing that curtain aside, he drew me inside. At first I was aware only of an enveloping blanket of warmth thrown off by heated stones that lay on a brazier.

Then of odors: sweat and the bodily smells of lovemaking. And other scents, heavy and sweet, that I could not put a name to.

Then of shapes: from the ridge-pole, a brass lamp swinging slowly to and fro that threw shifting patterns of light and shadow over the carpeted floor and the heaps of silken cushions.

Coiled upon those cushions, limp as sleeping cats, were a dozen naked women.

Pressing my arm, he chuckled, "You see, Odd Tangle-Hair—ha-ha— you see what Stavko sells?"

He uttered some words in a strange tongue, quick and curt, and one of the women—the same who had just now fetched me from the ship— rose and crossed to where a little table stood with a brass tray upon it. While the slave-dealer pushed me down on a soft bolster and lowered himself beside me, the girl approached, dropped to her knees, and set the tray before us. Taking from it a flagon, she poured hot, honeyed wine into a cup and held it to my lips.

"Nourishment, my friend," laughed Stavko, "for belly and soul."

The girl was hung neck, wrist, and ankle with jewelry that chimed when she moved. Her fingertips were dyed red with henna and her body, in the soft glow of the lamp, had the oiled sheen of dark polished wood. Black hair spilled over her shoulders in lovelocks, through which her painted nipples showed.

In short, she was quite simply a different being from the thick-ankled, raw-skinned, rough-and-ready beauties of Bergthora's inn. Nothing in my young life had prepared me to think that anywhere within the circling stream of Ocean there breathed such a creature as this.

The honeyed wine warmed me all the way to my stomach, the heat from the stones seeped into my aching joints, and the girl's scent made my head swim. I rolled back against the cushions, feeling myself dissolve in relaxation.

Surely, I thought, this is heaven, and Valhalla just a cheap alehouse with noisy guests.

"Is she not beautiful, sir? Belly like velvet, hips like a storm at sea. Her name is Jumayah, an Egyptian from Alexandria, and my favorite of them all. But mount her. Allow her to please you." He gave my arm an affectionate squeeze, almost, it seemed to me, as though he were assuring himself of the firmness of my flesh on the chance that I, too, might one day be for sale.

"What d'you mean—now?"

"Certainly now. I, myself, enjoy it most in morning—prepares mind for day's business. Please,"—his pink tongue darted out and over his lips—"you need do nothing, girl knows what to do."

Still kneeling, she separated my knees, put her hand between my legs, and began to touch me through the fabric of my trousers. I swelled, and Stavko, beside me, breathed, "Oh, magnificent, sir, oh, most impressive—"

"No!" I clapped my legs together and thrust her away.

"What is it? What is wrong?" The bulging eyes widened in dismay, in shock, in absolute despair. "Ah! Forgive me! I am so stupid—is *boy* you want! But I can produce one instantly—beardless with soft skin and—"

"Slaver, why was I brought here? Tell me at once or we say good-bye." I made to stand up, but he held me by the sleeve of my coat.

"Please, my good friend, please, you upset yourself for no reason. You were brought here on small matter of business—only that—but is too soon for talk."

"We have no business that I know of."

"So," he sighed, loosening his grip on me just a little when he felt me hesitate, "you are new to our ways, not yet true Varangian. All right. Please. Be comfortable. We take wine and cakes and talk business, yes? Later, perhaps...." he smiled on Jumayah, and with a flick of his finger, sent her back to the sleeping cats.

I let him draw me back onto the cushions and took another sip from the proffered goblet.

"What was it you said just now that I am not, Master Stavko—a 'Varangian?' Isn't that what they call the Eastern Sea hereabouts?"

"Yes, quite right. Is also name we give to you Norse merchants and soldiers who come to Gardariki to seek fortune. Aldeigjuborg is thick with them, Novgorod even more. There they have their own quarter of city. Prince Yaroslav values them most highly—warriors especially."

"Vikings, in other words."

"The same."

"You're not a Varangian, I take it, yet you speak our language."

"In my trade one speaks many languages—Rus, Wendish, Petcheneg, Bulgar, Greek—but my nationality, Rus—a Northman like yourself, except we are here longer time. You are ignorant of our history? I explain.

"Long ago Rurik the Dane came with his tribe, the Rus, to rule over Novgorod. Slavs invited him, for they were unruly and wanted master to keep order amongst them. House of Rurik still reigns, Yaroslav being fifth in descent from him.

"In time, of course, Rus and Slav mingle blood to where is only small difference between us now. Even most Rus nowadays barely speak Norse language. Disgraceful. But I—I speak very well, as proper Rus should, yes?"

He was evidently proud of this, although, in fact, he spoke it wretchedly.

"Prince Yaroslav, too, speaks very well language of old country," he went on. "Of course, his mother was Danish." He laughed and held up his hands in a gesture of helplessness. "Rus, Varangian, Slav! Is very confusing to newcomers. You will understand much better when you have been a while in Novgorod."

"Novgorod! Who's said anything to you about that?"

"What? Am I mistaken? You are not Icelander who was offered place in Harald Sigurdarson's hird?"

"I think it's time, Master Stavko, for you to say what you want with me."

"Ah! Again I am stupid! I begin things always wrong way." He leaned close, breathing anxiously into my face. "Is my pleasure, you see, to perform certain small services for Jarl from time to time...."

"Ragnvald? And what small service are you performing now?"

"Only to obtain promise from you, and in return to give, shall we say, indication of his high regard."

"I can't say I noticed his high regard much yesterday."

The slave dealer clapped his hands in delight. "Ah! Ha, ha! That is very good! You are ignorant of the ways of courts, my friend. That much is plain. Jarl's interest in you, of course, is not something he wishes to show openly, and so he employs me."

"I haven't the least idea what you're talking about, but it's time I was going, I'm feeling sick actually—"

"No, no, please, not yet. Listen carefully now. Is concerning this young upstart, Harald, and that one called Dag Hringsson who advises him. On his cousin's behalf Jarl is very troubled and thinks it would be useful—how plainly must I say it?—useful to know beforehand what are their intentions toward young Magnus, their schemes for seizing throne of Norway, other things, too, perhaps. And of course, a skald would know such things, yes?"

He let the thought hover between us, while his fingers slid into the leather purse that hung at his belt. The coins which he drew out glowed in the lamplight, and he dropped them one by one into my lap until twelve gold ounces lay there.

"Weigh them, bite them, sir, please."

It's wonderful what gold does to the mind. Its power over us doesn't strike home until one holds a quantity of it in his hands and feels the weight and warmth of it.

"From Ragnvald?"

"He has taken liberty of anticipating his cousin's wishes. By time you reach Novgorod she will know who you are."

"So this is the price of a skald's honor—forgive my ignorance."

A feeling rose in me that was part anger and part awe. That all this had been arranged between dinner and breakfast by a man who had done nothing but scorn me the whole evening long. I felt as though I'd grown suddenly older. I wanted time to think.

"Master Stavko, to whom would I give this information which is worth so much gold?"

"Ah, well, jarl's eldest son, Eilif, is always at court. And I myself am often there—I keep shop in Novgorod and another one in Kiev, my trade takes me everywhere. Anyone can tell you where to find house of Stavko Ulanovich and," he winked broadly, "no one will wonder why you ask, ha! Or, you will perhaps by invited to speak with Princess, herself."

"Are you acquainted with her, Master Stavko?"

"Alas, only from distance."

"She's quite a formidable old dragon, I gather."

"Dragon! What makes you say such a thing?"

What had? I wondered, aside from the impression made on me by her cousin, the Jarl.

"Then she has beauty?"

"Beauty!" he snorted. "Beauty is cheap article, I trade in it every day. Princess Ingigerd has much more than that—nor is she so very old, either, except in wit and shrewdness. But come now, friend skald, have we arrangement or no?"

Twice now in the space of a few hours, I thought wonderingly, someone has tried to tamper with my loyalty to bumptious young Harald before it is even a fact. Dag besieges me with reasons and the jarl with gold—both arguments, in their way, eloquent, though Ragnvald's somewhat blunter. Perhaps I had underestimated the boy. And a thing worth being bribed for may be worth the doing—if not precisely in the manner intended.

"Stavko Ulanovich, you may tell the jarl we have a bargain."

He heaved a sigh and hugged me again. Then, holding me at arm's length, he warned, "Sew gold in your coat lining and mention this to no one, you understand?"

"Of course."

It was a choice that would leave its mark on me forever and yet I made it so lightly, almost with no effort of the will at all. I would go with Harald to Gardariki. Once said, I couldn't think why I had hesitated so long. There was no going on with the Viper. I didn't like to admit it, but it was so. While here was a new world just beyond the tip of my nose— farther from home, it's true, but sometimes we must go the long way round to reach our destination.

Stavko, wiping his perspiring head, threw himself back against the bolster. "And now, my good friend, on to pleasanter business."

He crooked his little finger and the sleeping cats stirred. With slow grace they unwound themselves from their cushions, stretched, arching their necks and shoulders, raised themselves joint by joint, and padded silently forward to be admired.

"Feel them," Stavko chuckled softly at my elbow, "examine them, don't hurry."

They were short and tall, wide-hipped and narrow, big-breasted and small. They stood flat on their bare feet, with their arms loose at their sides, making no move to cover their nakedness, their faces were perfect blanks.

"Jumayah, my pearl, is not for sale. But others— Pechenegs, Chuds,

Volhynians, Finns, even Greek." He pointed out each in turn.

"Ah, it hurts me to part with single one, I am so very fond of them. But how they eat! I would soon be a pauper if I let my feelings guide me. And I am poor enough, for I am an honest merchant, not one of those thieves who sell sick slaves for healthy and pregnant girls for virgins. No, my friend, I am happiest when customer thinks he has taken advantage of *me*. Now, my friend, choose. A man of your importance—of your wealth, if I may say so—should have little girl to love him and care for him, no?"

I could not tear my eyes away from one thin figure whose yellow hair hung to her waist.

"Friend Stavko, shall I tell you something about slaves you may not have noticed, though they're your stock in trade? I say it with good warrant, having lately been one myself. They don't love you."

He started to protest.

"How much for the little Finn?"

"What? That one? Oh, no, no, no. Not for you. No, is good girl but inexperienced, moody sometimes. A man like you—"

"How much?"

"Why—ah—half a silver mark?"

I tossed one of his gold pieces at him. "Change it for silver."

He rummaged in the cushions behind him for his scales and his strongbox, while I told the girl in Finnish to dress herself.

Taking the fistful of coins he handed me, and shoving them in my wallet, I said, "No doubt we will meet again, Stavko Ulanovich," and departed, leaving him with his mouth open.

Outside, a blast of frigid air brought me back with a shock to the world of everyday. I was suffering with chills already and now my bones began to shake. But I gripped the girl by her shoulders and searched her with my eyes. She was taller, maybe a little older, not as pretty, her chin not as strong or her forehead as high. But her eyes, slanting and green as sea water—yes, they were *her* eyes.

The memory of my nightmare leaped back with all the overpowering feeling that a suddenly remembered dream can have and for an instant I hardly knew where I was.

"Who are you, girl? Are you Kalevalan?"

The green eyes, seeing something frightening in mine, widened a little. She stammered the name of some strange tribe.

And I felt suddenly a great sadness overcome me.

"You aren't her, are you? Not her little ghost come back to comfort me, to tell me my future with the all-knowingness of the dead. If only you were!"

She fixed her eyes on the ground, clutching one thin hand in the other, fearing, I suppose, a beating for some unknown fault.

"Still, who can say? May you not be a good omen for me anyway?" I took her face between my hands and kissed her, a lingering kiss, shutting my eyes against the memory of Ainikki, who had died because I'd been too late.

"You're free, girl, run far and fast!" I pressed a silver penny into her hand and closed her fingers on it. Without a word or a backward look, she bolted down the lane and in a moment was gone.

I stood for some time staring after her. Then, too restless to stay still, I waited out the hours until evening, pacing the streets and alleys of the town.

✝

That night we gathered once again in Ragnvald's hall. "Odd Thorvaldsson, will you accept from me the place of skald and first of all skalds in my hird, to ride with me, fight with me, and stand always at my right hand?"

Harald stood with Ragnvald on one side of him and Dag and I on the other, and addressed me in a voice that carried over the noise of feasting to the farthest corner of the jarl's stone hall.

Drawing his long sword, he placed on its tip an arm-ring of silver, cunningly carved in the shape of a coiled serpent biting its tail, and held it toward me. "The weight of this ring is eight marks and the value of it two-and-thirty milch cows. It is very old, having been taken from the Irish by my father's father."

Up and down the tables went grunts of admiration for the worthy gift.

I drew Wound-Snake and held it out before me so that the points of our two swords touched. "Wolf-Crammer, Feeder-of-Ravens, Ring-Giver," I answered him, using all the ancient kennings for a chieftain or a king, "I take the ring."

It passed from the point of his sword to the point of mine, singing as it slid along my blade and ringing on the hilt. I took it off and clasped it around my arm while cheers went up all around.

I was Harald's man.

Dag clapped an affectionate arm around me, and Ragnvald, smiling blandly, raised his drinking horn. At another table Stavko, too, lifted his cup. Each one of them believed that I played his game and all were wrong.

I played no game but my own.

✝

Earlier that day, as soon as they had returned from the hunt, I had sought out Harald in the stables and taken him aside, shown him Ragnvald's gold and even pressed him to take it for himself. As I expected, though he eyed it longingly, he couldn't, with honor, accept money from a man of lesser rank than himself. (I had kept back a portion of it anyway, just in case.) But the result was that he trusted me now as he might never have done otherwise. And that, I reckoned, would be worth a good deal more to me in times to come than the scant gratitude of the jarl and his royal cousin.

About Dag, I said nothing. I'd made him no promises, whatever he thought, and saw no reason to embitter Harald against him. For all I knew, his advice was well worth having. But if I offered it to Harald I would do so openly, for I would be straight with my new lord for as long as it suited me to be his man at all.

✝

We drank deep that night, skald and lord, sitting together on a bench, holding plump girls on our laps and shaping verses to the music of the harpers. My chills were drowned in the heat of mead and wine, and excitement drove me beyond the limits of my strength.

Harald's not a bad sort, I thought contentedly, once you've learnt the trick of managing him. And who knows what glorious adventures we two may share? Why, he reminds me a bit of my reckless brother, Gunnar— and what a good fellow he was!

Tomorrow we would sail up the river to Novgorod. My nerves hummed like harp strings.

But there was still one sad duty to perform.

☦

I awoke next morning in the Jarl's hall, where I had stayed the night, to find that my chills had turned to fever. My face was burning and my throat parched, but telling myself that I had no time to be sick, I drank several long draughts of cold water and splashed more of it on my chest and face and felt a little better.

Dressed and breakfasted, though I could eat very little, I made my way alone down to the dock where the Viper lay.

They watched me as I mounted the gangplank. Their new shirts were already soiled and their faces were pinched with hunger and cold.

"I have something to say to you all—"

"No, we have something to say to you," Starkad burst out in a barely controlled fury. He was their spokesman. "We can't go on like this, Odd Tangle-Hair, living like wharf rats, stealing our grub from the market place like common thieves. If there's nothing for us here, then let us, for the love of God, put to sea again and find some village or farm to loot. We'd a lot rather die that way, if it comes to it. Now we put it to you—we must have a captain and a steersman again. Make up with Stig and do it now, whatever you have to say to him, say it, because now he just—well, you see for yourself. Dammit Odd—!"

I looked at Stig. He was sitting on a sea chest as though he were all alone in the world, not moving, his eyes focused on nothing. A wine jug lay in his lap, though it was early morning still, and a soapstone mug of the kind they sold in the market place was in his hand. The irritating youth, Bengt, looking smug and important, sat beside him, though Stig paid him no attention.

"No, Starkad," I said, "it's no use. It can't be made up. There will always be a coolness between us, and a crew divided is no crew at all."

"And so?"

"And so one must leave."

With sudden violence Stig spat out a mouthful of wine. "One must leave!" he bellowed at me. "You've found the stomach to say it straight out at last? One must leave, Odd Tangle-Hair? Well, don't trouble yourself about it. I could fight you for this ship and win. You know I could. But I won't do it—that's how little I care! I'm a footloose man, and the company here begins to stink in my nostrils. One must leave, is it?" He thumped the hollow sea-chest and laughed, "Why, bless me, here I am packed already."

"The one to leave will be me."

He shut his mouth and stared. They all did.

"Leave the Viper?" Starkad said softly after a long moment's silence.

Before I replied, I ran my eye along the length of her. She was sorely battered but her lines were still lovely and her sinews strong.

"I never hope to sail a trimmer ship—but yes, Starkad, and all of you, I leave her to you. And for the refitting of her, take this." I poured into his hands all the gold that Stavko had tried to bribe me with. "There's enough here, I reckon, to keep you fat over the winter. And when summer comes, then sail out and plunder to your heart's content! But first, you must choose a captain for yourselves. And it's no matter to me whom you pick, but if I were in your place, I would trust my life to no other hands than Stig's. And so, old friends, good bye."

Einar Tree-Foot stood apart from the others, stiffly erect and looking straight ahead.

"Jomsviking," I said, "have you fared as far as Novgorod in your time?"

"I have not."

"All the same, I'd be glad of your company."

He answered with the merest nod, but his old cheeks colored.

With Einar beside me I turned to mount the gangplank. My foot was on the step when Bengt sneered in a loud whisper, "Young fool and old fool!" I rounded on him just in time to see Stig's hand, which held the stone mug, fly out to the side and catch Bengt in the teeth and Bengt roll backwards, choking, onto the deck.

And Stig—Stig looked away into the distance as though nothing at all had happened, and smiled, just for a moment, with the corner of his mouth.

Stig, who had helped me to steal Strife-Hrut's ship and escape from Iceland; Stig, who had taught me navigation and seamanship; Stig, who had been everywhere and knew everything worth knowing. It was thanks to him—and I knew it—that I stood here now, skald to a king's brother and on the verge of great adventures.

I lifted my cap and made him a low bow.

Then Einar and I swung down the gangplank and away.

POST SCRIPTUM

SKALHOLT, THE CATHEDRAL
NOVEMBER 19, ANNO DOMINI 1077

I, Teit the Deacon, write these words alone in my bed chamber. It is late and a winter storm howls outside my window. I have tried to pray, but can't. It is a week since I returned from Odd Thorvaldsson's farm, from that smoke-blackened hall under the volcano where the crazy old man lives like a hermit—no, not a hermit, like an animal. Because hermits are of God, but he is the Devil's creature. My dear father, Bishop Isleif, gives me worried looks and asks me if I am well. Am I? In body perhaps, but not in soul. And it is his fault. It was his idea that we should interview the old man, collect his reminiscences of the late King Harald of Norway.

Some seven years ago, the old man returned to Iceland, rowing up from the coast alone in a small boat. He was skin and bone, say his neighbors, and near dead from exposure. And though he spoke to no one, rumors swirled around him: that as a young man he had served with Harald in the Empire of the Greeks, and had returned with fabulous riches, which he buried beneath his floor. And that he was a heathen sorcerer, like his father before him.

"Never fear, my boy," said my father, always the optimist. "We'll get the old fellow to talk."

I was against it from the start, but my father has a way of getting what he wants. We came armed with food and a cask of ale, with sheaves of second-quality parchment, with pens and pots of ink. But when days stretched into a week, and the old man had not even mentioned Harald's name, insisting upon telling us *his* story before anyone else's, my father decided that he must return to Skalholt. "Keep him talking, my boy," he said, "and write it all down because it's not without some interest, the old fellow's life. These were our forefathers, after all." And with a cheery wave of his hand he left me alone with the madman, as winter closed in.

I stood it for another two weeks. Two weeks in which Odd Tangle-hair, as he calls himself (though the hair is now only a fringe of white) wove his life around me. No, sucked me into it is a better image, talking by the hour, while my inky fingers struggled to keep up, pouring out his tale of blasphemy and lechery and sorcery; of blood and lust. Filled with lies, of course, for who could believe half of what he says? It's all boasting and conceit. At last, thank God, the old man fell ill, coughing until he couldn't speak. And I made my escape, taking the pages with me.

I told myself that once safely home, those three weeks would pass like the shadow of a dream.

I was wrong.

On my first night under my own blankets, I dreamt such wicked things as I could never confess, even to my dear father. I am the same age now as the old man was when his tale began. And I feel my own blood stirring, though I fight against it. All through these last days, up to the moment of this writing, while I assist at mass, while I pore over the *Lives* of the blessed martyrs, even, God forgive me, while I kneel in prayer, always and everywhere the specter of Odd Tangle-Hair haunts me.

And now, my father says that when Spring comes, we will go back, and if the old man is still alive, hear more of his story.

I dread it.

AUTHOR'S NOTE

Despite the title of *Odd Tangle-Hair's Saga*, I have not tried to imitate the style or tone of an authentic Icelandic saga. Those amazing works of medieval literature, whose lean, spare prose breathes the cold Icelandic air, have already been written—and they are inimitable. I have instead written a novel with a modern sensibility, inspired by the facts and realities of Viking history. If readers are encouraged by it to read some of the sagas for themselves (which exist in many fine English translations) I will feel well rewarded.

Odd and his family are fictitious, but the crucial events in their lives—the conversion of Iceland to Christianity and the law and legal process relating to murder, feud, and banishment—all follow closely the accounts in the Icelandic family sagas. These anonymous works of literature, written mostly in the thirteenth century, relate events of two centuries earlier. While not precisely history, they bring us as close as we can come to the world of Viking Age Iceland.

A reader of *Njal's Saga*, one of the longest and best of the family sagas, will find described there a house-burning which inspired the one in our story. Violence is pervasive in the sagas. They exult in swirling battle scenes where arms, legs, heads are lopped off with a single slash of the blade. I have, if anything, toned things down a bit.

I have taken some liberties with the topography of Iceland, in particular, Mt. Hekla. I have climbed Hekla—well, half-way, before knees gave out—but the Hekla described in chapter three is mostly the Hekla of my imagination. I have also allowed myself some latitude in describing the battlefield of Stiklestad.

King Olaf, today the patron saint of Norway, and his young half-brother Harald Hardrada (the Ruthless) are historical figures, and both are the subjects of biographical sagas by the great Icelandic historian, Snorri Sturluson. If it seems to the reader that I have treated Olaf too harshly, his savagery against pagans is remarked on even by Snorri, who wrote in an age that was not squeamish about violence. In recounting the disappearance and recovery of Olaf's corpse after the Battle of Stiklestad, I have abandoned Snorri's version of events almost entirely ("The Saga of Olaf Haraldson," chapters 249, 251 and 258). It is doubtful how factual his pious tale is anyway.

The central fact of eleventh century Scandinavian history was the abandonment of heathenism for Christianity. In this period of transition, there will have been many who found themselves caught between the pull of their pagan heritage and the lure of the new faith. Egil Skallagrimsson, the hero of another of the family sagas, remained a fierce pagan throughout his long life, despite the conversion of his contemporaries. And there were others, even among converts, for whom old habits died hard. *Any man with sense prays to Thor in a storm*, one Christian viking is reported to have said. I have made Odd more articulate on the subject of religion than any real Icelander is likely to have been, but that is, I hope, a novelist's prerogative.

Parenthetically, no one knows precisely why Jesus is called the 'White' Christ (*Hvitakrristr*) in Icelandic sources. It may be a reference to the white baptismal robes worn by converts.

Of the Lapps, known to themselves as the Saami, and their shamanistic religion, I have given only what is recorded fact. A few of their spirit drums survived the zeal of eighteenth century missionaries and can be seen today in Scandinavian museums.

The berserkers certainly existed but did not long survive the coming of Christianity. They were more than fierce warriors, they were, in contemporary belief, shape-shifters, werewolves. Similar figures can be found in folk cultures around the world.

Concerning the Jomsvikings, the sources give conflicting accounts and scholars have even doubted their existence. I give them the benefit of the doubt and have worked into my story most of what we are told about them.

The Finland chapters are of a different character from the rest. Here I have recast the *Kalevala*, the great poetic epic of primitive Finland, into the form of a realistic narrative (with apologies to the Finns for the liberties I've taken with it). Some scholars have suggested that behind these tales of witches, sorcerers, and the miraculous *sampo* may lie a kernel of historical fact: namely, the struggle between two tribes of southern Finland for possession of a potent fertility fetish. (It should be noted that the ethnic nomenclature of Finns and Lapps in the Viking period is quite confused. I have preferred to use the modern names for simplicity's sake.)

A word about runes and rune magic. Although the Vikings credited their chief god, Odin All-Father, with the invention of writing, the runic script takes its origin from our own Latin alphabet, adapted by Germanic tribes in contact with the Romans. The connection with Odin guaranteed the runes a strong tincture of pagan sorcery. Runic writing could be used as well, however, for purely mundane purposes. Excavations at Bergen in Norway have brought to light hundreds of specimens of Medieval date, including shipping labels, bills of sale, love notes, and doggerel.

Teit Isleifsson, Odd's unwilling amanuensis, and his father are real characters. Isleif was Iceland's first native-born bishop, and his son lived to teach Latin and theology to the grandsons of Vikings in the cathedral school at Skalholt. It is only my fancy, however, that Bishop Isleif contemplated writing a biography of Harald. It would be another two centuries before Snorri Sturluson and his contemporaries composed biographical sagas of the Norwegian kings.

ABOUT THE AUTHOR

As a boy, Bruce Macbain spent his days reading history and historical fiction and eventually acquired a master's degree in Classical Studies and a doctorate in Ancient History. As an assistant professor of Classics, he taught courses in Late Antiquity and Roman religion and published a few impenetrable scholarly monographs, which almost no one read. He eventually left academe and turned to teaching English as a second language, a field he was trained in while serving as a Peace Corps Volunteer in Borneo in the 1960s.

Macbain is the author of historical mysteries set in ancient Rome, (*Roman Games*, 2010, and *The Bull Slayer*, 2013) featuring Pliny the Younger as his protagonist. *Odin's Child* is the first in his Viking series, *The Odd Tangle-Hair Saga*.

6/5   6/15

CPSIA information can be obtained at www.ICGtesting.com
Printed in the USA
LVOW07s0156290415

436391LV00001B/1/P

9 780991 305865